THE STIRRING SAGA OF A BITTER, BLOODY STRUGGLE AND THE VALIANT MEN AND WOMEN WHO ENDURED IT— THEIR AMBITIONS, THEIR DESTINIES, THEIR PASSIONS.

GLORIETA PASS
GORDON D. SHIRREFFS

Shirreff's Western sagas are "written by the hand of a master!" —*New York Times*

Quint squatted on his heels and looked at the thousands of soldiers spread across the land. He thought briefly back on his earlier days as a trapper and mountaineer, as dangerous and hard a life as one might live, and yet a life with a freedom that few people had ever experienced.

Beyond the slopes were the grasslands stretching almost limitlessly to the southwest. For the first time since he had settled there, fourteen years past, a vague but insistent disquiet came over him, fermenting deep within his very soul.

After this day of hate and hot, spilled blood it would never be the same again....

GLORIETA PASS

GORDON D. SHIRREFFS

LEISURE BOOKS NEW YORK CITY

A LEISURE BOOK®

April 1995

Published by

Dorchester Publishing Co., Inc.
276 Fifth Avenue
New York, NY 10001

Copyright © 1984 by Gordon D. Shirreffs

The name ''Leisure Books'' and the stylized ''L'' with design are
trademarks of Dorchester Publishing Co., Inc.

Printed in the United States of America.

To my daughter Carole,
who once rode those Southwestern trails with us.

The Civil War came to New Mexico Territory in July 1861. Lieutenant Colonel John Robert Baylor, Confederate States Army, in command of a battalion of the Second Texas Mounted Volunteers, occupied Fort Bliss, Texas, at Franklin, now El Paso, abandoned by United States troops the last day of March. It would be the base for a northward movement up the Rio Grande Valley. His first barrier would be Fort Fillmore, the southernmost occupied United States post in New Mexico, forty miles from Fort Bliss. Nearby was La Mesilla, in those days on the west bank of the Rio Grande and three miles from the fort. La Mesilla and the surrounding area were hotbeds of secessionism, and already the Stars and Bars flew above the town. The garrison at Fort Fillmore direly needed beef cattle for rations, horses for the cavalry and mules for the artillery and transport. There was but one place they could be obtained in all southern New Mexico— the Querencia Rancho of Quintin Kershaw on the San Augustine Plains 125 miles northwest of La Mesilla.

★ ONE ★

JULY 1861: PLAINS OF SAN AUGUSTINE

It was just after sunrise. A *zopilote*, the great land buzzard of Sonora, hung high in the eye of the sun, soaring with wide outstretched wings over the deep arroyo. It was a sure sign something was dead or dying there. It brought Quint Kershaw and his five companions to that area.

The young dun mare lay motionless on her side. Her legs stuck out from her bloated belly like the stick legs of a clay model. A swarm of early-rising bluebottle flies hovered close over her while others crawled over her in such a heaving mass it was difficult to see her coloring or determine how she had died or what might have killed her. The buzzing of the flies sounded inordinately loud in the still air of the arroyo. The body moved a little as though life still remained within it; then came the soft sound of escaping body gas mingling with the incessant buzzing.

Quint dismounted from his *bayo coyote* dun. The horses were distressed at the sight and smell of the dead mare. He withdrew his long-barreled Sharps rifle from its fringed buckskin cover, lowered the breechblock and slid in a .52-caliber linen-covered cartridge. His companions also dismounted and loaded their rifles.

Quint turned. "Take the horses back to where the ladies are, Vicente. Tell them they must remain where they are until I send for them. Moccasin, you scout ahead. I wouldn't want to be trapped by Apaches in this stinkhole."

The Delaware hunter and scout Black Moccasin had been with Quint for over twenty-five years. He quickly passed the mare and vanished into the thick brush farther up the twisted arroyo.

David Kershaw, Quint's firstborn, came to stand by his father's side. His clear, cold, light-gray eyes were exactly like Quint's, while his darker skin and broad face and underjaw betrayed his mixed blood. His mother had been Shoshoni. Francisco "Frank" Kershaw felt about in his jacket for the makings. He was younger half brother to David, handsome and arrogant in mien. There was some facial resemblance to Quint, otherwise he showed much of his mother's blood in his blue-black lustrous hair and great dark smoldering eyes. Guadalupe de Vasquez Kershaw had been *the* great beauty of northern New Mexico in her time.

Anselmo Campos tied his bandanna about his mouth and nose, then limped to the mare. He gripped the long flowing mane and pulled the head stiffly to one side to expose the bone-deep hole in her neck. He looked back at Quint. "Apache work, *patrón*," he said quietly. The thick and fleshy upper part of the mare's neck had been neatly excised as though by the scalpel of a surgeon. "When the Apaches can get flesh of horse, mule or burro, they shun the flesh of all other animals," a Spanish chronicler of the eighteenth century had recorded.

"Can we smoke to get the stink out of our nostrils?" Frank asked, wrinkling his fine patrician nose, slightly askew from a violent difference he'd had with David when they were boys. A thin scar on his lower lip was also a constant reminder of that incident. Dave had almost forgotten about it; Frank never had.

Quint shook his head. "Wait. We'll need to know where the herd is first, upwind or downwind."

Yndelecio Sepulveda could not help but grin at Frank's discomfiture. He was a Californio imported to New Mexico by Quint years past because of his mastery of the science of mules and their breeding. There was none better. He was intensely loyal to Quint and Dave; he hated Frank.

Twenty minutes dragged past. Moccasin returned as noiselessly as he had left. "Five more dead up the arroyo," he reported. "Two young stallion. Three more mare. Dead maybe two days." He looked down at the mare. "All like her. All *bayo coyotes*. All with neck meat gone."

"They must have had a helluva feast last night when they got back to their *ranchería*," Dave commented dryly.

Quint's big hands tightened on his rifle. "Some of the best stock we have. How many do you think they drove off, Moc?"

"Maybe twenty or so."

Dave shook his head. "Just how many we need to replace those broken for the army order."

"We saw smoke signals day before yesterday," Yndelecio said. "They were successful, all right. Inviting their neighbors for a victory feast of horse neck meat."

Quint nodded. The Mimbres Apaches and the Navajos were starting to run rampant now that most of the Regular Army garrisons had abandoned their military posts by order and had left for the war in the East.

"Speaking of smoke," Frank said.

"Where are the nearest herds, Moc?" Quint asked. He grinned ruefully. "Those the sonsofbitches let us keep."

"Where they usually are, Big Red. Upwind, beyond that long ridge."

Frank immediately took out his silver tobacco canteen and roll of thin-scraped corn husks and began to roll a cigarette. He lit up and drew in a big lungful of smoke.

"How many?" Quint asked.

"Three *manadas*. Maybe seventy-five to one hundred mares to the three."

"They were there yesterday, *patrón*," Yndelecio put in. "The largest *manada* is that of the *bayo naranjado*, the bright orange dun with the white mane and tail. The one the *patrón* knows and admires so well, eh?" He smiled.

Quint nodded. "Aye," he said softly, almost to himself. "Does the bright dun *yegua* still lead his *manada*?"

"Who else?" Anselmo cried. "He drives them and she leads them. They'll never be caught, eh, *patrón*?"

"That is so," Quint agreed.

Frank spat to one side. "Hell! They're only stupid horses! They can always be 'walked down.' It's just a matter of time."

Yndelecio shook his head. "Those two will *never* be caught!"

Frank looked quickly at him. "No one asked *your* opinion, *muleteer*," he sneered. "And I do not like to be contradicted! Understand?"

Yndelecio flushed. It was not being a muleteer that irritated him. He had been a muleteer since the time he was a boy in California. There was nothing disgraceful about that. But he had not been a muleteer for the years since Don Quintin had come to

California five years past to buy stud horses and jackasses with good blood for breeding purposes on the Querencia. Those of Mexican blood are masters of the science of mules; few of them were as skilled as the Californios, and none of them could match Yndelecio. No, it was not being called "muleteer" that annoyed him; it was Frank's tone of voice. Don Quintin and his half-breed son never spoke to underlings in that manner. Instead they treated them as equals. It was the Kershaw way. Not so with Don Francisco. Perhaps his way was that of his mother, she who had been a proud de Vasquez, a direct descendant of one of Onate's Orphans, those Spaniards who had early come to New Mexico more than 250 years before.

"Well?" Frank demanded. "Weren't you spoken to by one of your superiors?"

Yndelecio was uncertain. He wasn't afraid of the young man, although Francisco was notorious for his knifing and shooting escapades in Santa Fe and Taos. He looked first at David. David looked away. He wanted no part of this. There had been bad blood between him and his brother since they had been children.

"Look at me, muleteer, not my brother!" Frank shouted.

Quint lighted a cigarette. "That's enough, Frank," he said quietly. It was usually all he had to say in such circumstances. Men *listened* when Quint Kershaw spoke in such a tone.

Frank whirled. "You heard what he said, father!"

Quint usually treated Frank with kid gloves. He knew, or *thought* he knew, Frank loved him, but Frank had always felt Quint favored David. Perhaps it was true. Dave was much like his father; Frank was not.

Quint shook his head. "I heard nothing derogatory from Yndelecio in reference to you." He almost added, "Nor did you." He thought better of it. This time when he spoke the faint, clipped Scots burr was more apparent, a sure enough danger sign.

"Then it's his attitude!" Frank shouted. "He's always like that!"

Quint half smiled. "Perhaps you are imagining things," he suggested firmly.

"Damn it! No!" Frank's face had whitened a little under the tan.

David looked from Frank to his father and back again. "There

★ 4 ★

were Apaches around here a few days ago. Some of them might still be within hearing distance."

Frank turned on a heel and walked a short distance away to relieve himself. Quint followed him. Frank looked back over his shoulder. "We came out here to check the *manadas*, Frank," Quint reminded him. "We've been keeping an eye on them for weeks. You've only been here a few days. I don't want anything to interfere with our roundup of enough of them to replace those we're driving down to Fort Fillmore. *Anything*. You understand?"

Frank turned. He nodded. "That was why I came home, father."

Quint smiled. He put an arm about Frank's shoulders and squeezed him. "And we appreciate it! Now, let's get to business, eh, son?"

David watched them from a distance. Quint had a way with men. He was a born leader. He looked somewhat older than his years but acted younger. It was the way of that country with a man. One could *age;* one could not get *old*, that is, in the sense of losing those instincts, characteristics, and skills that kept one alive in a relatively constant hostile country. Quint's years did not show in his movements or reactions. He was still the rangy *montero Americano* who had come to New Mexico over twenty years ago. He was two inches over six feet tall and weighed one hundred and ninety pounds. His dark reddish hair showed no signs of gray. He was hawk-nosed and butt-jawed. There were two noticeable features about him that first struck an observer: the fearsome scar on his left cheek from the corner of his eye to that of his mouth, relic of a bone-deep furrow slashed by the rending talons of a mammoth grizzly. The wound had eventually healed and in so doing had drawn skin and muscle into a slightly sardonic look. The whitish scar stood out sharply against the saddle-leather hue of the weathered skin. Nothing in his lifetime could ever erase or darken it. Then there were his eyes of light gray, clear and cold-looking, which had sometimes been likened to the rime ice feathering the edges of a swift-running mountain stream after the first heavy frost of winter. Still, they were deceptive. The cold look in them belied another part of Quint's complex nature, a great warmth and deep humaneness. David could remember, as a child years past, seeing and playing with the necklace of fearsome grizzly talons taken from the body of the monster who had marked Quint for a lifetime. Up until not too many years ago Quint had always worn them in the field, hunting or at war. They were his "good medicine." For some years David had thought Quint had discarded them forever, until one day when he had seen his father on a wolf hunt stripped to the waist. There, hanging about his neck from a rawhide thong, was one of the claws. It was then David had realized his father must wear at least one of them always. It had been years before David found out who had really killed the grizzly. Luke Connors—Quint's perpetual friend and partner for the past thirty years or so and the only "brother" he ever had, albeit in the Indian fashion—had told David it had been Dotawipe, Mountain Woman—the Shoshoni "winter squaw," hardly more than a girl, and David's mother, whom he could not remember—who had done in Old Ephraim the grizzly, deadliest foe of all mountain men, and thereby saved Quint's life.

This day Quint was attired as usual, partly Apache style, some civilian garb and some military. He wore a battered wide-brimmed hat, a greasy-looking elkskin jacket, dark-blue army breeches with the twin yellow stripes of a cavalry officer, with the seat and inside of the thighs foxed with antelope skin where wear was greatest. His footgear was Apache, the desert moccasin, or *n' deh b'keh*, thigh-length, button-toed and thick-soled. There was nothing better for mountain and desert terrain.

"We'll check out the ridge before we send back for the girls, Dave," Quint said. "I wish to hell they hadn't insisted on coming along."

Frank couldn't help but grin. "Rafaela can usually get anything she wants out of you, Quint."

Dave slung his Sharps over his shoulder. "It wasn't really her who wanted to come along, Frank. She's usually got too much sense for that. It was Catherine. She wanted to see the *cimarrones* for herself. As usual, she got her way."

The eyes of the two brothers met hard, noted well by Quint. There was always an uneasy truce between them. Now, since Catherine Williston had accompanied their sister Rafaela, twin to Frank, down from Santa Fe on a visit, the old rivalry between the two young men had flared up again like a spurt of flame from a bed of long-smoldering embers.

"Up the ridge, lads!" Quint said cheerily. He didn't fool either of them. It wasn't a suggestion; it was an *order*.

★ 6 ★

TWO

THE *CIMARRONES!*

From the ridge top, the San Augustine Plains were an eye-staggering spread of sage-colored rangeland and blue-hazed mountains under a cloud-dotted sky more luminescent than the richest turquoise—a vast loneliness, a pastel landscape of typical New Mexican cast. This was real plains country in the true meaning of the word: an immense expanse of high grassland with the finest of grazing. The dry breeze blew perpetually from the southwest, rippling the grasses and giving the illusion of serried waves moving across a tawny sea to lap against the beaches formed by the lowest slopes of the mountains. Despite the apparent dryness of the country, it was well supplied with life-giving, spring-fed water bubbling up from the foothills. In early spring bright rivulets of melting snow flowed down from the mountains to the plains. The combination of nutritious grasses and good water made the rolling land a natural grazing ground, a home for countless antelope and herds of wild horses. It was the type of terrain that in less hostile times would have accommodated many cattle and sheep.

The plains trended from northeast to southwest, approximately sixty miles in extreme length, averaging perhaps ten to twenty miles in width. The mountains bounded the plains on all sides. To the east were the San Mateos, with the smaller Magdalenas northeasterly from them. Between them was a wide spreading pass to the east and the valley of the Rio Grande del Norte. To the distant north were the Gallinas, with the Datils west of them. On the western flank of the plains along the towering serrated spine of the Continental Divide were the Gallos, with the Tularosas south of them and still further south the rugged Mogollons. Closing the southern gap between the Mogollons to the west and the San Andres to the east were the Elk Mountains, with the Mimbres, sometimes called the Black Range, to the south.

The lower slopes and hillsides of the mountains were stippled with spidery cholla cactus, cane cactus, sage with scrub evergreens, piñons and juniper trees, while still higher were the darker evergreens marching in solid phalanxes up the mountain sides. Canyons and arroyos choked with green thorny brush twisted and burrowed into the stony mountain flanks. On the highest elevations were millions of board feet of prime saw timber. This was mostly western yellow pine with the remainder spruce and white fir. Highest of all were the stately ponderosa pines towering darkly against the sky. Dashing streams of cold water leaped and frothed, chuckling throatily, to the lower ground. Cold springs welled up from subterranean depths, forming pools from which leaked small rills. Much of the terrain was volcanic in origin, as indicated by dark rock outcroppings and bubbling hot springs. The mountains teemed with bears, white-tail and mule deer, beaver, and turkeys and were haunted by *leones fantasmas*, phantom mountain lions, so called because they were rarely seen by man or their prey.

Quint and his companions had gone to cover just at the reverse side of the knife-edged ridge top. Thick grass and broken rock gave them good protection. Below the ridge was low, rolling plain broken here and there by rock outcroppings, some of which were over one hundred feet high, and one low mesa. Antelope were thick everywhere. The bright dun mare stood on top of the mesa silhouetted in the alert posture of the hunted, head thrown up, long mane and tail floating out in the fresh breeze like liquid gold. Below her high station on the plain was the big *manada*, of which she was both leader and sentinel. Beyond her at the far end of the mesa was another sentinel, this time a big mule. There were actually three *manadas* in the area below the mesa. Quint and Anselmo had studied these three *manadas* over the past few years. Although they kept apart, and each was dominated by its own stallion, they were always within hearing and sight of each other, as though by an agreement for mutual protection.

"Before God, *there he is*," breathed Anselmo.

It was the *bayo naranjado*, a bright-orange dun with a flowing white mane and a tail that almost reached to the ground. He was magnificently outstanding among all the other fine stallions on the plains. A number of times he had been bold enough to come to the ranch and steal some of the best mares. Quint knew they could have easily killed him; they could not have captured him. They had tried, in fact had outdone themselves, to capture him, until at last Quint realized what the act would do. It wasn't only the stallion, but the dun *yegua* leader and the rest of his *manada* who would suffer. Stallions did not lead their *manadas* in the apparent sense of the word; they *drove* them, allowing a mare, or perhaps a wise old mule, to guide or lead it. Mules as sentinels were as useful to wild horses as antelopes were to buffalo. Stallions recognized mules and geldings as noncompetitive and so tolerated their company. The dun mare was a fitting counterpart to the stallion. She was as outstanding as he in appearance and spirit. She would run at speed ahead of her mates with head thrown high, white-star blaze on her forehead, long mane and tail shining goldlike in the sunlight.

Quint had a standing order on the Querencia—the stallion and mare must not be caught or harmed in any way. There was method in his order. The stallion was ultraselective in his choice of mares. He took only the very best for his *manada*, and always *bayo coyote* duns. Who knew but that someday the progeny of the stallion and his selected mates might eventually produce a breed of outstanding quality? Then too, to kill or capture the stallion would be to lose his *manada*, perhaps to a lesser master. The major problem was that though the *bayo naranjado* and his splendid mares could and would produce an outstanding breed, to capture their progeny when young might prove impossible with such leadership. It was only Anselmo and Dave who really understood Quint's true motive, although neither of them had ever mentioned it. To kill or capture the stallion and the leader mare would be to destroy something so essentially ethereal it did not appear to be real.

Anselmo borrowed Quint's field glasses. He studied the mustangs. "Never have I seen such large *manadas*," he said. "I've seen them as small as three. Half a dozen are common. Fifteen to twenty is usual. Thirty is extra large. But *this* . . ." His voice trailed off.

"How many, in truth?" Frank asked.

"Fifty to sixty, *patroncito*." He lowered the glasses. "I've heard of such *manadas*, but these are the first I've ever seen in such numbers."

"Look beyond," Yndelecio urged. "See the dust beyond the mesa? There might be as many as three to four more out there, perhaps not quite as large, but large enough. There are many three-months foals. *Many!*"

Anselmō handed the glasses back to Quint. "But we want as many stallions as possible to replace those we ship out, eh, *patrón*?"

"As many as possible, but I don't want to disturb the *manadas* too much. What do you think, Anselmo?"

The *vaquero* shrugged. "Colts, as you know, are born equally male and female. Thus many males have no *manada*."

Quint nodded. "The immature, the declining, and the mediocre. They've never tasted power and likely never will. Still, the mediocre on these plains might do well elsewhere. Look at the competition they have here. I'd say any stallion running here grouped with others of his kind is of a breed superior to the average mustang in other places. We'll try for the lone stallions first. We'll begin tomorrow."

"How many for starters?" Dave asked.

"We've got forty half-broken at the ranch. Thirty mules. About two hundred beef cattle. I'd like to replace the forty we're shipping out in ten days to two weeks."

Anselmo and Dave looked doubtfully at each other out of the corners of their eyes. "I guess we can do it," Dave said at last.

Quint nodded. "You *will*," he said firmly.

Frank yawned. "Supposing you can't round up that many by walking them down or trapping, Quint?"

"It won't be easy," Quint admitted.

Frank looked at his Sharps carbine. "There's always creasing. One shot barely grazing the spinal nerve along the top of the neck can do it. Stuns them temporarily. Then all you have to do is tie them up and break them." He did not look at his father as he spoke.

Quint shook his head. "Most shots either miss or kill, Frank. Another thing: Where do you aim? A place close to the withers? A foot behind the ears? A vertebra a little forward of the hips? No! I want no creasing here."

Frank shrugged. "Saves time, that's all."

"With that carbine?" Dave asked dryly. He was as good a rifleman as his father and Luke. "You won't get close enough to crease with that. I'd even think twice before I used a rifle. At that, you'd probably kill or maim as many as you capture."

Their eyes met. Frank at last looked away. "Well, you might be right, both of you." He smiled ruefully. "I sometimes forget who I'm dealing with."

Anselmo sensed the tension. "Don Francisco is right in a sense, *patrón*. That is, as far as the walking-down method. Creasing is too wasteful. Any shooting will scatter the *manadas* like fallen leaves before the winter winds."

Quint nodded. "It will have to be a combination, then, Anselmo. Some walking down, but mostly traps."

"The lack of water out here this season should make it a little easier," Yndelecio said. "We can fence in all but one waterhole, perhaps two at the most."

Each *manada* usually kept to a range seldom more than ten to twenty miles across and almost never grazed more than five miles from water. Unless they were disturbed, they watered at the same place and at the same spot on the bank. Yndelecio had once told of wild horses in California who would walk miles beside a flowing river to water at the same place, coming down the bank always in the identical spot.

Moccasin raised his head. "Someone comes."

Quint cased his glasses and reached for his Sharps. "Where?" he asked softly.

The Delaware looked down the long slope beyond the arroyo. He vanished into the brush. The others scattered. Rifle hammers clicked back to full cock. The ridge top now seemed deserted.

Minutes ticked past.

A soft whistle came from the lower slope.

"Stay put," Quint ordered. He moved noiselessly downslope.

Moccasin squatted under cover. He pointed toward the arroyo. "The women. They haven't smelled the dead mare yet." He grinned.

A short horrified scream came from the arroyo.

Quint grinned in turn. "They have now," he said.

Rafaela and Catherine had quickly retreated back to the shallow valley with the dry streambed. The horses and the three *vaqueros* now stood far upwind from the arroyo.

Quint stopped beside the *vaqueros*. "I told you not to let the women go off by themselves," he said coldly.

José Vilas smiled uncertainly. "I was with them, *patrón*. They would not listen to us."

Quint walked to the two women. Rafaela was twin to Francisco, although they were not identical, having been born in separate sacs. She was twenty-one now, tall for a woman, more handsome than beautiful, but striking to an extreme. Her dark hair, inherited from the de Vasquez line, had a coppery sheen to it, tinted by her Kershaw genes. She had immense clear gray eyes like those of David, certain legacy of her Scots blood. She had been well educated for a woman of her time, learning much from scholarly Tom Byrnes, with whom she had stayed in Santa Fe while at the School of the Sisters of Loretto. She had learned a great deal from Quint and his well-rounded library. She had matriculated at the Female Academy in Saint Louis, though she had disliked intensely much of the teaching there, which bound women of her station to a rigid status and code. When it was to her advantage, Rafaela could play the demure, seemingly helpless female that was currently so fashionable; but beneath it all she was a highly capable young woman. She loved ranch life and the open country and was a skilled rifle and pistol shot and a superb horsewoman. Quint knew it had not been she who had screamed in the arroyo.

Catherine Williston was not related in any sense to the Kershaws. She was an orphan, daughter of Charles and Catherine Williston, née Allan, and niece to Jean Calhoun, younger sister of her mother. Fragile Catherine Williston had traveled the Santa Fe Trail in 1837 so that she could have her unborn child where Charles lived and was in business. He had been a merchant trader of Santa Fe, not too successful, a profligate with a penchant for extremely young and virginal "housekeepers," who were actually pureblooded Digger, Ute, and sometimes Jicarilla Apache Indians, as well as half-breed girl children sold to him by slave traders, for he paid top dollar and had standing orders for the best they could get, the younger the better. Catherine had been born in Santa Fe. Her mother had died shortly thereafter. The arduous trip, childbirth, and perhaps a broken heart had been far too much for her frail physique. Charles had not long survived her. Before his death he had turned the child over to the then Jean Allan, who became her guardian. Jean had married Lieutenant Shelby Calhoun of the United States Dragoons and then taken Catherine home to Kentucky to raise as her own.

Catherine Williston was as pretty as a peach. If Rafaela's dark handsome beauty could be likened to soft summer moonlight, Catherine's was like bright summer sunlight. In appearance, at least, she had the coloring of the aunt who had raised her. Her hair was cornsilk blond, her eyes an immense hazel, her skin creamy, her mouth wide and soft, almost sensuous. But in contrast to Jean Calhoun's intelligence and quick humor, there was a certain shallowness with Catherine, perhaps not noticeable to the average observer, but readily apparent to Quint—a man with the trained eye of the hunter and mountain man, able to size up another human being almost on the instant. Then too, Quint, of all people, would have noticed such a difference. Jean had been lover to Quint on several occasions. He hadn't seen her for years. Sometimes she resided in New Mexico with her husband, now Major Calhoun, at their Rio Brioso Rancho in northeast New Mexico not far from Fort Union.

The girls had lighted up as Quint approached them. They knew they had been wrong in entering the arroyo against his wishes. "Well, ladies, I see you've learned something. Listen to *me* at times. I just might know what I'm talking about," he commented dryly.

Rafaela nodded. "You were certainly right. What happened to that poor mare?"

Quint grounded his rifle and leaned on it. "Apaches. Mimbres. They fancy horsemeat above all else. There are five more dead further up the arroyo."

"Is that all they took?" Rafaela asked.

Quint shrugged. "Perhaps a score or so of my best mustangs. They're very selective."

"You never seemed to mind that before. Provided, that is, they didn't take too many and not the *bayo naranjado* with his leader mare."

Quint shrugged. "It's their country as well as ours, and they have a prior right to it. Thank God they don't bother us too much, at least at the Querencia."

"Why not, Uncle Quint?" Catherine asked.

"We sort of respect each other. I leave them alone. They usually leave us alone. They never come near the Querencia."

"Why not?"

"Didn't you know it was haunted, Cathie?" Rafaela queried.

Catherine looked quickly at her. "What do you mean?" she asked uneasily.

"It's a long story. It happened long before Father established the *rancho* there."

"But *why*?" Catherine insisted.

Rafaela looked at her father. He shrugged. "Tell her. She'll learn soon enough."

"Massacre," Rafaela said shortly.

Catherine paled. She placed her slim gloved hand at her smooth white throat. "When?" she asked quietly.

"Years ago. It was raided by Mimbres Apaches with the help of some Chiricahua Apaches who were slaves there."

"Is that why there is a graveyard up behind the *rancho*?"

Rafaela nodded. "No Apache or Navajo in his right mind would come near such a place for fear of the vengeful spirits of the dead." She smiled a little. "Father had some captured owls brought there to live. That helps. Apaches believe Bú, the Owl, speaks with the voice of the dead. But there's more to their fear than haunting." She looked down at the Sharps rifle. "Indians, Mexicans, and unlawful New Mexicans who come here looking for loot find deep trouble instead. The people say, 'It's easier for them to raid us than the cold-eyed men of the Querencia led by the giant redhead with the pistols that never seem empty and the long rifle that always kills at incredible distances.' A raid on Don Grande Rubio, as they call him, brings instant and deadly retribution. It's cheaper and wiser to leave him alone."

Quint grinned. "And under their breaths they say, 'But wait for the chance, *compañeros*.' "

Rafaela looked sideways at her father. "They claim he and his *vaqueros* can shoot around corners. They can hit targets no one else can see. They can track a man or stolen horse on a pitch-black night in a pouring rain." She grinned a mite.

Quint waggled a modest hand. "Not quite *that* good, Catherine, but we're pretty good at that."

Catherine had always had a secret inner yearning for this

panther of a man, born in Scotland and christened Quintin Douglas Ker-Shaw, raised in the Red River country of Canada, orphaned and on his own at sixteen, with no known living relatives. He had left his Canadian Red River home after the death of his father, with nothing but a rifle and a few good books, legacy of his well-educated father. It was all he had to leave his only son—that is, in a material sense. He had given Quint far more than a few well-worn books—a strong body, deep sense of humor, a love of learning, a strong feeling for the underdog, and a stubborn Scots ambition and determination. His mother, who had died when he was a child, had willed him a strong sense of pride and tradition, an intense loyalty to relatives and friends, and a deep-seated humanitarianism. All this Catherine had learned from her aunt. No one had ever told her, but she knew with true feminine intuition that there had been a great deal more than friendship between her aunt and this stallion of a man. She wondered idly how it would be to be serviced thoroughly by him. She shivered a little in fear and anticipatory ecstasy.

"Are ye ready to see the *cimarrones*?" Quint asked.

They followed him. Catherine noted his catlike walk, sensitive to the ground he noiselessly trod upon, and the constant alertness common to Indians and men of his breed. Without it, he would not have survived his years of beaver trapping in Indian country and the savage war with Mexico.

Quint halted below the ridge crest. "Keep low. Don't speak if you can help doing so, but if you must, only in whispers. Don't move unnecessarily. If you do these things you'll see a sight you'll never forget."

★ THREE ★

Rafaela and David had told Catherine that Quint's personal horse preference over many years had been for the *bayo coyote* dun. The dark line running down the back of such a horse gave him or her the name of "coyote dun," or at times "*bayo lobo*," the *lobo* dun. The simplest designation, at least among the Anglos, was that of dun. The dark spinal line was usually accompanied by a black mane, tail, and hoofs. Often there were streaks around the lower legs and at times a transverse stripe over the shoulders. In the north such marked horses were often called buckskins or claybanks. The Spaniards, with their hair-splitting terminology as to horse color, called such a type the *barrosa* to denote a smudgy, dun-colored horse. Thus a large percentage of the *manadas* on the plains were of that type, and of these nearly the best were the personal choice of a stallion with an affinity for his own color. The best, of course, were the offspring of the *bayo naranjado* Quint had given the freedom of the plains. There were other *manada* colors, of course. There were some *manadas* of roans, one of blacks—though this was very small—and an occasional herd of whites or grays, sometimes mixed. Quint's standing orders were to deliver fresh mares in the vicinity of *manadas* of their own color, and always with a decided preference for duns.

The dun was, as Anselmo, that master of the science of horseflesh, often said, "of the race that dies before tiring. If you would lead the riders, pick the coyote dun. They have the *brio escondido*, the hidden vigor." Quint would then smile a little. "And the *huevos*, the great testicles, Anselmo?" he would ask. Anselmo at first would not smile in return. "Those too," he would agree, then slant his obsidian dark Mimbres eyes sideways to look at Quint. "Like the *patrón* himself, eh?" It was a standing joke they often shared and of which they never tired.

"She's not fully alert to us yet," Anselmo whispered to the two women. "But she's nervous about something. Her eyes are as alert as her nostrils."

"That far away?" Catherine whispered incredulously.

Anselmo nodded. "If a rider sights a lookout mustang on high ground as much as two to three miles off, he knows he's been seen. She hasn't spotted us yet, but she's suspicious."

"How can you truly know?"

"Watch the antelopes," Quint advised.

They ran here and there, then back again, then came suddenly to a rigid halt, staring intently toward the *manada* sentinel. She came down from her post on the high ground. The antelope dashed away, sometimes leaping like young goats, circling this way and that, jumping stiff-legged and landing on all four feet, rebounding from the ground as though impelled by coiled springs, then dashing away, only to come to a sudden and rigid halt again.

"There's the boss," Dave whispered. "See, Cathie? The orange dun with the long white flowing tail and mane."

Quint handed her his field glasses. She drew in a sharp breath. "My God! He's magnificent!" she cried.

"Speak lower," Quint warned. "Perhaps he's one of a kind."

"Have you tried to capture him?"

"We did—at one time."

She lowered the glasses and looked sideways at him. "He's the one Rafaela told me about, then?"

Quint nodded. "He has the freedom of the range."

"Your range?"

He shook his head. "It's his as well as mine, and yet it belongs to neither of us."

"That's Injun talk," she said tartly.

"Maybe so, but it has its merits."

Dave hissed. "She's coming toward us. I don't think she's seen or smelled us yet."

The wind shifted, bringing with it a sweetish rotten scent. The mare reared and galloped off toward her *manada*.

"She's smelled the dead mares," Anselmo whispered.

Catherine studied the *manada*. "Are all those mares his?"

Francisco grinned. "They sure are. What a life!"

Quint shrugged. "As long as he can last."

"What does that mean?" she asked innocently—*too* innocently, Quint thought. Dave and Frank were eyeing her with their lips slightly parted, like hounds after a bitch in heat. She glanced from one to the other of them and then slowly away.

Rafaela felt the situation. She knew horses. Her tutors had been of the best. When she had been a child growing up at her maternal ancestral *hacienda* near Taos, El Cerrillo de Vasquez, the Little Hill of the de Vasquez, she had learned to ride from Federico Casias, distant cousin to her mother, majordomo of the estate and an outstanding horseman in a country of outstanding horsemen. In later years, after the Mexican War, when she had come to live at her father's new grant here on the plains, she had graduated cum laude in equestrianism and horse lore under the uncannily skilled tutelage of Anselmo. Her twin, Francisco, was one of the great young horsemen bred in New Mexico. Few could compare with him; yet those who knew the twins felt that in many ways Rafaela was superior to her brother, at least in horse lore. A horse to him was merely something on which to get from here to there and a means of showing off. To her it was a way of life, inextricably mixed with the land itself.

Rafaela inched closer to Catherine. "Stallions are despots. Naturally polygamous. Guarding their *manada* the year round against all enemies and holding them to themselves against all challenging stallions. They are fiercely possessive and domineering. Only at foaling time can the mares drop out to be alone, perhaps only for a day or two, until their colts grow strong enough to run. The stallion's *manada* endures only as long as his vigor endures. Depending on his vigor and aggressiveness, his *manada* can number from three to as much as fifty."

"My God," she breathed.

Frank grinned. "He's got it, Cathie. The *huevos*. The *brio escondido*. Some men are like that too," he said suggestively.

"That's enough, Frank," Dave warned.

They looked at each other. Quint had long felt the latent animosity between his two sons, so different from each other. Or was it actual hostility? Years ago it had been a pony that had caused their first and only physical clash, in which Frank had come off a poor second best. Now the cause boded well to be a woman.

"Do the stallions fight much over the mares?" Catherine asked eagerly.

Quint nodded. "They are most savage during the breeding season, Cathie. Stallions with *manadas* must do constant battle with other stallions who have *manadas* of their own, both of them eager to add more mares to their personal harems. Then there are the outcasts, the older stallions and the younger ones without *manadas*, who are a constant threat. Stallions and their mares usually graze and water in the same areas. The stallions mark their personal range with piles of dung as much as two to three feet high with fresh droppings always on top. Sort of a private 'pyramid,' a notice to other stallions and a warning for them to stay away. Woe betide interlopers. It means instant combat, sometimes to the death. Stallions moving about the range are always on the lookout for such notices. They can respect it, or move into the territory to certain combat."

Frank rested his chin on his crossed forearms and looked out across the sunlit plains. "A stallion can pick up the scent of a mare in heat a long distance away," he said quietly, almost as though to himself. He did not look toward Catherine. "If she's willing enough she leaves frequent urinary notices whenever she can."

"Oh, Frank!" Catherine cried in mock disgust.

Quint had been noticing her perfume. It was almost as though she were a bitch in heat. Then the slow realization came to him that it was exactly like the perfume her Aunt Jean had worn, at least in Quint's time with her. Disquieting memories came to him of her breasts, thighs, and hips and her soft, loose, searching mouth.

Frank continued inexorably. "The stallions without mares dog the trails of the mares in heat and those of the stallion's *manadas*. They come stealthily by night to the grazing grounds. They haunt the watering places. The *manada* stallion approaches watering places very cautiously. He tests every yard of the ground before he lets the mares and colts drink. He sniffs about for the dung of a competing stallion. Of course, he must also be on the alert for other dangers—a lurking panther who'd like nothing better than a colt for dinner, or man, his greatest enemy."

It was very quiet on the ridge. The perpetual dry wind from the southwest ruffled the tails and manes of the mustangs and rippled the dry grasses.

"Quiet!" warned Anselmo. "She's coming back!"

She moved fast this time. She held her head high, circling almost playfully, leaping and curvetting. She became involved with the faint cloud of dust she delighted in raising as though that was her only interest.

Anselmo nodded. "She's seen us, but she hasn't picked up our odor yet. That's why she's circling, trying to pick it up. The dust play is just to make us think she's not really interested in us. They've an incredible sense of smell. When I was a *mestenero* out beyond the Llano Estacado, we'd go for days and weeks sometimes without changing our clothing, especially our underwear, when trailing a *manada*. That's so we wouldn't alter our odor, trying to get them used to our presence."

"Before God," Frank whispered. "You must have been ripe, eh, Anselmo?"

Anselmo shrugged. "It worked, Don Francisco."

Catherine focused the binoculars on the mare. She drew in a sharp breath. "I must have her," she murmured as though only to herself.

"See the star blaze?" Anselmo asked. "We call her Estrella."

Dave and Frank did not look at each other, but they had heard Catherine's expressed wish. Quint could almost feel the thinking processes going on in their heads. Was it to be a horse again, as well as a woman, that would bring them to loggerheads?

The mare snorted, startling Catherine. It was clearly audible for hundreds of yards, possibly a warning to the *manada*. The *bayo naranjado* ran swiftly from his position at the other side of the *manada* to halt and look intently toward the sentinel mare, slanting his ears in her direction, the very picture of intense alertness. The *manada* mares and colts also slanted their ears toward her.

"Horses talk with their ears," Quint whispered. "It won't be long now."

The mare came closer, snorting repeatedly.

"Listen to her," Anselmo said in delight. "She has rollers in her nose."

The stallion trotted closer to the mare. He halted, head held high, looking directly at the ridge crest where the man-creatures lay hidden.

The *manada* mares and colts tossed their heads high, nostrils dilated, then held still; a picture in sudden suspension of the wild and the free, waiting, waiting for the signal for flight.

The breeze shifted uncertainly, just a little, but enough for the sentinel mare to catch the foreign scent. Her warning snort was startling. She wheeled and raced toward the *manada*. Her hard little hoofs seemed hardly to touch the ground; a devil's tattoo on the hard earth. She plunged right through the center of the *manada* to take her post at its head. The stallion turned in behind her, snorting like a quick-firing pistol, squealing and biting at the flanks of the mares, driving them on, a pell-mell mass of horse-flesh pounding in unison past the rocky height where the mare had been sentinel, startling the smaller *manadas* beyond it into wild, dust-clouded flight. In a little while they were gone, the thundering tattoo of their hoofs on the ground slowly dying away while the busy wind was already dispersing the dust clouds.

Quint stood up. "Show's over," he said. He walked down the slope, trailed rifle in hand.

None of them spoke, still held in awe by what they had seen, as they followed Quint back to the horses.

★ FOUR ★

QUERENCIA

Querencia—there is no English translation for *querencia* (Spanish *querer*, "to love"). In a sense it refers more to animals than humans. It denotes not only the haunt, the lair, the stamping ground of animals, but their place-preference for certain functions. Who can explain this "*querencia*"? This attachment of living flesh for a particular parcel of earth? As Anselmo Campos, a creature of that country, half-Spanish and half-Mimbre Apache, had defined it upon first meeting Quint Kershaw on the San Augustine Plains and thereby attaching himself to the man for life, perhaps, "*Yo tengo raíces aquí*. I have roots here." None could have put it better.

The site for the Querencia had been selected in 1817 by wound-crippled Sergeant Major Eusebio Campos, retired from the Mexican Provincial Dragoons. He had patterned the original structures somewhat after his ancestral home in Estremadura but more like the *haciendas* of Chihuahua, at once a fortress and a home. The site had been selected on the long gentle easterly slope of a wide shallow valley through which a clear spring-fed stream flowed. Peachleaf willows and cottonwoods bordered the watercourse. The Datils and Gallinas formed a backdrop to the north; to the east were the San Mateos, whose southern two-thirds was concealed behind the Mimbres, sometimes called the Black Range because of the dense dark mantle of cedar and other trees that lined its slopes. To the south and west the valley widened to afford a panoramic view of sweeping tawny plains and the distant Continental Divide.

The original central building, or *hacienda,* had been built of rock and adobe in the shape of a squared figure-eight. The front, or western part, wherein lay the family quarters, was built around its private patio, and the rear portion, built around another patio, comprised the servants' quarters, kitchen, storerooms, and workshops. There were deep wells in each patio. The *hacienda* walls had been built of native rock set two feet in the ground on a bed of broken rock and gravel. The rock walls extended four feet up from ground level and were topped with adobe brick tempered with straw and pebbles. They were almost three feet thick. The few small windows were narrow, with the outer opening narrower than the inner like arrow slits in castle towers. Thick handwrought bars through which a musket could be thrust for firing closed the outer opening. There were funnel-shaped loopholes between the windows, the outer ends wider than the inner. At each corner of the building were ells so that riflemen could cover with enfilade fire an attacker's close approach to the walls.

The flat roof was supported by huge adzed timbers, or *vigas,* brought down from the mountains. The beams had been covered with diagonally placed willow withes painted in primary colors, then covered with brush and thick earth well packed down. The roof had a four-foot-high parapet with embrasures for riflemen. The front entrance of the house had an inner and outer door of thick hardwood planks bolted together, with the outer surface studded with nails to resist bullets, arrows, and fire.

A *torreón*, or defensive tower, had been built set apart from the southwest corner of the central building. It was fifteen feet high, windowless but loopholed with an embrasured parapet. It was situated so that if captured, attackers could not leap over to the house roof, or from the house roof to the tower if the house was captured. Arms were kept ready in both structures. The walled corral was to the east of the house. It was built of adobe with fifteen-foot walls without openings save for one large double gate of doubled hardwood planks bolted together. A favorite trick of Apache horsethieves was to wet a portion of an adobe wall and then, using hair ropes, saw down to form an opening. To forestall this, pieces of sharp bone and flinty pebbles had been mixed in the brick molds. In addition, the top of the wall had been troughed, filled with earth, and planted thickly with wicked spiked cholla cactus, to prevent their being scaled by thieves.

Beyond the main building were many loopholed outbuildings joined together by contiguous walls. Here were shops for blacksmithing, carpentry, pottery, and weaving as well as the quarters for the wives and families of the *vaqueros* and other employees. Beyond them were smaller corrals, cattle, sheep, and goat pens. In the time of Eusebio Campos, the fertile bottomlands of the stream had been used for crops and were still crosshatched with *acequias*, or irrigation ditches, fed by the *madre acequia* from the stream. The stream had rarely, if ever, gone dry in the summer, but for such an eventuality low earthen dams with sluices had been thrown across it to form *charcos*, or storage pools, for the stock.

Sergeant Major Eusebio Campos had planned well, but he had made one fatal mistake. It had led to the massacre of him and his people. The mistake had been to employ Indian slaves on his *hacienda*. There was nothing basically wrong with that time-honored custom, provided one used the right breed of Indian.

Eusebio had brought enslaved Apaches with him from Mexico. Throughout Mexican history the custom of the conquerors had been to defeat the Apaches, kill off all adult males and older boys, and enslave the women and younger children. *But* such slaves were kept hundreds of miles from their homeland and were never allowed to work in large groups. Eusebio's older slaves had been Opatas, docile and hardworking. His other slaves were of Apache blood, and Chiricahuas at that, *broncos* of the wildest order. The *rancho* was in Mimbres country, close kin to the Chiricahua. It was only a matter of time before the Mimbres struck, aided by the Chiricahua slaves. The result had been massacre, the destruction of the *hacienda* and captivity for the younger Mexican women and the children.

There were still relics of the massacre at the Querencia. Bits and pieces of rusted iron, fragments of wooden-handled tools and broken pottery. Mutilated musket balls or flint arrowheads still turned up after heavy rains. Some were still stuck in the walls. The graveyard was the main relic of the tragedy. When Quint had taken over the *rancho*, the little *camposanto* was thickly weedgrown. The wooden crosses, turned chalk-gray and ebony by the elements, were fallen or askew. There were a lot of them. They were unnamed. When the soldiers from Socorro had reached the scene, the bodies were so mutilated and decomposed it was impossible to identify them. Then too, the coyotes, wolves, and *zopilotes* had gotten at them first. The soldiers buried the corpses in a mass grave, placing as many crosses over it as there had been bodies. It was the best they could do. It had been Cristina, she of the tender heart and great encompassing love for humanity, who had seen to it that the cemetery was cleaned up, restored, and maintained.

It had been Anselmo Campos fourteen years past who had guided Quint and Luke to the lonely ruins. "There are ghosts here, *patrón*," he had said quietly. "At times, particularly about the date the massacre took place, their thin wailings may be heard on the night wind." Anselmo himself could have been considered a sort of relic of that time. His mother had been Luz Campos, youngest daughter of Eusebio, just fourteen years old. His father had been the fearsome sub-chief nicknamed Cuchillo Roja, or Red Knife, by the Mexicans. It was said that the hue of his knife was always that of fresh blood, for the old stain had little time to dry before he refreshed it with more blood. Many believed he was the devil incarnate. Father and son would have killed each other on sight.

The one blessing of the massacre had been the rather tenuous immunity the *rancho* had from Apache and Navajo raids. That immunity extended for about a mile or so on all sides of the *hacienda*, including the walled spring that fed the stream, just at the edge of the low hills east of the *rancho*. The rest of the sprawling land grant had been fair game until Quint and his *vaqueros* had won a grudging respect from Apache and Navajo. The combination of the haunted Querencia and the hardcase men who garrisoned it had kept an uneasy truce for fourteen years.

There was another blessing at the Querencia—Cristina. She was as much a fixture there as Quint's old Hawken rifle hanging over the fireplace in the study. She had been sixteen when she entered the service of Guadalupe Kershaw at El Cerrillo. She had come with Guadalupe, David, Rafaela, and Francisco to the Rio Brioso Rancho east of the Sangre de Cristos in the *cimarrón* country. She was in her early thirties now, a dark-eyed, dark-skinned, capable woman. She was pretty in a pronounced Indian way. She had skin like dark moist earth, glossy jet-black hair, high cheekbones, and a broad face with a strong jawline. Her eyes were huge and dark, like polished obsidian, but not like cold stone, for they held deep warmth and humaneness; her mother had been New Mexican, her father a Moache Ute, for she had been born in Ute captivity, then rescued by Mexican soldiers. She was a Genizara, one of mixed birth.

Guadalupe had insisted she be a virgin when she had employed her. In time Cristina had lost that virginity to Quint, as planned by Guadalupe herself. When Quint had become widowed, Cristina had moved easily into the role of foster mother to the four children. Indeed, she had delivered the youngest, tiny frail Guadalupe. There was a deep mutual love between the children and her. She had become a foster mother to them and house-keeper for the family. She loved Quint and the Querencia. Cristina was rarely without a smile and a cheery word. Quint had not married her. It would have been considered beneath his station, although he himself had never thought of it that way. There was no doubt in her mind that he liked her exceedingly well, but as for love? She would shake her dark head. Still, it was far better than not being near him and the children. It was she who had named the *hacienda*. Shortly after they had settled there, he had asked her one moonlit night for her opinion on the matter. "*Querencia*," she had quickly replied. So it was.

The Querencia was a good place, but hardly profitable. For fourteen years it had been a place of subsistence, just beginning to show a profit when Fort Sumter was fired on and Quint was immediately called up to reorganize his Independent Company of New Mexico Mounted Rifles, actually to be used as a "spy" or scout company, and in time of battle as sharpshooters. Before the Mexican War he had led them as Mexican Rural Militia in pursuit and chastisement of Indian raiders on the northeast frontier of New Mexico. When he had taken the oath of allegiance to the United States he had taken his riflemen with him as a lieutenant of United States Mounted Rifles to serve in the Navajo country, and during the Taos Revolt of 1846–1847 they had fought with honor at La Canada and Taos Pueblo. Since that war, his company had served a number of times in response to Apache and Navajo raids. Over the years the official unit designation had been almost forgotten in favor of Kershaw's Rangers. With the most recent orders for active duty had also come his commission as captain.

All of this was milling within Quint's mind when he returned to the Querencia from the *cimarrón* scouting on the plains. He left the others and entered his private *querencia* within the cavernous house. When he closed the door behind himself, it was a warning to others that he wished to be alone. The war had been in progress for three months now, but Quint's volunteering for active service in the East had been negated by his orders from Colonel E.R.S. Canby, Tenth Infantry, newly appointed Commander of the District of New Mexico. As desperate as his command was for good fighting men with leaders such as Quint, the need for horses, mules, and beef cattle was far more urgent. Quint had been ordered to remain at the Querencia to supply as many contract animals as possible and at the same time to keep an eye on the Mimbres and Navajos. Certainly, it was active service, but not the kind Quint had envisaged in the almost certainty of a War Between the States before Fort Sumter was fired on. War talk had been rife ever since 1860, and when one southern state after another had seceded, war was a foregone conclusion. It was only a matter of weeks now before Quint could supply the contract animals, then the likelihood for active duty against a threatened invasion of New Mexico from Texas would be a certainty. Quint would welcome that possibility, but the price he would have to pay by leaving the Querencia with the best of his *vaqueros* for such service would be overwhelming. It would cost him any future profits, at least until the war was over, and further, it might cost him, his family and employees the loss of the Querencia altogether. If he led his fighting men from there, it would be open to destruction and massacre by the Mimbres and Navajos, or perhaps the Confederates might occupy it for their own needs. In either case, he could not leave the women and children in occupation insecurely guarded by a few older men and those unfit for military service.

He opened a bottle of Pass brandy, filled his pipe and lit it, held it up to the sky for the first puff, then settled himself in his old sagging armchair to think and *think*.

The study was quite similar to that which he had built at the Rio Brioso before the Mexican War. Tall triple candelabra hand-forged in the blacksmith shop stood in diagonally opposing corners, matched by beehive fireplaces in the other corners. A built-in adobe bench covered with bright Navajo blankets extended the full length of one wall. Some of the furniture was of Mexican Colonial style, dark and solid, while other pieces were homemade of curved branches and willow withes bounded and covered with rawhide. Both end walls were lined with bookshelves filled with many books, much like the library he had once had at Rio Brioso. It had taken years for Quint to fill those shelves with classics from many disciplines. Those Regular Army officers who had visited the Querencia to contract for horses, mules, and beef and sample Quint's warm hospitality had often commented that there wasn't a military post in New Mexico Territory and possibly the entire Southwest that had such a library on military science.

The room had been decorated with items revealing Quint's colorful and adventurous past. There was a Comanche buffalo-hide war shield and a war lance taken in hand-to-hand combat, Jicarilla Apache basketry, Zuni, Hopi, and Pueblo pottery. There was a beautifully decorated Cheyenne buckskin shirt and a pair of Ute moccasins, the best that could be had. A huge grizzly pelt with head attached covered the center of the polished earthen floor.

The place of honor over one of the fireplaces was held by Quint's splendid muzzle-loading Hawken rifle. His nickname for it was "Auld Clootie," broad Scots for "Old Devil." In earlier times it seemed as though man and rifle were one and the same—a combination with a legendary reputation for deadly accuracy. Some of Quint's old trappings and accoutrements hung from pegs on the wall near the Hawken. His large and small powderhorns, tomahawk, Green River knife, possibles bag with bullet mold, bar lead, bullets, whetstone, wire worm, percussion caps, awl, nipple pick, firesteel, and flint. He didn't carry the Hawken now, but it was kept ready for instant use.

In 1860 Quint had seen the future in breechloaders. Christian Sharps had patented a single-shot breechloading rifle in 1848. The open breech was closed by a lever-activated vertical slide that was also a shear for cutting off the tail of a paper- or linen-covered cartridge to release the powder charge in the chamber. It was a powerful and accurate weapon that could be loaded with ease and rapidity. There was no question of the superiority of the Sharps over the Hawken in efficiency and speed of operation as well as pinpoint accuracy. Quint had purchased a dozen of them in St. Louis.

The Sharps New Model 1859 was just under four feet long, with a thirty-inch barrel, weighing about nine pounds. It was straight-breeched, with a vertical sliding breechblock. Caliber was .52 with a 475-grain conical bullet propelled by an average load of sixty grains of FFG black powder. It used "fixed" ammunition, consisting of a bullet fitted to a paper- or linen-covered cartridge treated with nitrate for quicker firing. The earlier cartridges had the "tail" sheared off by the rising breechblock to free the charge in the chamber to be ignited by the percussion cap. A later improvement used flat bases of gold-beater's skin through which the primer flame burned to ignite the charge. The bullets were lubricated with rendered lamb suet and one part beeswax to every three parts tallow. The weapon could be fired using regular musket percussion caps or by means of a pellet primer, a device fitted within the right side of the breechblock plate. A little brass charge tube held fifty tiny wafer-shaped pellets of mercuric fulminate enclosed in thin copper cups. When the hammer fell, it actuated a slide that impelled a pellet onto the nipple just ahead of the falling hammer. Thus the rifleman could fire the weapon fifty times without the necessity of capping the nipple for each shot. The pellet primer device was fitted with a cut-off for keeping them in reserve until needed, the rifleman meanwhile using conventional percussion caps.

Since 1836 Quint had carried a matched pair of Colt's Patent five-shot revolving pistols of .36 caliber with nine-inch barrels and sheathed triggers. They had been presented to him by William Bent of Bent's Fort. Over the years he had established a deadly reputation both as a rifleman and with his twin Colts. In 1851 Samuel Colt brought out a single-action six-shot .36 caliber percussion revolver. It was thirteen inches in overall length, with a seven-and-one-half–inch octagonal barrel, and weighed two pounds ten ounces. The powder charge was an average twenty-two grains of FFG black powder propelling an eighty-one–grain bullet. The cylinder was engraved with a depiction of the 1843 Texas Republic Navy battle with Mexican men-of-war, which in time gave rise to the nickname "Navy Colt." With a pair of these fine pistols and an extra loaded cylinder for each the pistoleer had twenty-four rounds ready for action. Quint bought a pair for himself and Luke Connors. He gave his twin Colt Patersons to Dave, who tactfully gave one back to him, suggesting that it be given to Frank. Frank, incensed because Quint had not offered the pair to him first, haughtily refused the proffered pistol.

Quint had eliminated another weapon from his early days. The last Green River knife he had carried had been worn thin by too much use and sharpening. It had been the last of a long succession of the blades. He had replaced it with a seven-pound bowie knife, a heavy, murderous weapon more suited to infighting than any other use.

He had grown to rely upon the Sharps rifle, and in time, with the custom of mountain men, he thought to christen it. He would have liked to call it Auld Clootie, but somehow he felt that name belonged to the old Hawken. It was Luke who, after witnessing Quint's five-hundred-yard shot to drop a Mexican *ladrón* driving off some rustled cattle, had come up with a fitting nickname. He had looked with appreciation at the smoking muzzle of the Sharps. "That *ladrón* is one for the wolves now. I still don't

believe that shot. Name it Satan, Big Red.'' The name had
stuck.

There was one other item hanging on the wall, which had been
a concession of Quint's at the request of Cristina, a gleaming
gold crucifix for which she had scraped and saved for years. It
meant much to her and little Guadalupe. There were times, in the
dusk, when Quint had been at the brandy, when he would look at
the crucifix, and questions about religion would enter his mind.
His mother had been Catholic; his father had not. He had been
christened Catholic in Scotland, but until he had settled in New
Mexico and married Guadalupe he had almost forgotten about it.
In the morning, the questions had vanished; the hangover had
not.

Cristina came into the room after dark, closing and barring the
door, and lighted one of the candles. She looked down at Quint,
asleep in the armchair. She bent and kissed him on the forehead.
Two powerful arms pulled her down onto his lap. An exploring
hand crept up under her skirt and several petticoats. ''Mother of
God,'' she whispered. ''Can't you wait?''

He grinned tipsily at her. ''Why?'' he asked softly.

She didn't have an answer.

★ FIVE ★

Quint hooked a leg around his saddlehorn and took out the
makings. As he shaped a cigarette, he watched the last of the
cattle strays being driven in to where the two hundred or so beef
cattle had been herded preparatory to being driven to the Querencia
and eventually to Fort Fillmore. The rest of his *vaqueros* with
Dave, Frank, and Anselmo were on the far side of the plains,
trapping mustangs near the springs at Ojo de Luera. He lit up

and as he did so saw a faint trace of dust to the east. He uncased his binoculars and studied the dust. In a little while he made out the rider, Black Moccasin—and he was in one hell of a hurry. Quint had kept the Delaware on watch in the trail to the southeast, which led eventually to Canada Alamosa. Quint rode to meet him.

Black Moccasin's horse was lathered. The Delaware accepted the makings from Quint. "Horsemen. From the south. Soldiers. Whites. Twenty-five. They got a little forked flag on a lance. What you call it, Big Red?"

"Guidon. They're not·ours, are they?"

Moccasin shook his head. "Texans, I think. Some wear gray clothes, or some gray clothes mixed in with regular clothes."

"Who's leading them?"

"Officer. Wearing nice gray uniform. Carries shiny sword. They don't look much like soldiers. But *he* does." Moccasin lighted up and eyed Quint over the flare of the lucifer. "You know him," he added.

"So?"

"Major Shelby Calhoun."

Quint whistled softly. He had known for months that the Virginian had resigned his commission in the dragoons and gone to Texas, but it was still somewhat of a shock. Shell Calhoun had been the very quintessence of the Regular Army officer and in the elite First Dragoons at that. Quint had known him for almost twenty-five years. At that time he had been on leave from the service to observe the situation in New Mexico and prepare maps and notes, which were later used by General Kearny and his Army of the West in the bloodless conquest of New Mexico. He had married Jean Allan before the both of them returned east, she with the infant Catherine Williston. Quint and Shelby had met again during the Mexican War.

"How far are they from here?" Quint asked.

"Twenty-five miles. They went into dry camp. I figure they'll march all night to reach Querencia early tomorrow."

"You figure that's ·where they're heading?"

Moccasin grinned. "Where else they get water outside of Ojo de Luera mebbe?"

Quint nodded. "And they'll be wanting more than just water, Moc. Horses, mules, and beef cattle."

"We get the boys and we shoot 'em up? Could ambush on trail at dawn. Get 'em all!"

"You bloodthirsty savage!"

They grinned at each other.

"Well?" Moccasin asked.

Quint shook his head. He couldn't stop the roundups now, nor could he spare the men from them to defend the Querencia. He'd have to take that task on himself with the few people at the ranch. "Go back to the ranch, Moc. Get a fresh mount. Head out to keep an eye on the Confederates. Tell Cristina what has happened. I'll send a rider from here to warn Dave. *Vámonos!*"

It was almost dusk when Quint reached the ranch. The mingled sounds of whinnying, neighing, thudding hooves and a few shouting men came from the big breaking corral where old Tobias Galeras and his horsebreakers were hard at work. Beyond the horsebreaking corral were the corrals holding the mules and those horses already half-broken at least, for the government contract. There was no way Quint could have them driven off into the plains to keep them away from the Texans. Shorthanded as he was, at the ranch leastways, such an act would be a gamble. There were always stray Mimbres and Navajo scouts sometimes within eye view of the ranch complex.

Cristina met him at the gate. "What will you do?" she asked anxiously.

Quint dismounted and took his Sharps from the saddle sheath. "Moccasin suggested we go out and ambush them."

She was horrified. "You wouldn't do that!"

He shrugged. "Why not? We'd save our animals, get rid of a bunch of Rebels and gain twenty-five horses we could turn over to the government."

She shook her head. "I know you too well. What else can we do, Quint?"

He looked toward the south. "Bluff," he answered quietly. "We've got one ace in the hole, at least. They had a dry camp last night and there isn't any other water between it and here. They've *got* to come here. Even if they wanted to, they couldn't turn back now. So, we have the water and we'll have to control it. A thirsty man will usually listen to reason."

"You'd deny men and horses water?" she demanded.

He slapped his horse on the rump and walked toward the house. "I *said*, they'll have to listen to reason."

"We can't stop them if they decide to take it and the horses and mules!"

He turned. "We'll see about that. Now get into the *casa*. We've got some figuring to do. *Pronto!*"

"Do you think they know you're on active duty?"

Quint nodded. "Of course. Calhoun was still on duty in Santa Fe when the orders were issued and my instructions to remain here and round up the animals were given me."

"Then it could be war right here," she said as she caught up with him.

"Why, so it could be," he said quietly. "After all, they are the *enemy*."

The three women sat in the study listening to him as he explained his plan. "I won't stop the horsebreaking. We can't lose the time. Cristina, you and Rafaela can handle firearms in case a shooting war starts; otherwise, you'll stay under cover so that they don't know you are women. Catherine, you can at least thrust a rifle barrel through a loophole for bluffing, and shoot it whether you hit anything or not if trouble starts."

"I won't want to shoot Uncle Shelby," she said quietly.

Rafaela looked at her. "There'll be plenty of other targets, Cathie."

"I don't know if I can shoot at anyone."

"You might just have to," Rafaela said firmly.

"We can always run away," Catherine suggested furtively. She did not dare look at Quint.

Quint explained their duties, then finished, "I want all the window shutters put up and all doors barred from within. Spare rifles and carbines in each room with loopholes so that you can move from one to another of them if need be. Rafaela, take half a dozen horses and picket them in the box canyon near the spring. Cristina, see that every available pot is filled with water in case we're unable to reach the wells. Then tell the women and children to remain indoors when the Texans arrive. Is everything clear?"

They nodded.

"Get at it, then," he ordered.

Quint walked to the horsebreaking corral. Old Tobias Galeras climbed to the top rail of the corral. Sweat streamed from his seamed face, the color of old saddle leather. He had been with Quint since the origin of Querencia. He studied Quint through sun-tightened eyes.

"How does it go, Tobias?" Quint asked.

"It goes well, *patrón*. I plan to keep at it until moonset. These soldiers who are approaching, are they Rebels?"

Quint nodded. "Texans," he said.

"Tejanos? Those sonsofbitches! Why do they come?"

"For our horses and mules without doubt."

"*Jesu Cristo!* Do you mean to let them have them? Before God! They'll have to kill me first!"

Quint shook his head. "No. Let me handle this. Tomorrow you must continue with the horsebreaking, but keep your guns hidden here in the corral in case of need. I'll let you know when and if you'll need them. You understand? *Only* when I let you know."

Tobias climbed down inside the corral and peered balefully between the bars. "*Desgraciado!*" he spat out. A fighting word. Tobias, like most New Mexicans, hated Texans with a passion—a hatred with a long history. He stamped away.

Quint was up before dawn. Just as daylight broke, Moccasin appeared. "They'll reach here after sunrise, Big Red," he reported. "What do you want me to do?"

"I'll have to depend on you to act like at least a dozen men stationed up on the hillsides overlooking the ranch. When and if I want you to shoot *near*, but not *hit*, any of these rebels, I'll take off my hat and hold it by my side."

The Delaware studied Quint. "And to *kill*?" he asked.

"When they start shooting, Moc. Not before!"

"*Bueno*, Big Red."

"Take my old telescope with you. Get some food from the kitchen and take plenty of water."

Moccasin turned to leave.

"Moc," Quint said quietly. He gripped him about the shoulders. "You take good care, now, you understand? I wouldn't want to lose you before the real shooting war starts."

Quint watched him walk toward the *casa*. Moccasin had been one of his beaver-trapping partners back in the thirties. Delawares were the only Indians white mountain men ever took into full partnership. Most Delawares could shoot as well as or better than most white men. Moccasin and his nephew Joshua, now out on the plains with David and the *vaqueros*, were two of the best riflemen Quint had ever known.

The sun came up. Half an hour later Cristina called down from the top of the *torreón*. "There's much dust on the road, Quint!"

He entered the *torreón* and climbed the ladder. She handed him the powerful field glasses, and he focused them on the dust. The sun glinted brightly from polished metal. In a little while he could make out individual horsemen and the guidon fluttering in the fresh morning breeze.

Before long he could clearly discern two officers. One of them was young wearing a sort of quasi-uniform, part military, part civilian. The other officer wore the full gray uniform of a Confederate field officer with the two stars of a lieutenant colonel on each side of his high collar and *galons*—the looped gold braid knots in the French style—from cuff to elbow on each sleeve. There was no mistaking Shelby Calhoun.

They descended the ladder and passed through the low, narrow passageway Quint had built from the base of the tower into the house. He smiled as he saw the anxious faces of the two young women. "Take your posts," he said. He went to the den and got the mate of his holstered Colt and slid it into the leather loops he had sewn inside the left front of his jacket so that the muzzle touched about where his elbow was and the butt was just inside the edge of the jacket front. As an afterthought he dropped a .41 caliber double-barreled derringer inside his left coat pocket. At close range nothing could beat the solid impact of slugs from the stingy gun. He returned through the passageway and leaned his Sharps just inside the *torreón* door, then stepped outside. A little later he heard Cristina drop the wooden bar in place behind the door.

Quint stood there in the bright sunlight watching the Texans approach. Shelby was riding in dragoon-style, with a single rider ahead as point, one far out on each side as a flanker and two others bringing up the rear.

Shelby stood up in his stirrups. "Hello, the ranch!" he cried. "Is that Quint Kershaw? Permission to enter, sir!"

Quint walked to the gate. The troopers were a confident, tough-looking, windburned lot sitting loose and easy in their saddles. The guidon was marked with the numeral 2 and the letter B, Second Regiment Texas Mounted Volunteers. The horses nickered and the packmules brayed as they scented water on the dry breeze. He opened the gate and let them pass through until they were halted at a command from the lieutenant.

Shelby dismounted and turned over the reins of his fine gray to an orderly. He removed his gauntlets and began to slap the trail dust from his uniform. "Well, we meet again, Quintin Kershaw," he said. "Almost always in time of war."

They respected each other but they had never been friends. Both of them were first-class fighting men in their own style.

Quint nodded. "You're wearing a different uniform this time, Shell."

"Lieutenant colonel, Regular Confederate States Army. At present attached to Baylor's Second Texas."

"How long has this been?" Quint asked.

The hard blue eyes held the cold gray ones. "Why do you ask?" Shelby said.

"Just curious."

"May fifteenth, to be exact. That was the date of my resignation. I thereupon tendered my services to the Confederacy and was immediately accepted."

Quint nodded. "Where was that? Couldn't have been Richmond. Perhaps San Antonio?" He smiled a little. "Fast work, if that was the case."

Shelby was nettled. "It so happened I was at Fort Davis, Texas, which your people abandoned last March. Colonel Baylor brought my commission from San Antonio and swore me in."

"Then your commission must have been all settled *before* you resigned your post of duty at Fort Marcy."

Shelby drew himself up a little. "Sir, are you accusing me?"

The lieutenant came quickly over when he heard Shelby's tone of voice. "Sir, permission to watah the horses?"

Shelby nodded. "Of course. Proceed, Lieutenant Jarvis."

"Wait," Quint said quietly.

Shelby wheeled. "Wait? What do you mean?"

"What's your purpose in coming to my ranch with half a company of troopers?"

"What does that have to do with watering our horses?" Shelby demanded.

"Just answer the question."

Shelby shook his head. He was tired and thirsty. "No need for that, sir," he said irritably. "We need water. You have plenty. It's common courtesy to extend watering rights to us. Do you question *that*, sir?"

"No. I am just questioning your purpose in coming to my ranch, *sir*."

It seemed to become quieter. The cries of the horsebreakers at work came faintly to them, mingled with the closer chinking of a bit or the thud of a hoof on the hard ground from the Texans' mounts.

Shelby smiled with only the facial muscles, not with his eyes. "We'll discuss that *after* the watering."

"We'll discuss it *now*," Quint said firmly.

Shelby spoke over his shoulder. "Lieutenant, water the command at once." He turned toward Quint. "I hope you're not foolish enough to try and stop us, Quint."

"The springs, wells, and *charcos* are covered by my riflemen. No one drinks here without my permission."

"The greaser sonofabitch!" Jarvis snapped.

Quint turned slowly and held the Texan eye to eye. Jarvis was a fighting man, and damned thirsty, but suddenly he wanted no part of this silent, cold-eyed man.

Shelby smiled. "No need to get upset, Quint. We happen to know most of your men are not here at the ranch. If you refuse to cooperate with us it will necessitate my taking over the ranch. You and your people won't be disturbed in any way."

"By what authority do you take over my ranch, Calhoun?" Quint demanded.

"That of the Confederate Territory of Arizona."

"Never heard of it," Quint lied. "Can you enlighten me as to its whereabouts?"

"Southern New Mexico Territory south of the thirty-fourth Parallel, from the Texas state line on the east to the Colorado River in the west."

Quint raised his eyebrows. "Is that a fact? But it doesn't apply here."

Shelby smiled thinly. "It includes virtually all of the Plains of San Augustine, which, I might add, includes the Querencia. By the authority vested in me, I am able to confiscate anything my government might require, offering payment in good faith with notes of the Confederate States of America. I can also accept enlistments of all male residents between the ages of eighteen and thirty-five and in sound health for service in the military forces of the Confederacy." He turned a little. "Lieutenant Jarvis, I am taking command here. Water your horses. Place a guard over the people of this place. Confiscate foodstuffs and forage as required."

"First Section, water your mounts!" Jarvis barked.

The lead Texans started to lead their horses toward the first of the *charcos*. Quint took off his hat and held it by his side. A rifle cracked like the splitting of a shingle on the hillside above the cemetery. A puff of smoke drifted on the wind. Dust spurted up just in front of the leading trooper of the First Section. He grinned. "Lousy shootin'," he said. "Is that the best you greasers can do?"

"It was only a warning!" Quint called out.

The trooper turned and looked at him. "Why, you greaser sonofabitch!"

Quint smiled. "Come closer and say that, you Texas sonofabitch!" He took off his hat. The rifle flatted off again. The bullet plucked at the crown of the Texan's hat. His face paled. Quint's almost did too. That damned Delaware was showing off again and *he didn't like Texans*.

"Goddamn!" the trooper cried. He dropped his right hand to the butt of his Navy Colt.

"Hold it, O'Neil!" Shelby snapped. He looked at Quint. "How long do you think you can hold us this way?"

Quint pointed at the *torreón*. A rifle barrel was thrust through a loophole. He pointed at the *casa*. Another rifle barrel appeared. "I've got men up on those slopes with Sharps rifles, every one of them a sharpshooter. They can cover every foot of open ground down here and all the *charcos* and the stream. Some are covering the springs. You can't get into the *casa* either."

Shelby looked up at the silent hillsides already hazing a little in the morning heat. Nothing moved. Shelby knew his man. Kershaw was not to be trifled with at any time. He and his command desperately needed that water. They could not retreat back to the Rio Grande without sufficient water for the trip. He looked at his command, then turned to Quint. "What are your terms, sir?" He hated to do it; he had no choice.

"Pile all your firearms beside the *torreón*. You can water your men and horses and stay the night. I want you out of here by dawn tomorrow. Your arms will be returned to you unloaded."

"Those mountains are quite likely full of hostile Apaches, sir. My command will be massacred."

Quint shook his head. "Once you're a sufficient distance from here I'll send on your ammunition."

"We didn't see any signs of Apaches," Jarvis blurted.

"They're out there," Quint said.

Jarvis studied him. "How do you know?"

Quint nodded. "I *know*. . . ."

Shelby watched his men stack their carbines and double-barreled shotguns next to the *torreón*, then pile their Navy Colts and bowie knives at the foot of them. Quint could be bluffing. If he was, Shelby knew his men. They were tough and resourceful frontiersmen from Bexar County, and many of them served as Indian fighters for their state. When night came there might be a chance for even unarmed men to overpower their captors.

The door of the *torreón* opened. Rafaela and Cristina quickly gathered the weapons and took them back within the tower. The door was closed and barred behind them.

"Part of your strong garrison, Quint?" Shelby asked. He did not smile.

"Amazons," Quint replied, straight-faced. "I warn you, both of them are expert with firearms."

After the Texans had watered their mounts and let them out to graze under a mounted guard, they made their simple camp in the open between the corrals and one of the *charcos*. Every now and then one of them would look up uneasily at those silent, heat-shimmering hills. They would be sitting ducks if the Querencia "greasers" opened fire.

Quint had a steer butchered for the troopers. He invited Shelby and Jarvis to quarter within the *casa* and dine with the family that evening. The long hot day passed slowly, as it always seemed to do at Querencia. The isolated *rancho* seemed almost to exist in a timeless vacuum on a planet otherwise uninhabited and the people there the only human life thereon. The thought was that of Shelby Calhoun.

The sun set. With the coming of darkness the wind reversed itself as it always did, creeping down the deeply shadowed canyons toward the lower ground. The Texans' cooking fires sprang up brightly in the darkness, sending thin smoke tendrils high over the *rancho*. The firelight reflected from the lean tanned faces of the troopers. Most of them were young. Like soldiers everywhere, they hadn't remained downhearted very long. It was a good place. Plenty of water and good beef, with the whitest of Mexican bread. The horses had been watered and grazed. The mingled music of a banjo, jews' harp, and harmonica drifted over the *rancho*. Tomorrow was another day.

★ SIX ★

Cristina had personally supervised Consuelo, the head cook, in preparing the evening meal, then—unusual for the times, at least for one of her past standing in the family—she had joined the company at table. In the old days in New Mexico the women of the family rarely ate with the men. It was a custom Quint had eliminated in his household. He believed, years ahead of his time, in the utter equality of women and men. It hadn't been easy for him at first, but he had grown to like it, for he enjoyed the company of women at table.

Shelby was related to Catherine by marriage and so knew her quite well. In fact he knew her too well, a matter that was kept secret between him and her. Rafaela he had known since she was a child. Cristina he knew mostly by hearsay. He covertly studied her at dinner. She had become somewhat heavy-bodied, rather squat and wide-hipped, with the full bosom of approaching middle age. Her heavy plaited hair was a glossy black. It was her great dark eyes that always called one's attention to her. They were seemingly unfathomable. He knew of Quint's relationship with her and how it had come about through the instigation of his first wife, Guadalupe. Shelby remembered her well. It would be difficult for anyone to forget Guadalupe Kershaw. He had seen her young daughter Guadalupe in Santa Fe at the home of Tom Byrne. The girl had been left as a haunting memory of her mother. The resemblance was startling. Rumor had it that Quint had found it difficult, almost impossible, to really accept young Guadalupe, because of the circumstance of her birth and her remarkable resemblance to her mother. Dark rumor had it that Cristina, who had been alone with Guadalupe at childbirth and delivered the infant, had somehow been instrumental in Guadalupe's sudden death, so that she might gain the child and Quint for herself. If so, she had succeeded beyond her wildest expectations. Now, for all intents and purposes, she was mistress to Quint and foster mother to the Kershaw children. Shelby wondered idly what would happen to Cristina once Quint found out that Shelby and his wife, Jean, had been divorced early that year. Quint had no legal ties to Cristina. He had a long-standing attraction to Jean and she to him. It should be interesting.

The dinner was a great success. Jim Jarvis, for all his being a Texan to whom "greaser" and Indian blood were anathema, was absolutely fascinated by Cristina and Rafaela. But it was Catherine Williston, not only by virtue of her blond Anglo beauty, but also because of her obvious interest in a man, *any* man, that received the bulk of his attentions. He was hopelessly infatuated with her.

Shelby turned to Quint when the dinner was concluded. "Can we have a word in private, Quint? It might be of interest to you."

Rafaela picked up the cue. "Shall we have dessert and coffee, then cards later?" she suggested to the others.

Shelby seated himself in the study and looked about it. "They say one has but to look about such a room to gain an insight into the character of the person who furnished and decorated it," he said thoughtfully.

"It can't tell you much more than you already know, Shell," Quint countered.

Shelby studied him. "On the contrary, I've long had a feeling we know very little about the inner man in each of us."

"Even after twenty-five years?"

"You know that fact as well as I."

"My family, my people, and friends know me fairly well."

Shell shook his head. "Only one, perhaps."

"Such as?"

"Luke Connors, that green-eyed wolf in the shape of a man."

Quint smiled a little. "You might be right at that. I sometimes think he knows me better than I know myself."

Shelby relighted his cigar. "Where is he now, by the way?"

Quint shrugged. "Who knows? He comes and goes. He's his own man, beholden to no one."

Shelby eyed Quint over the flare of the match. "You *know*," he suggested firmly.

"He's not here on the plains, if that's what you mean."

"That's exactly what I mean."

Quint leaned forward and refilled Shell's brandy glass. "Get to the point," he said quietly.

"He's been seen east of El Paso del Norte, and as far as Forts Davis and Lancaster on the Pecos. Some say he's even been in San Antonio."

Quint didn't change his expression. "Nothing wrong with that."

"I agree. *As long as he's a civilian.*"

It was difficult for Quint to maintain his expression. *Damn Luke, anyway!* His orders from Santa Fe, through Quint, had been to go no farther than Fort Davis, and then only if absolutely necessary to gather information about the numbers and disposition of the Confederate brigade of mounted infantry said to be organized in San Antonio for the purpose of a "major buffalo hunt" to supply the Confederate military. They had said the same about Colonel John R. Baylor's Second Texas Mounted Volunteers before they had marched from San Antonio to occupy Fort Bliss. There was little question that the brigade now forming in San Antonio would follow Baylor's command west.

Shelby sipped his brandy. "He *is* a civilian, isn't he?"

Quint nodded.

"He's been your shadow for over thirty years. He trapped with you, fought Indians, lived at the Rio Brioso, served throughout the Mexican War in your Rangers, and came here to the Querencia fifteen years ago."

"Time does fly," Quint commented dryly.

"Now, with a war going on and him quite likely to be a member of your Rangers, called to active duty last April, he suddenly leaves your side and is seen wandering around our soldiery and military installations in Texas, a sovereign state of the Confederacy." Shelby paused, bluffing a little. "He's not there now, of course."

Thank God, Quint thought. If that's the case he should return soon with his memorized report.

Shelby blew a smoke ring and poked a finger into it. "He might not be back soon. Recently he showed up at Fort Bliss, where the Second Texas is garrisoned. I doubt he knows I'm attached to them for special duty."

"Such as the forthcoming invasion of New Mexico," Quint suggested.

Shelby smiled. "It's not a military secret, then, is it?"

Quint shook his head. "Your ex–U.S. Major Henry Hopkins Sibley passed through Fort Fillmore last May and shouted out to the Federal troops there that he was now 'the enemy' and that he would soon return. Not very tactful of the old boy, was it? He's lucky he didn't get a bullet up his ass."

"Well, Henry was always partial to strong drink, Quint."

Quint grinned. "*Partial?* My God, Shell!"

"Your *compañero* Luke has not been arrested. But he is under surveillance as a suspected spy. If we find out for certain he is a member of your military forces, it will go badly for him, I'm afraid."

Quint lighted a fresh cigar. "You've forgotten one thing, Shell. Luke was born a Kentuckian. It is possible he went to Texas to enlist with the Confederacy. He's always been a southerner at heart, you know."

There was now some doubt in Shelby's mind. By God, if what Quint said was the truth, Luke Connors would be a great asset to the invading force. Few men knew New Mexico Territory as well as he, unless one also considered Quint, who in addition to having that knowledge was a born fighting man and leader.

Quint settled back in his armchair. "You didn't come in here to talk solely about the whereabouts and loyalties of Luke Connors," he suggested.

"Direct and to the point, this Quintin Kershaw," Shelby said.

"Wasn't that what Jean used to say about you? Direct and to the point, the Highland way of speech."

"It still stands good," Quint responded. He didn't want Jean brought into the conversation.

"I had a personal reason for coming here, one coupled with not only that of General Sibley but also that of General Earl Van Dorn, commanding officer of the Department of Texas."

"Former U.S. Major Earl Van Dorn. Another of your rebel turncoats."

Shelby paled. "Sir!" he snapped.

Quint waved a hand. "Get to the point! Damn it! Spit it out, man! What do you want of me?"

"Fine! We feel that your best interests would be with the Confederacy. I have the authority to offer you a captain's commission in the service of the Provisional Army of the Confederate States of America. Is that not direct and to the point?"

Quint studied Shelby. "Do you remember Carrizo Creek in 1846? You were on duty with Kearny's Army of the West. At that time you were a captain of United States Dragoons and one of the best professionals in the business. You offered me then a temporary commission as a lieutenant of Volunteer Mounted Rifles in the Army of the United States. Now you have the infernal guts to come here to steal my horses, mules, and cattle for your damned Rebel army and offer me a commission in it while I'm on active duty with the same army you had me commissioned in fifteen years ago!" Quint stood up. "Damn you, Calhoun! Because of the fact that you are here as my guest, the rules of hospitality prevent me from kicking your ass right out that door and driving you and your Texas thieves to hell off the Plains of San Augustine!"

Shelby stood up slowly. His patrician face was taut, white beneath the tan. "Rebels?" he said between clenched teeth. "Rebels? Why, damn you to hell, Kershaw! *We're Americans!* What are you? A Scots-born, mongrel Canadian drifter who came to this country without a cent to his name and connived his way into ownership of this grant of land! Who are you to shout names and obscenities against the glorious Confederacy! I should call you out for that!"

Quint took one step forward and raised a big clenched fist. He could not speak, so intense was his emotion.

"I'm unarmed," Shelby said quickly. "I'd have no chance with you and your rough and tumble, eye-gouging fighting style."

Quint slowly lowered his hand. "I'm not armed, Shelby. Nor would I attack you mountain style. You should know me better than that."

They stood there, two hardcase fighting men at heart. Shelby suddenly smiled a little and extended his hand. "I apologize, Quint. I went too far. You incensed me with your insults to my country. We gain nothing by shouting insults at each other, nor by physical conflict. Come, let us reason together like officers and gentlemen."

Quint nodded. He took the proffered hand and gripped it. "Fair enough. Just choose your words more carefully."

"I can say the same to you," Shelby countered.

Quint refilled the brandy glasses and offered a fresh cigar to Shelby. After all, what did he have to lose? He held all the aces, at present, anyway. It might be interesting, and he might learn more about the anticipated invasion.

Shelby lighted his cigar and puffed it into life. "I remind you, Quint, the northern boundary of the Confederate Territory of Arizona is the Thirty-fourth Parallel. Which would include most of the Plains of San Augustine, a good part of which was the original land grant of Eusebio Campos. It was granted to him in the year 1817. Governor Manuel Armijo of New Mexico somehow gained possession of that grant in his customary corrupt fashion. Your Dr. Tom Byrne when working here in New Mexico as a United States undercover agent before the Mexican War had realized the possible strategic value, to use a broad term, of the plains. But to control the plains and the Mimbres Apaches, it would be necessary that someone establish a fortified settlement here. The Spaniards had realized that but did nothing about it. The Mexican government, too, realized that importance by giving Campos a grant to establish a *colonia* here. We know how he failed. During my visit here in 1838 I gathered notes and observations about the plains which were incorporated into the military map prepared for Kearny prior to his invasion of New Mexico."

Quint nodded. "He showed it to me in '46. Beautiful work. In fact, it was that very map that first interested me in the plains. Later I accepted the grant from Tom Byrne in lieu of cash for my part of the Rio Brioso grant." He smiled. "They used to say the same thing about *that* country. Strategic value. The 'bastion of the northeastern frontier of New Mexico.' "

"Established and held by you, Quint."

"Only to eventually find myself out in the cold when your former father-in-law, Senator Allan, gained control and you and Jean took over the Rio Brioso, at least that part of it which wasn't sold to the government at an exorbitant price for the establishment of Fort Union."

Shelby shrugged. "Well, I'm out of it now. You sound bitter about the whole deal, but at the same time I think you were glad to get away from it. It was becoming too settled for a former mountain man like yourself. Come! Admit it! There must always be a challenge in life for you, Quint. One in which you pit yourself against great odds. It seems now that here on the Plains you've found another such challenge."

Shelby had neatly put his finger on the truth. "I'll have to agree to that," Quint admitted. "I can't say that I've missed the Rio Brioso that much."

"But *this* is different."

"It is. Moreover, it is all mine. Rio Brioso was, in reality, your father-in-law's. El Cerrillo de Vasquez was never mine. It was always The Little Hill of the de Vasquez. Now Rio Brioso is gone, and the only connection I have with El Cerrillo is to see that my children by Guadalupe get their income from it by right of lease. None of it is mine."

Shelby drained his brandy glass. "Can you be sure that this grant is yours?" he asked quietly.

"Of course! Why do you question it?" Quint studied Shelby. "Just what are you driving at? Is there something you are holding back from me?"

Shelby refilled his glass. "This land, or at least the major portion of it, including your Querencia, is south of the Thirty-fourth Parallel and part of the Confederate Territory of Arizona. When and if we invade New Mexico and conquer it, as we surely must, the entire territory will be ours. In that case, as owner of this grant who served against the forces of the Confederacy you will lose the Querencia. Further, we have already examined the original Spanish land grant and the Mexican grant to Eusebio Campos and find that it is correct." He paused. "However, we have found that the claim of Governor Armijo to the grant is fraudulent. He sold a bill of goods to Tom Byrne, who, perhaps unwittingly, gave you this grant in exchange for your quarter share of the Rio Brioso.''

"I don't believe you," Quint said flatly.

"The facts are indisputable. They are now on record in both San Antonio and Richmond. Quint, believe me, I have nothing to gain by lying to you about this.''

With his faults, Shelby was always the man of honor.

"Is there more?" Quint asked.

Shelby leaned forward. "There is. Resign your commission in the Army of the United States. Accept the Confederate commission I have with me. By that means, if you serve with us in the invasion of New Mexico, and we are successful, which we surely must be, you can be assured your ownership of this grant for you and yours forever, with the thanks and remunerations of a grateful government.''

It was very quiet. The low hum of conversation came from the dining room. The clock on the study wall struck the half hour. The silvery chimes died away.

"I'll be goddamned," Quint said at last.

"It's something to be deeply considered," Shelby urged. "Take your time. I might add that if we are successful, I eventually plan to retire from the army and take up residence at Santa Fe. There's a possibility I may be appointed military governor of New Mexico and in time the first civil governor of the Confederate Territory of New Mexico. You realize what that might mean to you.''

"Always the ambitious one, the seeker after power, eh, Shelby?" Quint queried quietly.

Shelby shrugged. "I'll wait for your final decision, Quint." He stood up and wandered about the room, brandy glass in hand, looking at the relics and accoutrements.

If Shelby was right about the illegal ownership of the Querencia by Governor Armijo, it could only mean one thing—the only legal owner then would be one of Eusebio Campos' descendants. If there weren't any, and the Confederacy conquered New Mexico and won the war, then they would have sole possession of the old grant. There was one fact they *didn't* know. There *was* an heir to the grant—Anselmo Campos, half-breed son of Luz Campos and the Mimbres Cuchillo Roja.

Shelby was studying a tinted daguerreotype on the mantel of one of the fireplaces. Before God, thought Quint. It's that of Jean and her son Alexander Calhoun, taken when he was quite young. The resemblance of the boy to Quint was startling. Shelby had known for years who Alexander's father really was. There had been no love between Jean and Shelby even before the birth of Alexander, but Shelby could not divorce her. The importance of being the son-in-law of the powerful and wealthy Senator Allan of Kentucky was too much for Shelby to lose. Quint should have thought of removing the daguerreotype before Shelby entered the room.

"I'm sorry about the daguerreotype, Shell," Quint said.

Shelby turned. "It doesn't matter now, Quint. In fact, it never really did matter. You know there has been no love between Jean and myself almost since the time we were married. I knew it after we left Santa Fe when we were first married. When Alexander was born it only widened the rift; it was not the cause of it. The boy became the apple of his grandfather's eye. I was a climber. An impoverished lieutenant from Virginia with 'first family' connections and little else. It was a golden opportunity for me to marry Jean. It would assure me of a fine career, money, and property. She loved you, and only you, before we married and she still does. Divorce had been long in coming. My joining the Confederacy was the catalyst."

"The boy. Is he still at the Academy?" Quint asked.

"He graduated in June. He's probably already with his regiment."

"Federal or Confederate?"

Shelby was a little nettled. "Federal, of course. He's absolutely devoted to his grandfather, who, as you know, is one of the most staunch Union members of Congress. He has had great influence over the boy. Alexander respected me. He never loved me. I've seen very little of him these past ten years. Only when he spent time at the Rio Brioso during vacations. He loves New Mexico, Quint."

"Now you've left him and his mother to pursue the jade of glory and prestige. I truly wonder why."

"I'm first a Virginian," Shelby reminded him rather tartly.

"Is that reason enough?"

"I . . ." Shelby started to say. He paused. He spoke again. "It is perhaps something you don't understand."

"Such as?"

"You're not American born."

"Do you mean *States* born?"

"Something like that."

Quint waved a hand to encompass something far beyond the narrow confines of the room. "New Mexico. Is that not the same as a state? It will be someday. Perhaps not in my time, but it will be. I want to work toward that. I want to be part of that future. I *am* a part of that future."

Shelby had no rebuttal.

★ SEVEN ★

Sergeant Ben Tate led five of his men through the pre-moon darkness. The remainder of Company B was wide-awake but feigning sleep. The six shadowy figures crawled along the stream concealed by the bank to reach a clump of willows closest to the *torreón*. One by one, crouching low, they ran on soundless stocking feet to the tower looming in the darkness. Sergeant Tate tried the door. It was barred from within. Two of his men pressed shoulders together and braced themselves against the wall. Lanky Joe Parnell climbed up their backs and stood up, inserting long strong fingers into two of the drain holes at the rooftop level. Charley Jeter, youngest and smallest of them, went up the human pyramid, got an arm and then a leg over the parápet, pulled himself up, and rolled over inside it. He tried the trapdoor, grinned, then eased it up. He leaned over the parapet. "Open," he whispered to Joe. He went down the ladder into the tower and unbarred the door. He passed out cartridges, pistols, and carbines to his comrades, then armed himself. He tried the low door leading into the passageway, which in turned led into the house. It was barred.

Sergeant Tate moved like a disembodied shadow to the window of the room where Colonel Calhoun and Lieutenant Jarvis were quartered with the door locked from the outside. He tapped on the shutter. The shutter was unbarred and pushed open. The window was too small for the officers to escape through. Tate passed in a brace of Colts for each of them. He vanished into the darkness.

Quint sat sleepily in a chair near his bedroom window. It was very quiet except for the ticking of a clock and Cristina's deep breathing. She lay fully clothed on the bed with a loaded carbine and pistol beside her.

Someone tapped on the door. Quint crossed to it. "*Quién es?*" he whispered.

"Rafaela," she replied, low-voiced.

Quint eased open the door.

Rafaela came into the room. "There are armed Texans prowling about," she reported tensely.

"How the hell did they get arms?"

"I heard noises in the *torreón*. I went through the passageway. The trapdoor was open and the door was unbarred."

Cristina sat up. "I told Catherine to secure the trapdoor."

"You should have attended to it yourself!" Quint growled.

"Let her alone," Rafaela said. "There's no time for that."

"What about the officers?"

"I tried their door. It's still locked."

"Where's Catherine?"

"She won't leave her room. I've already warned Tobias. He's gone to get the other two horsebreakers."

Quint slipped his derringer into a pocket and took his pair of Colts. He thrust one under his belt. "Stay behind me in the passageway, Cris. Rafaela, you catfoot down to the other end and stay in the living room. If anything happens to us, bar the door and sit tight."

"How can they get out of their room?" Rafaela asked.

Quint motioned her along the dimly lamplit passageway to the living room. He paused at the bedroom door and tried it gently. It was still locked. Just as he did so, there was a muffled explosion within the room. Part of the door lock flew out and smoke leaked through the hole. Quint flattened his back against the wall. The door was jerked open and a man leaped into the passageway, crouching to fire his outthrust pistol. Quint swung the Colt high and brought the long barrel down just behind the man's ear. He dropped the pistol as he went down. It struck the floor butt first. The hammer fell. The Colt flamed. The bullet fanned past Quint's face. Another man charged from the bedroom and thrust a pistol toward Quint.

"Drop, Quint!" Cristina cried. She fired just over his head. The man grunted in savage pain and fell over the unconscious man on the floor.

Carbine butts thudded against the door into the study. The Texans must have come over the roof, dropping onto the patio. Quint ran to the study with a Colt ready in each hand. The door crashed open and three men charged into the room. Quint fired each Colt alternately four times. The first two men went down, one of them falling heavily against Quint's legs, driving him backward. He fell over a stool. The third Texan shouted in triumph. Quint fired from the floor and missed. It was enough for the trooper. He whirled and ran for the patio. Cristina leaped across the two fallen men and raised her carbine. Just as the Texan reached the well, she fired. The big slug hit him in the middle of the back. He dropped his carbine, staggered sideways, hit the top of the well, and fell into it with a muffled scream. Seconds later there came the sound of a heavy splash.

Cristina closed the door and shoved a cabinet across it. She turned to Quint. "Are you all right?" she cried anxiously.

Quint stood up. He began to reload his pistols. "I'll make it," he said.

They peered into the smoky passageway. The two men were still lying there. The one on top moved a little. Quint and Cristina moved warily to them. The wounded man was Jim Jarvis. He opened his eyes and looked up at them. "You," he said to Cristina. "I thought you liked me." Blood trickled brightly from between his lips. He coughed hard. A flood of dark blood poured from his slack mouth. He rolled over and died.

Shelby sat up, feeling the knot behind his ear. He looked up at

Cristina. "You women learn well from the master killer Kershaw," he said grimly.

"What would you have done?" she asked.

He had no answer.

The muffled roaring of gunfire came from the outside. Quint ran to the patio, went up onto the roof, then crept on hands and knees to the parapet. The moon had come up. Gun flashes spurted from some of the outbuildings. The Texans were running for cover on the far side of the stream. Two of them lay sprawled on the ground. A rifle boomed just on the far side of the cemetery and another Texan staggered in his stride and fell into the shallow stream.

"Don Quintin!" Tobias shouted. "We have them damned Tejanos on the run! Shall we kill them all? *Degüello! Degüello! Degüello!* No quarter! No quarter! No quarter!" he chanted wildly.

Quint stood up. "No, you bloodthirsty old sonofabitch! Just keep them where they are! I've got their officer here." He turned and looked toward the stream. "You hear me, Texans?" he shouted.

There was a moment's hesitation. "We hear you, greaser!" a trooper shouted back. "What do you want us to do?"

"Have a few of your men bring over your arms! *All* of them, you understand! I want no more killing! Now *move!*"

The Texans buried their dead just after dawn light. A cool dawn wind crept up the slopes and rippled the grasses of the old *camposanto*. Quint allowed the Texans to fire three blank volleys over the graves. The echoes chased off into the distance, startling the birds, who rose squawking in disorganized flight.

At sunrise Dave and Frank with a few *vaqueros* rode up to the *rancho* on lathered horses. By that time the silent Texans stood to horse just beyond the gateway. Their guidon snapped restlessly in the breeze. Now and again one of them would look up the slope to the freshly mounded graves. They were a long way from Bexar County. Quint had allowed them three old packmules to carry their marching water. Shelby Calhoun insisted in paying for them with Confederate money. Some of the *vaqueros* would follow the Texans, carrying their unloaded weapons on packmules.

"March order!" Shelby commanded.

The troopers moved out under the command of grim-faced

Sergeant Tate, whose broken left arm was in a sling. Cristina had set it for him that morning.

Shelby mounted his horse and looked down at Quint. "You checked us neatly, Quint," he said. "But it was a near thing. We are still far from checkmate, you and I."

Quint nodded. "You made a good try," he admitted.

"You'll not reconsider our offer?"

"Last night should have proven that to you."

"Nonetheless, the offer still stands. I can hold the commission for you if you change your mind."

"Do you have it with you?"

Shelby took it out from within his coat.

"Let me have it."

Shelby handed it down to Quint. Quint ripped it into tiny fragments and cast them to the breeze. He looked up at Shelby. "You'd best get on the way. The sun is rising high. It bids to be a hell-hot day."

Shelby pulled on his gauntlets. He looked back toward the *casa*. The women stood on top of the *torreón*. "Jim Jarvis spoke much about your women after we went to our room," he said thoughtfully. He looked down again at Quint. "I envy you Rafaela, Quint. I would have liked to have had a daughter like her."

Quint nodded. "One of the best."

Shelby hesitated. "Catherine," he said, then paused.

"What is it, Shell?" Quint asked.

"She'll cause trouble here, likely between your sons, possibly even yourself. I saw her with Francisco in Santa Fe a few times and once at the Rio Brioso."

"I didn't know they were that close."

Shelby shrugged. "They were, as close as she can get to any man, then give nothing of herself. She's a tease, a trollop, perhaps worse than that."

"She's been much with other men?"

"Quite a few. It has caused Jean great grief."

"You're sure? Positive?" Quint demanded.

Shelby's eyes held Quint's. "I am sure. Positive, in fact." He touched his mount with his spurs. There was something outspoken, something dark, perhaps evil, about Catherine. How could he be so positive—except perhaps by personal knowledge? Then Quint knew. *For the love of God*, he thought.

Shelby looked back. "Good-bye, then, until we meet again, Quintin Kershaw. I'm sure we will—in battle smoke."

Quint climbed to the top of the tower. He looked full into the great blue eyes of Catherine. There seemed to be no feeling within them; it was like looking through tinted window glass into an empty room.

Anselmo and his *vaqueros* unloaded the carbines and pistols by the side of the trail. The Texans were five hundred yards away, watching them. Shelby Calhoun rode back. "A word with you alone, Anselmo Campos," he said.

Anselmo waved his men back to the *rancho*. "Talk," he said over his shoulder.

"You know this is part of the Confederate Territory of Arizona," Shelby began.

Anselmo grinned. "Have you told the Mimbres that? The men of the Querencia? You saw what they thought of that."

"It is true. It is only a matter of time before we invade New Mexico and make it part of the Confederacy."

"I'll wait. What is it you have to say to me? Get on with it! I have much mustang trapping to do."

"You are the only surviving kin of Eusebio Campos, are you not?"

"His daughter was my mother. There are no other survivors of his family other than myself."

"You are sure?"

Anselmo nodded. "Look in the *camposanto* for the others."

"I haven't much time, Anselmo. The fact is, this grant now known as the Querencia should legally be yours."

Anselmo stared at him blankly. "Are you without reason?" he demanded.

"It's true. Your grandfather's grant was from the Mexican government and was legal. In later years, when it was abandoned, Governor Armijo managed to get it—illegally, of course. He, in turn, sold it to Dr. Thomas Byrne of Santa Fe, who gave it to your Don Quintin in exchange for his share of the Rio Brioso grant up north. Therefore, whether or not this is Confederate or United States territory, the right to this grant is legally *yours*, and none other, Anselmo Campos."

It was very quiet except for the wind rustled dry grasses and the distant cry of a soaring hawk.

Anselmo studied Shelby. "*Verdad?*" he asked at last.

Shelby nodded. "*Verdad.*"

Anselmo was confused. He had never thought of such a thing. The Indian in him looked upon the land as belonging to all, yet to one. That was the way of the Mimbres. He believed in it, liked it.

Shelby smiled. "You can say nothing of the fact that you now know of this. When the time comes and we of the Confederacy invade and conquer New Mexico, we can drive him from the land and install you as rightful *patrón*. Will you remember that?"

Anselmo shrugged. "I can," he said carelessly. He spurred his dun and rode back toward the rancho.

"*Vaya con Dios*, Anselmo Campos!" Shelby cried.

Anselmo looked back. "*Vaya con Dios—acaso!*" he shouted. "Go with God—maybe . . ." He spat hard to one side and continued on.

Quint was seated on one of the top rails of the horsebreaking corral watching the horsebreakers at work. Anselmo climbed up and sat beside him. "All taken care of, *patrón*," he reported.

Quint passed him the makings. "Anything else?" he asked.

Anselmo looked sideways at him. "Just something the Tejano officer told me."

"About this land being legally yours?"

Anselmo nodded as he deftly rolled a cigarette.

"So?" Quint asked.

Anselmo looked blankly at him. "So?" he echoed.

Quint shaped a cigarette. "What is it you want to do?"

Anselmo was silent for a time. "Do you remember what I told you the first time we met here?" he asked.

"You said many things."

"Can you remember what?"

"You called me *patrón* almost immediately, as though you had been expecting me."

"True, and . . . ?"

"*Yo tengo raíces aquí.* I have roots here."

Anselmo nodded.

"There is more?"

"Fifteen years ago you came here to find me. At that time I agreed to be your man. You were the first white man I ever met who I knew I could trust. We became more than master and servant—with your permission, *patrón*, we also became good friends. I don't want to own this land. All I have ever wanted is to stay here in peace and work at my trade. This, you have allowed me."

Quint grinned. "In peace? Have you forgotten the Mimbres? The Navajos? The Mexican *ladrones*? And now the Tejanos?"

"The *patrón* knows what I mean. You understand?"

"I understand. So, what shall we do?"

Anselmo looked sideways at Quint. "The land is freely yours. All I want is to live out my time here with you, *patrón*."

Quint nodded. "Granted."

They gripped hands hard and looked into each other's eyes.

After a time Quint said, "You did a helluva job trapping these mustangs, Anselmo."

The *vaquero* waved a hand. "For nothing. After all, is it not my job?"

★ EIGHT ★

The contracted time of delivery was not far off. The corrals were full of the mustangs broken, or at least half-broken; the mules were ready, and so were the beef cattle. Still, there were not quite enough of the mustangs for the contract as well as those needed to replace them. The *vaqueros* used every trick and skill in the unwritten book of mustanging to fill the quota. No mustang can be caught by outright pursuit. They can be "walked down" by keeping after them, in mounted relays, changing horses frequently twenty-four hours a day, never letting the mustangs have any rest, until at last they can be lassoed. This took time, time that was not available. Water was short in New Mexico that year, as it had been in the previous year. The lesser waterholes on the plains had been fenced in, to force the mustangs to come to two of the larger ones. Snares were set under trees on known trails to the waterholes, where a mustang might run his head through a cunningly concealed loop suspended from a stout branch. It wasn't easy to fool them with this device. A caught horse could choke himself to death in a wild frenzy to escape before the arrival of his captor. Sometimes a water-soaked sack of salt would lure the wild horses to it. An added attraction could be a staked-out mare. A concealed man could then rope the unwary horse. Sometimes a stallion would approach the *rancho* after some of the captive mares and be roped. There was a major fault with these two methods. A stallion thus roped, usually the boldest of the bold, would be one of those who approached the *rancho* and would turn on his captor with a ferocity quelled only by killing him or maiming him with a bullet. It was a dangerous and wasteful method.

At times the mustangers would surprise a few strays from the lesser *manadas*. Then they closed in with long lariats and swung out loops, yelping loudly, leaning forward in their Californio saddles, riding like demons until a loop streaked out like a lightning flash to rope the mustang. Then grass and gravel would fly as the roping horse dug in his hoofs. The thrown mustang would go head over flailing hoofs. The fight would begin as soon as he got to his feet, circling away from the roper, trying to free himself, snorting, nickering and shaking his head to free himself of the lariat. The rider would pivot on his mount, letting the captive wear himself out running in wide circles. If the captive fought too hard, other riders closed in to throw ropes, snaring legs and neck until at last he stood, lathered, quivering from head to tail roots, while his captors sat their horses admiring him with a horseman's keen appreciation.

The waterhole traps worked best. They were built about the two most used watering places. Wing fences were built to blend in with the trees and brush. The gate was left open. Water was the bait and thirst the driving force that brought the *cimarrones* to the trap. The stallion would come first, sniffing the wind carrying the scent of water. He would be suspicious, snorting,

then wheeling away, kicking high and hard, and racing away. H
would come back slowly, dry-thirsty, unable to resist, to ent
the gate, giving away his freedom, perhaps his very life. One
one, in twos and threes, mares and colts would follow him, no
that the way was safe. They would line up about the wate
nuzzling it and blowing contentedly. A man would come soft
through the semidarkness to stand near the gate and whist
sharply. The mustangs would wheel and charge the nine-foo
high triple-strong fence. The man would wave his arms a
stamp his feet, making sure the wild ones saw him. There w
no need to close the gate. The man could return to his downwi
station to wait for more captives. The penned mustangs wou
not go near that open gate again, for man had been seen ther
During the night strays would trot to the water, hearing t
champing and low nickering of the mares, smelling the oth
mustangs, feeling that if *they* were there, it was a place of safet

There was one temporary blessing while the mustangers work
day and night to fill the contract quota. The Mimbres stayed we
away from these tough men of the Querencia. There was fai
chance of cutting one of them off alone, and even if it could
done, it was a great risk for one horse, rifle, and pistol. T
Mimbres knew the men of the Querencia all too well by no
Further, once the concerted drive was over, they would be ab
to conduct their horse-hunting activities with less danger. Aft
all, there were plenty of horses for both factions, although th
sudden frenzied drive of the white-eyes and the *nakai-yes*, t
Mexicans, had them wondering.

The *vaqueros* worked hard, led by Dave and Anselmo. Fran
worked intermittently and with little enthusiasm. His interest
work of any kind was always lukewarm. He was clever enough-
sly might be a better word—not to let his father know he was n
cooperating fully in the hunt. Even so, Quint had always bee
tolerant of Frank in that respect. Frank knew the reason and too
full advantage of it. In order to smooth over his rather obvio
love of David over Frank, Quint did not want Frank to think h
was picking on him, so to speak. For that reason, Frank ha
things easier than Dave around the *rancho*. He would purpose
fully wander away from the mustanging on the pretext he ha
seen a fine stray stallion, one of those without a *manada*, off b
himself. Frank would track him down and capture him. He ha

ined two fine stallions that way, one by "creasing" and the
her by snaring. He took them back to the *rancho* and told the
orsebreakers that they were his personally and that he would
reak them himself. He was never questioned. The traditions of
d New Mexico were ingrained in them. What the *patroncito*
anted, that he could have. It was sufficient.

During the roundup there were few people at the *rancho*.
afaela often joined the mustangers. She loved the excitement of
e hunt and the sheer outright virility of the *cimarrones*. Cather-
e would not join her. She didn't mind the roundup. The hunt
as exciting, and she loved fine horses. It was the thought of
mping out in the open on the hard ground, eating the coarsest
food, around men who had the rank smell of hard-living
tdoor men, reeking of stale sweat, rank tobacco, and manure.
esides, there was absolutely no way of bathing, and she must
ve her bath each day. Therefore, she stayed at the *rancho*.
ristina was busy, as always. The women of the place were
ccupied with their many chores. The few men were breaking
e horses eighteen hours a day or herding and guarding the
ttle.

Frank approached the *rancho* by a circuitous route. He didn't
ant to be seen. Supposing the word got back to his father?
here was a *bosquecito* a quarter of a mile from the ranch, near
e mouth of a box canyon where the spring that fed the stream
abbled constantly. The overflow pool had been embanked with
ck. A *choza*, a light structure of upright poles with a mud roof,
d been constructed there for the women of the *rancho* who
athed there. When they were there, usually as a group, bathing
d washing clothing, a guard was always posted overlooking
e spring area, but unable to see the bathers. In common with
e rest of the Querencia, the spring was taboo to the Apaches
d Navajos. It was too close to the scene of massacre. In fact,
me of the victims had been slaughtered there, dyeing the
ring pool and the stream with their blood. It was an unwritten
w of the Querencia that no male, outside of the one guard,
ight approach the spring except in time of danger.

Frank reined in behind a clump of willows as he neared the
ancho. A rider was approaching the spring. He could tell by the
at it was likely a woman. No man ever rode like that, at least
New Mexico. He put the glasses on her. The lovely oval face

of Catherine swam into his vision. She was riding sidesaddle on a cinnamon roan. She wore a long full skirt of military blue and quasi-military jacket with brass buttons twinkling in the bright sunlight. The material was stretched tightly across her full breast. A tiny army forage cap was perched on the side of her head. was the type of riding attire army officers' wives affected.

He dismounted and entered the *bosquecito*. There was a full view of the spring from there. There was no guard above it. She dismounted beside the spring and tethered the roan to a tree. She removed a towel and bathing materials from a saddlebag and placed them beside the pool. She took off her cap, then removed the hairpins and combs to let her cornsilk blond tresses fall thickly about her shoulders. She pulled off her tiny boots and began to strip off her silk stockings, giving Frank a fascinating view of her long, shapely legs. He drew in a sharp breath as she raised her skirt high to remove the stockings. She unconsciously rubbed the inner sides of her smooth white thighs. She didn't seem to be in much of a hurry.

Frank had propositioned her several times in Santa Fe. She had refused intercourse but had granted him liberties with her lush body right up to the point of penetration. She had teased and tantalized him. Once he had tried too hard, and she had threatened to cry rape. It was too dangerous to go on, but to his eternal shame he had ejaculated right in front of her, dribbling down her belly and legs. She had exploded into laughter. He had wanted to hurt her for that utter indignity. No one, but *no one* particularly a *woman*, could laugh at Francisco Kershaw. Still he had played her little game, feeling that some day he would possess her, then walk away from her to *her* eternal shame, or so he thought. It would have been worth the wait. There was no one quite like her in Santa Fe, that city of prostitutes and loose women. He must have her!

"Before God," he murmured.

She stood up and stripped off her jacket and full skirt to stand there in chemise and drawers. Then suddenly, she looked in his direction while she stripped to the buff, raised her arms above her head, stretching so that her bust seemed to thrust itself out toward him, then stepped quickly into the pool.

Catherine luxuriated in the cool clear water, soothed by the soft murmuring of Cristina's pet ducks on the pond. She was

★ 60 ★

t in thought. She didn't like the Querencia, much preferring
amenities and society of Santa Fe, in particular the army
ficers of good family stationed up at Fort Marcy, those who
re single and those whose wives were back in the States. It
s somewhat the same at the Rio Brioso near Fort Union, but
all her aunt's efforts to make the place comfortable and
easant for her, she much preferred the Santa Fe house, which
d been left to her by her father under the guardianship of her
nt. It was the only thing she had received from her father. The
oney she had came from her mother's side of the family. She
ood to gain much more when her grandfather died. She could
independent of any man. But she wanted to marry and marry
ell with a man of wealth and social position. She didn't have
y objection to older men. In fact, she preferred them. Perhaps
e was unconsciously seeking the father she had never known.
er Uncle Shelby was such a man, but he had no money and
tle influence now that he had divorced Aunt Jean. Quint
ershaw! There was a man. The New Mexicans had a saying
out such a one: "*Huevos con huevos*. Testicles with testicles."
short, a real "stud." She had heard of his reputation and
ew of his past relationship with her aunt. But then, he didn't
em to have much money, and not a great deal of interest in
cumulating it. However, in the future such a man with the
ght influence, connections, and her money might do exceedingly
ell. She didn't know, of course, that her Aunt Jean had thought
the same idea over twenty years ago and had not succeeded,
arrying Shelby Calhoun on the rebound. She did know her aunt
d something in her head for Quint. Now that she had divorced
elby and Quint was widowed, she might be deeply interested
him again. Perhaps she might snatch Quint from under her
nt's nose. Imagine Catherine parading such a barbarian in
ont of Jean and the relatives and friends in the capital. She
ughed out loud.

"What's the joke, Cathie?" Frank asked suspiciously.

She opened her eyes. He stood not fifteen feet from her,
evouring her with his eyes—the full cherry-tipped breasts, the
unded thighs and long shapely legs, the curly blond fleece at
r crotch. She quickly and inadequately covered her breasts
ith one hand and her crotch with the other.

Frank squatted, teetering back and forth on his boot heels

while he shaped a cigarette. "You make a lovely picture," murmured.

"If you were a gentleman you wouldn't have done this!" snapped.

He shrugged. "I've seen you like this before. Remember? the big bed in your house."

She smiled. "I remember what happened then. Maybe I safe enough from rape here, in that case."

His face tightened. "You cock-teasing bitch," he sa low-voiced.

"Get out of here! You make me sick!"

He shook his head. He could not lose his temper with h That would be to play her game. "I'll have to stay and gu you. There's no guard up on the hillside. You know the r here. No bathing without a guard. Supposing a Mimbres bu saw you? Supposing there were half a dozen of them? They have you flat on your back on those hard rocks. Two of th would pull your legs apart to let the first stud ram it to you. Af that they'd take turns. Then they'd leave you lying there, nak bruised, and bleeding, squatting in a circle, watching you unti last one of them would mount you again and the process wo be repeated all over again. You *might* survive. It might be be if you did not. Life as a captive white woman in an Apac *ranchería* would be pure hell for you once their women got you. They can be worse than the men with captives, far worse

She shrugged. "You can't frighten me. No Apache wo come here. It's taboo and you know it."

"They've been known to break taboos. They might if th saw you like you are now. Then there's always the *vaquer* Most of them are studs."

"They wouldn't dare! Not as long as they work for Un Quint."

He grinned evilly. "That leaves *me*, my heart. I'm not cc cerned about 'Uncle Quint.' "

"Throw me my clothes and turn your back!" she demande

He shook his head. "Not until you stand up and turn around front of me for the full effect."

"Then what happens?"

He looked around. "The grass is warm and soft. You wo

t me off this time. I've not had a woman in months. This time
u won't dare laugh at me."

She stood up reluctantly and turned slowly about.

"Mother of God," he murmured. He wet his lips. He stood
, unbuckled and dropped his gunbelt, ripped off jacket and
irt, then sat down to pull off his boots. Catherine had early
ining as a dancer. She pivoted and swung out a long leg,
tching Frank on the point of the jaw with her heel. The next
ck sent him sprawling backward, half-stunned. He flung him-
lf sideways, facedown, to avoid those murderous heels.

"Don't get up, you horny sonofabitch," she said. She full-
cked the Navy Colt she had snatched from his holster.

He looked along the pistol barrel into those great, cold-looking
ina-blue eyes and knew she wasn't joking. "I just thought you
ere asking for it," he said lamely.

"You were wrong, my heart."

"I think you knew I was watching you all the time," he
cused. "Didn't you?"

She shrugged. "You'll have to figure that out."

"I thought you might be asking for my love."

She laughed. "Love? Rutting in the grass like a pair of
ongrel dogs?"

"It'll do for want of anything else. You can't fool me, Cathie,
ou're cut from the same cloth I am. All right. You win again.
ll let you go and we'll keep this to ourselves."

"*You'll* let *me* go? Who has the pistol? You know I can use it
I have to."

He sat up and studied her creamy nakedness. *Jesu*, but she
as built! Was she playing with him again? Damn her! "What is it
ou really want?" he asked. "I know you well enough. You
ant *something*."

She slowly backed to her clothing. "Strip," she ordered. She
atched him as he did so. "Stand up. Turn around slowly." She
inned. "Not too bad."

He put his hand down and held his genitals. "Come on now,"
pleaded. "Stop playing. Let's get to it."

"I have a price, my heart."

"Name it!"

She tilted her lovely blond head to one side and studied him.

"You remember the day we were out watching the *manac* owned by that *bayo naranjado* stallion?"

He paled. "Not *him*, Cathie."

She laughed. "Quint has you scared to death about him, or it Davie?"

"Damn you! I'm not afraid of either one of them. But th stallion is another matter. I doubt if he'll ever be caught and if was I don't think he could ever be broken."

"It's not *him* I want, Frankie. It's his leader mare. The o with the star blaze. The one they call Estrella."

He shook his head. "It would be almost impossible to captu her as long as the stallion is around. Besides, they are not to t killed or captured."

"Why would it be necessary to kill?"

"Because if the mare is captured, the stallion would follo her into hell itself to get her back."

"Then capture her and kill him when he comes after her."

"Cathie, you don't know what you're asking. Isn't the *anything* else I can do instead of that?"

She shook her head. "Davie said he'd try if he could tal Quint into it."

He bent his head a little. "Dave? When did he say that? can't believe it. He thinks the same way Quint does about tho two *cimarrones*." He took a step toward her. "He hasn't sai that, has he?" He wouldn't have minded if any other man ha already gotten to her, or might in the future, but David w another matter.

She shook her head. "Not really. Besides, he just doesn want to bed with me. He wants to *marry* me."

"I can't imagine him interesting you or any other *whi* woman."

"You'd be surprised. He can be quite interesting and *amorou* when no one else is around. Not that he's gotten too far with m at least not as far as you did in Santa Fe."

"You haven't told him what happened then, have you?" h asked slowly and quietly. There was menace in his tone.

She shook her head. "But, I *might*, if you don't try for th mare." She smiled. "Well?" she added sweetly.

He nodded. "I'll try."

"I want more than just a 'try,' Frankie."

"All right! Damn it! I'll get her for you!"

"That's better!"

He eyed her up and down. He could not control his growing erection. "Can't we get at it now? Give me the pistol."

She slowly passed her free hand over her full breasts, down the soft mounded belly, then up and down her crotch, fingering herself, teasing, tantalizing, watching him all the time with mockery in her eyes. The bitch was trying to arouse him again to make a fool of himself. He started toward her. She raised the pistol again and shook her head.

"You bitch," he murmured.

She shrugged. "Not now, Frankie dear. But, after the mare is mine, you can have anything and everything you want. Now walk around to the far side of the pool and up the canyon a way."

He circled the pool and walked out from the shade of the trees into the bright hot sunlight. He could just make her out as she dressed quickly. She gathered up his clothing, mounted her mare, and rode out into the sunlight. She touched the mare with her heels and galloped her toward the *rancho*. Then at intervals she dropped his clothing, saving the trousers until the last. She rode swiftly down the long slope. The southwest wind carried her jeering laughter back to a madly cursing Frank.

★ NINE ★

The Querencia *mesteneros* had captured all the *cimarrones* needed. They removed the fences about the waterholes and herded the captives back to the Querencia. The plains were as they had been before.

Frank had supposedly left for Socorro, riding one of his best horses and leading two others. He moved by a circuitous route west-southwest to Caballo Springs, where the *bayo naranjado* seemed to have moved his *manada* to escape the traps at their usual waterholes. The mustangs had regulated hours for watering. One might almost set one's watch by their approach to a favorite watering haunt.

Frank's usual fault in capturing wild horses was his impatience. Other than that he had been quite good at it when younger. He was a born horseman, who had learned early from Federico Casias, distant cousin to his mother and majordomo at El Cerrillo in the days before the Mexican War. Anselmo Campos, who didn't like Frank, had still contributed much of his lore and skill to Frank's experience. The combined teaching of the two men, coupled with his innate ability to ride, had developed him into one of the finest horsemen, in a land where horsemanship was an art. Now in order to capture the mare for Catherine he must develop that most necessary of traits in being a *mestenero*— absolute patience. Patience like an Indian, or a peon in the fields, he thought with a wry grin. Quint had it, probably from his early experiences as a mountain man and his long association with Indians. David had it, perhaps even more than Quint, but then his mother had been Shoshoni, the half-breed sonofabitch.

Anselmo had been one of the best *mesteneros* beyond the Llano Estacado when he was still in his teens. He had always worked alone, which might have been one of the best reasons for his great success. He had lived constantly in close proximity to the *manada*, so in time they had come to accept him. Sometimes those less wild would often follow him docilely into captivity. He was never cruel or vicious in his conquest of them. He never maimed or starved mustangs, as did other *mesteneros*. However, in those earlier days, time meant nothing on the limitless plains, with thousands upon thousands of *cimarrones* to be had. One could take time. Such was not the case with Frank. Before he had left the Querencia, Catherine had subtly hinted she was considering a return to Santa Fe before the war came north, as it surely would, if rumor had any basis to it. So time was limited, and each passing hour triply important to Frank in his quest for the *estrella* mare.

He chose a place with a clear panoramic view of many acres of open plain and *bosquecitas* not too far from Caballo Springs.

There seemed to be a natural truce between the *manada* stallions as to watering times. Few stallions with or without *manadas* had the courage to water at Caballo Springs when the *bayo naranjado* was there.

For three days Frank lay hidden on a slope downwind from the springs. He lit no fires, did not smoke, and moved only after dark. He kept his three horses picketed half a mile away and downwind from the watering place. He hoped to God no wandering Mimbres or Navajo might find them. It was a risk, but a necessary one.

Each of the three days, the *manada* came to water during the late afternoon. The stallion always came first, testing the ground, smelling for the dung of a competing stallion or for signs of a lurking mountain lion. Even the faintest of suspicions caused him to stand alertly, to advance and retreat, to wait, then advance and retreat again, wary, watchful, and taut with suspicion. He took his time. Only at his signal would the leader mare bring the *manada* to the water. Even then the mares and colts would water only at another of his signals. They too were touchy, wary, alert to the slightest foreign sound or smell. The third day they had stampeded at an alien scent. A sleek shape launched itself from overhanging rocks—a magnificent tawny red mountain lion at least nine-and-a-half feet long from nose to tail tip. A colt died instantly as powerful jaws crunched into his neck. The stallion snorted a signal for instant flight, snapping and biting at the mares' flanks. The leader mare had been badly frightened. She had been within a few feet of the stricken colt. The stallion cut through the center of the *manada* at tremendous speed, scattering the panic-stricken mares and colts to right and left toward the *bosques* and breaks.

The mountain lion felt safe enough. Who was there to dispute his fresh kill? He dragged the colt into the brush and up the slope to an opening among the trees where he could see for quite a distance. He lay down, munching contentedly on his prey.

The *manada* was gone, scattered to all points of the compass. Darkness came. Faint moonlight began to illuminate the plains. The great stallion came back alone, downwind from the panther.

Frank couldn't believe it. Mountain lions were the bane of wild horses. They feared them like few other predators. No horse in its right mind would ever stalk such an efficient horse-killing cat. It was a tale Frank might never tell; no one would have believed him.

The lion raised his head. Blood dripped from his jaws. He looked down the slope. The horses would not be back that night. He began eating again. Then he raised his head and padded noiselessly down the slope to a bare patch of hard ground lighted by the moon. He raised his head and sniffed the night breeze. Hoofs clattered on the ground. The lion was startled. Before he could crouch to leap or speed away at a run, iron-hard hoofs struck his barrel. Frank knew his ribs had been staved in. The lion staggered sideways. Hoofs hit his rounded head. Jaws closed like the snap of a steel trap on the lion's head, peeling the scalp down over his eyes. In agony and half-blinded the lion tried to escape. The hoofs battered him into a twitching, smashed, and bleeding hulk until he lay still forever. The *manada* would not come back there until the menacing odor was gone.

The scavengers came before dawn, and when the sun rose the *zopilotes* arrived, hovering high above the springs. By afternoon, nothing remained of the mountain lion but cleanly picked bones and a skull grinning in the bright sunlight.

The stallion returned in several days. He scouted the area, then left to bring back his *manada*. The need for water, at a favorite watering place, overcame their fear of the faint remaining lion odor. Even so, the stallion had to drive them to the water as he had driven them from it a few days past.

Frank knew it would be almost impossible to trap the mare. As long as the stallion was around, no enemy could get near his *manada* wihout fighting him to the death. Frank knew better than to kill him outright. He would have to face his father after such an act. Somehow he had to cut the mare out of the *manada* and "walk her down." After dusk he watered his horses at a tiny spring rarely if ever used by the mustangs. Under cover of darkness he rode one of them and led the other three far downwind until he could circle back to Caballo Springs and to a point where he could overlook the route by which the *manada* came and went to the water. The *estrella*, as the sentinel mare, often was apart from the rest of the mares. She would lead them to water and then lead them away from it again and out on the plains for night grazing. At that time the mares and colts would be somewhat scattered, with her on one side of them and the stallion on the other, keeping a lookout for rival stallions. This would be the time for Frank to strike.

Frank concealed his horses in a deep-cut arroyo at the bottom of a ridge downwind from the herd. He took a position of excellent observation on a low ridge. The *manada* returned from watering. The lead mare took up her position on the slope below Frank and upwind. The mares and colts scattered to graze. Then Frank's break came. A stallion younger and bigger than the *bayo naranjado* came through the moonlight, looking for trouble. They closed, circling and wheeling, rising up on their hind legs, squealing in rage as they fought it out with iron-hard hooves and slashing teeth.

Frank ran to his saddled dun and took the lead ropes of the roan and chestnut. He rode up the ridge slope. Frank was not religious, far from it, but this time he crossed himself, then sank his spurs into the dun. He came down the reverse slope as though shot from a cannon, with the two extra horses hammering along behind him and the dun.

The *estrella* was completely surprised, so intent was she on the conflict between the stallions. She panicked, ran this way and that, losing valuable time, then finally raced down the slope and headed out for the open plains, with Frank not more than a hundred yards behind her. He had the odds now. She had nowhere to hide, no stallion to fight for her. She was on her own. Her hoofs drummed a tattoo on the ground. By God, she was fast! Frank fell behind a little but kept up the pressure on her until he felt the dun tiring. He drew up the roan and shifted to him bareback, letting the dun drop behind to run with the chestnut.

Strays and lone mustangs fled from the pursuit. A *manada* scattered at the urging of its stallion. Half an hour passed. She was still running at her best speed. Sweat glistened in the moonlight. He raced the roan at top speed. The mare's stride seemed to falter. He shifted to the chestnut and let him full out. He was the fastest if not the most durable of his mounts. The mare began to veer a little from side to side, as though seeking a hiding place. She could not shake the man-creature and his three mounts.

Frank eased up. The gap widened. She looked back and slowed her stride. She began to trot and then walk. Frank immediately increased his speed. She dashed off again at full speed, but now her stride was a little erratic. This time the gap was steadily closed up. On and on they raced through the bright moonlight. He could see her sides expanding and contracting spasmodically with her laborious breathing. Sweat glistened and lather foamed back from her mouth.

Frank switched back to the dun and kept him at a fast walk until the mare slowed, then he'd spur after her at top speed. She could never outlast the dun. He was a stayer who could go on all night if necessary. Desperately she veered and ran up a rough, broken slope. Halfway up she stumbled. She was tired and could not save herself. She went down hard.

Frank stood up in his stirrups and cast a long loop as the mare struggled to her feet. It settled neatly about her neck. He reined in the dun, who then dug in his hooves. The rawhide rope tightened about her neck, choking her. She went down again. Another rope settled neatly over one of her hind legs. She tried to get up, but the two ropes dragged her down again. This time she stayed down, breathing spasmodically, a terrible wheezing sound.

"Got you, you pretty bitch!" Frank yelled. He came off the dun at a run and threw a *bozal*, two half hitches, about her nose. When at last she got up, trembling from tail root to nose tip, he placed her in between the two extra horses and led them north through the moonlight until it died away at last. He rode all night long until he reached a place five miles from the Querencia where there was a small seep spring on a timber-clothed mountain slope where in years past a corral had been built and a *jacal*, a brush shack, had been constructed. On his way to Caballo Springs he had cached a supply of food there and repaired the old corral.

He led her into the corral. She began to struggle. He tightened the choke hold on her and she went down. The distressful, frenzied breathing of her choking to death did not bother Frank. He swiftly hobbled her, then eased off on the choker. She got unsteadily to her feet, trembling violently, with lather dripping from her jaws. Frank quickly blindfolded her. He spoke softly to her: "*Hoh, hoh, hoh, hoh, hoh . . . Shuh, shuh, shuh, shuh, shuh. . . .*" He rubbed her nose over and over again, then took off the blindfold, stroked her ears and forehead, and breathed into her nostrils, an ancient, widespread practice taught to him by Anselmo. It seemed to tone her down. He tied her to a tree that formed one of the corner posts of the corral. As strength returned, she fought the tree and rope until exhausted. He did not allow her any water. By late that afternoon she had a caged look in her eyes, as though she had begun to realize struggling against this man-creature was futile.

To the south the conflict between the two stallions was long over. The *bayo naranjado* was more than a match for the challenger until he realized the lead mare was gone. He was caught between the horns of a dilemma—to defeat the newcomer or hunt for the missing mare. At last he turned away, lather foaming at his mouth, blood streaking his sides, and trotted away to the south, leaving his fine *manada* to the new stallion. Perhaps he thought he could return and regain his mares after finding the leader mare. He picked up the trail at moonset and swung north, feeling his way more by instinct than anything else. He would not quit until he found her.

★ TEN ★

The contract animals were about ready to be driven the 125 miles southeast to Fort Fillmore. It would be up to the cavalrymen at the fort to complete the training of the horses and the quartermaster teams to break the mules to harness. The problem of Apache intervention wasn't too likely to come up. Quint intended to send enough well-armed *vaqueros* under Dave's command to counteract such an eventuality. The pressing problem was that the Confederates might advance up the Rio Grande Valley to La Mesilla a few miles from Fort Fillmore. Both town and fort lay well south of the designated 34th Parallel boundary of the so-called Confederate Territory of Arizona. The threat notwithstanding, the garrison must have the animals necessary to help defend their position or, if need be, to have good transport to the north if they abandoned Fort Fillmore. Quint knew from headquarters at Santa Fe that timorous Major Lynde, post commander of Fillmore, had secret orders to either fall back on Fort Craig on the Rio Grande, about one hundred miles north of Mesilla, or Fort Stanton, about one hundred miles northeast, in the Capitan Mountains and roughly the same distance east of Fort Craig, with the San Andres Mountains and the Jornado del Muerto between them. Such a maneuver would depend solely on the results of a possible Confederate advance north.

"Will you send Frank or Dave with the herds?" Cristina asked Quint one evening at dinner.

"David, of course," Quint replied.

Rafaela looked up from her plate. "I think Frank would like to take them, Quint," she said. She slanted her eyes at Catherine, who blushed prettily.

Quint shook his head. "It is to be Dave."

Dave smiled ruefully. "No one seems to bother about what *I* would like to do," he said.

Quint looked quickly at him. "Do you have any objection?"

Dave glanced at Catherine but did not answer.

Cristina caught Quint's eye and shrugged her shoulders suggestively. She had mentioned to Quint earlier that Catherine was getting anxious to return to Santa Fe. She had added that Dave was gathering up enough courage to ask Catherine to marry him, or to at least consider it. It wasn't to Quint's liking, but he knew better than to interfere. He was uncertain about Catherine. Besides, Dave was a half-breed, not exactly the type of husband she would have liked. Still, Dave was of age and had a mind of his own coupled with a powerful will, and if he wanted to ask her to marry him, there was nothing Quint could do about it.

Quint pushed back his plate and stood up. "You may have forgotten these are army contract animals. It's government business and an emergency. I'm on active duty and so is Dave. Dave is second-in-command of my company. Frank is a rather disinterested private. I can't depend on Frank too much. All of you know that. By the way, where has he been this past week or so?"

No one answered

Quint looked from one to the other of them. "Well, someone must certainly know. I'm waiting."

Dave shrugged. "I have no idea."

"He said he was going to Socorro," Cristina said. She looked at Rafaela as she spoke.

"Rafaela?" Quint said.

She looked up. "He left here with three horses. He wasn't going to Socorro. Tobias told me he took a week's supply of food with him. He's gone out on the Plains, Quint."

"So?" Quint asked.

Catherine looked up. "He's gone to walk down some *cimarrones*."

Quint was puzzled. "We've got all the mustangs we need. No one should go out on those plains alone now." He looked at Catherine. "Tell me the truth, Catherine."

When Quint spoke that way, no one could lie to him. He could perceive it the instant one spoke.

"Oh, all right, Uncle Quint!" she snapped. "He went to get me a mare."

Dave looked sideways at her. "Any particular mare?" he asked quietly.

Rafaela caught her breath. She had suspected why Frank had gone out there. She remembered what Catherine had said the first time she had seen the lead mare of the *bayo naranjado*'s *manada*. "I must have her," she had murmured, as though only to herself.

"Catherine?" Quint asked.

"The *estrella*," she blurted out.

"Jesus Christ!" Quint cried.

Dave shook his head. "He'll never capture her with the stallion around, and he might very well get himself picked off by the Mimbres."

"Maybe he plans to kill the stallion," Catherine said carelessly.

"Is that what he said?" Quint demanded.

She shrugged. "How should I know!"

Dave stood up. "I'd better go look for him, Quint."

"Not alone, Dave. Take some of the *vaqueros*. The Mimbres will know we're off the plains now. They'll likely be back, keeping out of sight, waiting their chance. We can't take too much time and risk too many men. I want those contract animals out of there in five days or less, if possible. We'll travel in pairs for protection. We can start at the Caballo Springs and work from there.''

Cristina followed Quint to their room. He began to change into trail clothing. ''Why must you go?'' she asked. He buckled on his gunbelt and settled it about his lean hips. ''If he's captured the mare and perhaps killed the stallion, I want to get to him before Dave does. If I don't, it might very well end up in a killing. You know they are always in an armed truce. Then there's that damned little empty-minded bitch in there. She's gotten in between them and is likely playing one of them off against the other.''

Cristina nodded. ''She's no good. But I think Dave may be in love with her.''

Quint shrugged into his jacket and put on his hat. ''God forbid! She'd break his heart if he let her.'' He looked at her. ''And Frank, what's his interest in her, as if I didn't know?''

''You're right, Quint.''

Quint rolled his eyes upward as he reached for his Sharps. ''Dave only thinks he's in love with her.''

She hesitated. ''How would *you* know?'' she asked boldly.

He looked at her, then away. It was the same situation that always came up at similar moments when they were alone. God knows she meant a great deal to him. She had been a mainstay in his life both before and after the death of Guadalupe. There were times when Cristina's devotion to him reminded him of Mountain Woman, mother to David. How long had that been? Almost twenty-five years . . .

''I'm sorry,'' she said softly. She came to him and pressed her dark head against his broad chest. He drew her close.

''Ready, Quint?'' Dave called from the passageway.

It was after dark when the group reached Caballo Springs. Each of them had a lead horse. They would start searching at first light. They found no traces of Frank that day or the next. It was Dave, riding alone, who noticed that the *manada* of the *bayo náranjado* was missing, both him and the leader mare. A younger stallion was now dominating the mares.

The following day, results were the same.

''Maybe he did go to Socorro after all,'' Quint suggested.

Dave shrugged. "The stallion and mare are missing. Doesn't that strike you as odd?"

"Possibly. There's also another possibility."

Dave looked at him. "Apaches?"

Quint nodded. "If so, we'll never find him now. One white man with three fine horses, a Navy Colt, and a Sharps carbine would be a prime target for the Mimbres. Dave, I've got to get those contract animals started south."

"Go, then," Dave said shortly. "I'm looking for Frank."

"I'll need you to take them."

Dave walked to his horse. "Send Anselmo or go yourself."

"Wait, then. I'll go with you, Davie."

Dave mounted and set spurs to his horse, turning him away from Quint and some of the *vaqueros*. "I'll go alone!" he shouted back. "If I'm not back in the next few days, start them south. If I get back in time, I'll catch up with them."

Yndelecio came to Quint. "There will be trouble if Dave finds him, *patrón*."

"I know."

"Do you want me to trail them?"

Quint shook his head. "You and the boys go back to the *rancho*. I'll search a little longer."

Dave rode to the north. A thought had come to him. There was no trace of Frank or the two missing mustangs. Somehow the searchers should have turned up something, some clue, anything at all. Dave felt that he was still alive. If *he* had captured the horses, or the mare at least, and didn't want to take them back to the Querencia until broken, where would he have gone? The name Mary Magdalene came to him. The northernmost end of the plains had a mountain thought to resemble the profile of Mary Magdalene, at least to the early Franciscan friars who had come that way. The resemblance had always escaped Dave. The mountain was said to have an enchanted reputation among the Apaches and Navajos. It had existed long before the coming of the Spaniards. Whether that was true or not, no white man had ever been attacked by Apaches or Navajos on that particular mountain. Superstition or not, it was a well-proved fact. Quint and Luke had known about it the first time they had seen the Plains and had taken advantage of it. There was a small corral and a *jacal* there, built long ago for the use of the

Querencia. It had not been used in many years. Dave reasoned that if he wanted to break a horse in privacy, that would be the place he would have gone. Frank knew about it. It was a long chance, but the only one Dave had left.

Quint started north after an hour's delay. It wasn't until he was an hour on the way that he noticed an almost indistinguishable thread of smoke streaking skyward to the west. He looked about. There was another such smoke tendril to the south. No need for conjecture. The Mimbres were aware of the searchers and might have noticed the main group riding east toward the *rancho*. Quint was raising thin dust in the late afternoon sunlight. They would be aware that it was a lone rider and fair game. He'd have to be doubly cautious and yet remain on Dave's trail, to keep him unaware that he was being followed and still evade any possible Apache pursuit.

Frank awoke with a start. He reached for his Colt. It was still dark, that intense darkness just before the dawn when the spirit is at lowest ebb, and a favorite time of Apache approach and attack. The wind was shifting uncertainly before dying away with the coming of daylight. It soughed through the tops of the towering pines.

A horse nickered and then was still. Frank peered through one of the paneless windows downslope to the corral. The mare had been quiet all night. Another day or two and he might be able to ride her in triumph to the Querencia. His horses were picketed a quarter of a mile away from the mare. She nickered again. The Apaches never came to that mountain. What was it, then? White men? Mexican *ladrones*? He pulled on his boots and reached for his carbine. He cocked and capped it. He moved noiselessly outside. The faintest trace of gray light pewtered the eastern sky.

The mare stood close to the fence on the other side of the corral, gnawing steadily at the upper bar. Something moved just beyond her, a large shadow, but there wasn't enough light to make a shadow. Frank ran toward the corral, slipped on the mat of pine needles, and came down hard. His right hand closed on the small of the stock and his forefinger pressed the trigger. The Sharps flashed and boomed. In the light of the muzzle flare he saw the stallion plunging toward him with bared teeth. The shot echo bellowed through the trees and died away as he rolled

★ 76 ★

deways from the path of the stallion and behind a big pine. The
allion thundered past him. Frank snatched a thirty-three-foot,
ght-plaited rawhide reata from a corral post. He rolled between
e bars into the corral just as flailing hoofs smashed into the top
il, missing his face by inches.

Frank retreated while he coiled the reata. "You murdering
nofabitch!" he yelled at the raging stallion. "Come to get her,
? Good! Come on, then! We'll see who gets her right now!"

The big dun prowled outside the corral like a night-hunting
ountain lion, never taking his eyes from Frank. The sky grayed
en became a pearly gray. Visibility became better. Frank was a
p roper. He spread out the loop on the ground behind himself.
e stallion rounded the corral and hammered at the broken top
il with his hoofs. Frank held the reata loop at his left side half
t of sight of the stallion, stepped out with right leg forward,
en pitched the loop in a diagonal position, performing one
volution, then settling perfectly over the dun's head, to be
awn swiftly taut.

Hell broke loose. The stallion plunged and then pawed for the
y. He twisted this way and that, lunged both ways along the
nce line, rearing and showing his belly while his hoofs flailed
rrows through the quiet air, a powerful mass of sheer raging
ergy. He reared up on his hind legs and pitched straight down
ith his head between his pastern joints, then flung himself to
e ground.

Frank came hand-over-hand along the taut reata while it cut a
oove in the top rail. The rotted rail snapped, allowing enough
ack in the reata so that the dun could rear back up onto his feet.
e turned sideways, reared and fell again, backward this time,
agging Frank forward to the fence line. Frank dug in his boot
els and moved backward, fighting to get enough slack to make
dally about the snubbing post behind him. The reata slackened
lly as the raging stallion broke completely through the bars,
rs laid back, mouth open and teeth bared, slavering yellowish
am, eyes afire with hell light. His powerful jaws closed with a
cious steel trap snap on Frank's left thigh, peeling off pants,
awers, and a layer of flesh. Frank screamed with excruciating
in and utter rage. He dropped the rope and retreated, facing
e horse, who reared high above him with flailing hoofs. At that
stant the mare kicked out and knocked Frank flat an instant

before the dun's hoofs flashed right where his head had bee
The stallion reared back for another surefire try at breaki
Frank's skull like an eggshell.

A gun cracked flatly twice like the quick splitting of a shing
over the knee. The dun was seemingly flung sideways. Blo
sprayed over Frank. Three more shots cracked out. The d
vomited blood all over Frank. Some of the spray hit the mar
She screamed in mortal panic, reared back, snapping her teth
and raced around the corral until she reached the broken fen
opening, leaped through it, and fled downhill through the fore
The dun lay still, partly over Frank's lower legs and feet.

"Stop her! Goddamnit! Stop her, whoever you are!" Fra
shouted.

Dave stood at the break in the fence, empty, smoking Colt
hand, looking at Frank with set face and cold gray eyes. For
fraction of a second Frank almost thought it was Quint becau
of those icy-looking eyes.

"Get up," Dave said coldly.

"I'm pinned down. Can't you see?"

"Too Gawd-damned bad he didn't land on that stupid head
yours."

Dave brought up his horse, looped the reata about the sauce
shaped saddlehorn, and dragged the dead dun off Frank's leg
The left pant leg and exposed flesh were soaked with the mi
gled blood of man and horse. Frank pulled himself up to his fe
and hobbled across the corral without a word of thanks.

"Well, you really did it this time," Dave said. "Where
you think you're going?"

Frank did not turn. "I'll take your horse," he said.

Dave shook his head. "Sit down and let me take a look at th
leg of yours."

Frank reached the horse. He quickly dragged the Sharps rif
from its saddle scabbard and checked to see if it was loaded.

"Hold it!" Dave snapped.

Frank turned slowly, rifle at hip level, cocked and cappe
aiming at Dave's belly. "Drop the Colt," he ordered.

Dave dropped the Colt. "You've gone loco, Frank."

Frank mounted. "I'm going to get that damned mare. I'm n
letting her get away after all the work and time I've put in
her."

"You'll never catch her now."

Frank spurred the horse. "We'll see about that!"

Dave ran to pick up Frank's Sharps. By the time he loaded it, ank was out of sight in the thick timber. Dave ran through the ber to where he had seen Frank's three mounts.

The sun was just up. The mare had gone about a mile into the en below the timber. She stood still, looking back upslope. here was the stallion? Why hadn't he followed her?

Frank knew he'd not be able to ride her down again, not with smell of horse blood on him. He'd never get within two ndred yards of her. He ground-reined the horse, crawled ty yards into a low spot, then parted the thick grass to look at r. She seemed interested in Dave's horse. Perhaps she thought might be the *bayo naranjado*. She trotted a little closer and n stopped.

Frank raised the rear sight of the Sharps. He wasn't the leman Quint and Dave were, but he was competent enough.

She was a beautiful sight, with her glistening hide, tail, and ne like liquid flowing gold in the bright sunlight, head up and rt in manner and bearing, a born aristocrat of her breed.

Frank set the trigger with a slight click. He sighted on her, w in a deep breath, let out half of it and held the rest. He iched the trigger and began to tighten his whole hand, aiming rely to graze the spinal nerve along the top of her neck about foot behind the ears. He couldn't miss.

"Frank! Frank! For Christ's sake! No! No!" Dave shouted arsely from far upslope.

At the sound of the voice, Frank winced involuntarily. The arps bellowed. Smoke and flame plumed from the muzzle. e shot echo rolled along the ground. The mare jerked, was ng sideways, then crashed to the ground; she kicked her legs asmodically and lay still. Bright blood glistened in the sunlight. ere was no need to verify the shot. She was gone forever from Plains of San Augustine.

Far downslope a lone horseman heard the shot. He quickly smounted, pulled his rifle from its scabbard, slapped his horse the rump, and dropped into shelter.

Frank lay still, breathing hard, head down and eyes closed.

"Get up," Dave ordered.

Frank did not move.

"Get up!" Dave shouted harshly.

Frank looked up. "Go to hell, you half-breed bastard," [h]e snarled.

Dave dragged him to his feet. "I ought to kill you," he sai[d] low-voiced.

Frank laughed shortly. "Cain and Abel, dear brother."

The big rock-hard fist caught Frank full on the mouth. Fra[nk] staggered back. He plunged forward and began to throw punche[s.] He was no match for Dave in this type of rough and tumble. [He] had learned that fifteen years ago and still bore the marks of th[e] encounter. Still, he was no weakling, and he had never lack[ed] courage. Twice he drove Dave back with the fury of his attac[k.] Once he staggered Dave so that he dropped to one knee. Da[ve] was like Quint, all spring steel and rawhide in his rangy fram[e.] Frank went down at last, flat on his back and unable to get u[p.] Blood leaked from his mouth and nose. Two teeth were loos[e.] He blinked his eyes. The pain in his bitten leg was intense, and [a] slow weakness was overcoming him.

"Get up," Dave ordered. "I'm not through yet."

"To hell with you!" Frank shouted.

Dave dragged him to his feet. Powerful, slugging blows dro[ve] him staggering and falling down the slope until he went dow[n] flat on his back without striking a retaliatory blow. He cou[ld] hardly see Dave through eyes that were almost closed. His brea[th] whistled wetly through his nose and mouth.

"Get up," Dave repeated mechanically.

Frank shook his head. He was sure he was going to get th[e] boot. There was nothing he could do about it.

Dave strode forward, reaching out with big hands for h[is] brother.

"That's enough, Dave," Quint said from behind him.

Dave turned. Quint found it difficult to recognize both h[is] sons, Frank because of the bloody wreck of his handsome fac[e,] Dave because of the sheer atavistic hate etched on his features[.]

"Keep out of this," Dave said.

Quint shook his head. "Watch yourself," he warned. "I[']ll take nothing from you. Now get out of my way!"

Dave raised his bloody fists. "Keep out of this, old man," [he] repeated.

Quint studied him. "He's beaten, Davie. Badly beaten. You've had your revenge. Now let him be. Get out of the way."

Dave threw a right and then a left. That was all he got off. Both were evaded. A left smashed into the pit of his stomach. His head came down involuntarily as he bent forward in agony. A knee rose up to meet his chin; a fist hit him behind the ear. He went down on his knees and tried to get up. A boot heel caught him on the jaw and put him into the deep sleep.

Quint stepped back. He was hardly breathing. He looked down at Dave. "*Old man*," he said to himself. "Why, you half-breed sonofabitch!" He grinned lopsidedly.

Quint poured brandy on Frank's bitten leg and bandaged it with a strip of his shirttail. He reset the broken nose as he had fifteen years ago and pulled out the broken teeth. He washed the blood from Frank's face, and all the time Frank never said a word. Quint shaped two cigarettes, placed one of them in Frank's mouth and the other in his, then lighted them.

"You forgot me," Dave said from behind Quint.

Quint tossed him tobacco canteen and cornshuck wrappings. He squatted on his heels and looked from one to the other of his sons as he smoked. He thought briefly back on his earlier days as a trapper and mountaineer, as dangerous and hard a life as one might live, and yet a life with a freedom such as few people had ever experienced. He looked down the slope to the dead, once lovely *yegua* whose like he might never see again. Beyond the slopes were the grasslands stretching almost limitlessly to the southwest. For the first time since he had settled there fourteen years past, a vague but insistent disquiet came over him, fermenting deep within his very soul. After this day of hate and hot spilled blood, it would never be the same again.

★ ELEVEN ★

Quint gave his orders when he returned to the Querencia. Frank, seconded by Yndelecio, with ten *vaqueros* was to take the horses, mules, and cattle to Fort Fillmore. Dave was to take charge of the *rancho* and the breaking in of the new stock. Now that the contract animals were to be delivered, there was nothing more for Quint to do before he left for Santa Fe to report to Colonel Canby as per his previous orders.

The night of the day Frank had left for Fort Fillmore Quint and Dave correlated their thoughts and ideas as to what should be done at the Querencia. Dave was concerned that the Confederates would return.

Quint shook his head. "Keep a lookout for them. Half a dozen good riflemen in the hills along the trail they'd have to take could make their approach difficult if not impossible. There are not enough stock here to make the trip worthwhile, in any case. Even if they did reach here you could hole up and make it impossible for them to get water. Besides, if there is any possibility of an invasion, it will be up the Rio Grande from El Paso del Norte to La Mesilla and Fort Fillmore. If successful there, they'll likely strike farther north to capture Fort Craig or bypass it, whichever is most opportune at the time."

Dave nodded. "Then what?"

Quint shrugged. "*Quién sabe?* If successful there, they'll probably strike further up the valley to Albuquerque and possibly Santa Fe."

Dave shaped a cigarette. "And?"

Quint shook his head. "I don't know. They might try for Fort Union and the military stores there."

"And then up into Colorado and Denver to seize the gold and silver mines."

"It's a trenchant thought," Quint admitted.

"Have you any idea of what Canby wants of you?"

"I think so. He might want me for his staff, considering my knowledge of the country and my experience."

Dave grinned. "Fat chance. You're a *fighting* man, Quint. He'll not keep you behind a desk at Fort Marcy."

"I agree."

"Then perhaps you'll be ordered back here to recruit the Rangers up to full strength and take us to war?"

"That I don't know, but it's what I want to do. However, if I do not, the responsibility will be all yours, Dave. You're second-in-command."

Dave's eyes widened. "Jesus! I never thought of that."

Quint grinned. "It will make a man out of you, sonny."

"If so, who will I leave in charge? The best *vaqueros* will be with the company."

"All we'll have left is Cristina. She can manage as good as any man, provided she has a few older men to remain with her."

"There's always Frank, when he returns from Fillmore," Dave said hesitantly.

"No! Absolutely not!"

Dave looked at his father. "If I command the Rangers, I don't want him in the company."

Quint smiled, a little ruefully. "You think he'd serve under *you*? Or *me*, for that matter?"

"Would he serve under *anyone* in the war?" Dave asked quietly.

Quint didn't have an answer to that little enigma.

Quint sat alone in the study after Dave had swayed a little woozily to bed, slightly brandy-stricken. Everyone else was asleep. He hadn't been in Santa Fe in quite some time. He had counseled with Guadalupe then. She was still in school there. He had wanted her to attend school in St. Louis, where Rafaela and Catherine Williston had studied, but she had refused at first. Then she had reluctantly agreed, but the war had intervened. The Santa Fe Trail would be too dangerous now with the lack of Regulars to keep it safe. A few militia and volunteer units would take over that duty, but it would still be dangerous. Then too, the caravans would be fully taken up with military transportation. Best to let her stay safe in Santa Fe.

Jean Calhoun might be in her Santa Fe home or still out at Rio Brioso. It was safe enough there, close to the Santa Fe Trail and Fort Union. The *hacienda* at Rio Brioso was a small fortress in itself. Quint had planned it that way, although the original structure had been burned during the Taos Rebellion. Shelby Calhoun had it restored as it had been originally. He closed his eyes and thought of her. The last time they had been intimate had been fourteen years ago, before he had marched north with Sterling Price's force of Regulars and Missourians to recapture Taos and quell the rebellion. He wondered what her status would be now that she was divorced from Shelby.

The lamp guttered low and flickered out. Faint moonlight crept through the two windows opening on the patio. Cristina would be sound asleep by now. It would be simple to rouse her for lovemaking. She was always ready for that. This night, warmed by the good Pass brandy, he could not dispel Jean from his mind. He rested his head on the back of the chair and closed his eyes.

Years of living in hostile country on the razor edge of imminent danger had honed a sixth sense in Quint. He opened his eyes. For a moment he wasn't sure whether or not he was dreaming. She stood in one of the patches of moonlight, looking at him. She was naked. Her long silken hair hung loose over her bare shoulders and barely covered her full breasts. He could just make out the nipples through the fine strands. She was absolutely motionless except for the rise and fall of her soft breathing.

He closed his eyes. A memory-picture formed in his mind— Jean Allan naked in the bedroom at Tom Byrne's *casa* in Santa Fe, and again eight years later, when she was Jean Calhoun. It's the brandy and wishful thinking, he reasoned.

He opened his eyes. She was still there. She held out slim hands with tapered fingers. "Quint," she breathed.

He could not believe it. It was impossible!

She seemed to glide toward him. The faint odor of lilac perfume came to him. Jean had worn such a scent.

"Jean?" Quint whispered.

She stopped in front of him, placed cool smooth hands on each side of his face, tilted his head back and kissed him open-mouthed, thrusting her tongue between his lips. She twisted quickly and dropped into his lap, a warm, perfumed, tantalizing bundle of sheer femininity. She placed her arms about his neck and kissed him again.

Quint turned his head away from her sensuous, brandy-wet, loose, and searching mouth. Jean had never quite kissed with such absolute whorish abandon. "Kiss me," she whispered. "Again and again." She pressed down in his lap, feeling his sudden, unwanted erection within his trousers.

Quint pushed her back. "What the hell is this?" he demanded. "Are you drunk, Catherine?"

She shook her head. "Not yet, just enough to make it interesting. After all, you've a head start."

"Supposing someone came in here?" he asked for lack of anything else reasonable to say.

She shrugged. "You're the *patrón*, aren't you? The lord of the manor. You can have or do anything you want here."

He could not get enough leverage from the deep soft chair to unseat her. She slid a hand underneath her buttocks and squeezed his genitals as hard as she could.

"*Jesus!*" he gasped. "Take it easy!"

She grinned like a pleased cat. "*I* should be saying that soon, once you get *that* into action. I've heard about you. A stallion in human form, they say."

He wiped the sweat from his forehead, his forearm brushing against one of her breasts. By God, but she was a luscious piece! No wonder Frank and Dave had clashed over her. "Let me get up," he said hoarsely.

She shook her head. "You're my own captive stud." She giggled.

"At least let me get my pants off."

She widened those great china-blue eyes of hers. "Why? What did you have in mind?"

He finally managed to shove her off his lap. "Go lock the door, Cathie," he whispered. "Then hurry back. I warn you— you'll be sorry."

She started toward the door, looking back over her shoulder. "Like my Aunt Jean?" She giggled again. "I can hardly wait." She ran to the door. He was after her in a second. He closed in on her, placed a hand over her mouth, twisted one of her arms behind her up toward her shoulder blades and marched her through the dark passageway to her room. She struggled.

"Take it easy, you would-be whore," he hissed. "We'll be better off in your bedroom, where your screaming won't disturb the others."

She nodded eagerly, in slightly fearful trepidation. He shoved her into the doorway of her room and slapped her rosy buttocks stingingly with a callused leathery palm. He closed the door on her angry shriek. He returned to the study, where he closed and locked the door behind himself. He felt almost regretful. Christ, what a mounting he could have given her! He was about due. He picked up the brandy bottle and went into his bedroom. He did not see Cristina slip into bed just ahead of him.

Dave was waiting in Catherine's dark room, stripped to the buff and sitting on the bed. She didn't see him as she stumbled, whimpering, toward him with her buttocks aflame. She reached for the brandy bottle on the nightstand and drank deeply. She lowered the bottle, wiped her full lips with the back of a hand and then replaced the bottle on the stand. "That sanctimonious sonofabitch," she murmured angrily.

"Here's another one," Dave said. He slid a hard hand up between her smooth thighs, wrapped his other arm about her breasts, and pulled her down on top of him, rolling over so that she sprawled wide-legged on the bed. He gripped her long hair, bent her head back and kissed her hard enough to bruise her soft lips while he thrust questing fingers up into her sweat-damp crotch.

She tried to scream, but he sealed her loose mouth with savage kisses while working his hand further up between her thighs. "You're drunk," she finally gasped.

He grinned. "Why, so I am!"

"Let me go! I'll not tell Quint," she cried.

He shook his head. "I watched your pretty little performance in there. Now raise and spread your legs!"

She shuddered. "Let me go," she whispered. "Some other time?"

He shook his head.

She placed her hands on each side of his dark, sweating face. "For God's sake, Davie," she pleaded. "I'm a virgin."

"Raise those damned legs!" he snarled. "Raise and spread, you two-bit whore!"

She did as she was told. A moment later she regretted it as he rammed into her with a violence that almost forced an agonized scream out of her. He thrust in hard and suddenly, then with a touch of panic he learned she had been telling him the truth. She couldn't escape, she thought. Maybe this half-breed son of Quint's might be better than the old man after all. So long as she was finally going to be forced, she might as well enjoy it. I'll pay for it tomorrow, she thought, but tonight is another matter. She began to respond, painfully at first, then she forgot the pain in the hot ecstasy of a few moments of unbridled passion.

Quint stripped and reached for the brandy bottle.

Cristina raised on her elbow. "What about me if you don't want her?" she asked.

He handed her the bottle. He lighted a candle and looked down at her as she threw back the coverlet. She still had a body he found hard to resist, although in the years since he had taken her virginity from her, when she was sixteen years old, she had gained some flesh. She was full-breasted with dark-brown nipples, dark of hair at her crotch, with a brown skin the color of moist earth and velvety smooth. Her legs were rather short and sturdy, her buttocks large and well-rounded.

"Why didn't you take her?" Cristina asked.

"She's a mindless whore."

She nodded. "But in the dimness you might have mistaken her for that aunt of hers, the blond *gringa* woman of yours up north."

He looked down at her. "You've no right to say that."

"I'm sorry," she said, suddenly contrite.

"You know I've had nothing to do with her for years."

"But not through choice, *mi vida*."

He sat down on the bed and placed a hand alongside her rather broad jaw. "I'll be leaving soon for the north. Would you prefer I slept elsewhere tonight?"

She shook her head. "Don't leave me tonight, or any other night while you're still here."

He lay down beside her and caressed her body. Soon they were into the old full rhythm of the act. She never seemed to tire of it or him. It was not always true of him. As they worked smoothly together without speaking, the lovely oval face of Jean was before him, her great eyes searching his face, almost as though the vision was attempting to speak with him, perhaps to tell him she would be waiting for him in Santa Fe.

Cristina moaned a little. "*Lado del lado de mi corazón*. Side of the side of my heart. *Alma de mi alma*. Soul of my soul . . ."

★ TWELVE ★

A hard rapping came at the bedroom door. Quint awoke in the darkness, rolled up off the bed onto his feet, and reached for his bedside Colt. He walked to the door. "*Quién es?*" he queried. He was not yet fully awake.

"It's Dave, Quint. Luke just showed up. He's got one helluva story for us."

"Is he all right?" Quint asked quickly.

Dave laughed softly. "Who can harm that human wolf? He's at the brandy already."

Cristina lighted the lamp. "I'll get him something to eat. He's always hungry."

"And thirsty. Bring in a full brandy bottle with the food."

Luke Connors was sprawled in Quint's big armchair with a brandy bottle in his hand. "*Buenos días*," he said casually.

Luke was just short of six feet tall, a lean lath of a man, all spring steel and rawhide, Kentucky-born and -bred until the age of fifteen, when he had left Connors Fork of the Licking River forever to try his fortune in the Big Shining Mountains of the Far West. His hair was a ruddy brown streaked with gray at the sides. His face was a leathery saddle brown bisected by a crooked beak of a nose. His eyes were a piercing bottle-green, sunlight-squinted, and seemed endowed with the ability to look a hole right through anyone. His age was somewhere around fifty-five years, maybe more, certainly not less. He looked his age; men aged fast in the mountains and deserts of the Southwest. He had been baptized Matthew Mark Luke John Connors by his father, a self-ordained ridgepole evangelist. Luke had been the only name that stuck. Those who knew him best—although they were mighty few in number—sometimes called him Wandering Wolf, his Kotsoteka Comanche name given to him by the Lords of the Plains when he had lived with them for a time. He had the stamina and vitality of an Apache warrior. He had been one of the famed quartet of beaver-trapping partners with Quint, along with François Charbonne—part Cree, part French—and Black Moccasin, the full-blooded Delaware who was still with Quint. Luke strayed away at times over the years, never said much about where he had been or what he had been doing, never announced his going or coming, but always came back.

This time he looked as though he had been stirrup-dragged behind a galloping mustang for hundreds of yards through a dusty prickly pear patch. He was thinner than usual, almost gaunt. His left boot toe was split wide open, revealing a black-nailed big toe. Both boots were badly run down. His right trouser leg was ripped from hip to knee. The crown of his hat was almost torn off.

"Where . . . the . . . hell . . . have . . . you . . . been?" Quint asked.

Luke drank, wiped his mouth with the back of a dirty hand, belched, and grinned. " 'Sta bueno! Mother's milk!"

"You hear me?" Quint demanded.

The hard green eyes focused on Quint. "I hear you. I was in the Confedrit Army, Big Red."

"Jesus," Dave breathed.

Luke hiccupped. "Jesus warn't there, Davie. I heard he had been made an orderly sergeant in F Company of the Second Texas. I was in Company B myself. Our orderly sergeant was either Satan or his twin brother. I warn't sorry to see the last of him, the Tejano sonofabitch! Why . . ."

Quint grinned. "Get on with the story!"

"The secesh captured the entire garrison of Fort Fillmore a week ago and took over the post."

Quint stared. "My God!"

"Are you sure?" Dave demanded.

Luke eyed him. "You ever hear me lie?"

"Do I have to answer that? How did you hear about his?"

"I didn't *hear* about it, Davie. I was there." He looked solemnly at Quint. "*Verdad,* Big Red."

Cristina brought in the food and a replacement brandy bottle. "My God, Luke! What happened to you?"

Luke shrugged. "Fortunes of war, Cris." He picked up a thick sandwich and sank his long yellowed teeth into it, looking exactly like a famished wolf.

"Go on, Luke," Dave said.

"Let him eat," Quint said. "But a few questions, Lukie: Were you followed here? Have the Rebels advanced beyond Mesilla and Fort Fillmore? How many troops do they have?"

"No to the first two, Big Red. I figger mebbe about three hundred men of Baylor's Battalion of the Second Texas Mounted Regiment."

Quint stood up and held a lamp close to the large-scale map of southern New Mexico hanging there. Fort Fillmore had been built in Doña Ana County in 1851, located at the edge of the sandy foothills on the east side of the Rio Grande on the old road from Las Cruces to El Paso and about seven miles from Las Cruces. Fort Fillmore was thirty-eight miles north of Fort Bliss at El Paso del Norte, called Hart's Mills and sometimes Franklin on the American side of the river, or generally just El Paso. Fort Bliss had been evacuated by United States troops in March. La Mesilla had been settled a year before the fort was built about three miles from it and on the west bank of the Rio Grande. It had been a depot on the Great Southern Overland Mail stagecoach line of Butterfield and Company on the well-traveled emigrant road between Texas and California, crossing the Colorado River at Fort Yuma. The Southern Overland was joined at El Paso by the San Antonio and San Diego Mail, originating in San Antonio. There were no habitations between La Mesilla and the Santa Rita copper mines about ninety miles to the northwest. La Mesilla had always been a trouble-ridden town with a strong secessionist element there before the war.

Fort Fillmore had originally been built to keep an eye on Mesilla, settled the year before by Mexicans. Thanks to a badly made map and the decision of the international boundary commissioners, Mesilla was at that time adjudged to be in Mexico. There being no extradition treaty, the place became a refuge for fugitives who were chary of the laws administered on the east, or American, side of the river. One of the vital issues at the time had been the plan for a proposed southern railroad route south of the Gila River to the Pacific Ocean. In addition, the Mesilla Valley was a highly desirable agricultural area coveted by the United States. It wasn't until 1854 that the American flag had been raised over Mesilla. Isolated Fort Fillmore, in addition to keeping an eye on Mesilla, was occupied with punitive expeditions aimed at the troublesome Apaches infesting southern New Mexico.

The greatest concentration of New Mexican southern sympathizers was in Mesilla. In March of 1861 a convention of politicians and the well-to-do from the western and southern portions of the territory had met and declared that part of the territory below the 34th Parallel to be under the jurisdiction of the Confederate government. Soon after that, the secession leaders had warned all Union sympathizers to get out of the town and the newly formed territory. A bright new Confederate flag made from a United States flag by redesigning it with parallel bars of red and white with a blue canton and thirteen stars for the Confederate states—and aptly nicknamed the Stars and Bars—was brazenly hoisted in sight of the nervous garrison of Fort Fillmore. The *Mesilla Times* was bitterly anti-Union, threatening with death anyone who refused to acknowledge the usurpation of that part of New Mexico. There had been a strong pro-Union sentiment among the native population, but they had been over-awed by the fiery secessionists. United States troops in New Mexico were demoralized. Their pay was half a year in arrears. Most of their officers had resigned to serve the Confederacy. Fort Fillmore, in common with other military establishments, was virtually without horses and mules. There was a lack of ordnance stores and the artillery necessary to properly arm a single fort. Throughout New Mexico there were only fourteen understrength companies scattered through half a dozen posts. There was virtually no news of events back East since the February Ordinance of Secession by Texas had closed the Southern Overland Mail.

"A hell of a mess," Luke said around a third sandwich.

"Anyone with the least knowledge of fortifications would not have placed Fort Fillmore where it is. Down in a basin commanded and halfway surrounded by hills covered with chaparral. An attacking force could come through that brush unseen to within five hundred yards of the post. A couple of artillery pieces mounted on the hills could render the fort helpless. The only water supply is a mile and a half away. The post commander, ol' Major Lynde of the Seventh Infantry, is a doddering old fool scared of his own shadow."

Quint nodded. "It's been an open secret for months that Fillmore should have been abandoned in favor of Fort Craig."

Luke shook his head. "I was at La Mesilla July twenty-fifth. In order to throw off suspicion I had enlisted in the Second Texas when I was at Fort Bliss, figgerin' to desert when I got all the information I needed. I saw Shelby Calhoun while I was there. He's a lieutenant colonel in the Confedrit Army now. I ain't sure he noticed me. He came and went a lot on some sort of secret business. Still, I was a mite worried the Tejanos might suspect I was a spy, and knowin' them like I do, they might hang me without benefit of trial, like they say. They were signin' up every man they could get. Wasn't very many, by the way. I think they thought the New Mexicans and the Regulars would bust their asses to get into the Confedrit Army, but it didn't work out that way. So, when they heard my Kentucky accent, they grabbed me. Ol' Shelby had left Fort Bliss with half a company and was said to have gone north on some kind of reconnaissance or something."

Quint nodded. "He did and showed up here looking for horses, mules, and cattle, claiming that everything south of the Thirty-fourth Parallel was part of the Confederate Territory of Arizona."

"What happened, Big Red?"

Quint quickly told the tale.

Luke cracked up. "Jesus God! He'll never forgive yuh for that. Why in hell didn't yuh either wipe out his command like piss ants, or at least run 'em off without their shootin' irons?" He grinned like a hungry wolf. "The Mimbres would have taken care of them then."

Quint shrugged. "It's not considered to be *civilized* warfare, Wandering Wolf." He grinned back.

"I've seen the elephant," Luke murmured.

"Get on with the story, Luke," Dave urged.

"We marched up to Mesilla," Luke continued. "Ol' John Baylor was in command. He's a bobcat, I tell you, with bristles on his belly. Tough as an old boot. He's a born Kentuckian, like me. Texan for twenty years. When *he* talks, people *listen*. We occupied Mesilla. The secesh in Mesilla gave him all the inside information on Fort Fillmore. The garrison was demoralized, ol' Major Isaac Lynde, the post commander, was a Vermonter and loyal enough, but he was a frightened, tired old man. The main reason he had stuck it out there was because he had orders to wait for Regulars marching east to Fillmore from Forts Breckenridge and Buchanan in Arizona, which they had abandoned. Colonel Canby wanted Lynde to hold Fillmore until those Regulars were safe. Then he could pull out and head for either Fort Craig or Fort Stanton." Luke shook his head. "Lynde knew what was in the wind, but he did nothing to fortify Fillmore or improve the morale and effectiveness of his command. Them ain't *my* words. They were printed in the *Mesilla Times*. Yuh won't believe this, but some months earlier Lynde had quartered and fed ex–U.S. officers on their way to Texas to join the Confederacy and even provided them with transportation south." Luke lighted a cigar. "I guess he had no confidence his men would fight if attacked. Personally, I was surprised he hadn't already surrendered. His whole damned garrison was asleep the night we occupied Mesilla. They didn't know anything about it until the next day. If I had been Baylor, I would have hit 'em at dawn after the night we got there. As it happens, it didn't make much difference anyways. Seems like Lynde had been gettin' ready to leave, packin' and such. Problem was he didn't have enough horses and mules for all his transport."

Quint looked at him quickly. "What do you mean? I sent Frank down there with horses, mules, and cattle before Baylor reached Mesilla."

Luke held up a hand. "I'll get to that, Big Red. Before we had reached Mesilla we made what the military call 'demonstrations' against Fillmore. One time we drove off forty horses from the post herd. That was one of the reasons they were so short. Another reason was Mexican horsethieves had been ahead of us and got a nice haul.

"Late on the afternoon of the twenty-fifth, the Fort Fillmore garrison marched toward Mesilla. They sent two officers with a flag of truce, demanding the surrender of the town and the Texans. They were told if they wanted the town they'd have to come and take it. Their artillery opened fire, but they fired too short. We had no artillery, by the way."

"Where were you all this time, Luke?" asked Dave.

Luke grinned. "I was a sharpshooter, on account of my big Sharps. A bunch of us were in some adobes right in the middle of their advance. They didn't know us 'Texans' was waitin' in the adobes. We could hardly miss. Two officers was wounded, seven or eight troopers wounded, mebbe four or five of them killed. The guns were limbered up, and the Federals retreated into Fort Fillmore. Baylor sent out scouts that night. I was one of them. The Federals were busy digging breastworks. We reported this to Baylor. He went an express down to Fort Bliss for artillery. Early on the mornin' of the twenty-seventh a little after daylight, we saw dust on the road north of Mesilla about fifteen miles away. We hit the saddle and took out after the dust. Our scouts had come back from Fillmore. The Federals had taken out in such a hurry they left the garrison flag flyin'.

"Lynde was headin' for San Augustine Pass in an effort to cross it and head for Fort Stanton. We caught up with the first stragglers. There were a lot of them half-dead from thirst. We found more of them exhausted, sleepin' alongside the road. We went on over the pass in pursuit of the main body. The bushes alongside the road was full of more stragglers unable to go on.

"Their cavalry gave us a little resistance but got to hell outta there when we charged. They left behind wagons loaded with supplies and some of their artillery." Luke's voice died away. He looked sideways at Quint. Luke's dry, flippant manner of speech at such times was mostly a cover-up for his inner feelings. This time Quint could see the deep, sick hurt in his eyes. Luke was Union to the core.

"For five miles the road was filled with fainting soldiers. They threw down their arms and begged us for water. Coupla hundred of them had drawn up in line of battle at the San Augustine Springs. We charged again, cutting off more stragglers from the springs. We disarmed them and gave them water. Our hosses was about spent. It didn't matter. Major Lynde sent for

Colonel Baylor and asked for conditions of surrender. Baylor insisted it be unconditional. The articles of surrender were then written out and signed by both parties. Lynde gave the order to stack arms. Most of his officers and men had tears in their eyes and hate against Lynde for his cowardice in surrendering to an inferior force without artillery. Lynde did allow their colors to be burned rather than surrender them. The Texans captured eight companies of infantry and four of cavalry, all Regulars, about seven hundred men in all, and four fine pieces of artillery. I think we had about two hundred men all told. . . ."

Quint felt sick. "What about Frank and my contract animals?" he asked quietly.

Luke drained his glass. "I was one of the men sent back to Mesilla. We saw a cloud of dust. Our lieutenant sent me and three others to see what was causing it. I found Frank with a face full of bruises riding far ahead of the stock. I told him what had happened and that I was desertin' right there and then and that he'd better, by God, turn them animals around and head to hell outta there as fast as he could go. I suggested he drive them up north to Fort Craig. He offered me a drink of brandy. I had the flask up to my mouth when he pulls a pistol on me. I might have tried somethin' with most other men, but not with Frank. He looked as mean as a bee-stung grizzly. He disarms me and orders me on ahead of him. He didn't tell his *vaqueros* what had happened. We ride right into Mesilla and he delivers the animals, the *vaqueros*, and me to the Tejanos. He tells my lieutenant who I really was and that I enlisted in the U.S. Volunteers." He shook his head. "I always knew Frank never had much use for me, but I never thought he'd turn me in like he done, knowin' them Tejanos wouldn't waste a minute hangin' or shootin' me. What the hell got into him, Quint?"

"You saw his bruised face," Cristina said.

"Looked like he run into a buzzsaw."

"He did. It was David," she said.

Luke looked at Dave. Dave nodded. "I wondered when somethin' like that was goin' to happen," Luke said. "You picked a great time for it, Davie lad."

Quint shook his head in disbelief. "I never thought . . ." His voice died away. He could not speak of it.

Dave smashed a fist into his other palm. "Wait until I get my hands again on that sonofabitch! You should have let me finish him off, Quint.''

"He won't be back," Quint said.

"Did he take off with the money for the stock?" Cristina asked.

Luke shook his head. "He enlisted in Baylor's Second Texas the day he got to Mesilla.''

"We'll not mention his name again," Quint said. "How did you escape, Luke?''

"They locked me in the guardhouse at Fillmore. Shelby Calhoun came up from Fort Bliss with the artillery and verified Frank's story about me. That night the guard fell asleep. I had to kill the sonofabitch with a cot leg. I stole a cayuse in Mesilla. I got as far as Rio Alamosa before my hoss went lame. I walked most of the way from there at night, hidin' out by day. There was smoke signals in the hills. Mebbe the Mimbres saw me. I don't know. I reached here this mornin'. That's it.''

Dave looked at his father. "Now what?''

Quint stood up. "I've got my orders for Santa Fe. Luke's information must be taken up to headquarters there immediately. Dave, saddle my dun and a horse for Luke. We'll need a pair of extra mounts.''

Cristina placed a hand at her throat. "You two are going alone?''

Quint nodded.

"Luke said there were Mimbres in the hills.''

"And Confederates at Fort Fillmore and La Mesilla.''

Luke yawned. "He'll be all right, Cristina. I'll take good care of him like I always done.''

Quint grinned. "That'll be the day.''

"Yuh know as well as I do, every time I ain't around to back yuh up yuh get shot, or stabbed, or somethin' big and hairy gets his teeth and claws into yuh. So, yuh see, I ain't got any choice, Big Red.''

"What about Catherine, Quint?" Cristina asked. "She planned to return to Santa Fe with you.''

"There's no time. She couldn't keep up. We'll be riding night and day straight through. She'll have to stay here until a more opportune time.''

Catherine stood listening behind the ajar door leading into the passageway where her bedroom was situated. She bit her full lower lip, turned on a heel, and ran to her room. She dressed quickly, crammed some extra clothing into a bag, slipped a small pistol into her jacket pocket, and left the house. It was still dark. She ran to the stable where the family riding horses were kept and saddled a dun mare. She led the dun and a small sorrel, more of a pet of Cristina's than anything else, out of the stable and behind it, skirting the rear of the long row of quarters and shops. She led the horses upslope past the old cemetery and then north until she was in the area beyond the springs. She planned to follow a small canyon that twisted its way through the hills until it met the Socorro Road. If she moved fast, she'd be able to reach that point before Quint and Luke made it to there. The problem was that she wasn't exactly sure which of two similar canyons was the right one. She'd have to take a chance on that. If she selected the wrong one, she could always (God forbid!) return to the *rancho* and face David. She shuddered a little at the thought.

The false dawn was just tinting the eastern sky when Quint and Luke rode from the Querencia. Their mounts had pommel and cantle packs. The two led horses carried extra forage bags. Quint wore full field uniform. Luke's only concession to his status was to wear a pair of yellow-striped blue breeches and a belt with a big U.S. buckle.

Quint looked back. Cristina and Rafaela stood in the grayness, watching them. At last Rafaela turned back to the *casa*. Cristina stood alone, wrapped in her shawl against the dawn chill. She held up her arm in mute farewell. She was still standing there, a short, lonely-looking figure, when they rounded a turn in the road and lost sight of her.

Despite the urgency of their mission, a feeling of exhilaration had begun to rise within Quint. The air was crisp and cool. A faint dry wind crept along behind them from the vast plains. The *barrossa* felt good between his thighs. He could feel the weight and hardness of his sheathed Sharps just under his right leg. The road to Socorro was empty and wide open before them.

Luke turned to look at Quint. He grinned. " 'Sta bueno, Big Red," he suggested.

" 'Sta bueno, Wandering Wolf," Quint agreed.

They grinned at each other.

The éastern sky exploded silently into a glory of luminescent pink and gold as they passed the junction of the road with the mouth of a canyon empty of life.

The sun was up high. The canyon began to fill with heated air. There was no wind. Dense tangles of wait-a-minute bush, the catclaw acacia with its vicious curved thorns partly hidden by pretty little fuzzy yellow flowers, thrived ten to twenty feet high in the poor soil of the canyon. The thorns ripped and tore through Catherine's clothing to reach and rake her soft creamy flesh. Sweat dripped from her face and body. Her sweat-damp long hair hung in front of her face. She no longer looked up to see how much longer the thicket continued. Surely she should be somewhere near the canyon mouth by now.

It was noon when at last she let the horses shift for themselves. She sat on a flat rock ledge in dubious hot shade and pulled off her left boot to inspect a large blister.

It was deathly quiet in the canyon. Nothing moved. There was no wind. Catherine looked up suddenly.

They were twenty feet from her. Six men stood watching her. Their hair was thick-maned and glossy black, bound about their temples with buckskin bands or white cloth. They wore buckskin shirts and apronlike garments hanging from their waists to their knees. Their footgear was knee-high, folded just below the knee, the button-toed, thick-soled Apache moccasins. White bottom clay streaked their broad faces. It was their eyes that frightened her. They were like polished obsidian with no warming light in them.

She started to run. She didn't get far. Then her clothing was torn from her. She was forcefully thrown flat on the hard hot rock of the ledge. Two warriors pried her long, lovely legs apart until she thought they would break from their hip sockets. The biggest of them stripped off his apron and gripped his penis while he grinned at her with his deeply pockmarked face. He was on her like a hound after a bitch in heat. After the third rape she hardly felt anything anymore. She was unconscious while the last one had his turn.

Catherine was in agony as she opened her eyes, hoping against hope they had gone. They were still there, squatting in a circle watching her like cats watching a mousehole. Then Frank's warning words came back to her: "... *One of them would mount you again and the process would be repeated all over again. You might survive. It might be better if you did not. Life as a captive white woman in an Apache ranchería would be pure hell for you once their women got at you. They can be worse than the men with women captives, far worse.*"

They dragged her to her feet after the second round was over. By now she was beyond caring, hoping they'd kill her and get it over with. They gathered up her clothing and cut switches from the catclaw, motioning her to go ahead of them. She forced her bleeding way through the dense thickets. Every time she slowed down, the switches would sting her buttocks, back and legs. When she fell, they'd drag her to her feet and shove her along, until they reached their horses and the two she had brought with her. They hoisted her to the bare back of the sorrel and tied her ankles together under the barrel of the horse. Her fair skin was aflame with the touch of the hot sun. They led the sorrel behind them as they made their way to the south and west. The last thing she remembered was falling forward onto the neck of the sorrel into a complete blackness.

★ THIRTEEN ★

THE SIBLEY BRIGADE, C.S.A.

Louisianian Henry Hopkins Sibley had arrived in San Antonio, Texas, from Richmond, Virginia, in August in 1861 with the provisional rank of brigadier general in the Confederate States Army. During the Mexican War he had been brevetted major for bravery. After the war he had served on the Great Plains. He had invented the Sibley tent, patterned after the Plains Indians' *tipi*, and its accompanying stove, both of which had been adopted for use by the United States Army.

When Sibley had been stationed in New Mexico, he had been promoted to the permanent rank of major on May 13, 1861. That same day he had resigned to offer his services to the Confederacy and had "gone south" to Texas for that purpose. While in his native Louisiana he had been offered the colonelcy of a regiment but had declined. He had bigger game in mind—a vision of conquering New Mexico for the Confederacy. This plan he had presented to President Jefferson Davis. The president was already well aware of New Mexico's strategic importance. Sibley knew the resources of the territory, its people, and the condition and morale of the United States forces stationed there. One of his major goals was to capture the large stocks of war materiel stored in the territory. With them he could arm the many southern sympathizers he felt sure would rise to the support of the Confederacy once an invasion force appeared in New Mexico. Sibley's strategy, as outlined to Davis, would call for a virtually self-sustaining campaign. He maintained that if his invasion force was initially supplied and equipped in Texas, they could secure all other needed war materiel and supplies in the territory. Further, they could live on the land, first securing the agricultural production of the La Mesilla-El Paso del Norte region and later that of New Mexico proper. Thus, according to him, the campaign would cost little, yet there could be immeasurable gains.

General Sibley's orders were simple:

SIR: In view of your recent service in New Mexico and knowledge of the country and its people, the President has entrusted you with the important duty of driving the Federal troops from the department, at the same time securing all the arms, supplies, and materiels of war.

He was to proceed immediately to Texas, where he was to raise initially two full regiments of cavalry, one battery of howitzers, and whatever other forces were necessary for his campaign. Once he was into New Mexico he was to take (hopefully) into his force all "disaffected" Federal officers and enlisted men. Upon clearing the territory of the enemy, he was to establish a military government.

Upon arrival in San Antonio, Sibley immediately established his headquarters and set about raising his brigade. He was undeniably anxious. Already Lieutenant Colonel John R. Baylor of the Second Regiment Texas Mounted Rifles had cleared all Federal troops from the old Gadsden Purchase and had created the Confederate Territory of Arizona south of the 34th Parallel with headquarters at La Mesilla. Thus Sibley was all the more convinced of the easy prospect of taking over the entire territory.

The first regiment to be formed was the Fourth Texas Mounted Volunteers. Ohio-born James Reily of Houston, Harris County, was commissioned colonel and put in command. His second-in-command was the already famous William Read "Dirty Shirt" Scurry of Clinton, De Witt County.

The Fourth Texas trained at Camp Sibley on the west bank of Salado Creek, six miles east of San Antonio. The De Witt and Caldwell counties Davis Rifles formed Company B; the Victoria County Victoria Volunteers were the basis for Company C. The San Andres Light Horse of Milam County became Company D; Milan County also contributed Company E. The Polk County Lone Star Rangers were Company F, while Germans from Austin, Washington, and Fayette counties became Company G. Houston and Madison County men formed Company I. Company K was from Cherokee County.

Virginian Colonel Thomas J. Green formed the Fifth Texas at Camp Manassas two miles above Camp Sibley. He was a fighting man of the first water. Some of the companies were from the counties of Colorado, Bexar, Washington, Anderson, Travis, Fayette, and Parker. B Company were Falls County men and had been designated as lancers. C Company was formed from the Grimes County Rangers, while the Jackson Cavalry of Austin County became Company G, also designated as lancers.

The Seventh Texas trained at Camp Pickett on Salada Creek. William Steele, born a New Yorker, was colonel. His regiment had Germans from Comal County in Company B. The Williamson County Grays formed Company C. D Company had been the Angelina Troop of Angelina County. The Trinity County Cavalry became Company E; the New Salem Invincibles were from New Salem, Rusk County. Company I had been the Anderson County Buckhunters. Men from Bexar, Walker, Houston, Leon and Tarrant counties composed the remaining companies.

Each of the three regiments consisted of approximately nine hundred men—a total of twenty-seven hundred for the entire brigade. General Sibley appointed the field officers. The men themselves elected their company commanders.

The original premise was that the enlistees were to supply their own horses and weapons, but there were still many shortages. The brigade was armed with a miscellany of practically every small arm then in existence—squirrel guns, single- and double-barreled shotguns, military muskets both smooth-bored and rifled, common rifles, big-bored bear guns, and sporting guns of many varieties. Most of the men brought their own revolvers. The lancers of companies B and G of the Fifth Regiment were armed with a pair of Colt Navies and lances decorated by red pennants.

A grand review of the brigade was held in October. It was almost time for the march to Fort Bliss. The Houston *Tri-Weekly Telegraph* covered the review with these inspiring words: "A finer brigade of men and horses I do not believe can be found in the Confederate Army. Most of the men have entered the service for the war, not for pay, but for the love of country." The Fourth Regiment marched to San Antonio late in October. They had no band, but as they drew near the city the stirring strains of "The Texas Ranger" welled from a thousand throats. General Sibley bade them farewell: "Though you are still green saplings bending to discipline, you will make the best soldiers in the world." So a thousand of the best young strong-faced men, with lithe bodies, born horsemen, soft-spoken as most Texans, rode off to the war.

The main road to Fort Bliss consisted of almost seven hundred miles of hardly more than wagon ruts, passing through vast, rolling plains, bleak and inhospitable deserts, and rugged mountains, many of which were haunted by hostile Indians. Water at many of the springs would be inadequate for large groups of men and horses; therefore, it was necessary to divide the regiment into three sections marching one day apart. In addition there would be a long wagon train and a herd of beeves. Daily travel would be limited by how far the herd could be driven and the distance between water holes.

The planned Confederate invasion and conquest of New Mexico Territory and perhaps much, much more had begun.

FOURTEEN

FALL 1861: SANTA FE, COUNCIL OF WAR

October 1861

Citizens of New Mexico, your territory has been invaded, the integrity of your soil has been attacked, the property of peaceful and industrious citizens has been destroyed or converted to the use of the invaders, and the enemy is already at your doors. You cannot, you must not, hesitate to take up arms in defense of your homes, firesides, and families. Your manhood calls upon you to be alert and to be vigilant in the protection of the soil of your birth, where repose the sacred remains of your ancestors, which was left by them as a rich heritage to you, if you have the valor to defend it.

> Henry Connelly
> Governor of the Territory
> of New Mexico

Quint and Luke waited in Colonel Canby's Fort Marcy headquarters while the commander of the District of New Mexico was finishing reading some dispatches in the outer office. They had just come in carried by an officer courier from St. Louis. Quint and Luke were in excellent, long-familiar company. Present were Governor Henry Connelly, Dr. Thomas Byrne, and Ceran St. Vrain, newly appointed colonel of the First Regiment of New Mexico Volunteers.

Henry Connelly had been Virginia-born, and Kentucky-reared

and -educated. In 1824 he began in New Mexico as a merchant trader and later spent twenty years in Chihuahua, Mexico, in the same line of business. During the Mexican War he had been instrumental in the negotiations between Governor Manuel Armijo, then Mexican governor of New Mexico, and James Wiley Magoffin, civilian emissary for the United States, which resulted in the bloodless conquest of the territory by General Kearny and his Army of the West. At present he was a merchandizer and rancher resident of Los Pinos near Peralta on the Rio Grande.

Irish-born Thomas Byrne had studied for a degree in medicine at Trinity College in Dublin. He had immigrated to America and for a time served as a surgeon with the elite First Dragoons, then commanded by Colonel Alexander Allan, later United States Senator from Kentucky. When Tom Byrne left the army, he went to Santa Fe and established a front as merchant trader financed by the immensely wealthy Senator Allan. He had done some small practice of medicine. He also served as an undercover agent for the United States in the years preceding the Civil War. His services had been invaluable. In a broad sense he had accepted Quint Kershaw as a protégé, originally because he had realized Quint's potential value to the then rather nebulous dream of Manifest Destiny, and later specifically for the annexation of New Mexico to the United States. It had been Tom who had helped Quint get established, by making him one of four partners in the vast Rio Brioso grant in northeastern New Mexico in close proximity to the Santa Fe Trail, an ideal site for a future military post when and if the United States acquired the territory. Quint at that time had no funds to invest, but had agreed to perform as *hacendado* as his share. Later, at the conclusion of the Mexican War, Tom had been instrumental in offering Quint the sole rights to the Querencia grant in exchange for his rights to the Rio Brioso grant.

Ceran St. Vrain was a giant of aristocratic French descent. His full name was Ceran de Hault de Lassus de St. Vrain. He was a round-faced, solid block of a man with graying hair and beard and had once been a mountain man and trapper. He had been born in Missouri and came to San Fernandez de Taos as early as 1825. Ceran had once been a partner of the Bent brothers, who had established Bent's Fort on the Arkansas. He had taken out Mexican citizenship to facilitate the firm's merchandising in

New Mexico. He had married a Mexican woman. During the Mexican War he had commanded the Santa Fe Company of Volunteers, serving with Colonel Sterling Price's command during the fighting against the insurrectionists at La Canada and Taos Pueblo. Quint had served as scouting officer of the company. Ceran had accepted the colonelcy of the First New Mexico Volunteers because of his prestige, prominence, and immense popularity among the native New Mexicans who had flocked to serve under his command. He had only agreed to the appointment with the understanding that he would resign in favor of Kit Carson, his lieutenant colonel, as soon as the regiment was fully mustered. Carson at this time was guarding the Santa Fe Trail with four companies of the First New Mexico.

Quint and Luke dozed in their chairs after their forced ride from the Querencia. Those in the office could hear the pleasant voice of Colonel Canby in the outer office intermingled with the voice of another, perhaps younger, man. Then a woman spoke. Quint opened his eyes. He listened closely. Then she laughed, a sound as of many tiny silver bells hung where the wind could swing them. Quint stood up slowly, unaware almost that he was doing so, oblivious to the others in the office, and walked toward the door. It was *her*. *It had to be her!* He opened the door to look directly into immense clear eyes of a darkish cornflower blue. *Jean! God, but she was beautiful!* Maturity had brought with it a different aspect of beauty, all the more pleasing to Quint. Her hair was still cornsilk in hue and texture. Her complexion was fine and clear, the cheekbones and rather bold nose dusted with infinitesimal freckles and tinted by the sun and wind of northeastern New Mexico. The mouth was a treasure, full-lipped with a touch of the sensuous to it. The teeth were perfect. It was her eyes that had always fascinated him. They hinted of intelligence, with a constant flicker of mischief apparent. He knew them well. They could change almost imperceptibly and slowly into a smoldering blue when she made the passionate love with him he remembered in every intimate detail from years past. There had only been two such occasions, some years apart, but even so, he had never forgotten them.

She extended a slim gloved hand. "Well, Quintin Douglas Ker-Shaw," she said with a smile. "Have ye no' forgotten your manners?'' She had mimicked his faint clipped Scots tone of voice to perfection.

Quint smiled. ''I apologize, Mrs. Calhoun. I've been away from polite society so long I seem to have forgotten them.''

She raised her eyebrows. That delicious laughter came again, thrilling Quint. ''*Mrs.* Calhoun? You've no' forgotten my ain Christian name, Quintin?''

''Jean, then,'' he murmured. The touch of her hand sent something electrifying up his arm, into his body and very soul. Her hand lingered, then with a slight, quick, intimate pressure she withdrew it. He knew then and there she would again be available to him for lovemaking.

''You've not met my son Alexander,'' Jean said. She turned toward the young officer courier. ''Alec, this is the legendary Quint Kershaw you've often heard about from me, Tom Byrne, and, of course, your grandfather Alexander, who, of course, knows of him only by hearsay.''

Quint smiled as he extended his hand. ''Only the better lies, I hope, Jean.'' He met the firm grasp of a tall young second lieutenant of dragoons.

Alexander Calhoun was a little awed. ''Whatever the tales were, Captain, I enjoyed them, lies and all. I hope to hear more, perhaps from your own lips, sir.''

Colonel Canby looked up from his desk. ''You might hear such in New Mexico, Lieutenant, but not from Captain Kershaw himself. Kershaw, Lieutenant Calhoun has arrived from St. Louis with important dispatches by way of Denver City and Fort Union.''

There was much of his mother in young Calhoun. He was quite handsome in a chiseled way, with fine blond hair, a strong nose and firm chin. It was his eyes that would draw immediate attention—clear and light gray, with intelligence and humor within them. Those eyes were the indelible mark of his Kershaw blood, similar to those of David and Rafaela, for Alexander Calhoun was the true son of Quint.

Canby stood up. ''Lieutenant Calhoun has come just at the precise moment with important information for our meeting, Kershaw. He smiled. ''In addition he brought his beautiful mother with him from the Rio Brioso so that she might offer her services and the facilities of the Rio Brioso to the government. I have invited her to attend our meeting.''

The dingy office seemed to brighten when Jean entered it. The other men knew her quite well. Tom Byrne had delivered her during his days as surgeon with the First Dragoons. She was like his own daughter, he being childless.

Colonel Edward Richard Sprigg Canby was forty-four years old, Kentucky-born, graduate of the military academy, veteran of the Seminole and Mexican Wars. He had very much the look and carriage of a soldier, tall of stature, erect and well-formed. His countenance was weathered and somewhat careworn. He was inclined to be reserved and silent, a kindly man, always courteous in manner. He was intelligent and industrious. At the start of the war he had been serving as major of the Tenth United States Infantry at Fort Defiance, New Mexico, in the Navajo country. He had been appointed commander of the District of New Mexico in May of 1861, with the rank of colonel, succeeding Colonel William Loring, of North Carolina, who had resigned and defected to the Confederacy after his plot to turn everything over to it was disclosed to the loyal commander of Fort Stanton by a drunken officer. Earlier, Loring had urged the United States Government to ship Regular Army troops from New Mexico to the east for service while at the same time admitting he could not hold the territory with the troops he would have left. Canby was one of the few senior officers in New Mexico who had remained loyal to the Union. Upon assuming command of the District of New Mexico in May, he had intercepted a letter from former U.S. Major Henry Sibley (then at Fort Bliss wearing Confederate gray) in which Sibley had written to other officers in New Mexico, including Loring, urging them to defect to the Confederacy. Canby had immediately issued orders to Major Lynde at Fort Fillmore to place Sibley under arrest as a traitor, but he had already passed safely into Texas on his way to accept a commission in the Confederate Army. Canby and Sibley were related by marriage, their wives being distant cousins.

Much depended on Edward Canby. His troops were demoralized. They had not been paid in months. Almost all the senior officers had defected. The few Regular Army troops under his command were being slated to go east to more active theaters of war. He lacked enough troops to adequately garrison the few military posts that had not already been abandoned. Supplies were limited, and more from the East were long in coming, if they came at all. He had little faith in the native New Mexicans as volunteer or militia material.

Jean was the center of attraction. She usually was in the company of men, which she preferred to that of women. Still, she had the quality of being liked and admired by the women of her acquaintance, because of her character, kindness, warmth, and generosity.

Quint studied her. In fact, he could hardly keep his eyes from her. She was free of marriage now, as he had been for fourteen years. The same overpowering, possessive feeling for her had returned to him full force. Now and again she glanced at him, then away again. He knew then that she felt the same as he did. There never had been any need for them to explain how they felt about each other. It had a magnetic quality, drawing them irresistibly together whenever they met. It was perhaps not truly a feeling of possessiveness between them but rather one of soul partnership, and that too might be inadequate to explain it. She could have been his back in 1838. Or would *he* have been *hers*? Both of them were strong-willed, individualistic to a high degree, and above all ambitious. She had had an advantage then of intelligence, vitality, beauty, and great wealth, coupled with powerful political ties through her father. All Quint had had at that time was his ambition, powerful vitality and drive, and his Hawken rifle, and not a *centavo* to his name. If he had accepted her proposal of marriage at that time it would have meant returning east with her, a penniless adventurer without formal education, married to the daughter of one of the most influential and wealthy men in Congress. Jean had told him at that time he had all the qualities necessary for success. Paradoxically she had also said his future would be in New Mexico. "The future for you is here in New Mexico, Quintin Ker-Shaw," she had prophesied. Years had passed since their parting. Now fate had thrown them together once again, but this time with a curious twist—their son, Alexander, was with them now, not knowing Quint was his real father. It was a secret few people knew, but one of them was Shelby Calhoun. Luke Connors knew about the relationship, and Tom Byrne as well.

Alexander surreptitiously studied Quint. All his young life he had heard about this so-called living legend. Although Alexander had been in New Mexico a number of times before he entered the military academy, and during summer leaves from there, he had never met Quint. Still, he felt as though he knew him well. He felt himself irresistibly attracted to this rangy, tall, scar-faced ex—mountain man. There was another attraction for Alexander in Santa Fe, one that he had tried to keep within himself. Some years ago he had met Guadalupe de Vasquez Kershaw, then still a child, a student at the Academy of the Sisters of Loretto. Although not much more than a boy himself, he had been instantly attracted to this demure, elfin, little female creature, quiet and thoughtful, mature far beyond her years, and filled with deep religious fervor. It was almost as though she were not of this earth, a fairylike creature who might vanish like a puff of smoke if she so desired. As a boy he had become accustomed to the dark, flashing beauty of the higher-class women of New Mexico, the *gente fina*, those of pure Spanish ancestry, but he had never seen anyone remotely like the tiny, fragile, and Madonna-like Guadalupe.

No one in New Mexico, not even his mother, had known the two reasons he had returned home as officer courier, with orders to remain on duty there. As a top-ranking graduate of the military academy he could have chosen the elite engineer branch of the service, or perhaps that of heavy artillery. He did have a preference for artillery, and might have chosen it, except for the two reasons that had brought him to the territory. He had chosen the dragoons first, with mounted rifles as a second choice. He had been posted to the First Dragoons, recently redesignated as the First Cavalry. Upon graduation he had been ordered to temporary duty in Washington, through the influence of his grandfather. He usually could have his way with the old man but rarely used that prerogative. This time he used it and obtained the assignment in New Mexico. His reasons were sound enough. He loved New Mexico for itself. Both his parents were there. At that time he had not known of his father's defection to the South. He knew many Regular units would be ordered east. Volunteer units must be raised to replace them. They would need trained officers. He knew the territory fairly well and spoke fluent Spanish. Assignment to a volunteer unit would assure him of rapid promotion, perhaps the beginning of a prestigious military career in the Southwest. The other principal reason was his attraction to Guadalupe, a spiritual experience he had kept solely to himself. She was not quite fifteen years old.

Colonel Canby pushed back the last dispatch he had been reading and reached for his pipe. He was rarely seen without an unlit cigar in his mouth, but when he felt the need for deep thinking and the solace of burning tobacco he always smoked his pipe. "Light up, gentlemen," he suggested. He looked at the large map of the Southwest hung on the wall. "Manifest Destiny," he mused. "I wonder how many Americans east of the Mississippi had any idea of what it meant and the reality of its accomplishment. A great dream that became a reality. Now it is in fearful jeopardy from those people down south."

"Are we not comparatively safe here in New Mexico, sir? The war seems far away," Alexander said.

Jean shook her head. "Listen to *him*. You've been too long in the East, Alec."

Canby nodded. "The government is so involved with events in the East, particularly so after Bull Run, they've almost forgotten we exist out here. Two years of drought have cost great loss in crops and the raising of stock. Our cavalry is virtually dismounted now. We have not enough teams to haul guns and transport wagons. We've been forced to retrain cavalrymen and infantrymen as artillerymen. The abandonment of most of our forts in Arizona and Texas and some here in New Mexico have lost us what control we had over the hostile Indians. Now the Apaches think that they have been the cause of our problems and that the day of the white man in this country will soon come to an end. They are beginning to run rampant, destroying the control over them it has taken years to establish."

"But do not the Confederates have much the same problems?" Alexander asked quickly.

"They do," Canby agreed. "But there are some differences. Their troops are almost completely of Anglo descent. Most of them are fine horsemen, skilled with weapons and experienced in Indian fighting, led by veteran officers, in fact, natural-born fighting men."

"We have our Regulars, sir," Alexander reminded him.

"Certainly, but not enough to repel a full-scale invasion. We too have men such as the Texans.'' He looked at Quint and Luke. "But Lieutenant, far far too few. The vast majority of the population here are native New Mexicans of mixed blood, hardly literate, ninety percent of whom still speak only Spanish fifteen years after their annexation to the United States. Many of them live in abject poverty worse than the black slaves on the southern plantations. There is no middle class. There are only the rich and the poor, with very few exceptions. The *ricos*, one-fiftieth of the population, own everything that is worth owning. They hold all the social, economic, and political power. Up until we came here they were a law unto themselves. There has been no tradition of self-government here. The territory is unique in the United States. Isolated, little known, with a background of Mexican institutions foremost of which is the power of the Catholic Church. Further, there is an inbred fear and intense hatred of Texans among them. These are the men we must recruit, but I have little faith in their ability to be trained in time or to stand and fight the Texans.''

Governor Connelly nodded. "We have some few advantages, of course, young Calhoun. The population for the most part is loyal to the Union. The majority of the *ricos* are also loyal. According to the report we have received from Sergeant Connors here, the Texans seem to have been left to carry out the invasion on their own, dependent upon living off the country. They may not have it quite as easy as they think.''

"Then there is the country itself, Alexander,'' Quint added. "It might just be our greatest ally. Water is scarce after a two-year drought. Winter is coming, and a cold and bitter one has been predicted. Hostile Indians will certainly cause us a great deal of trouble, but they are not choosing sides. A Texan is as much an enemy to them as a New Mexican. They'll run off the Rebels' stock, raid their supply columns, ambush their patrols, and harass their outposts. Every mile they take from us in their advance will have to be guarded by garrisons they leave behind. Remember, the Apaches may be the best guerrilla fighters in the world.''

Alexander was puzzled. "If that is so, why would the Rebels want New Mexico in the first place?''

Canby stood up and walked to the map. He placed a finger on the El Paso area. "New Mexico is the key to a conquest of the Southwest. Texas still has dreams of expansion and is still smarting over the defeat of her claims in the Compromise of 1850 to the territory as far west as the Rio Grande. It might be that she only wants to establish a protectorate over New Mexico, but I doubt that. I think they want outright annexation now that the Compromise of 1850 is no longer binding them as part of the United States. Last February they passed an ordinance to secure the friendship and cooperation of New Mexico. They delegated Simeon Hart, of Hart's Mills in the El Paso area, and a certain Philemon Herbert as commissioners to New Mexico for the express purpose of stirring up insurrection here. Hart reported that the people of Arizona, which as you know is part of New Mexico, were one hundred percent in favor of joining Texas and the Confederacy.

"The greatest concentration of Arizona secessionists is at La Mesilla, Doña Ana County. Last March a convention of those people was held there. They declared that part of New Mexico south of the Thirty-fourth Parallel to be the Confederate Territory of Arizona."

"Why didn't we drive them out?" demanded Alexander.

Canby looked at Luke. "Sergeant Connors, please enlighten the young man with the information Captain Kershaw and yourself brought me early this morning."

Alexander's face was a montage of incredulous disbelief, shame, and horror when Luke finished his report.

Canby pointed with the stem of his pipe to the La Mesilla–Fort Fillmore area. "Here now is a solid springboard for their invasion of the north. I think they believe they can rally many of our Regulars and native New Mexicans to their cause. They claim the western boundary of their Arizona Territory runs all the way to the Colorado River. There are many Anglo southern sympathizers in western Arizona. California also has many of them. To the north, the Utah Mormons are still smarting over their treatment of the United States and might well be sympathetic to the southern cause. You already know the situation in Colorado.

"There can be great advantages in a successful invasion. The northern Mexican states of Coahuila and Chihuahua are virtually independent of their government and possibly ripe for inclusion in the Confederacy. Our State Department has been warned of this possibility. The southwest areas of Colorado and Nevada, and California, of course, are rich with gold and silver mines.

The Confederacy has urgent need of these invaluable resources. It might be the real objective of the invaders. Just before the start of war our then Secretary of War John B. Floyd sent great stores of ordnance and small arms to depots in California and other areas in the Southwest. It is estimated there are from six to eight thousand stands of rifles and about twenty-five to thirty pieces of artillery in danger of being captured by invaders.

"Perhaps one of their major goals would be the conquest of California and possibly Baja California, which would give the Confederacy a Pacific Ocean coastline over twelve hundred miles long, which would effectively counteract our naval blockade of the East Coast and the Gulf of Mexico. Remember, Lieutenant, there are three major deep-sea ports along the Pacific Coastline—San Francisco, San Diego, and Guaymas in Mexico."

"Perhaps weightiest of all, Alec, above and beyond the practical, would be the *moral* victory if the South is successful in these areas. The North might not be able to reverse that conquest. Such a feat would insure recognition of the Confederacy by the major European powers, a recognition they must have in order to win the war at all," Tom Byrne explained.

Quint nodded. "As to New Mexico itself, there are the military stores in the active posts and the depots in Albuquerque, Santa Fe, and particularly Fort Union. Control of Fort Union and those captured stores would open the way to an invasion of Colorado and control of the western terminus of the Santa Fe Trail."

"I had no idea," Alexander started to say. His voice died away. He looked at Canby. "How has the recruiting progressed, sir?"

"Why do you ask, Lieutenant?" Canby said.

Alec flushed a little.

"Go on," Jean urged.

The young officer took the bull by the horns. "I thought I might be appointed to a volunteer unit. With my training and knowledge of Spanish and the territory, I think I could command a company, Colonel," he said a little uncertainly.

Canby shook his head. "I have a policy of not appointing Regular Army officers to volunteer units. We must fill up their ranks in the main with New Mexicans of Spanish descent. At present the prejudice against us Americans is so great that if the field officers, for example, are taken altogether from the

Americans, it will delay, if not defeat, the organization of these regiments. It's not a sound military reason, I grant you, but it's a necessity forced upon us by the very nature of these people. I hardly think that with your American birth, prestigious family, and background I could promote you to the temporary wartime rank of a captain in command of a line company possibly composed one hundred percent of native New Mexicans who speak little or no English.''

"Alexander speaks fluent Spanish and has lived with the people,'' Jean put in quickly.

Canby waved a hand. "Granted, Mrs. Calhoun, but there is more to the command of these people than a speaking knowledge of their language. You say he's lived with them. Fine! But not as *one* of them, rather as the son of the *patrón*, a product of the upper class and an American as well. Those Americans such as Colonel St. Vrain, Lieutenant Colonel Carson, Captain Kershaw, and others have lived long in New Mexico, before the American annexation. They've married New Mexican women and have made their living here. They've served in the Mexican War and have fought Indians in this territory. As such, each of them is worth a regiment to our cause. I can't honestly say I have their favorable opinion of the Mexican character, at least in some cases, but then, perhaps I do not have their experience in such matters. Therefore, the best we can do at present is recruit, organize, and train the native New Mexicans as quickly as we can, officered by either other native New Mexicans or Americans such as I have just described.''

"Your point is well taken, sir,'' Alexander admitted.

Canby smiled. "Besides, I will have need of you on my staff, young sir. It isn't often I can find a young officer from the military academy, from a prestigious Eastern and New Mexican background, who speaks fluent Spanish. As such I am immediately promoting you to the rank of temporary first lieutenant assigned to my staff as aide.''

Alexander smiled. "In that case, Colonel, I'll readily forego any thoughts I had of serving in one of your volunteer regiments.''

Beautifully done on both sides, Quint thought.

"How goes the recruiting and other preparations, Colonel?'' Alexander asked, already interested in his new assignment.

"I have written to Governor Gilpin of Colorado, requesting

volunteer troops as quickly as they can be trained and sent down here. The First New Mexico is about at full strength. The Second and Third Militia regiments are partially organized. The Fourth Regiment is being recruited at Fort Union, the Fifth at Albuquerque. With the exceptions of the Fourth and Fifth regiments all other company units will be for three months' service only. We're entitled to recruit thirty-two such companies. At present we have just nineteen. I have just been informed in the dispatches brought me by Lieutenant Calhoun that those thirty-two companies, of which we have nineteen only, are to replace my Regulars, who will be ordered east for service as soon as possible."

"That could lead to disaster!" Ceran exclaimed.

"I intend to resist that order," Canby continued. "We cannot hold this territory with raw native troops. Even now I'm scraping up every man I can find. Fort Craig has only three hundred Regulars and one hundred and eighty volunteers. In addition there are Captain Graydon's spy company and a few miscellaneous small units of militia. Fort Craig is our keystone of defense against a Confederate advance up the Rio Grande Valley. If the enemy should advance up the Pecos, we'll have nothing to stop them except Fort Union. Fort Stanton in the Capitans was abandoned last August by my orders. It could not have effectively halted a Confederate advance along the line of the Pecos. I plan to reinforce Fort Union with Colorado troops, providing I get them, and in time. One of our major problems is to discern whether the Rebels will advance up the Rio Grande, up the Pecos, or possibly the Canadian. Perhaps all *three* . . ."

It was very quiet in the office. They could hear a clerk's pen scratching in the outer office and the ticking of the clock.

Canby looked at Quint. "What I cannot understand, Captain Kershaw, is why those contract animals from your ranch were virtually herded right into the hands of the enemy at La Mesilla. Surely your men must have known the enemy was in possession of both town and fort? Perhaps you can explain that, Sergeant Connors?"

Luke looked at Quint. Quint nodded. It would only be a matter of time before the truth was known. "They knew all right, Colonel," Luke said quietly. "It was just that the man in charge of the herd was planning to defect to the Texans."

Canby looked quickly at Quint. "Surely not one of the men in your company, Captain?"

"All of them were," Quint admitted. "The truth is, sir, that the man in charge was my own son Frank. He delivered the stock, then enlisted in the Second Texas."

"But he was a New Mexican! Son to you and his mother, of the oldest New Mexican stock."

Quint nodded. "There was a conflict between him and his half brother David. It evidently triggered his actions."

Canby eyed him. "Is not David your second-in-command? Was it a problem of military origin?"

Tom Byrne caught Canby's eye and shook his head. Quint had told Tom what had caused the break, and Tom, of course, knew of the long-standing rancor between the two men.

"A war like this makes enemies of father and son, brothers and old friends and associates," Henry Connelly put in.

Canby wisely avoided the subject. "What is the condition of your company at present, Captain Kershaw? How many have you mustered?"

"I had over forty men at the Querencia. At least ten of them were turned over to the Texans, probably to be paroled. I haven't heard about that possibility. So at present they are lost to my command. I'll have to leave some men to guard the Querencia to defend it against possible attack by the Apaches, once they know its weakness, or the Texans. They've been there already, as you know."

"Under the command of Colonel Shelby Calhoun," Luke added.

Jean and Alexander looked quickly at Luke.

Quint continued. "I can assign some of the older men and those unfit for military service to the Querencia. It's either do that, risky as it is, or abandon it altogether. It would make a good outpost for the Rebels. And I would not like to see it destroyed by the Apaches. I can recruit perhaps twenty more men in the Socorro area who would be willing to serve with me. How soon will you need us, Colonel?"

"As soon as possible, Captain."

"Here, sir?"

Canby shook his head. He turned again to the map. "I want you to return to the Querencia and make your arrangements.

★ 116 ★

When ready I want you to make a reconnaissance out to the line of the Pecos, at least as far south as the Rio Felix area, to scout for signs of a possible Rebel advance. Colonel Carson has scouts out along the Canadian and the upper Pecos. At present we have no troops for observation in the entire southeastern part of the territory. I would, of course, also like information as to enemy movements in western Texas, their strength, type of units, and numbers of artillery. In fact, every scrap of information I can get, no matter how trivial.''

They all knew the great peril of such a reconnaissance. The country was overrun by the Mescalero Apaches, perhaps even Kiowas and Comanches. The closest Union troops would be at Fort Craig and Fort Union.

Canby refilled his pipe and lighted it. He spoke between puffs. ''I realize your command will be too small for such a dangerous mission, but your men are frontiersmen, skilled Indian fighters—led by an experienced man like yourself, Kershaw, the possibility of success might very well be good.'' He didn't sound very convincing. ''Further, although I hesitate to say this, I will have to risk your unit rather than lose a single man of my well-trained Regulars. The mission is absolutely necessary. I know of no one better equipped than yourself to undertake it. I will not *order* you to do this, however.''

''It's not necessary, sir,'' Quint said. ''I've left my company in charge of my son Lieutenant David Kershaw. He can handle it about as well as I can. Thirty men, or double that number, or many more, experienced and well armed, could hardly move across that country without being seen by hostile Indians, no matter how carefully they travel. The Rebels would soon know what we were about. The severe drought of the past two years would make finding enough water for so many men and horses extremely difficult, if not impossible. As such, it is an impossible mission.''

There was a pause. Canby took the pipe from his mouth. ''Then you refuse to go? Is that it?''

''I'll go, sir!'' Alexander said eagerly.

Canby shook his head. ''Well, Kershaw?'' he asked quietly.

''I didn't say I wouldn't go, Colonel,'' Quint said. ''I merely stated it was impossible for such a number of men.''

''How many men will you need, then?'' the colonel asked.

Quint held up two fingers. "Myself and Sergeant Connors, if he's willing to ride with me."

Luke nodded. "I thought you'd never ask, Captain," he murmured.

Canby shook his head. "Two men? Are you mad, sir! I can't allow it!"

Quint raised his hand. "You don't understand, sir. Luke and I can move through that country virtually unseen, traveling by night and hiding out by day. We can move faster than a company, with less if any noise, no dust, and blend into the landscape, covering far more ground at greater speed and with at least a twenty-five percent better chance of survival."

Ceran nodded. "He's right, Colonel. If any two men can do it, it's them."

Canby shrugged. "All right! All right! You've convinced me. I hope to God it doesn't strike my conscience in time to come. How soon can you leave?"

Quint stood up and looked directly into Jean's eyes. He had been about to say, "Within the hour, Colonel." He did not. "Within the next twenty-four hours, sir," he said.

Tom Byrne had sensed what was going on. "You'll stay with me, of course, Quint. Jean, you and young Alexander are welcome too, unless the colonel wants him to quarter here at Fort Marcy."

Canby nodded. "I do, Tom."

Tom stood up. "Then it's settled. Quint, you and Luke will have dinner with us this evening. Guadalupe will be there, of course." He did not look at Alexander as he spoke. He knew of the interest the young officer had in the girl. Somehow he must help Jean and Quint explain Alexander's true relationship with Guadalupe. He could not bear to see the two young people he loved be so hurt, but he had convinced himself that in the long run it would be all for the best.

★ FIFTEEN ★

1861: DENVER CITY, THE PIKE'S PEAKERS

Colorado Territory was isolated by six hundred miles of rolling plains from the borderland of the States. Southern menace was apparent. Secessionists plotted and conspired to drag the territory and hopefully the entire Southwest into the Confederacy. Colorado was surrounded by hordes of hostile Indians ready and eager to strike if the chance presented itself.

The Confederate leaders were resolute men. They knew about the plan for the Texans to invade New Mexico, detach it from the United States government, then seek control of the rich silver and gold mines of Colorado Territory. Their task would be to insure that Colorado would be ready to fall.

In July Samuel H. Cook and two associates began to raise a mounted company in the South Clear Creek mining district for service in Kansas, eventually to become the nucleus of the First Regiment of Colorado Volunteers.

In August James H. Ford was authorized to raise a company of infantry. This was the beginning of the Second Regiment of Colorado Volunteers. Theodore H. Dodd was appointed first lieutenant of a company to be mustered at Canon City, slated for the Second Colorado.

Ohioan John P. Slough, a prominent lawyer of Denver City, recruited Company A of the First Colorado Volunteers and soon was promoted to colonel of that regiment. John H. Chivington, another Ohioan, was presiding elder of the Rocky Mountain District Methodist Episcopal Church and an abolitionist to the core. Six feet five inches tall, a bull-strong giant with a powerful voice, he was called "the fightin' preacher against whom the devil himself had mighty poor odds." He had been offered the chaplaincy of the First Colorado but had refused, preferring a strictly "fighting position," as he put it, and was then commissioned major.

The First Colorado was rapidly recruited. Company B came from Central City and Blackhawk. C Company was recruited in Denver City and the Buckskin Joe Mining District. Company E hailed from the mining towns of Oro City and Laurette. South Clear Mining District supplied Company F. Men from Nevada, Empire City and Clear Creek formed Company G, while Company H hailed from Central City. The Germans of Denver City, Central City, and Clear Creek Mining District were recruited for most of Company I. Company K came from Central City and Denver City.

The Coloradoans as a whole were big, confident, self-assured men, with weather-beaten faces marked with the stamp of physical courage. They were well qualified for combat, although perhaps not for military discipline. They were hardy, individualistic, a wild, tough bunch of men with rugged energy and a tendency toward lawlessness. Most of them hailed from the East and Midwest. Some were of Irish extraction, others of Scottish, German, Canadian, English, or Welsh descent.

By late autumn three companies under Lieutenant Colonel Tappan had been sent to garrison Camp Wise on the Arkansas River two hundred miles southeast of Denver City. The remaining companies stayed at Camp Weld under the command of Major Chivington. Well armed and trained, these tough Coloradoans would be a force to be reckoned with in battle.

★ SIXTEEN ★

Maria, Tom Byrne's cook of many years, had concocted an outstanding dinner, outdoing even herself in the preparation of classic New Mexican dishes. The dinner was served in the low-ceilinged dining room ablaze with candles. There was a thin consommé with noodles and another soup, this one thicker, with bits of meat and vegetables. Beef had been roasted, boiled, and chopped, then stewed with a gravy of red-hot peppers. There was boiled chicken and rice, the rice thickened with butter, the whole topped with slices of hardboiled eggs. Hot *mistela* was served, a fragrant brew of ancient forty-year-old brandy made from El Paso grape wine, sugar, spices, and chimaya leaves sealed in a jar with dough and simmered. The thinnest of tortillas, always a test of the maker's skill, were served warm at the table, as well as *sopapillas*, a puffed yellow thin-walled pastry filled with butter and honey, crumbling into sweetness, topped with powdered sugar. There was a round yellow cheese of goat's milk sliced to bone whiteness. *Empanaditas*, pastries filled with mincemeat, were served hot from the oven. There were silver pitchers of fruit syrup prepared by stirring constantly for three days as the mixture simmered over the coals. Thick brown chocolate had been beaten to a froth in a copper bowl and served in silver cups. There were champagne and red wine. The bread was that incomparable New Mexico type, the whitest of white. For dessert there was fine sponge cake and boiled custard pudding seasoned with cinnamon and nutmeg and thick with raisins and piñon nuts scattered through the yellow richness.

Jean leaned back in her chair at the conclusion of the magnificent dinner. "Tom, I do believe you've a plot to destroy any woman's figure who dares to dine with you."

Tom smiled. "I don't believe I've ever seen your figure any different than it is now, Jean."

Quint nodded. "*Verdad*," he murmured.

Jean was lovely in a cream taffeta with a pattern of rosebuds on a brown satin trellis and a full-looped skirt. She wore a fichu with deep lace flounce. Her creamy shoulders and throat were bared to the soft and uncertain light of the flickering candles. Guadalupe wore a simple black silk gown that Quint had not seen before, with a filmy mantilla. The gown was perfect for her velvety black eyes, red lips, developing bust, and softly rounded figure.

Alexander was resplendent in the dress uniform of an officer of dragoons; the blue, yellow, and gold, accented by lustrous polished brass, set off his fine complexion, light hair, and light-gray eyes. He wore the bare shoulder straps of a second lieutenant, not having had time to place the single silver bar of his new rank on them.

Quint himself wore his best uniform, kept for some years in Tom's care. He could hardly remember the last time he had worn it, at some function or other in the city. The times he had been called to duty were always for field service of the hardest type, where he usually wore the trousers and an elkskin jacket with the bars pinned to the shoulders.

Luke had been invited to the dinner, but he had begged off, not because of his rank as sergeant but because he was always ill at ease in such company. Too, there was Rosa, an old acquaintance of his who ran a small monte parlor, nothing of the style and caliber of La Tules's old place, but good enough for Luke. Rosa had been Luke's faithful inamorata for the past fifteen years, at least when he was in the city. They had a beautiful understanding.

After dinner the party adjourned to the library. Tom knew how to decorate a room, Quint thought. It was low-ceilinged, in common with the rest of the rooms, and had a beehive fireplace. The furniture, for the most part heavy dark polished wood in the Mexican Colonial style, was supplemented with deep leather armchairs brought over the Santa Fe Trail. The walls were shelved in dark polished wood and lined with leatherbound volumes on many subjects and disciplines. The library was probably one of the best and most complete west of St. Louis and north of Mexico City. It had been Tom who had helped establish Quint's library at Rio Brioso and later at the Querencia.

Quint listened idly to the gay conversation among the others. The good brandy was warm within him, and the cigar was one of Tom's excellent havanas. He watched Jean as she walked about the room. She had the slim waist of a horsewoman, and her gown at times molded itself against one of her long, well-shaped legs. Jean wasn't a great beauty in the classic sense. Her type was Nordic or Celtic, perhaps a combination of the two. Each of her features was fine individually, but taken together they lacked that homogeneity required for the popular concept of pure beauty. That had never been a problem with Quint. He had never been drawn to classic beauty as he had been to Jean.

Guadalupe seemed fascinated by Jean. Guadalupe's mother's last request had been to name the child after herself. Perhaps she had sensed something secret to herself, for tiny Guadalupe had grown into a living image of her mother. It was almost as though she were the physical reincarnation of Guadalupe. In the mental sense she was almost at the opposite pole. Guadalupe had succeeded to Rafaela's place in Tom's household while being schooled in Santa Fe. She had not succeeded Rafaela in the old man's heart; there was ample room for both of them, and Jean as well. Still, Guadalupe did seem closer to him. There had been another such girl-woman in his heart years past, but not in the platonic sense. Luz, a Genizara, had been many years his junior, loving him as much as he loved her. Since 1846 he had never spoken of her, and none of his friends or associates had mentioned her name to him. In a way Guadalupe was much like Luz, more so than her own mother. Guadalupe and Luz both had lacked the deceptive inner mental strength of Guadalupe de Vasquez Kershaw.

Guadalupe loved Cristina, Rafaela, Francisco, and David. David had always been unable to resist her every wish and desire. In Cristina she had all the foster mother a child could desire. Most of all it was Quint she loved and wanted to be loved by in return. Her silent adoration of him was obvious when she was in his presence. He had always treated her well, many times perhaps better than the other three children. He could be adamant when his will was crossed, particularly in matters concerning their welfare. With Guadalupe it was something else. Quint was one of those people unable to conceal their true feelings. As the child grew, Quint could not look at her without seeing her mother. Quint had never mentioned it to anyone, but it was always there. It was difficult as well for him to show strong emotion, except in lovemaking with a woman he truly cared for, or in red battle, when he reverted to his Norse and Celtic ancestry. His lack of visible emotion might come from his Scots forebears or from his long and close contact with Indians, or perhaps a combination of both. He had paid a heavy price for it at times. With Guadalupe it had been proven costliest of all.

Quint had watched with alarm the eye play between Alexander and Guadalupe while at the table. It continued now in the living room, almost as though the two of them were unconscious of the others present. There could be no question that whatever Alexander felt for her, she would respond in turn.

Tom seated himself in his armchair near the fire, brandy carafe and humidor of fine havanas close at hand. "Ye mind the fine, informative discussions we had here in this room during the thirties before the war, Quint? Manifest Destiny! That was about all that was in our minds at the time." He looked at Jean, then at Quint. "At least it was one of the uppermost interests," he added dryly.

Quint could never be near Jean without experiencing that almost overpowering impulse to become part of her, physically and mentally. There never had been the need to explain to each other how they felt.

"Quint?" Tom asked. "Are ye with us this night? Ye seem to be far away, lost in those deep thoughts of yours."

Quint smiled. "Sorry, Tom. Perhaps I'm tired from that damned long ride here."

"What glorious times those must have been," Alexander suggested. "With prospects of battle, conquest, and well-earned glory."

Tom shrugged. "It wasn't quite like that here, Alec. The fighting was done elsewhere, *after* the peaceful conquest."

"We *bought* that conquest," Quint said.

"You sound a little bitter, Quint," Jean suggested.

He nodded. "For some of us it *was* a bitter time."

Alexander looked at Quint. "But there was the fighting at La Canada and Taos Pueblo."

"That was against the insurrectionist Mexicans and Taos Indians," Quint said quietly. "It was the poor deluded Taos Indians who paid in bloody coin for it. I've never been proud of my part in that."

"You were doing your duty," Alexander said.

"It was the moral sense to which Quint refers," Tom put in. "They were but fighting for their freedom and their land, both of which we had taken from them. There is no glory or satisfaction in such a victory."

Quint closed his eyes. The acrid smoke and stink of that bloody hand-to-hand battle around the Taos church came back to him in every horrible detail.

"I was born at that time," Guadalupe said softly.

They were startled. They looked at her. She was usually so quiet.

"My mother died because of me," she added. "I never knew her."

"Look in the mirror, dear," Jean almost said. She well remembered Guadalupe de Vasquez. Perhaps if it hadn't been for her Quint might have married Jean and returned east with her. *Perhaps?* Well, one would never know now. But supposing, just supposing . . .

Guadalupe had slipped into a momentary depression. Quint found himself, as usual, unable to communicate with her.

Tom leaned toward the girl. "Child, it was not your fault. Your mother knew long before your conception she should not have another child. I had warned her. She knew the consequences."

Guadalupe looked slowly, almost accusingly at Quint.

Quint looked away from her. "I didn't know, child. She never told me."

"Couldn't you have understood, father?" she almost pleaded. She gathered her courage. "Or did you force yourself on her?"

A memory-picture of a passionate, sensuous Guadalupe came swiftly to Quint in sporadic fashion like the slides in a magic-lantern show being operated too fast and irregularly. His memory had not failed him. She had never mentioned her condition to him.

★ 125 ★

"This is not the time and place for such a subject, Guadalupe," Tom said gently.

She did not look at him, still looking steadfastly at her father. "With apologies, Dr. Byrne, you are not the judge of that time and place," she countered.

Tom shrugged. He looked at Jean.

There were quick tears in the girl's eyes.

Jean sat beside her and placed a hand on her arm. "Come with me, dear," she suggested softly.

Guadalupe shook her head. "If he forced himself on her, knowing her condition, it is the same as murder." It hurt her deeply to say so, but it was something she had held back for years. Paradoxically it had never altered her deep love for him.

Quint stood up. "I did not know," he repeated mechanically. "But I know this: If I had known, you would not have been conceived. Have you ever considered that?"

"Then you are blaming my mother's death on me!" she cried.

Tom was horrified. "For the love of God, Guadalupe!"

"I'll leave now," Quint said quietly.

Guadalupe shook her head. "I've made a fool of myself. I'm tired, and the wine has not helped matters."

Jean helped her from the library. The door closed behind them.

"She'll be all right in the morning," Tom said. There was little certainty in his tone. "It is not like her to be this way. Perhaps it was the wine after all." Both Quint and he knew better.

Alexander stood up. "I'll bid you both good night as well, gentlemen. There is some paperwork I must have ready by tomorrow. I would have liked mightily to accompany you on your mission, Captain Kershaw."

Quint smiled. "There will be another time, Lieutenant Calhoun. Wait here a moment. I have something for you." He returned to the library with a small plush case in his hand. He held it out to Alexander. "These are yours."

Alexander opened the box. The candlelight shone on a pair of epaulets with silver-bullion first lieutenant's bars on them. He looked up at Quint. "Yours?" he asked.

Quint nodded. "I have no further need for them, Alec."

"An honor, sir," Alexander said quietly.

"Let me put them on for you, son," Quint said, almost without thinking. He removed the epaulets on the coat and replaced them with his. "Wear them with honor," he said.

Jean returned as Alexander was leaving. She looked beyond him at Quint, then back at Alexander. Father, son, and mother, she thought to herself, the three of them together for the first time in their lives.

When Alexander left, Jean sat down. Tom filled her brandy glass. "He'll be a real professional someday," she predicted. "The very quintessence of the professional frontier soldier."

"Amen to that," Tom said. He yawned. "The dinner was excellent. The company beyond reproach. It's time for my bed, children." He looked at Quint. "I can't understand why Guadalupe acted in such a way."

Jean shook her head. "*Men!* She *had* to know!"

"But why this night?" Quint asked.

"Because, you great dummy, she knows how dangerous your mission to the south will be."

"I have a feeling both of you feel I might not return," he said.

Her eyes met his. "It is a good possibility, isn't it?"

Tom looked up. "It's war again. This territory seems to breed war. Indians, Mexicans, outlaws, and Rebels, it's all the same. There is a poetry about this land of ours, this Tierra Encantada, the Land of Enchantment, but beneath it all there is violence and cruelty. Like a beautiful woman who enchants one, then, when she is aroused, rends and tears at one with teeth and nails."

Jean's eyes met Quint's and they held the gaze. "Why a woman, Tom?" she asked. "Could it not be a man as well, who destroys with fist and boot rather than teeth and nails?"

Tom shrugged. "Perhaps. But can a man enchant a woman? True, he can attract, but it is the female of our damnable species that really enchants." He studied Jean. "You should know that by now, lass."

"It's late," Quint said. "We'll be leaving before dawn."

Tom shook his head. "Bide a bit, Quint. I'm off to bed. It's been a long time since you've seen Jean."

The door closed behind Tom.

"Brandy?" Quint asked.

She nodded. "Brandy is the drink for heroes," she quoted.

"Por todo mal, mescal;
Por todo bien, también."

She held out her glass and then translated thoughtfully, as though only for herself:

"Brandy helps everything bad,
And the same for everything glad."

The fire was dying. A thick bed of ashes covered the last embers. One of the piñon logs stacked vertically in the fireplace crumbled a little. Fine ash and a shower of tiny sparks spurted from the fireplace. The fire would soon be out.

The brandy was shining wet on her full lips. "Do you remember the New Mexican superstition about a fire of piñon logs you once told me long ago?"

In the dimming light of the guttering candles she looked lovelier and more desirable than ever. Quint shook his head.

"You said that if a piñon log blazes up when first lit and the logs stand upright against the chimney until they are charred, sweethearts will be true."

He narrowed his eyes. "How long ago was that?"

She studied him. "Fourteen years ago this month, in this very house."

He remembered then. They had made love with a warmth and passion he had never forgotten. After that he had not seen her for nine long years. They had repeated the performance at that time. It had been the last time, up until now.

"You do remember?" she asked.

"Of course."

"Why did we do it?" she asked rhetorically. She knew, of course.

"The lovemaking? It seemed to me that at that time we could not resist."

She shook her head. "Not *that*, Quint. Why did we part, knowing then, as we know now, we were in love with each other?"

He could think of nothing to say.

"But you became happy with Guadalupe," she murmured, as ough to herself.

"I was," he admitted. "Perhaps if you had stayed here . . . ut no, it wasn't in the cards at that time, was it?"

"Not at that time, nor nine years later," she reminded him.

"By then we were both married, Jean."

He shaped cigarettes and placed one between her lips. He ghted both of them and looked deep into her eyes. "A problem at seems to have vanished," he said softly.

They sat down opposite each other, near the fire, and close gether. "Have you thought of telling Alexander who his father ?" he asked.

She shook her head. "I didn't think it was the time."

"Why did you come to Santa Fe?"

She shrugged. "To offer my services to the government. To e with my son as long as I could." She placed a cool hand gainst the great scar on his left cheek. "And I had heard you ere ordered here."

He placed his hand atop hers and pressed it against his cheek. What do I say now? What happens now?"

"You're glad to see me?"

"What a question to ask," he said.

She leaned closer and touched his lips with hers.

"Wait," he said. "We must settle the issue of Alexander's arenthood and his interest in his own half sister."

She widened her eyes. "*Now?*" she queried.

It was very quiet in the big cavernous *casa*. The ticking of the randfather clock sounded inordinately loud. The last standing iñon log snapped and threw out sparks.

"You must keep him away from her, Jean, at least until I eturn," he warned. "Perhaps at that time he'll be assigned lsewhere. That will give us time. Perhaps he'll lose interest in er and she in him."

"He's only been here one day, Quint. It might be months, ven a year or more, before he's ordered away. Can't you make er return home? Or to school elsewhere?"

He shook his head. "The Querencia is too dangerous. It will oon be undermanned. The Santa Fe Trail is endangered by ostile Indians and possibly the Confederates. No, she must

remain here. Tom knows the situation, I'm sure. It will be up
the two of you to keep that situation under control."

She nodded. "Agreed."

He leaned back and studied her. "I've only a few hours l
and a long ride tomorrow," he suggested.

She stood up. "I'll be in my old room. Give me a little time
She walked to the door and looked back over her shoulder. "It
the same room as before. I'm sure you can find it."

"I think so." He smiled reminiscently.

She closed the door behind herself. The slight jar disturbed t
last piñon log. It crumbled in a shower of sparks and a cloud
fine ash.

Quint waited a reasonable length of time. He drained
brandy glass, selected a full bottle from the liquor cabinet, ble
out the candles, and left the library. He walked down the lo
hallway to the room. He tapped lightly on the door.

"*Quién es?*" she called softly.

"*El diablo,*" he replied. He grinned.

She paused. "Then enter, my heart."

He opened the door, stepped inside, and closed it before
turned to look at her. His breath caught in his throat. She wore
red silk dress with a daring décolletage revealing the deep clea
age and twin mounds of her breasts. The unhampered nippl
thrust themselves against the thin silk. The soft candle flam
picked up the highlights of her hair and the soft wetness of h
lips. She stood with her hips back against a low table beside t
bed and her hands braced behind her on the tabletop so that h
breasts were forced out.

"Do you remember?" she asked.

"It can't be, Jean."

She nodded. "It is. The same gown I wore the first time w
made love together in this room."

"But how? Why?" he asked, puzzled.

"I left it here when I returned east. Tom, the old sentiment
dear, kept it here for me. I had almost forgotten about it until
returned here today." She smiled. "You'd better bar the door.
wouldn't want to be surprised by our children."

He barred the door and then started a fire under the vertical
stacked piñon logs. They flared up immediately. He looked bac
at her over his shoulder. "That's half the superstition." He aros

d went to her. She tilted her head far back and let him kiss
r. He drew her close and fumbled with the tiny buttons at the
ck of the gown. She had thought of everything. Only a few of
e buttons had been fastened. He peeled the gown down over
r breasts and down about her hips. She wore no brassiere or
dergarment. They kissed passionately. He pushed the gown
wn over her hips. It dropped with a faint dry rustling sound
ke a cricket in tall grass. She stepped free of the gown and
cked it across the floor. She wore the finest of silk hose over
r long legs and black, gold-heeled slippers on her feet. She
cked off the slippers. He peeled the stockings off, then rose
owly, passing his hands up the outside of her thighs, then to
r belly and up under her breasts. She ran her hands through his
air, then bent his head back to kiss him, thrusting her tongue in
etween his. parted lips. He stood up and stepped back to view
r from head to foot, hardly believing what was happening.

"It's almost the same, isn't it?" she pleaded. "Please! Tell me
's almost the same!"

He nodded. "It is, but not *almost—exactly*, Jean."

He picked her up and placed her on the bed. She placed her
ands on each side of his face and drew his head down to meet
r searching lips. "Do I please you?" she whispered.

"*Huerito*, little blonde one," he murmured.

"Brandy," she said.

He stood up and stripped while she drank, all the while
watching him. He took the bottle from her hands, drank, then lay
own beside her. He blew out the candle.

They came together with a consuming passion engendered by
e long years they had been apart. The outside world had
anished. There was nothing beyond their searching lips and
aressing hands. There was no restraint between them. There had
ever been any before.

At last they fell apart from each other, exhausted and dewed
with perspiration. He slid his right arm beneath her neck. She
ested her head against his shoulder. They savored the quiet
noment. There was no need to speak. The fire filled the room
with warmth. Quint closed his eyes and drifted off. He had had
ery little sleep during the long arduous ride to Santa Fe. There
vas no sleep for her. She raised herself on her elbow and studied
is features and lean, muscular body, with its scars of bullet,

knife, and claw. She wondered fearfully how he had managed to survive all those years of danger. She reached across him for the bottle. She was a little drunk, but not enough to interfere with lovemaking.

She lay back against the pillow and looked at the moving fire-light patterns on the ceiling. "For how long this time?" she asked aloud.

He opened his eyes. "For what?"

She sat up, wrapped her arms about her knees, then rested her cheek on the knees. "Us," she replied simply.

"I'll be back, Jean."

"To whom?"

He raised up on his elbow. "You, of course, if you'll have me."

"God forbid that I would not! But what about Cristina?"

He had let Cristina drift out of his mind. "I hadn't considered her," he said quietly.

"Hasn't she always considered you?"

"Of course."

She knows about us, doesn't she?"

He nodded. "Yes."

"*Everything?*"

He shrugged. "I really don't know."

She studied him. "Evidently you don't know about those parts of your 'legend' in dealing with women."

He sat up and drank. "Tell me," he suggested.

"You know of the *cantina* songs written about you. Some of them refer to me as the blonde *gringa*, although my name is never mentioned. Everyone, including the Americans, knows damned well who they're referring to, the ultrapolite sonsofbitches. They don't need proof, Quint."

He nodded. "I suppose."

"Have you ever asked Cristina to marry you?" she asked.

He shook his head. "If I had, we'd have been married years ago."

"Has *she* asked *you*?"

"A New Mexican serving woman asking her *patrón* to marry her? You know better than that." What a damned hypocrite I really am, he thought.

"Is that the only reason?" she persisted.

★ 132 ★

"Damn you! I don't love her, not in the sense I loved Guadalupe and you too, for that matter."

She nodded. "Then there's nothing to hold us apart now, is there?"

He closed his eyes. How could he take Jean back to the Querencia as his wife? How could he ever face Cristina? She'd have to go. Before God, *how could he face her?*

She kissed him quickly. "I shouldn't have brought that up."

He drew her down close. In a little while they were at it again. Later, as they lay quietly side by side in the dying firelight, he turned to her and whispered, "Does that, at least, answer your question?"

When she awoke in the cold stillness of the predawn he was gone. She lighted a candle. The piñon logs were deeply charred, but they were still stacked upright. *"Gracias a Dios,"* she whispered.

★ SEVENTEEN ★

JORNADO DEL MUERTO

Space was the keynote of the Pecos River country, from its origin far to the north in the towering Sangre De Cristos, five hundred miles south, to its juncture with the Rio Grande. Its character was vast limitless stretches of plain, desert, hills, buttes, mesas, and lofty mountains of bare-earth colors and hazy purple distances to rest the eye. Pink at dawn, powder-white at noon, it was a land of changing hues that sank in a deep sea of sky at midnight when looming blue-black mountains thrust upward like volcanic-islands.

It was late afternoon, five weeks after Quint and Luke had left Santa Fe to scout the line of the Pecos. They were hidden in a deep, brush-filled arroyo low on the western slope of the San Andres Mountains with Salinas Peak towering above them to the north. They lacked water, food, and a pair of fresh horses, in the order of urgency named. Their one remaining horse was lame and just about done in. They had been out of food for two days and water for twenty-four hours. They had not stopped moving during those twenty-four hours, taking turns on the horse while the one on foot loped alongside. They had to keep moving. The Mescaleros had first seen them five days ago on the Rio Hondo not far from where it joined the Pecos. They had crossed the Sacramentos south of Fort Stanton in the Capitans, abandoned since last August and now said to be occupied by Rebels.

The closest water might be at Ojo del Muerto, the Spring of Death, thirty-five miles west of their position across the Jornado del Muerto. The next water would be at the Rio Grande, beyond the distant Fray Cristobals west of the Jornado. There was always the risk that the Confederates had moved upriver from La Mesilla while Quint and Luke had been scouting far down in West Texas, despite their orders from Colonel Canby that they must not go farther south than Rio Felix in New Mexico Territory. They would have to leave their hideout at dusk and reach the springs before dawn. Darkness would cloak the first part of their journey, but there would be a full moon that night, illuminating the light-colored surface of the desert as though it were daylight. Anything moving on that desert would stand out like a fly caught in amber.

Luke finished removing a thorn from his left foot. He held up his *n' deh b' keh*, the thigh-length, thick-soled, button-toed moccasin of the Apaches. There was no better footgear designed for desert travel, and Quint and Luke preferred the shoes over any other kind of footgear. Luke peered at Quint through a hole in the sole the size of a silver dollar. The rest of the sole was paper-thin. "My last pair," Luke said.

Quint nodded. He was in the same fix. They had each gone through a pair of boots and one pair of the desert moccasins on their reconnaissance from the junction of the Gallinas and the Pecos rivers twenty-five miles south of Las Vegas along the line of the Pecos to the Fort Lancaster area in West Texas, about 375 miles, traveling mostly by night through hostile country held in the dry vise of a two-year drought. In all that distance, the first

Confederates they had seen were troops moving west on the route of the Butterfield Overland Mail on the San Antonio–San Diego Mail line. They had remained near the stage line for a week, freezing cold at night, existing on meager rations and with very little water, tallying the number of troops moving west— mounted riflemen, artillery, transport columns, and herds of beef cattle. A friendly Mexican muleteer from the San Antonio area had told them the troops were the Fourth Texas Mounted Regiment, part of General Sibley's Brigade moving in three sections one day apart because of the shortage of water in the springs and water holes. The Mexican estimated the numbers of the entire brigade at about three thousand men with two batteries of twelve-pounder bronze howitzers. They had no heavier artillery. That had been sufficient information for Quint. That same night, Luke and he had returned north along the Pecos headed for Fort Craig on the Rio Grande 120 miles north of El Paso.

They had traveled through the habitat of the Mescaleros, a vast domain between the Rio Grande to the west, the Pecos and beyond to the east, and from the Llano Estacado in the north far south into Mexico. They were of Apache stock, known as the Mescal Makers and Eaters of Mescal. They moved about freely, wintering on the Rio Grande or farther south, ranging the buffalo plains in the summer, following the sun and food supply. In that land they owned nothing and yet everything. It was an enormous and untamed land, far too big for the Mexicans, who had claimed it as theirs for almost three hundred years. They held only the upland sheep pastures in the north and the narrow fields beside the rivers. The Apaches regarded it as their own land and believed absolutely that the Mexicans existed merely to raise stock and crops for them. Raiding was the business of the Mescaleros, and like Falstaff they considered it no sin to labor in their vocation. They haunted that country and the old Royal Highway from Chihuahua north to Santa Fe by coming over the crest of the San Andres or slipping through Mocking Bird Gap.

It was not quite dusk when Quint and Luke risked venturing out toward the Jornado. The horse had been fitted with buckskin boots for silence. Long shadows crept down the mountainsides inking in the hollows. The moon would rise in about three hours. It was that time of the day when light was deceptive, and hopefully it might help prevent two big men and a horse from being easily seen. It really wasn't much of a hope, but the risk was worth the time it would save.

They moved swiftly downslope and then out onto the silent, timeless, brooding solitude of the Jornado proper. Here the desert was stippled with scattered mesquite and creosote bushes with some tobosa and black grama grass. Now and again Quint or Luke would glance back over a shoulder. The mountains were shrouded in a purple haze. Nothing moved; nothing living could be seen except an occasional hawk circling, ever circling. There was always the impression that one was being watched from the seemingly lifeless mountain heights.

"There might be water at Laguna del Muerto," Quint said.

Luke shook his head. "Ain't likely. 'Lessn a wandering rainstorm passed right over it in the past few weeks, which is damned doubtful." He looked far across the desert. "Them·old Spaniards were sure involved with death all the time. Jornado del Muerto, Laguna del Muerto, and Ojo del Muerto . . ."

Quint nodded. "They had good reason to be, around here anyway. It's not the most healthy country I've ever been in."

The wind shifted. Dust-devils appeared, mysteriously whirling swiftly and aimlessly in a senseless rhythm of their own, then vanished to reappear in the distance, only to repeat the process over and over again, times without number, ad infinitum.

The Jornado had in prehistoric times been the channel of the Rio Grande until immense lava flows had blocked it, diverting it to the west and its present course. In the time of the Spaniards, the Jornado had become part of the old Camino Real, the Royal Highway to the north, starting 360 miles to the south of El Paso del Norte about the time of the great colonizing expeditions to the north.

They loped on and on through the darkness, moccasin soles softly slapping and hooves padding the hard graveled surface.

The Camino Real crossed the Rio Grande at El Paso to follow the east bank of the river to the north. There had been *parajes* at regular intervals along the route. These were so-called places of the King's Axe, permanent camping grounds with water, wood, and grazing set aside for travelers. The one at Fray Cristobal, north of El Paso, was on the east bank of the river. Here the highway divided, the right-hand fork continuing north on the Jornado east of the mountains, while the left hand fork crossed the river to the west bank, where it also continued north. The two forks joined together at Albuquerque about 140 miles to the north. There was another *paraje* at a place called Perrillo, Little Dog. Its name had come about in a curious way. When Onate's colonists had been marching up the Jornado in the year 1598, they had run out of water. They were desperate, perhaps doomed. A little dog belonging to one of the men trotted into the dry camp with muddy paws and wet muzzle. They backtracked his trail and found some pools of potable water left by a vagrant shower. To commemorate their little savior they named the place Los Charcos de Perrillo, The Pools of the Little Dog. In later years the name had been shortened to Perrillo. Just beyond Perrillo was the ominous-sounding Laguna del Muerto, Lagoon of Death, a mere sinkhole occasionally filled with water during the rainy season. It had gained its name because sometimes there was water there and at times none. If there wasn't any for thirsty travelers, death was the usual result. The full journey of the Jornado was a hazardous six-day stretch for pedestrians or wagons. It saved distance and cost many lives. There was great heat in the summer and intense cold during the winter. It was haunted, *always* haunted, by Apaches.

They seemed to be in a timeless void: a barren, lunarlike world without life or work of man. On and on they pressed, throats brassy dry, breathing with difficulty, moving west on a self-imposed race against time and the rising of the full moon.

Luke threw a glance over his shoulder. "Christ," he murmured.

The sky over the San Andres had almost imperceptibly lightened. In a little while Salinas Peak was tipped with moonglow. The Jornado gradually lightened. The Fray Cristobals seemed no closer, the San Andres no farther away.

Luke stopped suddenly. "Go on," he said. He pointed behind himself. There were dark stains on the light-colored soil. His footprints were marked in blood.

"I'll wait," Quint said.

Luke ripped off his left moccasin. "Go on, damn you," he growled. "I'll catch up."

The bottom of his left foot was swollen and black with blood-soaked dirt. He tied his filthy bandanna about it and put on the moccasin. He tore off his rear shirttail, ripped it into strips, and bound them about moccasin and foot. He got to his feet and limped after Quint and the sorrel.

Luke looked back over their trail. "I wonder how far back those footprints go, Big Red. Mebbe I'd better backtrack and wipe 'em out."

Quint shook his head. "Look." He pointed behind them.

The thinnest wraith of smoke rose from the heights into the windless air.

They slogged on, breath harsh in their dry throats. The first foul greenish feeling of fear worked through their souls and minds. *Apaches!*

They were more than halfway across when the sorrel went down at last. They tried getting him up onto his feet. It was no use. Luke wrenched his head up and hard to one side. Quint's razor-edged bowie sliced cleanly across the distended throat. They held dirty hands under the dark gush of blood and lapped it up. They removed their Sharps rifles, cartridge belts, canteens and field glasses from the saddle and went on.

Luke looked back. "That's one for the wolves. He was a good one."

The moon came full up. The Jornado became a ghostly landscape frozen in silence and bluish light.

They did not look back now. They knew the smoke would still be there.

The ground became more difficult to cross. They were on the limit of the *bajada arenoso*, the ancient soil flow from the mountains ahead. The scant vegetation thickened. They were on a gravel and detritus flow from the higher slopes where the rains ran down. In the spring for a short time the otherwise barren soil flourished and bloomed, then died away, leaving the desert dead-looking but hardy with vegetation.

Quint looked back. "By God," he croaked. "Maybe we'll make it at that."

"Mebbe with a bushy-haired murderin' reception committee," Luke said, low-voiced. "Look ahead."

This time the smoke rose from a high spur of the Fray Cristobals like lank hair stretched across pale bluish-gray denim.

They stopped to relieve themselves. Colt cylinders were inspected to make sure nipples were capped and chambers full. Sharps were loaded.

Twenty minutes later they reached an Apache post office, a small mound of rocks surrounded by short sticks of mesquite. Fourteen warriors had passed that way a day ago and would return the same way.

They took advantage of every scrap of cover afforded by the thickening brush, haunted by the uneasy feeling the hawk-eyed Mescaleros could hardly miss seeing them if they chanced to look in that direction.

The smoke no longer ascended from the San Andres or the Fray Cristobals.

They worked their way upslope. The faint west wind brought the odor of burning to them from the direction of the springs. They went to ground instantly.

"Patrol from Fort Craig?" Luke whispered.

"*Or* Reb scouts. If they made a campfire in this area they're as simple as kit beavers."

The faint sound of chanting voices came to them. "*Hoo-hoo-hoo-ahoo . . . Hoo-hoo-hoo-ahoo . . .*"

An almost indistinguishable sound arose, materializing into the soft thudding of many hooves.

Luke gripped Quint's wrist.

Something smoothly rounded with what looked like a tall reed rising above it appeared moving eerily along the tops of the brush as though self-impelled. The Apache's head looked enormous in the deceptive light of the waning moon. A pony's head tossed up and down. The sound of rawhide-booted hooves became louder underlying the low chanting. "*Hoo-hoo-hoo-ahoo . . . Hoo-hoo-hoo-ahoo . . .*" More heads appeared. White bands of bottom clay had been streaked across noses and cheeks in sharp contrast to the dark faces and thick manes of hair. The thin reedlike objects resolved into lance shafts topped by murderous-looking steel blades. The lead warrior rode into an open area. A water-bloated greasy, shining horse intestine hung over his pony's withers, serving as his canteen. The lead warrior rode on, followed by the rest of his party, softly chanting. Victory chant, thought Quint. Someone had died at Ojo del Muerto. Twelve warriors rode past toward the Jornado. They led five saddled horses equipped with cantle and pommel packs. The butts of scabbarded carbines or rifles thrust up from the sides of the saddles. Clothing hung over the saddles. They vanished downslope.

The chanting and hoof thudding died away. It was tomb quiet again. Minutes ticked past.

The tail-ender appeared. He was not chanting. His head moved from one side to the other, then to the rear, back again to the front, then repeating the ritual all over again, a constant vigilance. He too vanished downslope. Minutes drifted past.

Luke looked at Quint. "I'll never get used to them bushy-headed bastards."

Quint shrugged. "Who wants to?"

They could go to the springs now. No Apache in his right mind would go near that place of death for at least twenty-four hours, fearful of the lingering spirits of the newly slain hovering around for vengeance.

They spread out. The stench of burning cloth, leather, and human flesh was stronger. Quint stopped and thrust his full-cocked Sharps forward. A naked human figure lay huddled facedown at the base of a ledge. Quint hooked a foot under the belly and heaved him over on his back. The arms were outflung. The head was horribly misshapen. The skull had been crushed to let out the vengeful spirit. The distorted features were black with blood and dirt. The bloodstained yellow beard was full of sand.

An owl hooted. That would be Luke. Bú, the Owl, was considered by the Apaches to be a bird of misfortune, its call the mournful cry of the recent dead. Quint repeated the cry.

The stench of burning flesh was almost overpowering. The wind came up suddenly, fanning the ashes from the campfire. Flame danced up, illuminating two sprawled naked corpses beside the fire, partially tangled in bloodstained blankets. The beard of one of them had half burned away and was still smoldering. The other man lay facedown. He wore only a blood-soaked shirt. Three feathered arrow shafts protruded from his back like some strange deadly foliage.

"Secesh scouts," Luke said from behind Quint. "I found another one of them back in the brush. They must've come up on him whilst he was takin' a shit. Never even gave him time to finish, looks like. Full of arrers like a pin cushion."

They walked down beside the fire. A pack of playing cards lay scattered between the two dead men. Quint picked one of them up. The dignified and austere face of a man looked up at him. He read the name beneath it—President Jefferson Davis. A wooden keg canteen lay crushed in the sand. TEXAS and C.S.A. were burned into one end of it, 2ND TMR into the other. Quint showed it to Luke.

Luke nodded. "Baylor's Battalion, Second Texas Mounted Regiment." He grinned. "My old battalion," he added.

"You found only one man?" Quint asked.

"Yep. Why?"

"The Mescaleros had *five* saddled horses."

They vanished instantly into the brush. An instant later a gun report thudded upslope. A bullet richocheted from rock and plopped into the spring. The shot echo raced along the slope and died away.

"Yuh see the flash?" Luke whispered.

Quint silently pointed out where he had seen it.

Fifteen minutes later Quint parted a creosote bush and peered at a man standing behind a waist-high ledge with a carbine in his hands, gazing intently down toward the springs. Luke was moving softly up behind him. Quint tossed a rock down the slope. The Texan whirled and raised his carbine. Luke tapped him hard behind an ear with the butt of his rifle. The Texan went down. The carbine clattered to the ground and went off. The slug sang thinly into space.

The trooper was hardly more than a boy. They carried him down to the springs. Quint bathed his forehead. A pair of clear blue eyes looked up at him. "Thet you, Clay?" he asked wildly.

Quint stood up, shaking his head. He pointed at the two bodies.

The Texan sat up. "*Jesus!* They get *all* of them? Where's the other two?"

"In the brush. Dead," Luke said laconically.

The Texan covered his face with dirty hands. His body shook a little.

"Where you from, sonny?" Luke asked.

"Harris County," the Texan replied.

"He means just now," Quint explained.

"My cayuse ran away before moonrise. I went after him. I was comin' back when I heard noise here. I crept back and saw them 'Paches eatin' our rations around the springs. I ran like blazes, fell into a hollow, bumped my *cabeza*, and went out like a snuffed candle." He touched the lump on his forehead. "I came to. They was lookin' all over for me. I lay still. They took my hoss. Then they left. I was comin' down to see if any of the boys was still livin' when I saw yuh.''

"Why'd yuh shoot?" demanded Luke.

"Figgered you was Lincolnites maybe, or greaser bandits. We saw some of them over near the Rio Grande the day before we come here. You fellas Lincolnites?"

Quint shook his head. "You've got the wrong name. We're *Federals.*"

"Yuh ain't wearin' uniforms."

Luke grinned. "All you got on is a pair of army pants and a belt buckle with a star, Texas, and C.S.A. on it. You're our prisoner, sonny."

"Well, anyways, thet's better than being caught by them 'Paches, even if you are greasers."

"Jest who are you and what were yuh doin' out here on the Jornado?" Luke asked curiously.

"Private George Sutherland, B Company, Second Texas Mounted Regiment," the young trooper replied. He could hardly have been more than seventeen or eighteen years old. He looked at the big bearded man. "Thet's my elder brothah Clay. Never figgered he'd end like this. He was so all-fired anxious to lick you greasers, I guess he forgot they was hostile Apaches in this goddamned country. Beats me why us Texans would want it, but orders is orders, ain't they?" He studied Luke. "Ain't I seen you somewheah's before?"

Luke squatted in front of him, tilting his head to one side. "Now that's right interestin', George. Where do you think it was?"

"El Paso? No. It was later. Ah! La Mesilla!"

Luke glanced sideways at Quint. "Do tell," he murmured.

"Come to think of it," George said slowly. "You were in my company at the Battle of La Mesilla when we whupped the Lincolnites." He grinned. "You greasers ain't much for fightin'. Man, the way we captured them all at San Augustine Springs was a right caution. Never fired a shot and they outnumbered us fifty to one."

"Not quite," Quint said.

The boy looked at Luke. "But you was there. Then another greaser showed up at La Mesilla with horses, mules, and cattle for the garrison of Fort Fillmore, *after* we had captured it." He grinned again. "The greaser in charge of the herd captured you and turned you in, then enlisted. He was smart—for a greaser, that is." He studied Luke. "Then they put you in the *calabozo* for a spy and deserter and was goin' to hang yuh. So you killed your guard and got away. Now, if they catch you again, they'll hang you for murder, spyin' and desertin'."

Luke smiled thinly—a wolf's grin. "One charge would be enough for the job, but like it says in the recipe for rabbit stew, first yuh got to catch the rabbit. Besides, sonny, you ain't about to go back to your *amigos* and tell them yuh seen me. You're still our prisoner. Remember?"

Sutherland smirked. "Accordin' to the rules of war you got to take me back to your people or parole me. Then, when our boys march up the Rio Grande and capture your Fort Craig, then go on up north, they'll release me and let me fight alongside of them against you cowardly greasers."

Luke stood up and looked down. "Providin' we take yuh back with us, Sutherland. Another thing, you little Tejano sonofabitch, we don't like the word *greaser*. We don't have to take you anywhere. We can just leave you here alone without a cayuse or a gun. Or . . ." His voice died away significantly.

The Texan looked from one to the other of them, the wolflike Luke and the tall man with the scarred face and the cold gray eyes. For a moment he thought he was going to embarrass himself, but he only dribbled a little.

Luke suddenly looked up. He placed a hand over Sutherland's mouth and dragged him into the shadowed brush. "Quiet," he hissed. Quint had followed them into the brush. He looked questioningly at Luke. Luke touched finger to lips, then pointed upslope.

"More Apaches?" the boy whispered.

"They won't be back, at least for a while," Quint whispered. "Now, shut up!"

Luke vanished into the brush. Fifteen minutes later he came back. "Greasers. Upslope. Watchin' the springs."

"Some of ours, or Rebels?" Quint asked.

Luke shook his head. "I heard some of their talkin'. They're *ladrones* from down south, mebbe Chihuahua, from the looks of them. Six of them. Six lovely hosses." He grinned. "They must have been tailin' these Tejanos."

The Texan nodded. "We saw six of them near the Rio Grande the other day."

"You're sure they're *ladrones*, Luke?" Quint asked.

Luke nodded. "Chico Vaca's bunch. Remember them?"

They had a fearful, bloody reputation along the border and as far north as Socorro. Vaca was a former Comanchero, and a thief, rapist, and murderer; a two-legged predator of the human race, more demonlike than human.

"Three horses, apiece, eh, Luke?" Quint suggested.

"*'Sta bueno!*"

"I'll need a gun," Sutherland said.

Quint handed him one of his Colts butt-first. The Texan's hand closed on the grip, a finger was thrust into the guard to rest on the trigger, a thumb curled about the big spur hammer. The muzzle pointed at Quint. Sutherland's blue eyes looked into Quint's gray eyes.

"Don't get any ideas, sonny," Quint warned.

The moon was far on the wane; dark shadows crept down the eastern slopes of the Fray Cristobals. The area around the springs was shadowed now. The two bodies lay blanketed, as though asleep. There might be others in the brush and shadows, though.

Aurelio worked his way down the slope toward the springs to get a better view of the sleeping Texans. He studied the two motionless figures. Where were the others? Where were the fine *caballos*? He turned to crawl back. A hand slapped off his sombrero, gripped his greasy hair, and yanked his head back. His throat was cut from ear to ear. He died without a sound.

Chico Vaca looked down the slope. Where the hell was Aurelio? He turned to Ramón and pointed toward the springs. Ramón wasn't anxious to go. A pistol muzzle was waved beneath his nose. He went.

Ramón crawled belly-flat. He couldn't see much from that position. He got up on his knees. An arm was hooked about his throat and drawn noose tight. He struggled a little like a mouse caught in the steely talons of an owl, then lay still.

Chico waited impatiently. He didn't trust any of his men, particularly Aurelio and Ramón. That was why he had sent them out first. He turned, pointed to the right and then at José, pointed to the left, then at Bartolome, for an encircling, flanking movement. They crawled into the rustling brush.

José lay belly-flat one hundred yards from Chico. Damned if he was going down to those eerie, silent springs. He heard the faintest of husking sounds to his left. He turned his head quickly. A rifle butt smashed into the back of his neck, neatly breaking it.

Bartolome crept closer to the springs. There was something strange about the two motionless figures lying there. He got up on his knees and stared at them. The knife thrust into his back and up under the rib cage into his heart; at the same time a dirty callused hand was clamped over his mouth.

Santiago, Chico's *segundo*, crawled up beside his chief. "There's something wrong here, Chico," he whispered. "Where are the Tejano's horses? There are only two men at the fire. They never move. Where are the others? Where are our men? For the love of God, Chico, let's get to hell out of here!"

Chico shook his head. "There is nothing wrong. Besides, we can't get back to the river without water. Go see what has happened."

Santiago shook his head. "Go yourself."

Chico could not stand insubordination. "Go!" he snapped.

"Go to hell!" Santiago cried. He legged it for the horses. Halfway there a rifle barrel was thrust out from under a creosote bush and in between his churning legs. He fell headlong, furrowing the hard ground with his face. He was silently killed before he could get up.

Chico stood up and peered uncertainly into the dimness. There was a tall bush in his line of vision, a bush that seemed to have more substance than the others. He walked a little closer. Faint noise came from his left. He whirled. There was another of those damnable man-shaped bushes twenty feet away, *and this one had a head*. Noise came from behind him. He whirled and raised his pistol.

"He's *yours*, Texan!" Quint shouted. "Get him before he gets you!" He dropped flat on the ground.

Sutherland fired as he jumped to one side. Chico's pistol flamed and bellowed. The slug whispered past Sutherland's left ear as he fired twice more. Chico went down on his knees, dropped his pistol, cried out once, then rolled over and lay still, staring at the sky with eyes that would see no more.

"Good shootin', Texan," Luke said. "Give me a hand with their horses. They'll be needin' water."

Later they dragged the *ladrones* to a deep cleft and rolled them into it, pushing loose rock in on top of them. Quint watered the horses while Luke and the Texan dug a hole in the soft overflow ground from the springs. They buried the four Texans and mounded the grave with big rocks. Luke sprinkled gunpowder on the rocks and ignited it; hopefully, it would keep the wolves and coyotes from digging up the grave. Sometimes it worked.

The stars winked out one by one. The false dawn pewtered the sky far beyond the dark San Andres.

Quint took off his hat and bowed his head. "Though I walk in the shadow of the valley of death I fear no evil," he began.

"Look behind you, Big Red," Luke said quietly.

Sutherland stood twenty feet away at Quint's back. He held Chico Vaca's fine silver mounted revolver in one hand and Quint's Colt in the other. Both weapons were cocked.

"Well?" Quint asked.

"I appreciate all yuh done, suh," Sutherland said, "but I ain't goin' to no greaser prisoner of war camp. Keep your hand off that knife, Luke!"

Luke smiled easily. "I was only goin' to cut a chew," he protested.

Both pistol muzzles moved in a short arc between Quint and Luke. "Don't risk it, sonny," the Texan said.

Luke shrugged. "How far do yuh think you'll get with us after yuh?" he asked.

"I've thought of that. I'll take your rifles and all the horses."

"That's gratitude for you," Quint said dryly.

Luke rested his hands on top of his hat. "Yuh might not get the both of us, sonny," he suggested.

The young Texan was uncertain. He liked these two grim greaser-killing New Mexicans.

"The Mescaleros might be coming back," Quint said. "If they do, we won't live long enough to talk about it."

"That's a trick!" Sutherland accused.

Quint shrugged. "You want to wait and see?"

Minutes passed.

Quint looked at the false dawn light. "If you're planning to go, there isn't much time until your dust will be seen."

Sutherland backed away a little. "You won't follow me?" he asked.

Quint shook his head. "Listen to me! Shooting might sure as hell bring the Mescaleros back. You'll soon be so damned busy keeping ahead of them trying for the river we won't be able to do much but the same. If we're on foot, we won't get away. Afoot they can outrun a horse on the side of a mountain."

Sutherland placed Quint's Colt on the ground. He took the reins of a blocky roan and then mounted. "Thanks for everything, *compañeros*. Too bad we ain't fightin' on the same side. See yuh later, mebbe through the battle smoke." He spurred the roan up the slope. The rattling sound of the hoofs faded away. A moment later a shrill yell came faintly to the springs.

Luke grinned. "Fresh little Tejano sonofabitch."

Quint nodded. "Would you have killed him?"

Luke shrugged. "I would have tried to wound him."

"Think you could have made it? He's a damned good hand with a six-gun."

"I ain't sure, Big Red."

They rode from the springs, leading the extra horses. Just before they entered a narrow gulletlike pass that would take them to the Rio Grande, they looked back out across the sunlit Jornado. A faint wraith of thin dust rose from its hard surface. The dust was moving against the wind. There was no need to put the glasses on that dust source. They drummed their heels hard against their mounts' sides and vanished into the pass.

★ EIGHTEEN ★

FEBRUARY 1862: NEW MEXICO TERRITORY, FORT CRAIG

Kershaw's Rangers, officially Kershaw's Independent New Mexico Volunteer Mounted Rifles, arrived at Fort Craig late on the afternoon of a bright day of February sunshine. It was windy, clear, and with that chilling dry cold common to winter in New Mexico. Lieutenant David Kershaw took charge of the beef herd the company had driven from the Querencia and drove them a few miles north of the fort to the grazing land along the west bank bottoms. Corporal Anselmo Campos drove a *remuda* of thirty mules to the quartermaster corrals on the post.

Quint and Luke turned aside from the herd in order to report in at post headquarters. In the weeks since they had returned from their Pecos River reconnaissance they had gone back to the Querencia to scout the Mimbres and round up as many cattle and mules as possible. Cristina and Dave had asked them about Catherine Williston and were shocked to learn she had not traveled with them to Santa Fe. They had found out about her absence hours after she had left the *rancho*. Dave and some of the *vaqueros* had tracked her into one of the twisted canyons east of the *rancho* and then lost the trail. They had found some blood on a flat rock ledge. Half a mile beyond the ledge they had come across traces of a small party of horsemen riding fast to the south. They must have been Indian raiders, Dave had deduced. No Mexican would go into that area except under extreme duress, and white men avoided it like the plague. No one wanted to speak of Catherine's possible fate. Quint, Luke, and Anselmo had scouted the Mimbres and at the same time looked for the young woman. They had drawn a complete blank. The only poor solace they had was that she might have died alone in the waterless canyons or had been killed by Apaches. None of them mentioned the only other possibility in the back of their minds—a living hell as a white slave in an Apache *ranchería*.

The cold wind swept across the mesa, driving clouds of fine graveled dust across the hard-packed parade ground. The dust eroded the adobe walls, etched the warped wooden doors and shuttered windows, sifted into the interiors, and gritted between the teeth. The huge garrison flag stood out almost at right angles to its warped whitewashed flagpole, resembling nothing so much as a wrinkled sheet of brightly painted tin with frayed and raveled edges. Grayish white Sibley, bell-, and wall tents bellied in the wind. The smoke from the tin stove stacks of the tents and the chimneys of the adobe and lava rock buildings streamed off at right angles from the lips of the stacks and chimneys. Reflected sunlight flashed from earth-polished spades and. picks, rising and falling where fatigue details worked steadily at deepening the ditches in front of the two bastions or raising the ramparts. The faded grayish canvas tilts of long lines of transport wagons and some ambulances flapped and fluttered in the cold blast. The clanging of farriers' and blacksmiths' hammers pounding anvils came from the quartermaster shops mingled with the faint popping of firearms from the improvised rifle range overlooking the Rio Grande just east of the fort. Militia and volunteers in dusty, ill-fitting uniforms marched and countermarched on the parade ground. Over at the post cemetery, tactfully situated near the isolated tents of the smallpox hospital, the post band struggled valiantly against the wind while playing the doleful funeral march "Roslin Castle." Hardly a day passed at Fort Craig without at least one funeral. The rows of mounded graves had grown perceptibly in recent months.

Fort Craig had been built in 1853 to replace Fort Conrad, which had been situated on a mesa west of the Rio Grande near the Valverde fords. Fort Craig was situated on a high gravelly promontory surrounded by the Rio Grande on three sides of its base. Its primary purpose was to protect the north-south wagon road situated west of the river and the post. To the west were the rugged, somber San Mateo Mountains. To the east was the river whose east bank was a cut-up area of *pedregal*, or *malpaís* (bad underfoot). Directly beyond the *malpaís* was the Jornado del Muerto, which was flanked to the east by the Sierra Oscura to the north and the San Andres to the south, continuing all the way down to El Paso del Norte. Immediately south of the *malpaís* were the Fray Cristobals and beyond them the Sierra Caballo. The north-south road west of the fort was the old Camino Real from El Paso del Norte on the Chihuahua side of the Rio Grande and Hart's Mills, also known as Franklin on the American side.

The view east from the fort was a forbidding one of bleak and sterile sandhills, *malpaís*, and barren mountains. The west bank of the river north of the post had fine grass for grazing, reedy bottomlands, and tolerably thick willows and some cottonwoods. The river was inhabited by soft shell turtles and many large catfish. The river lured many species of ducks, swans, pelicans, wild geese, brant, hill cranes, blue herons, bitterns, and several species of snipe. There were mixed grasses on the mesas. The foothills were thick with chaparral, prickly pear cacti and long-thorned brush hard on horses and mules. High on the mountains were woodland types of vegetation. Despite the apparent barrenness of the country it was rife with game.

Fort Craig covered about ten acres. Originally it had been a collection of small adobes and *jacals*, shacks made by planting poles in the earth and plastering them with adobe clay. In time twenty-two permanent buildings had been constructed of adobe or lava rock. With the advent of the war Fort Craig had become a sprawling, well-organized military base, the keystone for the defense of southern New Mexico. It was the only Federal position standing in the way of a Confederate invasion of the north. Two large bastions had been constructed, one at the southeast corner, the other at the northwest corner. Each bastion had four embrasured cannon. Two of those in the northwest bastion covered the north wall with enfilading fire, while the other two guns protected the west wall. The southeast bastions covered the south and east walls in the same manner. The large storerooms had been bombproofed by digging the floors below ground level. The roofs had been lowered and protected from plunging cannon fire by layers of logs piled and banked high with earth. In addition to the real guns protecting the fort, the bastions also held "Quaker" guns, cottonwood logs shaped like guns, painted black and mounted on wagon wheels, very convincing and menacing when seen from a distance.

Fort Craig was commanded by Major Thomas Duncan, Third Cavalry. The Third Cavalry had been the Regiment of Mounted Riflemen since its inception in 1846 to guard the Overland Trail. They had been redesignated as the Third Cavalry in August of 1861, when the First and Second Regiments of Dragoons had been renumbered as the First and Second Cavalry, while the original First and Second Cavalry had been changed to the Fourth and Fifth, all because of regimental seniority. None of the five regiments had been pleased with the changes. The dragoons and mounted riflemen still proudly referred to themselves as such. The post garrison consisted of units of the Second, Third, and Fifth Cavalry, Fifth and Seventh Infantry. Captain Theodore H. Dodd's Independent Company of Colorado Volunteers had recently joined the garrison. Captain Alexander McRae of the Third Cavalry commanded a Provisional Field Battery of six bronze smoothbores, consisting of three six-pounder guns, two twelve-pounder field howitzers and one twelve-pounder mountain howitzer. The battery was manned by men of the Third Cavalry. A section of two twenty-four–pounder bronze howitzers was commanded by Lieutenant Robert H. Hall, of the Tenth Infantry. The total post complement consisted of about one thousand men. There were also several thousand troops, mostly volunteers and militia, with some Regulars on picket and outpost duty. Colonel Benjamin S. Roberts, Third Cavalry, now colonel of the Fifth New Mexico Volunteer Infantry, was commander of the Southern Military District of New Mexico Territory with headquarters at Fort Craig.

A Regular Army sergeant major wearing on his sleeves the three chevrons and arcs of his rank received Quint and Luke in the outer office of headquarters. "Colonel Canby is in closed conference now, sir," he said. "He didn't want to be disturbed, but the conference likely won't last much longer. I know he is anxious to receive your report."

Alexander Calhoun came into the outer office, slapping trail dust from his uniform with his gauntlets. His face lighted up when he saw Quint. "Captain Kershaw! I've just arrived from Albuquerque with dispatches for Colonel Canby." He grinned ruefully. "I've been stationed here for a month now and haven't slept here more than a few nights. However, the colonel did promise me I could remain here on his staff after this last trip." He looked back over his shoulder and lowered his voice, "I'm certainly glad to see you have returned, sir. I've been pleading with the colonel for a field assignment, but at present there seems to be no opening for me in any Regular unit, and as you know, the colonel is reluctant to assign Regular officers to volunteer or militia units. I even asked assignment to Dodd's Colorado company, but *they* turned me down. It seems as though they don't want any West Pointers giving them orders. Now I need *your* help, Captain."

"In what way?" Quint asked. He suspected what was about to come.

"Your company is back here ready for field duty, isn't it?"

Quint nodded. "Scouting, patrolling, and so forth."

"Couldn't you use me in it, sir?" Alexander pleaded.

"It's not exactly a Regular unit," Quint said.

Luke grinned. "And it ain't exactly a volunteer or militia unit either, Lieutenant."

"But there is bound to be a battle soon," Alexander continued. "I want to be in it with a fighting unit."

"We're not exactly a line-of-battle unit," Quint said cautiously. "In time of battle we'll function as scouts, skirmishers, or sharpshooters. I doubt you can qualify for those tasks, at least during the present. In time, however . . ."

Disappointment was obvious on the young officer's face.

"It's hard and dangerous duty," Luke put in." The odds are always against you, and the stakes are far too high."

Alexander shook his head. "That doesn't matter. That's where the glory is! I'm an expert pistol and rifle shot. I'm an excellent horseman. I'm strong and in fine physical condition! By God, Captain Kershaw, I don't want to spend the rest of this war sitting behind a desk here in headquarters splattering ink like a damned civilian goosequill clerk!" His voice died away. His face became fixed. "Oh, Lord, now I've done it," he added under his breath.

Quint turned quickly. Colonel Canby had come into the outer office. He smiled and extended his hand to Quint. "Sorry to keep you waiting, Captain Kershaw. We're ready now for your report, and I want to brief you on events that have taken place

uring your absence. Sergeant Connors, you'll come too, of
ourse. Lieutenant Calhoun, you might as well join the party.
'm considering temporarily assigning you as one of my scout
fficers. I want you to gain as much experience as possible
efore the Rebels begin their march north. I can't think of a
etter set of instructors than Captain Kershaw, Sergeant Connors,
nd the rest of the so-called Rangers. Please bring in your
ispatches and those intelligence reports lying on your desk over
here. They've been gathering a little dust in your absence." His
xpression had not changed as he spoke. He turned and reentered
is office.

Alec was wide-eyed. "My God, he must have heard me."

Quint shook his head. "Coincidence."

Luke nodded. "Or mebbe, Big Red, you don't suppose some-
ne close by, whose name I won't mention, might have been
vorkin' on our good-natured commandin' officer while we were
one?"

Alec flushed a little. "Well," he started to say.

Quint walked into the colonel's office to hide his grin.

Luke stopped beside Alec's desk as he gathered up his dis-
atches and reports. "Sonny, mebbe yuh think yuh made a smart
nove, but if you ride with Kershaw's Rangers you're goin' to
eed a helluva lot more than being an expert shot, an excellent
orseman, and being strong and in fine physical condition."

"Such as?" Alec asked.

"*Escuche!* You don't make but *one* mistake in this line of
usiness. These ain't my words, mind you, because I ain't got
he education to put it the way they were, so I'll say it like it was
aid original. *Eternal vigilance is the price of safety. We are not
masters of this land. Those who lack this knowledge run the risk
f an abrupt death. A man learns the measure of himself and
thers here. There must be a symbiosis between man and the
and. A man might pick his life way, but the mountains, plains,
nd deserts also pick the man, inexorably eliminating those who
lo not measure up.*" Luke turned to enter the colonel's office.

"Wait," Alec said.

Luke turned.

"This philosopher of yours sounds like an educated man for a
mountain man or frontiersman."

Luke nodded. "He was, and *is*. . . ."

★ 153 ★

"Captain Kershaw?"

Luke nodded. "Keno, Lieutenant." He entered the office.

Lieutenant Colonel Benjamin Stone Roberts, as commander o
the Southern Military District of New Mexico Territory, wa
second-in-command to Colonel Canby. He was a balding, round
faced man with deep creases from the side of his nose to th
corners of his firm straight-lipped mouth. He had gingery-colore
whiskers from hairline to tip of chin. The twang of Vermont wa
in his speech, not unpleasant but sharp and decisive, like th
quick closing of a Sharps breechblock. He had been in comman
of Fort Stanton when the war started and had been ordered t
evacuate it. Rumor had it his eyes had filled with tears when h
had ridden from the burning fort in a rainstorm. He was
first-class soldier with the reputation of being a fighting man.

Colonel Christopher "Kit" Carson, commanding the Firs
New Mexico Volunteer Regiment, had brought his regimen
from the north to serve under Colonel Canby. He was a legend i
his own time. Kentucky-born, of Scots descent on his father'
side, he had been in New Mexico by 1826, at that time seven
teen years old. He had been a trapper and fur trader and ha
gained a great reputation while serving with John C. Frémont
the Pathfinder. Kit had been active in the occupation of Califor
nia during the Mexican War, serving as a lieutenant of Mounte
Rifles. During the six years preceding the war he had been agen
to the Utes. Kit was barely five-and-a-half feet tall, slightly stoop
shouldered, long-bodied, with short bandy legs. He was wide o
shoulder and deep of chest. His hands and feet were small, bu
he had great strength and tremendous vitality and was a super
horseman and dead shot. His skin was fair, his hair very ligh
and fine, eyebrows and lashes light-colored. His face was oval
with very young-looking blue eyes as clear as a boy's an
woman gentle. His voice was soft and thin, unobtrusive, an
almost feminine. In most respects his appearance and deportmen
were completely misleading, considering his highly adventurou
life. Pound for pound he had the fighting aggressiveness of
wildcat. Kit was now fifty-two years old, a little man whose
heart was big. Men would follow him unquestionably whereve
he might lead.

"What are the conditions in the San Augustine Plains generlly and the Querencia Rancho specifically?" Roberts asked Quint.

"The plains, with the exception of the immediate area around the Querencia Rancho, are fully under the control of the Mimbres Apaches, with at times some incursions from the Navajos," Quint replied. "In my opinion the plains will not be even under partial control until the war is over and my *vaqueros* return in full strength from military service. Even so, I believe troops will have to be assigned there and several forts built in selected areas to control the Mimbres in the future. As long as my company was there rounding up the last of the stock we had some control. I know for a fact the day we left the *rancho* to drive the stock here, the Mimbres moved right back in again, putting the Querencia virtually under siege. You all know of the superstitious fear Indians have of the Querencia area because of the massacre there many years ago. It's a precarious situation. Once the Apaches are assured the Querencia is so lightly garrisoned, it may very well overcome their fears. The plains have been swept clear of all beef cattle. The only mules are at the *rancho*. They have just enough horses to exist. The mustangs, of course, are still running free. Most of the sheep have either been driven closer to the *rancho* or have been wiped out, along with some of the sheepherders by the marauders. Those sheep that are still on the Plains might starve if the predators and the winter don't finish them off first."

"Now, about the Texans: Do you think there is a possibility of them returning there?" Canby asked.

Quint shook his head. "No, sir. There's no stock left for them. On the other hand, if they are successful in this invasion, I wouldn't be surprised if they established a small outpost there to control the Mimbres and replenish their stock of horses. That's one reason I agreed with my people, who want to maintain the Querencia rather than to abandon it until the war is over."

"Captain, it occurs to me that by serving your country here you will suffer grievous losses at your Querencia. If it were possible, I'd release you from duty here and have you assigned to that area to hold it for your government and yourself." He hesitated. "But we need you here, Kershaw."

Quint shrugged. "If we lost this war and the territory, there will be no Querencia, as far as I am concerned. I would refuse to

swear an oath of allegiance to the Confederacy. That is why
prefer to serve here. Think no more of it, sir." He smiled
"Begging your pardon, Colonel, but let's get on with this damne
war and settle it when and how we can. I'll worry about th
Querencia later."

"What is the present situation of the Texans south of here
sir?" Quint asked.

"They are slowly moving north and have occupied Fort Thorn
which, as you know, is about seventy miles south of Fort Craig
abandoned by our government in 1859. We know they had abou
thirty-seven hundred troops in the La Mesilla–Fort Fillmore area
but they have been plagued with disease, so many of their sick
and convalescent did not accompany the advance to Fort Thorn
General Sibley is in command of the advance, an estimate
thirty-six companies, twelve mountain-type howitzers, a long
wagon train, and a herd of beef cattle. The column left Thorn on
February seventh on their march north."

"If the Rebels left Fort Thorn a week ago, they should be
nearing us about now," Quint said.

Canby nodded. "Captain Graydon keeps in close contact with
them, but he has very few men. I want you to join him
Kershaw, but act as an independent command. How soon can
you be ready?"

"We're ready now, sir. What are my orders?"

"Keep a screen in front of the enemy. I want immediate
reports on their activities. Avoid any clashes. If attacked, fire
and fall back. Under no circumstances are you to bring on a
general engagement. With the exception of my Regulars, I can't
be too sure of the volunteers and militia fighting other than a
defensive battle, or one in which we have the advantage of
position. You are free to leave now, and good luck."

Quint and Luke turned toward the door. Quint looked back
over a shoulder at young Calhoun. "Well," he drawled, are you
coming with us, Lieutenant, or have you changed your mind?"

Later that day Quint sat in Kit Carson's orderly tent, reading a
letter sent from Santa Fe by Jean some weeks past.

My Dearest:
    I am sending this letter to you by Alec. He has been
ordered to duty at Fort Craig. Although he assumes he will

be assigned staff duty with Colonel Canby, he told me he hoped to serve with you and your Rangers. On the one hand I fear the terrible danger to which he might be exposed while serving in such a capacity. On the other hand I know of no one to whom I could entrust him in war other than yourself and your company as well. I long to see both of you back here safe and sound before too many months have passed. You know I love you and have always loved you since that day long ago when first we met.

Your beloved, as always,
Jean

Quint folded the letter. The faint fragrance of lilac came from the paper. A quick vision of Jean came to him as he had last seen her, sleeping quietly beside him in bed. He had missed her after leaving Santa Fe, but not so much as he had in the past few weeks, particularly at the Querencia, when he had made love to a more than willing Cristina, who seemed to sense that Quint was already lost to her. All during the lovemaking, the face and body of Jean seemed to be there with him, not those of Cristina. The worst of it was that he felt Cristina knew it full well.

★ NINETEEN ★

The evening was dark and bitter cold. An icy wind swept mercilessly over the position of Pino's Battalion of the Second New Mexico on the east bank of the Rio Grande opposite Fort Craig. They were keeping a watchful eye on the Confederates who had crossed the river from the west bank at the Panadero

Ford earlier that day and were now bivouacked two miles east of the river. It was a dry camp buried safely from enemy musketry and artillery fire. The subdued light of their many fires showed fitfully against the black volcanic rock of the *malpaís*, although the Texans and the fires themselves could not be seen. For the New Mexicans the night was beginning to take on the aspect of a Norse hell of cold and ice rather the more conventional one of fire and heat. The infantrymen had crossed the river after the Texans, wetting themselves to the hips in the cold, fast-moving water. Unlike the enemy, they could not light fires, for fear of alerting them and inviting a howitzer shell or a shower of bullets.

Quint and Alec crouched in a narrow hollow between two outlying ledges of *malpaís*. Luke and Paddy Graydon were somewhere out in the blackness, feeling out the left flank of the Confederates. A few of the Rangers were hidden behind Quint's position, while Dave had the remainder of the company out in front of Pino's position as pickets and to act as skirmishers in case of an attack. Captain James ''Paddy'' Graydon had sent his ragtag, bobtailed company of militia as a reserve for Pino. As Paddy had said to Quint, ''Big Red, my boys are hell on wheels when it comes to spying and looking for Tejanos, as long as they don't get shot at too often. If they were here and heard someone prowling around in the darkness, they might shoot blind. I want to make damned sure whatever is moving and making them nervous ain't me and my old *compañero* Luke.''

The bawling of many cattle and the braying of mules came on the wind. ''They're thirsty poor sonsofbitches. Wouldn't take too much to stampede them to the river. Maybe Paddy is right after all,'' Quint said.

Alec shrugged up his coat collar and thrust his hands deep into his pockets. It was all he could do to prevent his teeth from chattering like castanets and his body from shivering uncontrollably. ''If they're that thirsty, sir, the Texans must be too. If the stock is stampeded, maybe the Texans will have to return to the river. If Captain Graydon's scheme works, they'll be out of beef rations and transport animals to haul their wagons and artillery. Then Colonel Canby can attack them on this side of the river and drive them back south. How does that sound, sir?''

Quint shrugged. ''Logical as hell.''

''You don't sound very positive.''

"Call me Quint, or maybe Big Red," Quint suggested.

"It's not regulation, sir."

Quint grinned. "Who's to know out here, Alec?"

"All right, Quint. Why aren't you sure about my logic, as you call it?"

"You don't know Texans, Alec. They can raise hell and put a prop under it if they have to. They're born fighting men, believe me. They'll head for Valverde Fords if they have to go on foot, dragging their artillery."

"But certainly Canby will fight for Valverde. If he can stop them there, they'll have to surrender."

"You're using too many ifs. Certainly Canby will fight for Valverde, but what if *he's* defeated? The Rebels can then head north to the big supply depot at Albuquerque. If Canby surrenders, then they'll have his arms, horses, and mules."

"And if he's defeated and doesn't surrender?"

Quint shrugged. "He'll likely fall back to Fort Craig."

"I doubt if we'll be defeated. Remember, we outnumber them."

Quint nodded. "In total numbers. But outside of our Regulars, Dodd's Colorado company and maybe Carson's First New Mexico, I wouldn't depend too much on the volunteers and militia. If they break and run in battle, our best troops *will* be outnumbered. The Texans are, as a rule, tough fighting men. They are led by experienced officers. Another thing, perhaps the most important: They must have water and gain those fords. If they are defeated, that will mean the end of their invasion."

Alec was silent for a time. "What do you think Sibley's chances are to make his invasion a success?" he asked at last.

Quint stood up and looked out into the darkness. "What the hell are they doing out there?" He shook his head and sat down again.

"You didn't answer my question, Quint."

"He's always been short of provisions. He has no United States currency or gold coin. The merchants and suppliers in El Paso and Chihuahua won't accept Confederate paper money. He had planned a start in October, but that had been impossible. It really wasn't his fault. There had been little financial support from his government and the State of Texas. So he started his invasion far too late in the year and wasn't equipped for a winter campaign. He had neglected also to take into consideration the two-year drought in New Mexico with subsequent losses in crops and stock raising. Sickness and disease has plagued his command from the start. Sibley seriously underestimated the hatred and animosity the native New Mexicans have had against Texans for decades. They'll give him nothing, sell him nothing, do everything in their power to hinder him. Mexican thieves have been running off his stock and killing his scouts and patrols for their horses and weapons. They and the Apaches menace his supply routes. He was forced to leave many of his men behind the advance to guard his conquests and keep his supply lines open. The advance north from La Mesilla has been harassed by freakish cold, sleet, snow, and strong winds.''

Alex whistled softly. "Then why, why, does he persist in this invasion?"

Quint looked at the young officer. "Because the man is an incurable optimist and dreamer. Now, one rule of war *not* in the regulations is to sleep when you can. God knows, there might be days and nights in the near future when it will be impossible to get any. Get some now, before the night's activities begin. I'll take the first watch."

Quint hunched his thick nonregulation Chihuahua poncho up about his shoulders and stood up, leaning against the ledge, looking off into the darkness toward the distant fire flicker of the Texans' bivouac. On February 12, Sibley's column had been seven miles south of Fort Craig. On February 16, he had developed a reconnaissance in force. Canby had advanced from Fort Craig to the river bend to meet the threat. There had been some long-range skirmishing. Canby had opened up with his artillery. Sibley had countered by sending out skirmishers, then withdrawing his main body out of artillery range. The afternoon had passed with no activity. At sundown Canby retreated to Fort Craig, leaving strong picket lines behind.

It was obvious that the Federals controlled the road from La Mesilla to Albuquerque passing west of the fort and within artillery range. Sibley must have felt the fort was too strong to be taken, at least by his force and inadequate artillery. He sent out his engineers to look for possible fords below Fort Craig, obviously for the Texans to cross the Rio Grande, outflanking Fort Craig by marching north to Valverde on the east bank.

February 17 and 18 brought on a typical New Mexican dust and sand storm that effectively paralyzed all operations. At dawn on the nineteenth, the Confederates marched northward in full view of Fort Craig and began fording the river opposite Paraje. By three o'clock, the entire brigade had completed the crossing. After dark the men standing guard at Fort Craig could hear Texans' voices on the wind and see their many campfires. Colonel Canby assumed that the Confederates intended to move upriver from Paraje to occupy a bluff that was about one thousand yards across the river immediately opposite Fort Craig. This projection of *pedregal* held a slight command of Fort Craig. Artillery planted on the summit might easily shell the fort. Colonel ordered colonels Kit Carson and Miguel Pino with their regiments of New Mexico Volunteers to secure the bluff. The New Mexicans held the position that night and the next morning.

At daylight on the twentieth, the Confederate Army of New Mexico moved out. They moved upriver, then right obliqued into a large ravine in the *pedregal*, blazing a new road in the process. The rocky *pedregal* and heavy sand held them to a march of only seven miles by four o'clock. The teams had become exhausted. There was no choice but to make a dry camp.

Colonel Canby crossed the river with his cavalry and McRae's battery to contest or harass the Texans. Carson's and Pino's regiments came down from their position on the bluff to join Canby's command. The *pedregal* was as difficult for the Federals to cross as it had been for the Confederates. They moved slowly eastward toward the enemy bivouac. The Texans set up an ideal defensive position on a *pedregal* mesa. Canby realized that the ground in front of the mesa was not suitable for cavalry or artillery attack. He deployed his infantry and sent out skirmishers to draw enemy fire so as to locate the guns. The Texans had obliged by opening fire. The bulk of Canby's infantry took their positions, but Pino's Second New Mexico panicked and nothing could be done with them to restore order. The combination of the panic and approach of nightfall prompted Canby to discontinue the attack. Colonel Roberts made a diversionary assault against the Confederate right, allowing Canby to withdraw safely back across the river, leaving the volunteer infantry behind to continue holding the strategic bluff commanding Fort Craig while the cavalry and artillery returned to the post. The Confederates remained in their camp in sight of Fort Craig and less than four miles away. That night Colonel Canby gave Paddy Graydon permission to raid the enemy camp.

An owl hooted faintly.

Quint kicked Alec in the side, then echoed the owl cry. In a little while the cry came again and was duly sent back by Quint. A moment later two shadowy figures ran noiselessly toward the rock ledges and scrambled over into the hollow.

"Well?" Quint asked.

Paddy grinned. "We got around their flank. Ain't but a few guards around the beef herd. Whole picket line of horses and mules not far away. By God, Big Red, them animals is thirsty!"

Luke nodded. "We'd best go back and get the mules right away." He and Paddy vanished into the darkness behind the ledges heading for the two condemned mules held by some of Paddy's men.

Alec yawned. "How did they ever make him a captain, Quint?"

Quint smiled. "He's long been a resident of New Mexico. Next to Kit Carson and Luke, there probably isn't a more colorful character than him. He's an old Regular Army man. Before our Regulars abandoned Fort Buchanan in Arizona he operated a saloon there. He recruited a company of Unionists who had been dispossessed and driven north by secessionists. To them the war is a very personal matter. Graydon's Independent Spy Company has been serving as a sort of jack-of-all-trades unit—spying, scouting, policing, and foraging."

Luke and Paddy led up the two old condemned mules. Each of them was loaded with a wooden box containing a dozen twenty-four-pounder howitzer shells. "Mules is right sociable, young sir," Paddy explained to Alec. "We can light the fuses on these shells and start the mules toward the Rebel mules. They'll sure as hell want to meet up with their friends over there. When the shells go off . . ." He grinned. "Them thirsty mules will sure as hellfire stampede for the river."

Quint reached under his poncho and brought out a *guage*, a big leather flask filled with El Paso brandy. "I'll drink to that, Paddy." He handed it to Paddy.

Paddy drank deeply. "Mother's milk," he gasped.

Luke took the flask and drank. "Keno," he husked.

Alec shook his head as Luke offered him the flask. "We're on duty," he said.

"Hear! Hear!" Paddy cried.

Quint took the flask and downed a good one. He waited a moment for the potent liquor to hit bottom and silently explode. 'Salud y pesetas," he toasted. He looked sideways at Alec. 'There's nothing in the regulations that says you have to die of cold and thirst while on duty, is there?"

Alec shook his head and took the proffered flask. He drank a little, then more. He blinked his eyes. He tried to speak but couldn't. He finally made it. "Captain Graydon," he said hoarsely.

"Aye, lad?" Paddy said.

"When I was on staff duty I noticed that no other company besides yours ever had such a consistent roster muster after muster. Even the Regulars. How did you manage that?"

Quint took out one of his Navies and checked it for loads and percussion caps. "Tell him, Paddy," he suggested.

Paddy relieved himself while speaking over his shoulder. "You mean the same names muster after muster with nary a change?"

Alec nodded.

Paddy buttoned his trousers and reached for the brandy flask. "It's simple. Me and my boys were always too busy to bother with paperwork. Whenever we lost a man who had enough of army life and took off, it meant a lot of paperwork. So supposin' Jesus María Barella of Polvadera deserted to see Rosita and Pedro Velarde of Bosquecitas happened to come by, we snapped him up, rechristened him Jesus María Barella, signed him up, gave him a caballo, a musket, a nice new blue suit, and the first pair of real shoes he ever had, a bellyful of issue bacon and hardtack, him swearin' all the time he was not Jesus María Barella of Polvadera but was Pedro Velarde of Bosquecitas. Well, if we was to bother huntin' down Brother Barella when we had our hands on Brother Velarde, we'd never get the god-damned war over with. So we'd keep a close eye on him until he got used to being around, and in time he'd get used to his new name. Some of them turned out to be better soldiers than the ones that deserted."

"Speakin' of the goddamned war," Luke reminded Paddy.

The flask made the rounds until it was empty. They led the patient mules off into the darkness toward the Confederate picket lines. The bluff loomed up, high, somber, dark, and mysterious. The cold wind rustled the brush. The odor of stale campfire smoke came on it. A mule brayed suddenly from the picket lines. Hard hands clamped over the mule muzzles to prevent them from responding.

The odor of manure and ammonia drifted to the silent figures moving slowly through the brush. They heard the voice of a mounted herder as he sang "Ellen Bayne" to keep the beef herd quiet. The singing was mingled with the bawling of the cattle and the braying of the aroused mules. A light flared up, revealing the yellow bearded face of a Texan herder as he lighted his pipe. They halted.

"These poor mules will get killed," Alec whispered.

"It's a fine thing to die for one's country," Paddy said.

Lucifers were scratched across belt buckles and applied to the fuse tips. Tiny specks of fire hissed up them.

"*Carajo!*" Paddy cried.

They slapped the mules on their rumps and then started running back to safety of the ledges.

Paddy looked back. "*Vaya con Dios,*" he said, crossing himself.

The specks of fire winked and bobbed in the darkness.

Paddy halted. "They're almost there."

A herder shouted.

The two mules brayed in unison.

Luke stared. "Jesus! They're comin' back!" he yelled.

"*Vámonos!*" Paddy shouted.

They plunged through the chaparral. The catclaw clung to their legs and clothing.

Quint looked back. "They're gaining, by God!"

A multiple shattering roar exploded behind them and the whole area was lit up. The faint popping of firearms came from near the herd. The mules and cattle raised a horrible din, but they did not stampede. Bits of jagged metal whizzed through the air.

Luke yelled hoarsely as he staggered in his stride. "I'm hit, Big Red!" he cried as he went down.

Quint handed his Sharps to Alec. He picked up Luke's rifle and gave it to Paddy. He lifted Luke up across his shoulders and staggered on through the stinking smoke and clinging brush, cursing all the way. A bugle gave brassy tongue into the night. More firearms popped.

"Goddamn you to hell, Paddy!" Quint raged. "You and your half-assed ideas!"

"Goddamn *you* to hell, Big Red!" Paddy retorted. "You and Luke volunteered, didn't you? Don't cry to me!"

Quint had no answer

They placed the moaning Luke on the ground behind the ledge. Paddy thrust his rifle on top of the ledge. "Go get the horses, young fella," he said to Alec.

Luke moaned loudly. Quint felt about his body. Luke's hair was soaked in back. Quint held his hand up. It was dark with blood.

Paddy looked down. "He hit bad?" he asked.

Luke shifted. "Christ yes! Mortal, I think. Quint, for God's sake don't bury me in this godforsaken country. Cremate me and scatter my ashes over the Querencia. Go on up Socorro way and tell Theresa—no, make that Maria—what happened to me." He closed his eyes. "Get a half dozen of them Tejanos for me, old friend."

Quint thumb-snapped a lucifer into flame and examined the back of Luke's head. There was no wound, just the wet stain of blood on his hair. He sat back on his heels. "Get up, you damned faker," he said.

Luke moaned. "I'm dying and he curses me."

Quint winked at Paddy.

"For shame, Big Red," Paddy scolded.

Quint yawned. "First time I've ever seen a man get a mortal wound being hit by a mule steak," he drawled.

Paddy slapped his thighs. "I'll be go to hell! I always claimed Luke never knowed what hit him."

Luke sat up. "Bite my hairy old ass, the both of you," he growled.

"Me and Big Red will recommend you for a brevet commission, Luke. The general will be right pleased with you. A real live hero," Paddy said, straight-faced.

Luke eyed his two grinning companions. "By Jesus, either of you two jackasses ever mouths off about this I'll sculp yuh with a dull knife."

Alec led the horses to them. He eyed Luke. He opened his mouth to speak.

"Shut up! *Sir!*" Luke snapped.

Alec shut up. He looked at Quint and Paddy, then shrugged. "I met a courier from the colonel," he said. "Quint, he wants you and Luke to scout as close to the Confederates as you can get. You must warn him the instant they start their march toward Valverde. Paddy, he wants you to stay with Pino's regiment."

"What about you?" Quint asked him.

Alec shrugged. "I'm to return to the post for duty."

"Staff?" Quint asked.

Alec shook his head. "One of Captain McRae's officers took sick with pneumonia today. I'm to join McRae's battery at least until the officer is fit for duty again." He shook his head. "Damn! Just when I was enjoying serving with Kershaw's Rangers."

Quint smiled. "We enjoyed having you, Alec. Maybe you'll be back with us."

Quint and Luke watched the two men ride toward the river.

Luke looked sideways. "He'll make a helluva soldier someday, Big Red."

Quint nodded. "I think he's one now."

They rode back toward the Confederate bivouac.

"You still want me to go up to Socorro and tell Theresa, or was it Maria, about your wound?" Quint asked.

They rode on a little way.

"No need to bother," Luke said at last. "I don't think either one of them ever gave a good goddamn about ol' Luke anyways."

"That's the way it goes, Wandering Wolf."

They grinned at each other.

★ TWENTY ★

MORNING, FEBRUARY 21, 1862: VALVERDE

It was two hours before dawn of February 21, east of the Mesa del Contadero not far from the edge of the Jornado del Muerto. The sound of many thudding hoofs muffled by deep sand mingled with the creaking of artillery and wagon wheels, the muted voices of many men, and the thirsty braying of hundreds of mules. Now and again the shifting wind blew the ashes from dying campfires to reveal faint winking red ember eyes. The advance detachment of Sibley's Brigade of Texas Mounted Rifles was starting their march north to the Valverde Fords. Man, horse, and mule, they had been waterless for twenty-four hours.

A dark man-figure rose from behind a rock ledge, faintly silhouetted against the sky, then moved noiselessly downslope. Twenty minutes passed. The faint hoot of an owl came upslope. Quint stood up and waved on Joshua and Anselmo. They led their booted horses to where Luke waited. He motioned them on and led the way south to the primitive rutted road the Texans had virtually made in their march from the Rio Grande. They crossed the road and left the horses with Joshua. The Jornado was just east of them.

Here the discordant sound of the braying mules and thirsty horses was louder. During the night Paddy Graydon's company had run off most of the beef herd, driving it across the river. Beyond the mule herd and picket lines of the horses the flickering, flaring light of many campfires reflected from the worn grayish white tilts of many transport wagons and the bronze barrels of four stubby howitzers. A scarf of smoke trailed over the camp as the Texans brewed coffee and cooked their scanty rations for the day's march. Guidons and company flags flapped listlessly in the wind.

Quint put the glasses on the encampment. "Fourth Texas," he murmured. He scanned the men. They were young for the most part, mostly in their twenties, with weathered brown faces, sun-tightened eyes and the look, stance, and walk of horsemen. The Lone Star Brigade flag was planted beside an ambulance. A heavy-set officer got out of the ambulance and walked to the nearest campfire. He wore the gray uniform of a Confederate general officer. On each side of the buff-colored collar was a wreath, within which was a large center star, with a smaller star on each side of it, the insignia of a brigadier general. The officer was bushy-haired, with a large hooked nose jutting out over a luxurious flowing mustache and short beard. Quint had known him before the war, when he had been a captain in the First Dragoons and a paymaster at Albuquerque.

"That the Old Man?" Luke asked.

Quint nodded. "Henry Hopkins Sibley himself."

Two officers wearing the insignia of lieutenant colonels followed by a sergeant approached General Sibley. The powerful glasses clearly picked out Shelby Calhoun as one of the officers. Quint could not identify the other officer. Just as he was about to pass the glasses to Luke he noticed something familiar about the sergeant. The sergeant half turned and looked in Quint's direction for a moment, almost as though he sensed he was being watched. Luke took the glasses.

"Who's the officer with Calhoun?" Quint asked quietly.

Luke studied the officer, then turned to Quint. "William Read 'Dirty Shirt' Scurry. He commands the Fourth Texas in the absence of their colonel, a James Reily." Luke paused. "You see the sergeant with 'em, Big Red?"

Quint nodded. "My son Frank."

Luke looked down at his Sharps. "Just when I was figgerin' on makin' wolf bait out of ol' Henry Hopkins Sibley too." He looked at Quint.

Quint shook his head. "It's not guerrilla warfare . . . *yet*."

The officers were in conference with Sibley. They nodded and returned to their commands. Frank walked after them. When Scurry turned aside, Frank continued following Calhoun, evidently assigned to his service.

Anselmo took the glasses and studied Sibley. "The others are gone, *patrón*. No danger of hitting Frank now."

"It'll be a cinch," Luke added.

Quint looked sideways at him. "Go ahead."

Luke raised his rear sight and full cocked the hammer. For a long moment or two he sighted, then he lowered the rifle. He let down the hammer to half cock. "That ain't really why we came here," he said quietly.

Quint turned to Anselmo. "Go back to Joshua. Tell him to return to Fort Craig and report that the Rebel advance party is moving north toward Valverde and it looks like the rest of the brigade will soon follow. Also, we're going to try to stampede their mule herd to the river. If we succeed they'll not be able to take most of their transport wagons with them. As soon as you tell Joshua bring our horses back here."

When Anselmo returned they led the horses to the south, then circled around behind the mule herd. The mule herders were on the other side of the herd, leading some of the mules toward the wagons and roping others. The eastern side of the big herd had no guards.

Luke nodded. "They figgered a mule would be too smart to go out there on the Jornado. A horse might, but never a mule. Which proves they're smarter than a horse, and next thing to a man, if the truth be known."

"Or smarter," Anselmo added.

They sheathed their rifles and unrolled their blankets. They mounted and drew their pistols. Quint nodded. Three shots cracked out, followed by a staccato of reports, as they emptied their pistols. The mules began to move. The three stampeders warwhooped and flapped their blankets. That was too much for the thirsty mules. They took off at a dead run right through the south end of the camp, raising dust, pounding through the campfires, scattering ashes, burning brands and sparks, knocking over some of the shouting, cursing Texans, and then headed for the river road with three whooping madmen racing their mounts right through the camp. A few scattered shots followed their course, and then they too were into the darkness behind the running herd on their way to the Rio Grande and the Federal positions.

Quint and Luke cautiously returned to the Confederate camp

just at dawn. The camp had been abandoned. Slowly rising smoke tendrils came from the dying fires. Thirty baggage wagons stood deserted. They picked through some of them. They were filled with the entire kits, blankets, books, and regimental papers of the Fourth Texas.

The Sibley Brigade was on its way to Valverde across a level sandy plain that the higher-ranking Federal officers thought it would be impossible for the Texans to cross. The sand was hub-deep. They were short of teams, and those they had were worn-out and unfed and had been without water for well over twenty-four hours. The men and saddle horses were in the same condition.

Quint watched them from a distance. The men were pushing and pulling the wagons and artillery through the soft clinging sand. "No question about it, Lukie," he said. "They're committed to Valverde lock, stock, and barrel."

Luke nodded. "Then what are *we* doing *here*?"

"A good question," Quint said.

They mounted their horses and rode toward the river.

The quick crack and reverberating report of the reveille gun boomed hollowly across the Rio Grande, awakening the echoes on the opposite heights. Lights had flickered on throughout the fort before reveille, twinkling through the darkness. The steady, incessant spine-tingling rumble of the big field drums beating the long roll followed the thundering report of the gun. Sparks and smoke poured out of the stacks of the mess kitchens. The mingled aroma of woodfires, frying bacon, and boiling coffee came from the kitchens. Doors slammed. Mules brayed. Horses whinnied. Men shouted. Booted feet pounded on the cementlike *caliche* clay of the parade ground. Long lines of seemingly faceless men stood at attention in the darkness answering roll call and coughing incessantly. The wind billowed tents and wagon tilts. It snapped out the company guidons and drove fine grit across the parade ground.

The grayness of the false dawn pewtered the eastern sky above the dim shapes of the hunched heights across the Rio Grande. Noncommissioned officers passed along the ranks, inspecting men, arms, ammunition pouches, and haversacks. One day's cooked rations were to be carried in the greasy white haversacks.

The sun rose in a vast and noiseless explosion of rose, pink, and gold. The huge garrison flag rose in unison with the sun, snapping out in the freshening breeze to its full glory of red, white, and blue. A spontaneous cheer broke out from the ranks.

Four companies of the Third and one of the First Regular Army Cavalry stood to horse. Two sections—four guns of Captain McRae's Provisional Battery manned by enlisted men of the Second and Third Cavalry, and Lieutenant Hall's battery of two twenty-four-pounder howitzers—waited for the command to move out. The Regulars were from the crack Fifth Infantry and Seventh Infantry. Captain Dodd led the independent company of Colorado Volunteer Infantry. There were four companies of the Third and Fifth New Mexico Mounted Volunteers. Captain Kershaw's Independent New Mexico Mounted Rifle Company was to provide advance scouting for the force. The field force was commanded by Colonel Roberts. The orders were to advance to Valverde, cross the river, and hold the fords before the enemy reached there. Most of the Federal infantry were still across the river opposite Fort Craig, where they had been since the night before.

Quint led his shrunken command out ahead of the Regular Cavalry. Out of an original company strength of thirty-five, he had only twenty men. Some of them had been assigned as scouts with the troops across the river. Others had been used as couriers. Dave and Luke were there, and Anselmo, with Black Moccasin and Joshua, the fighting Delawares. Others were the Americans Frank Scott, Jim Hunt, young Mick Casey, and elderly Otto Schmidt, a Bavarian American who acted as gunsmith for the company. Native New Mexicans were José Ochoa, his cousin Ramón Ochoa, Juan Trujillo, Marcos Perez, Jesus Padilla, Diego Chacón, Aurelio Díaz, José Vigil, Pedro Sanchez and the inseparable brothers Pablo and Ignacio Baca.

Valverde, the Green Valley, was seven miles north of Fort Craig. Quint's company had formed an escort for Colonel Roberts earlier that year when he had reconnoitered there. The Rio Grande flowed from a northerly direction, then turned easterly at the far northern end of Valverde to flow roughly at about a forty-five-degree angle to the southeast for over a thousand yards, then almost abruptly turned east again, flowed for about another thousand yards, then turned abruptly again to flow almost due south. Thus the river flowed in a great irregular curve from north to southeast and then east again before continuing on its southern course. The river formed the western boundary of Valverde, whose northern and eastern sides were formed by an ages-old dry channel of the Rio Grande. The northern part of the valley was bounded by the junction of the old channel with the present river. The valley itself was about seven to eight hundred yards wide across the midsection. The river averaged about one hundred and fifty yards wide. The southerly part of the valley was bounded by the three-hundred-foot-high Mesa del Contadero, a huge mass of sand rock covered by lava and inaccessible to horses. Its precipitous western base was washed by the river. The mesa extended for about three miles in an easterly direction, forcing travelers from the south to leave the Jornado by means of a canyon to enter Valverde. Small hills and sandy ridges stretched from a *bosque* of venerable cottonwoods bordering the old channel at the foot of the mesa across the valley to a smaller mesa in the north. Beyond the old channel and the sand ridges and hills was the Jornado del Muerto.

There were four possible fords at Valverde. The lowest and best was at the foot of the mesa. The next one was about six hundred yards due west, three hundred yards beyond which was another ford. The fourth ford was another four hundred yards upstream, where the river turned to the southwest. There were sand bars and flats along the westerly bank of the river from the second lowest ford, extending intermittently to beyond the highest ford. There were other sandbars at the crossing of the third ford, one of which was just above it, the other just below. The best ford was the lowest one. The others, due to quicksand, were rather treacherous. The river was four to five feet deep, a muddy brown in color, cold and swift-running.

The valley was filled here and there with thick cottonwood *bosques* with open spaces between them. Valverde had been a King's Axe on the Royal Highway, a place where water, firewood, and grazing was plentiful for travelers on the Jornado. It was the best fording place for many miles. During the years 1820–1825 there had been a pleasant little village there, but Apache and Navajo raids, and at times even those carried out by Kiowas and Comanches, had eventually forced its abandonment. Here and there low, eroded adobe and rock walls might still be seen. The shallow trace of an *acequia*, an irrigation ditch, was still visible. It was all that remained of Valverde. No one lived there now.

The day was warming up and bidding to be fair, clear, and very windy. The Valverde trees swayed and rustled in the strong wind. Dust and fine sand were driven across the open spaces. There was no sign of the enemy.

Quint ordered Dave to hold the company on the west bank while he, Luke, Anselmo, Joshua, Jim Hunt, and Frank Scott crossed the river. The horses were left with Jim and Frank while Quint led the others forward to the thick *bosque* at the mesa foot. Frost had long since touched the cottonwood leaves with gold. Those still on the branches were stiff and papery, dancing and chattering in the rising wind, the piled-up windrows crackling crisply underfoot. They reached the far side of the *bosque*. Dust was rising beyond the old channel near the canyon mouth.

Luke shifted his chew. "The big fight will be here," he prophesied.

Anselmo looked sideways at him from behind a thick boled tree. "How do you know?" he asked.

Luke shrugged. "Last night I seen a powderhorn in the sky. A good sign, that, or mebbe an unlucky one. My grandpappy was said to have seen such a powderhorn the night before the Battle of Oriskany when the Colonials fought the Indians."

"What happened to him?" Anselmo asked curiously.

Luke yawned. "He didn't come back. His sculp is mebbe still hangin' in a Seneca lodge."

"Listen!" Joshua cried.

The sound of many galloping horses and the shouts of men came on the wind. A few moments later the first Texans topped the far bank of the old channel and plunged down into it at full gallop. An officer was leading the way followed by a guidon bearer. The guidon bore the numeral 2 and the letter B.

Luke quickly took Quint's field glasses and focused them on the officer. "Second Texas, Company B, some of Baylor's boys. That was my old company. The officer is Major Pyron. Use'ta be command B. Guess he got promoted."

Anselmo grunted. "We goin' to let them water their horses?"

Quint led the way back through the *bosque*. There were at least 150, probably more, of the Texans. He looked back. The lead riders were urging their mounts over the near side of the old channel. Dust was boiling up farther to the east about where the canyon entrance was located.

"There come more of 'em, Big Red! Mebbe the whole brigade!" Luke called out.

Quint nodded. "Roberts said the lower ford is the key to the whole position! We've got to slow them down at least until we get reinforcements!"

The area between the *bosque* and the ford was one of low sand hummocks, fallen logs, and uprooted brush heaped there when the river overflowed the bottomland. Jim Hunt had already taken the horses farther back close to the river.

Quint hurdled a big fallen log, turned, and rested his rifle on top of it. The others joined him. "Shoot for the horses when I give the word and use your Maynard primers," he ordered. "After the first volley, fire at will until they break, retreat, or take cover."

"Every man his own turkey," Luke added quietly. "They's a lot of thirsty Tejanos comin' this way, hell for leather."

At 150 yards Quint spoke sharply. "Fire! Then fire at will!"

Five rifles simultaneously blasted flame and smoke. Breech-blocks were instantly dropped and long cartridges shoved into chambers. Breechblocks snapped up; hammers clicked back. The rifles crashed again.

Clouds of green top knotted mountain quail rose, whirring, into the air. Rabbits bounded off. Turkeys gobbled frantically and took wing for short flights.

Four of the leading horses had gone down in a tangle of thrashing hoofs. The guidon bearer threw up his arms, letting go of the guidon staff, which was immediately caught by another trooper, who leaped his horse over one of the fallen horses and came on through the powder smoke without losing a stride. The bugler blew the charge incessantly. Major Pyron waved his slouch hat. "Come awn, Texas!" he shouted. High-pitched warwhoops came from the charging troopers.

Ten horses were down with their riders. Riderless mounts ran aimlessly back and forth through the dust and powder smoke.

The bugle stuttered retreat. The Texans retreated to the *bosque* and out of sight. A few moments later their carbines began to crack flatly. Bullets whispered close overhead. Frank Scott had jumped up on the log to see better through the smoke. He sighed softly and fell backward with a bullet hole in the center of his forehead.

"They might be lining up to come back," Quint warned.

A bugle rang out from the west bank of the river. Duncan's squadron came to a dust-shrouded halt on the high ground. The enemy fire rattled steadily. The bullets made a crackling sound as they passed over Quint and his men. Sometimes they thudded into the logs or kicked up spurts of dust from the hard ground to ricochet eerily into space. Dust was rising thickly from the area of the old channel as hundreds more Texans joined their comrades now engaged with the four Rangers behind the logs.

Duncan's squadron of the Third Cavalry crossed the ford and reached the east bank. "Dismount! As skirmishers! Fight on foot!" The bugle stuttered out the calls. The horse-holders each led four horses back into the dubious shelter of the sand hummocks and fallen logs.

Major Duncan stopped beside Quint. "How does it look, Kershaw? What's the situation?"

"They're thick in the *bosque*, Major. Reinforcements pouring in along the old channel. They're extending their line from the base of the mesa to our left. They mean to take the ford."

Duncan nodded. "They know its importance."

"What are my orders?" Quint asked.

"Major!" a sergeant shouted. "Look!" He pointed to the far left. At about one thousand yards distance a group of men and horses were at the water's edge.

"Goddamn!" Duncan swore. "I haven't enough men to extend that far and still hold this position."

Quint waved a hand. "I can harass them at least, Major."

"Good! Lieutenant Claflin, commanding Company G of the Second, has been ordered up the bank. So you won't be all alone. Get to it!"

Quint, Luke, Joshua, and Anselmo ran back to their horses, then galloped directly toward the Texans. Bullets hissed past them as the enemy in the *bosque* and along the old channel bank opened fire on them. They dismounted two hundred yards from the Texans, who were watering. Quint and his companions began firing. Several horses and men went down. The rest of the men began a scattered fire, but when Claflin's troopers added their fire-power to Quint's detail, the Texans broke in confusion and galloped back toward the sand ridge.

"Good work, Captain!" Claflin barked. "We'll take over now!"

The uproar of firing rose in intensity from the far right flank. The Confederates charged spiritedly into the heavy carbine fire of the dismounted cavalrymen and were driven back. The Federals charged in return, driving the Confederates from the *bosque*. Smoke drifted in among the trees marked with the stabbing orange-red flashes of musketry. Then the Federal cavalrymen fell back under heavy defensive fire. The Texans charged back into the *bosque*. Quint turned and saw Dave leading a dozen of the Ranger company to the support of Duncan, who would need every man he could get in the bloody, desperate, up-and-down, back-and-forth struggle. Captain Brotherton's company of the Fifth Infantry reinforced Duncan. The Texans manhandled a section of light mountain howitzers into position and opened fire on the Federals.

Quint looked at the sun. It should be close to ten o'clock. A courier from Colonel Roberts splashed across the ford with orders for Duncan to fall back and give the artillery on the west bank a chance at the Rebels. McRae's and Hall's guns opened fire on the *bosque*. The guns roared and spat flame and thick smoke. Shells whirred overhead like the flight of huge partridges. They burst in the *bosque*. Leaves drifted down, and branches fell. Fragments thudded into the trees and the bodies of crouching men. Dust and smoke thickened throughout the *bosque*, eerily illuminated by the flash of the bursting shells. It was beautifully directed fire. The Confederate guns tried counterfire against the Union batteries, but they were outranged. Shells collided in flight with splitting cracks, flashing and smoking, sending whizzing fragments through the air. The cannonading boomed over the incessant popping of musketry. Here too the Federals had an advantage. Their firearms were of better quality and had greater range, while the Texans for the most part used carbines and even double-barreled shotguns. The deadliest fire came from the handful of Kershaw's Rangers, with their long-barreled, big-bored Sharps rifles. Every time a daring Texan moved from cover or otherwise exposed himself, he drew instant fire from the sharpshooters.

The Confederate artillery suffered. One gun had a wheel shattered. Its team of mules were killed or crippled. The gun was abandoned, but a group of Texans ran to it under heavy fire and carried it off by hand. Another two-gun section was bravely served, inflicting casualties on the far right of Duncan's position, but accurate rifle fire caused many casualties among the artillerymen. Quint put the glasses on the one light howitzer still being served. An officer was loading it assisted by only a few men. A shell burst nearby and set fire to the grass under the howitzer, but the Texans courageously kept up the fire. In a little while, that howitzer too was out of action.

Quint put the glasses on McRae's battery across the river. Young Alec Calhoun was in charge of a section. The powerful lenses picked out his face, running with sweat that was cutting streaks through the powder blackening. He seemed to be in his element. Quint handed the glasses to Luke.

Luke studied the battery. "By God," he said softly. "He's your son, all right, Big Red. He's *gloryin'* in this."

The sun reached its zenith. A lull came over the battlefield. It was a warm day for February and would get warmer. The wind had increased, blowing almost at gale intensity and clearing the battle smoke from Valverde. Colonel Roberts had held control of the battle thus far. Reinforcements were sent to extend his left as they arrived on the scene, covering the constantly lengthening Confederate line as their reinforcements arrived at Valverde. Colonel Kit Carson's First New Mexico, nine hundred men in eight companies, had arrived some hours earlier and had taken position on the west bank near the Valverde road in order to resist any possible flanking movement by the Texans. Captain Selden's battalion of the Fifth Infantry with Dodd's Independent Company of Colorado Volunteers was sent up the west bank to deal with a Texan advance menacing an upper ford. The battalion crossed the river up to their armpits in the cold, swift-running water, holding their rifles and ammunition pouches up high, feeling for quicksand with their feet. They re-formed on the east bank, fixed bayonets, and charged, driving the bold

Texans back. After that they kept up a galling fire on the right flank of the enemy.

It was comparatively quiet at that time on the far right flank. The cries of wounded and dying men of both sides lying between Duncan's position and the edge of the *bosque* came drifting to the Federals.

"Jesus," Dave said quietly. "Listen to them."

Quint nodded. "This is always the worst part."

There was one yellow-bearded Texan lying fifty yards in front of the position. His back was against a sand-drifted boulder. He stared accusingly at the Federals. Quint put the glasses on him. His eyes were wide, but they did not see, nor would they ever see again. His dirty hands were twisted in the bloody folds of his checked shirt. Quint put down the glasses and turned his head away. It was always like this after battle. The burning excitement died away and was replaced by cold, sickening reality.

A faint cry rose higher and higher. Quint looked over the log. A Texan was laboriously crawling toward the Federal position seventy-five yards away. Black Moccasin raised his rifle. Quint shook his head. The Delaware looked curiously at him but lowered his rifle.

"Watah! Watah!" the Texan cried hoarsely.

"I'll give you *watah*, you Texas sonofabitch!" a Regular Cavalryman yelled. No one laughed.

A rifle cracked from the Rebel position. The slug thudded into a log near the cursing cavalryman.

"Watah! Watah!" The cry was much feebler now.

Quint leaned his Sharps against the log, picked up his canteen, and vaulted over the log. He held his hands up high. A Texas rifle cracked, but the slug sang high overhead. No Texan would shoot *that* bad, Quint thought as he walked toward the wounded man. Maybe someone knocked his rifle up to prevent him from hitting Quint. *Maybe* . . . He passed the yellow-bearded Texan and could have sworn the staring blue eyes slanted sideways to look at him.

The wounded man lay facedown with outstretched arms, fingers digging into the hard earth. He was still breathing. Quint put down the canteen and knelt beside him. He gently rolled him over. The gray eyes opened. The swollen tongue was protruding through between the cracked lips. His chest rose and fell spasmodically, and his labored breathing whistled through his mouth. He couldn't be more than eighteen years old.

Quint slid an arm under the boy's neck and raised his head a little. "Where are you hit, son?" he asked.

"Right knee," the Texan gasped. "You got watah?"

Quint nodded. He held the canteen to the boy's mouth and let him drink a little. He cut away the trouser leg and turned his head quickly away. The leg below the knee was almost severed, but dirt had clotted the blood flow. He cut the trouser material into strips, applied a tourniquet, doused the wound with brandy, and bound it with the remaining strips. He smiled at the boy. "That will have to do until a surgeon sees to you," he said. "I think you'll live."

A dirty hand gripped Quint's sleeve. "What about the leg? Will I be able to keep it?"

Quint shook his head. There was no use in lying. "I'll have to get you to a surgeon as soon as possible."

The Texan narrowed his eyes. "You ain't one of us! You're a gawddamned *greaser!*"

Quint smiled a little. "Yup, and you're a gawddamned *Tejano!* Now that we've settled that, I'm going to have to pick you up and carry you. Think you can stand it?"

The boy nodded. "I'll have to," he answered grimly.

The sporadic firing had stopped on the right flank as both sides watched the little drama being played out on the blood-stained field. Quint picked him up and placed him across his broad shoulders.

"Which way we goin'?" the Texan asked. "Your way?"

Quint shook his head. "You're going home to Texas, sonny." Before God, he thought, I hope he makes it home, although the odds might be a thousand to one.

The powder-begrimed Texans watched Quint as he carried the boy to their lines. A sergeant came forward. "I'll take care of him, suh. He's my little brothah Jesse. I can't thank you enough, suh."

Quint nodded. "You'd better check that wound, Sergeant. It's a bad one."

"Captain, suh." A voice spoke behind Quint.

Quint turned. An officer wearing the insignia of a major smiled and extended his hand. "Major Charles Lynn Pyron, suh.

That was a mighty brave thing to do for an enemy, considering the circumstances."

Quint shrugged. "He's hardly an enemy now, Major. I'm Captain Quintin Kershaw."

"A typical Kershaw act, I'd say," Shelby Calhoun said as he approached them.

"Thank you, Shell," Quint said quietly.

Shelby studied Quint. "You can still reconsider our offer of a commission. You'll be sure to be on the winning side."

Quint half smiled. "It doesn't look like it this day, does it?"

"The day is young."

"We've held you thus far, Shell."

Shelby nodded. "Granted. But our full force is on the field now. You've held us with Regulars so far, but your greaser boys—I can't call them *soldiers*—will run at the first chance they get."

"Colonel Calhoun, sir! Colonel Green wants to see you at once!" someone called.

The voice was too familiar to Quint. He turned as Frank rode up and drew rein. They looked at each other for a moment, but neither of them spoke.

Shelby mounted his horse. He leaned from the saddle and held out his hand to Quint. "Each of us must make the decision he feels in his heart he must. Good-bye, Quintin Kershaw." He gripped Quint's hand, touched spurs to his horse, and rode off, followed by Frank. Once Frank looked back, but his father was gone into the thickness of the *bosque*.

Quint walked slowly back toward the Federal lines. The last time Shelby had spoken with Quint had been at the Querencia. Then he had said prophetically in parting, "Good-bye, then, until we meet again, Quintin Kershaw. I'm sure we will—in battle smoke."

During the lull in firing caused by Quint's act, both Confederates and Federals had taken the opportunity to administer to the dying and wounded of both sides. When Quint reappeared, they all returned to their own lines.

Quint vaulted over the log and came face to face with Colonel Roberts. The Vermonter was abristle. "Captain Kershaw!" he snapped. "Who gave you authority to do that?"

"I did it on my own, sir."

"There was no flag of truce!"

Quint shook his head. "There wasn't time. The boy might have bled to death."

"Succoring the enemy, eh?"

"No. That poor lad can never be an enemy of ours again, Colonel."

Roberts studied Quint for a moment. At last he murmured, "A brave and humane deed, sir."

"All in the day's work of killing and being killed, sir."

Roberts looked toward the quiet enemy lines. "What's your analysis of the situation? Do you think they've had enough?"

"No, Colonel."

"Reasons?"

"There are hundreds of them over there. We've hardly dented their manpower. Their artillery is intact. They won't admit we've held the advantage thus far. Their full force is on the field, according to one of their officers. He said that we've held them with Regulars thus far. I quote: 'Your greaser boys—I can't call them *soldiers*—will run at the first chance they get.' "

Roberts shrugged. "He might have a point there, but we've still plenty of Regulars and two fine batteries of artillery with heavier metal than theirs. They'll have to contend with them before they get a chance to make our 'greasers' run."

The battlefield was quiet. Roberts had ordered that the men be allowed to eat their rations and rest before further activity started. Quint was ordered to take his unit—with their scant numbers one could hardly call them a company—and report to the center of the line for duty as pickets and skirmishers.

As Quint turned to go, Roberts stopped him. "Just who was the officer who gave you that information?" he asked curiously.

"Lieutenant Colonel Shelby Calhoun, Colonel," Quint replied. He nodded. "The very same," he added quietly.

Roberts shook his head. "I find it hard to believe of Calhoun. Serving against his country in the Rebel army."

"War makes strange bedfellows, sir," Quint quoted. He rode off followed by his Rangers.

★ TWENTY-ONE ★

AFTERNOON, FEBRUARY 21, 1862: VALVERDE

The sun was slanting to the west. The success of Captain Selden's infantry battalion in their ferocious bayonet charge after fording the Rio Grande had encouraged Colonel Roberts to order McRae's battery across the river to take up a position on Selden's right flank in order to support any further movements. Selden's infantry had come under a galling fire from two well-served Confederate six-pounder guns and had been forced to fall back. McRae's battery was supported by the infantry of Captain Brotherton's company of the Fifth Infantry, Captain Ingraham's H Company of the Seventh Infantry and two selected volunteer companies—Captain Mortimore's of the Third New Mexico and Captain Hubbell's of the Fifth.

Quint's sharpshooters dropped back to the line of Selden's battalion as McRae's guns opened up on the Confederate gun section that had caused Selden so much trouble. The Rangers had lost four men. Diego Chacón was missing. Jim Hunt had caught a musket ball through his left shoulder and had been taken back across the river. Joshua had been sharpshooting in front of Selden's battalion. A solid shot had taken off his head. Pedro Sanchez had been shot through the head and had died on his feet without uttering a sound. He had a wife and two children back at the Querencia.

The day had turned warm, almost like early summer. The wind still swept the battlefield. Quint grounded his rifle and leaned on it. Sweat dripped from his face, ran down his sides, and greased his palms. His eyes burned from the incessant powder smoke. His throat was brassy dry. He had nearly been hit twice. A bullet furrow grooved the forestock of the Sharps. A ball had plucked his hat from his head. The fighting had been going on almost ceaselessly for five hours.

Luke bandaged his left forearm. A shell fragment had skinned it, leaving an angry red mark. "They got Sanchez," he said between his teeth as he tightened the bandage knot with them. "Not much of the company left, Big Red."

Quint nodded. "Better than a third gone of the twenty we had when the fracas started."

Luke grunted. "I heard a staff officer go by yelling we had them whupped. I yelled back, tellin' him to go spread that among the Texans. They don't know that yet, or mebbe they're too stupid to know about it."

Quint shrugged. "Neither, most likely. They probably think they got *us* whupped. There's a helluva lot of fight still left in them."

McRae's six-gun battery had begun a spirited duel with the two Confederate guns that had driven Selden's infantrymen and Quint's Rangers from their advanced position. Quint's last orders were to remain as battery support until required elsewhere. Two sections, four guns had participated with Hall's two twenty-four–pounder howitzers firing from the west bank in support of the Federal right flank. Hall had been ordered to cross the river and station his battery with the right flank. During the movement one of his guns broke its trail and was useless. McRae had been joined by the remaining gun section of his battery before he crossed the river to join the left flank. Now he had six bronze smoothbores, consisting of three six-pounders capable of firing solid shot, spherical case shot and canister, two twelve-pounder field howitzers and one twelve-pounder mountain howitzer on a field carriage. The howitzers could not fire solid shot. They fired shell, canister, and spherical case shot. Shot was used against infantry, and shells and spherical case shot against cavalry, while shot and shell were used in firing into flanks and against artillery. Shell was not as accurate as solid shot but had a greater effect on cavalry because of its aerial dispersion, breaking into twelve or fifteen pieces that could ricochet three or four times. A canister shot was a tin cylinder with iron heads filled with musket-ball-sized projectiles packed in sawdust. The balls were usually of cast iron, except in the case of the mountain howitzer, which used leaden musket balls. It took two seconds to reach five hundred yards. If it was fired at too short a distance, the balls would not have time to spread out for maximum effect. If fired too far they diverged too much. The maximum effective range was between four hundred and four hundred and fifty yards. At short range on hard dry ground, canister shot was fired with the gun depressed, allowing the balls to ricochet from the ground. All ammunition being used by McRae's battery was fixed, with the charge attached to the projectile for single loading for greater rapidity in serving and firing.

The battery thundered, spitting out flame and thick wreathing smoke. Solid shot plowed up earth in front of and next to the enemy gun section. Shells burst just overhead with lightninglike flashes. Quint put the glasses on the Confederate guns. Men were thrown this way and that from the heavy firing. Soon the enemy guns discontinued firing and were withdrawn behind the sand ridge. McRae ordered cease-fire. The smoke rapidly drifted off. The battlefield was comparatively quiet again.

Quint and Luke walked over to the left flank of Selden's battalion where the Coloradoans were posted. Captain Dodd turned to Quint. "It's quiet, Kershaw," he said. "It's getting *too* damned quiet. What do you think the Rebels are doing behind that sand ridge now?"

Quint shook his head. "I don't think they're planning to leave," he replied dryly.

"There's Colonel Canby," Luke said. "Just got here from Fort Craig with reinforcements. Mebbe we'll see more action now."

Dodd laughed. "I doubt it," he said dryly.

Quint and Luke started to walk back toward the battery. They noticed some of the Regulars of the Fifth Infantry pointing excitedly toward the far right flank of the Texans.

"Lancers!" a lieutenant shouted. "They're charging the Coloradoans!"

"Come on!" Quint shouted to Luke.

The lancers had topped the sand ridge and were pounding downslope toward the far left flank of the Federal lines. There were less than half a hundred of them, splendidly mounted, riding at top speed with leveled lances from which depended little fluttering red pennants. There was no question about the objective of the Texas boys from Falls County—it was the Colorado boys from Canon City.

"Form square!" Captain Dodd shouted. "Load with buck-and-ball!"

The lancers hammered closer, shouting in high-pitched voices. Firing on other parts of the field slackened and died as the combatants watched the drama being played out. The tattoo of the hoofs on the hard ground was louder. The bronzed, set faces of the Texans could easily be seen.

"Fire!" roared Captain Dodd.

The company's smoothbore muskets blasted flame and smoke. Buck-and-ball, a .69-caliber one-ounce ball and three buckshot, smashed into the leading lancers. Horses went down thrashing. Troopers were flung from their mounts' backs to the hard ground. The rest of the company galloped on through the smoke, a blood-tingling example of desperate courage against great odds and superior arms.

"Load!" Dodd commanded calmly. "Fire!" There was a pause. "Fire at will!"

Cartridge bases were ripped open with the teeth. Charges poured into smoking muzzles. Ball and paper patch followed. Ramrods rattled in barrels. Percussion caps were pressed on nipples. Muskets were raised and fired through the wreathing smoke at point-blank range. All this was done faster than it could be told. Some of the few lancers who made it to the front rank of the Coloradoans were transfixed with bayonets and pitchforked from their saddles. The lancer captain was down with a severe wound. A lieutenant staggered back through the smoke, bleeding from multiple wounds. A very few lancers were left unhurt. The company had been shattered—a gallant, furious, and futile charge had been more than a forlorn hope; it had been a disaster. The Pike's Peakers had held the flank.

Quint lowered his rifle and opened the smoking breech. He reloaded without looking at what he was doing. His eyes were on the bloody scene of carnage in front of the Coloradoans. He looked away. Luke shot a badly wounded horse. "This kind of fightin' sure takes the shine outta war," he said grimly.

"What shine?" Quint asked.

They walked slowly back to the battery.

One of those strange, inexplicable lulls came over Valverde

battlefield. The Texans were very quiet, hidden from view by the great natural rampart of the sand ridge west of the old channel, a position of great natural strength stretching for over fifteen hundred yards in a great arc with the concave side toward the Federal position. The Federal infantry and cavalry ate their rations and refilled their ammunition pouches and canteens. The artillerymen refilled their limbers. Stretcher bearers picked up the wounded, those closest to their respective positions. Those farther out were left to their moaning and crying out. The dead lay where they fell, like bloody bundles of rags, slowly stiffening, staring with eyes that could not see; they were thickest where the lancer charge had been shattered. The living watched the sand ridge with slitted eyes, wondering what was going on behind it. The afternoon dragged on. The wind blasted, blowing dust and sand, thrashing the tree branches, snapping the flags and guidons.

Quint attended an officers' meeting held by Colonels Canby and Roberts. Canby was calm and in control of himself and the situation. His usual unlighted cigar was in his mouth. He studied the terrain through his field glasses, speaking out of the side of his mouth around the cigar: "They're in too strong a position for a frontal assault, gentlemen. We'll keep McRae's battery strongly supported by Selden's Regulars and the Coloradoans. Hall will stay on the right flank, supported by Duncan's command. I plan to advance the right and center, using the left flank as a pivot to sweep the enemy northerly like a great closing door and enfilading the enemy position behind the sand ridge. Lieutenant D'Amours, extend my compliments to Colonel Carson and have him cross the river to our center. Captain Plympton's battalion of the Seventh will support McRae. Captain Nicodemus, my compliments to Colonel Pino and have him bring his Second New Mexico across the river to take up position as reserve for the left flank and additional support for McRae's battery." Canby lowered the glasses. "Everything clearly understood, gentlemen? Good! To your posts! Good luck to you all!"

Major Donaldson, Canby's chief aide, beckoned to Quint. "How many men have you in your company, Kershaw?"

"Fourteen, counting myself, Major."

"Casualties?"

"Two killed. One missing. Two wounded."

"Where are the rest of them?" Donaldson looked closely at

Quint. "You've got a lot of greasers in your company, haven't you? Have they skedaddled?"

Quint shook his head. "Not my boys, Major. Two of them were out skirmishing with me. One was killed, the other missing. Some of the others were detached back at Fort Craig for duty there. I haven't seen them since."

The officer nodded. "Sorry, Kershaw. The colonel and I haven't much faith in the native New Mexicans. Your company, of course, is quite different. What were your last orders?"

"To act as support for McRae until further orders."

"We can use some of them as sharpshooters with Carson. He specifically asked for you and a Sergeant Connors. Supposing you split up your company, half with McRae, the other half with Carson."

Quint nodded. "I'll have my son take the McRae detail."

"Sorry about your casualties, Kershaw."

Quint shrugged. "Part of the game, Major. Part of the game."

Kit Carson formed his regiment on the right of center, deployed them as skirmishers, and advanced toward the sandhills four hundred yards away. Confederate infantry fell back slowly before the advance. Suddenly a squad of their cavalry appeared and charged diagonally across Carson's front, trying for Hall's single twenty-four–pounder hammering away at the left flank of the enemy. There were at least 250 cavalrymen charging hell for leather. The throbbing beat of the hoofs on the hard ground carried through the First New Mexico as they halted on command. The fluttering guidons and a flag carried by the Confederates identified them as the Fourth Texas. Carson calmly gave his orders to volley fire at his command. The orders were repeated in staccato fashion by the company commanders.

"That's Major Raguet leadin' the charge," Luke said.

The charge reached eighty yards from the right of the First New Mexico. "Fire!" roared Carson. The volley crashed out. "Load! Fire at will!" The orders rang out. A continuous sheet of flame spat out from the volunteers' line. Horses went down, reared, or were flung sideways. No cavalry could stand such concentrated fire. The Texans broke and fell back in full retreat, leaving at least one out of every five horses and troopers lying on the field. Hall dropped a shell right in their midst, scattering horses and men like chaff before a strong wind. The orderly retreat became a panicky stampede.

The sun was slanting low down when the Federal right wing began its great swinging movement with the axis on the left of center. The far right flank crossed the old channel and swept along the base of the mesa, driving the Texans precipitately in disorganized retreat.

Quint had just reached the edge of a *bosque* and was reloading when a Texan stepped from behind a tree, raising his double-barreled shotgun and aiming it at him. Juan Trujillo was just next to Quint. He ran forward, clubbing his rifle. The Texan whirled and fired one barrel point-blank into Juan, then half turned as the rifle struck him heavily on the shoulder and fired at Quint. One of the shots just scraped Quint's right temple. Luke fired from behind Quint and dropped the Texan. Blood flowed from Quint's superficial wound.

"Yuh hit bad, Big Red?" Luke said.

Quint shook his head. "Not too bad, Luke. Hardly felt it."

"Go on back and get it taken care of."

"There's still fighting to be done."

"We can take care of it, Big Red!" Kit Carson shouted as he rode past. "Here, take my *caballo*! I make too big a target on it. Bring it back when yuh get patched up." He grinned. "I'll need it later, when we run these secesh back onto the Jornado!"

Quint bound his bandanna about his head, mounted the big gray, and galloped back toward one of the ambulances he could see not far from the river behind the left flank. He was halfway there when he heard a hoarse yelling rising from the sand ridge. A charging line of hundreds of Texans had emerged from behind the ridge seven hundred yards from the Federal left flank and came pouring down the slope running like great lean hunting hounds, their flags and guidons slanted forward. They yelled like demons straight out of hell's own smoky doors. Four pieces of their artillery fired over their heads into the Federal ranks supporting McRae's battery.

Plympton's infantry battalion was taken up by the heated fighting on the center and right. There was a wide gap between his left flank and the right flank of the First Cavalry companies to the right of McRae's battery. The gunners were loading and firing double-shotted canister like automatons. The canister was thrust into the hot smoking muzzles and rammed home. The gunner on each gun thrust a priming wire through the vent into the cartridge. A friction primer was inserted in the vent. The firing lanyard hook was inserted into the primer ring. The lanyard was jerked, the friction spark firing the charge. The gun or howitzer blasted flame and smoke, leaping back in recoil. The gunner pressed his leather thumbstall over the vent to prevent an inrush of air. The piece was rolled back into position in time to have the sponge withdrawn from the powder-blackened water in a bucket and thrust into the hot smoking muzzle to douse any lingering sparks that might predetonate a new charge.

The commands cracked out over and over again: *"Load! Ram! Ready! Fire! Thumb the vent! Sponge! Load! Ram! Ready! Fire!"* The guns were being served and fired at the rate of two to three shots per minute, a rhythm only used when firing at objects not difficult to hit, in this case about 750 massed ferocious Texans howling to drink blood out of a boot. The Texans leaned forward against the leaden canister as though running into a strong wind, leaving sprawled bodies behind them or leaping high over the fallen in front of them, never slacking their long-legged strides carrying them down the sloping plain at great speed.

"Move up the Second!" one of Canby's aides shouted to Colonel Pino of the Second New Mexico. *"Fill in that gap, for God's sake!"*

Some of the Second New Mexico had remained on the west bank of the river near the second upstream ford. Their officers were trying to get them to cross the river to take up their designated position. Those that had already crossed the river, hardly more than two companies, were hesitant and fearful as they saw the hated and feared Tejanos bounding toward the Federal lines. The battlefield was a bedlam of roaring cannon, musketry firing, shouting men, and whinnying horses. Smoke swirled over the field and the combatants.

Quint dismounted beside the ambulance and drew his pair of Navy Colts. He checked the loads and caps while a medical attendant quickly cleansed and bandaged the scalp wound.

The Texans were battle-wise enough to throw themselves down on the ground and fire their small arms when they saw the flashes of McRae's guns, then leap to their feet after the charges had passed over, reloading on the run. These tactics kept casualties to a minimum while deceiving the Federals into thinking they were doing far more damage with their guns than they actually were. Meanwhile the Confederate guns hammered away, causing the infantry supports of McRae's battery to keep their heads down in the protected positions they had taken behind the battery. Thus many of them were unable to see the swiftly approaching danger, and even when warned, exhorted, and threatened to advance in order to defend the battery, they flatly refused.

Captain Lord's small cavalry reserve came galloping up from the right, intending to charge the Texans, but came under the fire of both friends and enemy alike and turned away to the left and rear to avoid the fire.

"You'd better go to the rear, Captain," the medical attendant suggested.

Quint shook his head and began to walk toward the smoke-shrouded battery, a cocked Colt in each hand.

Many of the Regulars and the Coloradoans closed in on the nearest enemies. For a few moments they held the assault and even drove it back in places.

The main Confederate storming party deployed in an advancing crescent formation nearly a half-mile in length. They fired their double-barreled shotguns, muskets, and revolvers as they came on. Those on the right took advantage of a clump of cottonwoods, moving cautiously from tree to tree, picking off the cannoneers. One by one the guns were stilled.

The yelling Texans closed in on the undefended battery. Colonel Shelby Calhoun was in the lead, thrusting forward the glittering sword carried by his grandfather in the War of 1812. Frank Kershaw was close behind him, carrying a big-bored double-barreled shotgun. Alec Calhoun stood behind the double-shotted mountain howitzer. His hat was gone. His face was powder-blackened. He stared at the man he thought was his father.

"Surrender those guns!" Shelby shouted.

Quint was running now. He could see Dave reloading his pistol. The gunners were firing their pistols and clubbing with their rammers in savage, bloody, hand-to-hand fighting.

"Surrender!" Shelby repeated. He stretched forth his left hand to place it possessively on the howitzer barrel.

"God forgive me! Get out of the way, Colonel!" Alec shouted.

He jerked the lanyard. Just as he did so, Frank shoved Shelby to one side. The blast hurled Shelby to the ground, shredding his left arm to bloody rags. The Texans behind him were driven back and blasted, broken and bleeding, to the ground. Alec snatched up a fresh charge and ran to the howitzer muzzle. A bullet hit his left shoulder and spun him about. He dropped the canister and went down under the trampling feet of the yelling, cursing hand-to-hand combatants struggling for the precious guns.

Frank Kershaw placed his left hand on the hot barrel of the howitzer. "It's ours, goddamnit! It's ours!" he yelled excitedly.

Dave Kershaw came through the smoke. His pistols were empty. He threw them into the faces of a pair of Texans and snatched up a rammer, laying it about him like a berserker.

The two companies of the Second New Mexico who had crossed the river to support the guns had broken and fled, carrying many of the Regulars with them. The battery was completely surrounded. Captain McRae was dead beside the guns he had refused to abandon. Lieutenant Mishler had been killed instantly.

Frank was still yelling insanely, flourishing his double-barreled shotgun, when he saw a grim-faced Dave come through the smoke with upraised rammer. "Surrender, you sonofabitch!" Frank yelled.

A trooper knocked the rammer from Dave's hands. "Do as he says, greaser!" he cried.

Dave looked about. The fight was lost. He shrugged and raised his hands. Frank threw his shotgun up to his shoulder, cocked both hammers, and aimed point-blank at Dave's face. For an instant the two brothers, now deadly enemies, stared at each other. Dave sensed sudden death. He turned sideways and held his left hand across his face just as Frank's shotgun blasted flame and smoke. The charge partly struck Dave's face, his left forearm and hand, and raked his shoulder. He staggered sideways and went down on one knee, blood pouring from his face and shattered hand and forearm.

Frank grinned as he swung the shotgun to aim at Dave again.

Quint came through the swirling smoke. He saw no one but Frank. For long seconds father and son stared at each other. Frank hesitated. Quint strode forward and swung one of his long-barreled Colts, slashing it across Frank's contorted face. Frank staggered back. He managed to raise his shotgun again.

"He's our prisoner, yuh loco bastahd!" a Texan sergeant yelled at Frank.

"Shoot!" Quint said grimly. "Shoot! Ye won't kill me, Frank. But I'll track ye down wherever ye go. I'll find ye, mind. *I'll find ye and kill ye!*" The clipped Scots burr had returned to him.

The battery was taken. Triumphant yelling Texans were turning the guns toward the river, preparing to open fire on the panicky Federals streaming across to the west bank. Already the Texans were shooting rifles, shotguns, and pistols at the retreating soldiers struggling through the armpit-deep water.

Quint turned from Frank. He knelt beside Dave. He swiftly made a tourniquet to stop the flow of blood from the shattered forearm. He stuffed his bandanna inside Dave's jacket to staunch the flow of blood from the shoulder wound. He did not look up as he worked, but he knew there was a curious ring of Texans about him. At last he stood up, then helped Dave to his feet, placed his right arm about his shoulders, and turned to walk him toward the river.

"Yuh ain't goin' nowheres, greaser," a big Texan said. He grinned as he raised his pistol.

"Shut yore mouth, Clint Beasely!" a young trooper cried. "Let him go! He saved my life at Ojo del Muerto and buried my brother Clay and my squad mates after the 'Paches killed 'em! Ain't no one goin' to harm thet man!"

Quint turned and half smiled. "Hello, George Sutherland," he said quietly. "Can we go now?"

A sergeant came forward. "Go ahead, suh. After what you done here, we ain't got the heart to keep yuh."

The guns of McRae's battery roared into action again, firing across the river and into it, sending up spouts of water and foam or bursting just overhead with whiplike cracks, showering the retreating Federals with whizzing fragments. The red of blood tinted the brown of the silt carried by the swift current.

Quint helped Dave into a loaded ambulance, which instantly headed for the river. The Federals were in full retreat from the battlefield, the infantry marching in good order down to the fords, covered by the cavalry. Hall's twenty-four–pounder was

aken back across the river. The shouting of the victorious
Texans could be heard in the intervals of the cannonading.

Luke brought up a horse for Quint. "Yuh left your Sharps at
the ambulance," he said as he handed it to Quint. "We'd best
get back over the river, Big Red. Won't be anybody but Texans,
the wounded, dying, and dead around here in a little while."

They crossed the river at the lower ford and drew rein on the
west bank. Thinning smoke swirled above the battlefield. What
looked like bundles of rags at a distance were the wounded and
the bodies of the many dead. They turned away and rode toward
Fort Craig.

Dave Kershaw was lying in the small officers' ward of the
post hospital. It was the day after his surgery. He vaguely
remembered seeing his father and Luke the evening before. His
left hand was gone, so badly shattered there had been no hope of
saving it. His left shoulder was bandaged, and another bandage
was aslant across his left eye. The sight in it wasn't completely
gone as yet, but it was only a matter of time before it would be.
The surgeon had told him that morning the war was over for
him.

Quint, Luke, and Alec came into the room. They were dressed
for the field and ready to ride. A medical orderly had told Dave
that Colonel Canby had ordered Regular Army captains Howland
and Lord, each with fifty men, to march from Fort Craig to the
northern district to observe enemy movements and to bolster the
northern defenses. Captain Kershaw and Sergeant Luke Connors
were to accompany them as scouts, with a few of Kershaw's
Rangers. Lieutenant Alexander Calhoun, First Cavalry, was to
be second-in-command of Captain Howland's detachment. He
had just been discharged from the hospital that morning. They
had removed a minie ball from the back of Lieutenant Calhoun's
left shoulder. The ball had struck him while he was defending
his guns at Valverde. The rifle had been fired at such close range
that the muzzle blast had set fire to his uniform and the ball had
almost exited through his back. It had been a simple matter, or
so the orderly claimed, to merely cut out the ball through the
back rather than probe for it through the front.

Quint felt Dave's forehead. "How does it go, Davie lad?" he
asked cheerfully. His joviality was forced.

Dave nodded. "I'll live," he said quietly. He looked down at the bandaged stump of his left arm. He looked up. "You're about to ride," he added. "I heard about it. How many of the company are going with you?"

"Just Anselmo," Quint replied quietly.

Dave was puzzled. "But what about the rest?"

Luke shook his head. "There's not that many left, Davie."

"How many?" Dave asked after a time.

Quint rolled a cigarette and placed it between Dave's lips. He lighted it. "We got hit damned hard, Dave. Frank Scott, Pedro Sanchez, Juan Trujillo, and Joshua killed. Jim Hunt, Aurelio Díaz, Marcos Perez, and you wounded. It's said Pablo Baca was drowned crossing the river before the battle and his brother Ignacio left without orders to find his body. He hasn't been seen since. Diego Chacón, Mick Casey, and Black Moccasin are missing. No trace was ever found of them after the battle. They may still be alive, as prisoners."

"Black Moccasin?" Dave asked incredulously. "I can't believe it!"

Luke looked at Quint. Quint shrugged. "He vanished right after Joshua was killed."

Luke nodded. "Someone heard him say he was tired fightin' white man's battles. Might be he's just mournin' Joshua. He might show up one of these days." There was no conviction in his tone.

"They say you were hit too, Quint," Dave said.

Quint touched the plaster strip on his right temple. "A creasing is all, Davie. Could have been worse."

"Yeh, another half-inch and you would have been one of the killed." Dave held a hand across his right eye. "My God," he murmured. "That's at least half the company gone. What happens to the rest of us while you're up north?"

"I've promoted Otto Schmidt to orderly sergeant, Davie," Quint replied. "Colonel Canby said you could remain on duty until the campaign is over. As soon as you're fit, you can take command and see if you can recruit to full strength again."

Dave nodded. "What's the situation at present?"

"Sibley lost most of his supplies when we destroyed his supply wagons and ran off his beef herd, horses, and mules. He can't retreat to Mesilla for more. We're in the way. They broke amp on the twenty-fourth and started north up the valley. They aptured Socorro and established a hospital there. From what we ear they have only five days' rations left, so they'll be forced to march north to Albuquerque. Canby has sent orders for the ommanding officer there to remove all the supplies he can and hen torch the rest.''

"You mean to say we're not going after them?'' Dave lemanded.

Quint shrugged. "Colonel Canby felt the Rebels might lay siege to Fort Craig. There aren't enough supplies here at present, and not much chance of getting more, to withstand a siege. He had to reduce the garrison. He ordered most of the militia and some of the volunteers away, as being the least valuable. That leaves him with about eleven hundred Regulars plus several regiments of volunteers, Carson's First New Mexico for one, and Dodd's Independent Colorado Company as well. His hope is to organize a picked force of partisans from the volunteers to harass the Texans with surprise flank attacks.

"Canby held a council of war after the battle. He saw three possible courses of action: He could attack the Confederates again, committing major Federal forces to battle. He could abandon Fort Craig, circumvent the Confederates, and march rapidly northward to get above them and impede them, as well as uniting with our forces up north. He could retain Fort Craig while waiting for the reinforcements he had requested. Once here he could launch concerted operations. If successful, that would force the Confederates to retreat down the Rio Grande. Thus Fort Craig would stand in the way if they were forced to retreat from the north. The northward movement of the enemy forestalled the first choice. Canby did not want to abandon Fort Craig, leaving behind his sick and wounded as well as abandoning an important strategic point. That left the third choice, to remain here. That would enable us to cut off any Confederate retreat, to prevent them from receiving any reinforcements and supplies from the south, and maybe to take offensive action using Fort Craig as a base. That's the situation at present, Davie lad.''

Luke grinned. "Old Sibley won't find the going easy, Davie. His Fourth Regiment lost so many horses that they were reduced to infantry, turning over what horses they had left to build up one of the mounted regiments. I sure wouldn't have wanted to issue *that* order to a bunch of Texans. Marching *afoot*! My God!"

"The weather has turned bitter cold. There isn't much forage up north and very little fuel. The native New Mexicans hate them and will do everything they can to impede them," Alec added.

"We'd best get on our way," Quint said at last.

They all shook Dave's hand. Alec and Luke wisely left Quint alone with Dave. "What happened to Frank?" Dave asked quietly.

"He was alive the last time I saw him."

"Could you have killed him?"

"If I had, I would have been instantly shot down."

Dave studied his father. "You wouldn't have done it in any case."

Quint shook his head. "No," he admitted.

"The difficulty was between him and me. He really loved you, Quint."

What could one say?

Quint gripped Dave's hand again and walked to the door. He turned. "Let's not waste too much time in that bed, Lieutenant. Remember, there's a war still to be fought."

Dave nodded. "I'll remember." He looked down at his stump.

"Vaya," Quint said.

Dave looked up. "Has it ever occurred to you how much Alec Calhoun resembles you?" he asked suddenly.

So he too either knew, or at least suspected, the relationship between Quint and Alec.

"Father?" Dave asked.

"It has, son, it has," Quint said. *"Vaya,"* he repeated.

"Vaya," Dave echoed.

The door closed behind Quint.

It wasn't until Quint was gone half an hour that Dave suddenly realized he wasn't sure at all just what Quint had meant.

★ TWENTY-TWO ★

MARCH 1862: APACHE CANYON

Kozlowski's Ranch, a hostelry on the Santa Fe Trail not far from Pecos Ruins, was thirty-five miles from Bernal Springs and about twenty-seven miles from Santa Fe. It was an hour before midnight when Quint, Luke, and Anselmo reached the vicinity of the ranch. There was still some faint moonlight. The ranch buildings were dark.

Quint pointed to the right for Luke and to the left for Anselmo. They vanished into the deep shadows of the trees. Quint led the horses to one side of the road. A dog barked and then another. Quint moved noiselessly along the road. A shadowy figure appeared out of the brush and trees at the right side of the road. It was Luke. He made the sign for all clear. A few moments later Anselmo showed up. The dogs were making a racket.

"No signs of the secesh," Luke said.

Anselmo nodded. "I went past the ranch. Road is empty, *patrón*."

They led the horses toward the main house. A light showed in one of the barred windows. A moment later light appeared at the bottom and edges of the front door.

Quint approached the door and wisely stood to one side. He whistled sharply. "Andy?" he called. "It's Quint Kershaw!"

The door opened a fraction. "Step out into the light," Andrew Kozlowski ordered. "I got double-barreled shotgun here, mister, loaded wit buck-and-ball!" He opened the door, allowing a shaft of yellowish light to fall on the bare ground.

"Goddamnit, Andy!" Quint said. "Can't you recognize my

★ 197 ★

accent? I sure as hell can recognize yours!'' He walked into the rectangle of light and held up his hands.

"Goddamnit!'' Andy cried. "Sure as hell! What you doin' here, Big Red?'' He stared. "In uniform too! You ain't wit them Rebels, then? Or you in a U.S. uniform as disguise?''

"You know better than that,'' Quint replied. "We're scouting for Major Chivington and the advance of Colonel Slough's force from Fort Union. We've been marching all day from Bernal Springs. Have you seen any Rebels around here?''

The Pole had been a Regular Army soldier in the dragoons. He nodded. "I heard rumor from travelers heading east that there were some Rebel pickets at Pigeon's Ranch. I sent a couple of my boys to take a look. They seen them, all right. I was figurin' on sending a message to Fort Union about it. You got here just in time.''

"We've got orders to camp here tonight, Andy, and stay here all tomorrow.''

Andy nodded. "Welcome. You headin' for Santa Fe?''

"That was our plan, but these pickets at Pigeon's might be the advance for a body of Rebels.'' Quint turned to Anselmo. "Go back and tell Major Chivington it's all right to advance here. Tell him there are Rebel pickets at Pigeon's Ranch.''

The force encamped on a small cedar-covered rise near the spring. The officers gathered in the ranch house for coffee and a council of war.

Chivington paced restlessly back and forth. "As you all know, my orders were to advance to Kozlowski's, remain here all day tomorrow, then continue on toward Santa Fe and attack and overwhelm the small garrison that is said to be there. The presence of these enemy pickets at Pigeon's Ranch changes the picture.''

"There are only a few of them, Major,'' protested Captain Cook, commander of F Company, the mounted unit of the First Colorado. "It might not mean anything.''

The major shook his head. "Or it might mean much.''

Captain Walker, commander of the Third Cavalry unit, nodded. "Who knows how many more of them are in the pass? The Rebels might have been greatly reinforced since our last report about them. I suggest we advance through the pass and feel them out.''

Chivington looked at Quint. "Captain Kershaw, what's your opinion? You know this area better than most of us."

"I'd suggest sending ahead a picked party of, say, twenty mounted men under one of your officers first thing in the morning and before daylight."

"That was my thought too, Kershaw. I'll designate Lieutenant Nelson of F Company to that duty. He can select his own men. I'd like to have you and your scouts go along."

Quint grinned. "You're good at reading minds, Major."

Chivington waved a ham of a hand. "That used to be my profession when wearing the cloth, Captain." He grinned back.

The scouting party left Kowzlowski's before daylight. It was pitch black. No talking was allowed. They rode the five miles to Pigeon's Ranch and halted a quarter of a mile from it. Quint, Luke, and Anselmo moved ahead on foot.

Pigeon's Ranch was the largest hostelry on the Santa Fe Trail between Las Vegas and the capital. It was operated by immensely popular Alexander Valle, a Franco-American nicknamed Pigeon because of his peculiar style of dancing, cutting pigeon wings, and strutting with great dignity through the measures. He was well known as a genial and obliging host. The ranch was at the eastern end of Glorieta Pass in a narrow defile. The buildings, Santa Fe Trail, and an arroyo took up practically all the space in the canyon at that point.

Quint came out of the main house, shaking his head. "They've been gone since yesterday afternoon," he said.

Lieutenant Nelson shrugged. "I had a feeling they'd be gone, Kershaw. Well, we've done our job. Best to get back to Kozlowski's."

The dawn light was deceptive as they rode back toward Kozlowski's Ranch. The air was chilly. The men were quiet. The only sounds were the thudding of the hoofs on the hard road, the creaking of saddle leather, and occasional blowing of a horse. Anselmo was riding ahead as point. He suddenly turned his horse on the forehand and came quickly back.

"What is it?" Nelson asked.

"Four mounted men, sir. I don't think they're ours."

"Are you sure?"

Anselmo nodded.

Nelson turned. "Cock your pistols," he said to the first four.

Quint took one side of the road and Luke the other. Nelson rode on unconcernedly, but he held a cocked Navy Colt across his thighs.

One of the four shadowy figures riding through the dimness called out as they neared the column. They were within fifty feet.

"Now!" Quint said. He rode forward quickly. Luke did the same.

"For Christ's sake! These aren't our boys!" one of the four horsemen shouted.

Quint grinned as he raised his cocked Colt and aimed it at the face of the leading rider. "Too late," he said quietly. There was nothing they could do. There had been no chance to resist.

Quint disarmed one of the Texans. He looked at him closely. "Don't I know you?" he asked. "By God! You're Lieutenant McIntyre! You were on Colonel Canby's staff before Valverde!"

McIntyre looked quickly away. "You're mistaken," he insisted.

Quint shrugged. "Well, you can explain that to your court-martial when you reach Fort Union, mister. The war is over for you."

Later Major Chivington heard Nelson's report and then smashed a big fist into the palm of his other hand. "By Jehovah! I'm going to take the bull by the horns and go on! If the enemy are there, I'm going to find them!"

The command moved out promptly at eight A.M. with the scouts ahead and the infantry leading the advance toward Pigeon's Ranch and Glorieta Pass.

Glorieta Pass was at seventy-five hundred feet elevation. It was an area of lofty mountains, red adobe earth, vivid green cedars, and pines. The atmosphere was crystalline, the sky incredibly blue with marvelous white clouds. When the sun shone it was brilliant. The pass itself was a narrow transverse opening through rugged heights. The extremities were very narrow, the middle nearly a quarter of a mile wide. Both flanks of the pass were shut in by irregular crests one to two thousand feet high. The abrupt sides were thinly covered with cedar bushes, stunted oaks, and pines. These growths were thicker on the lower elevations just above the floor of the pass. There were large cottonwoods and some yellow pine along the arroyos. At the farthest end of the pass a stream had worn a deep, narrow, and tortuous channel through solid rock that some called Apache Canyon. Glorieta Pass is where the Santa Fe Trail wound through the southern extremity of the Sangre de Cristo Mountains. The western portion, or Apache Canyon, was around seven miles in length, narrow at both ends, and about a quarter of a mile wide in the middle.

Beyond Pigeon's Ranch, a local glacier flowing from Glorieta Mountain had deposited in eons past a series of terminal moraines, two of which were low bluffs merging to the south into bold and rocky elevations, lying nearly parallel to each other and not far apart. The northern ends of these had been broken through or washed away by a large and rapid stream caused by the melting of the immense deposit of ice in the pass and on the mountainside, leaving a narrow and deep depression that in time had borne the Santa Fe Trail.

Glorieta Pass had nothing to do with glory. The word could mean variously an arbor, bower, a shelter, or even a roadway turnaround. Legend had it that when Don Juan de Onate brought his colonists into New Mexico from Mexico in 1592 they brought with them a statue of *La Conquistadora*, Our Lady of Conquests, the famed Virgin of Guadalupe, patroness saint of Western Hemisphere Catholics. Each evening before vespers the servants of Our Lady made her a *glorieta*, a tiny bower or shrine, from native flowers and vegetation to protect her from the chill of the night. There was no record she had ever slept in Glorieta Pass, but *La Conquistadora* slept in many other *glorieta* all over the Southwest.

It was two o'clock by the time the advance reached the summit of the divide. The scouts moved cautiously down the slope toward a narrow gulch where the trail made a short turn. They dismounted and proceeded on foot. It was very quiet.

Anselmo was ahead. He stopped short near the turn and faded into the brush signaling back to halt the scouts. He came back swiftly. "Texans ahead," he whispered.

"How many?" Nelson asked.

"Twenty, mebbe more. They're in the trees and brush."

"Do you think you were seen?"

Anselmo looked at the officer as though he had dealt him a mortal insult.

Nelson signaled on the advance scouts. They moved quietly

down the road. The low murmuring of voices came to them. Nelson sent a squad to the right, one to the left, then led the rest of the men along the road. It was all over in a few minutes. The Texan advance picket had been completely surprised, netting the Coloradoans two lieutenants and thirty enlisted men. Not a shot had been fired. The main body of the enemy, units of the Second and Fifth Texas with a two-gun section of artillery, had advanced from Santa Fe. "Hellsfire, Major," one of the Texan officers said to Chivington, "we were only looking for better forage. Not much around Santa Fe." He smiled. "Our boys are led by a real fightin' man—Major Charley Pyron, Second Texas. If you're lookin' for a fight, you've come to the right place. You-all'll get your asses whupped."

"If you're an example of those fighting men you're blowing about, letting yourselves get surprised as you did, we haven't got much to worry about! Get to the rear, you damned Rebels!" Chivington roared.

Nelson spoke out of the side of his mouth to Quint, "I wish I felt as sure about that as the major does."

The cavalry moved forward to enter Apache Canyon. The infantry column closed up. They threw aside their knapsacks, overcoats, and other impedimenta, then double-timed after the cavalry.

Quint, Luke, and Anselmo galloped up beside Captain Cook, the commander of F Company. "Can we ride with you, Cook?" Quint asked. "Not much use for scouts right now."

"Glad to have you, Kershaw!" Cook cried.

The Texans were in full view five hundred yards ahead, about three hundred of them supported by two mountain howitzers emplaced one on each side of the road. Both howitzers plumed flame and smoke the instant the gunners saw the Federal cavalry advance. The thundering reports rolled along the mountainsides. Both shells cracked spitefully fifty yards ahead of the Coloradoans.

Chivington deployed two companies of the First Colorado and one of the Third Cavalry dismounted as skirmishers on the steep slopes to the left, and one company of Coloradoans to the right. Their incessant firing as they moved along the mountain sides made it too hot for the gunners. The howitzers were limbered up, and the whole Texan force retreated about three-quarters of a mile west. The Federal skirmishers leaped from rock to rock, like mountain goats, following the enemy. The Texans had enough of the sleet of rifle balls coming down on them. They retreated again for about a mile and three-quarters, crossed a log bridge over a deep and narrow arroyo, then took up a position along a ridge almost at the western end of the canyon. Again the Coloradoans advanced along the mountainsides, the company on the right now joined by a dismounted company of the Third Cavalry. The Texans deployed their dismounted companies on each side of the canyon to support their guns.

Major Chivington galloped up to Captain Cook. "Cook! As soon as they give way again, charge across that bridge and give them hell! I want those guns!"

Cook nodded. He turned to his command. "Sabers and pistols, boys, and don't let a damned thing stop you!"

Captain Downing's Company D was well beyond the left flank of the Texans, firing their Springfield rifles down from the heights. The Texans were badly shaken. This wasn't at all like Valverde. Who in the hell were these fighting madmen they had run into?

"All right, Cook!" Chivington shouted. "Go on in! We'll keep up the fire!"

Cook mounted and drew his saber. "Mount! Form fours! Trot!" The company moved forward at a steady trot. Pistols were drawn and cocked. "Gallop!" was the shouted command. The steady beating of the horses' hoofs on the hard road set up an insistent counterrhythm to the crackling rifle fire and the thudding detonations of the enemy howitzers. Smoking shells whined and split with lightninglike flashes, spewing burning-hot fragments. The ridge where the guns were stationed was a solid line of cracking rifles and muzzles spitting fire. Bullets whistled past the swiftly moving cavalry. "Charge!" Cook shouted. Company F chorused a hair-raising yell as they headed for the log bridge.

"Jesus Christ!" a sergeant yelled. "They've taken away the bridge!"

Company F turned their horses to one side or the other as though by command, so as to gain more running ground, then turned again and charged the bridge hell-for-leather and to the devil with the hindmost. They thundered toward the deep arroyo in fours, then leaped the arroyo, over one hundred cursing, shouting Coloradoans. Captain Cook was down with a ball and three buckshot in his thigh; a moment later another ball struck him in the foot. Only one rider missed the leap. His mount fell back on him to the bottom of the arroyo.

Then the Coloradoans were in among the fleeing Texans, Navy Colts spitting until they were emptied. Steel whined against steel as sabers were drawn. Back and forth the troopers charged among the Texans, laying about themselves with their bright blades like farmers scything wheat, the horses knocking men down to be trampled to death. The troopers were oblivious to the rifle fire pouring into their ranks from the ridge.

Quint emptied his Colts, swerved his horse to avoid a double-barreled shotgun being thrust at him, looked down into the black-bearded face of a yelling young Texan aiming at him and then turned away, sickened, as a bullet tore into the Rebel's contorted face. The Texan went down backward, tilting his shotgun upward. Reflex action tightened his hand and fingers on the triggers. The shotgun fired into the blue. Quint turned to glance back at his savior and looked into the grinning face of Luke.

"You owe me one, Big Red!" Luke shouted as he plunged back into the battle.

The Texans were smashed. They broke and fled from the onslaught over the ridge. The howitzers had been limbered up, and hauled away in the nick of time. The Coloradoans began rounding up prisoners. The rifle fire from Downing's Company D of the First Colorado and Company C of the Third Cavalry, now far beyond the left flank of the retreating Confederates, forced many of them to turn aside from the roadway at the bottom of the canyon to seek shelter in a branch canyon. Here they ran full into more Coloradoans, Wynkoop's Company A and Anthony's Company E, who gathered them into the fold.

The sun was setting. The shooting died away. The battlefield was littered with the dead, dying, and wounded. Some horses were down. Now and then a pistol shot finished one of them off as too far gone to save. Then that too was over. The agonized cries and screams of the mortally or severely wounded began to rise.

Lieutenant Marshall of Cook's Company F picked up a Rebel musket. He grinned at Quint and Luke. "Here's one they'll never have another chance to kill one of us with!'' he cried. He lifted it by the muzzle high overhead. Quint saw that the hammer was at full cock and the nipple capped. ''Wait, Marshall!'' he shouted. The musket fell with great force on a rock. It exploded and the charge caught Marshall full in the chest. He dropped instantly. Quint ran to him, took one look at the shattered chest and wide-open staring eyes, then shook his head as others ran up.

''What's the butcher's bill?'' Quint asked Lieutenant Nelson.

Nelson shrugged. ''Our losses are about five killed and fourteen wounded, no prisoners, and none missing. Haven't made an accurate count of the Rebels yet, but they've had about thirty killed, over forty wounded, and we've gathered in about seventy or so prisoners.'' He smiled. ''Not bad for a bunch of Pike's Peakers who were as green as spring grass when it comes to this sort of fighting.''

They gathered up their dead and wounded and withdrew back to Pigeon's Ranch in order to procure water for the men and horses. That night two companies arrived at the ranch with the news that Colonel Slough and the main column could be expected late on the twenty-seventh of March. At dawn of that day Major Chivington sent out burial details to the scene of battle and detachments of foragers to collect the corn and flour abandoned by the Confederates in their flight. Chivington's command breakfasted heartily on the Confederate provisions, then withdrew back to Kozlowski's Ranch, because the water at Pigeon's Ranch was insufficient for the command's needs.

★ TWENTY-THREE ★

It was just before dawn on the morning of March 28 when Quint, Luke, and Anselmo returned to Kozlowski's Ranch from scouting Johnson's Ranch, at the western end of Apache Canyon, to find that the main column under Colonel Slough had reached Kozlowski's at two o'clock that same morning. Major Chivington had briefed Colonel Slough thoroughly on the events at Apache Canyon.

Colonel Slough sat in conference at a table in the ranch kitchen. The room was crowded with other officers. He looked up as Quint entered the room. "Well?" he asked peremptorily.

"The Confederates have about a thousand men at Johnson's, Colonel," Quint replied. "Infantry and cavalry. Four pieces of artillery, about seventy wagons fully loaded. They have at least five hundred horses."

Slough hesitated. "Does it look like an advance, Captain?"

"Not at present, sir. They are deployed to command every approach to Johnson's Ranch, as though expecting an attack. We learned Major Pyron, who commanded against us at Apache Canyon, had sent a message to the Confederates at Galisteo to join him as soon as possible. Galisteo is about fifteen miles from here. They marched the night of March twenty-sixth and had a rough time, what with the bitter cold and getting their cannon and wagons over the mountain roads, which are literally not much more than trails. They reached Johnson's Ranch about three in the morning of the twenty-seventh. Their teams are worn out, and the men seem to be exhausted."

Slough nodded. "Well, we've had a tough march too, but we're not going to take up valuable time resting." He looked about at his officers. "We'll try to get the jump on them. Major Chivington, I want you to take your command up into the mountains to the south, then march westward until you find the rear of the Rebel forces. If the opportunity arises, you will attack them. I know I can depend on you for that." He allowed himself a faint little smile. "Meanwhile I plan to advance into Glorieta Pass with the rest of my command to feel out the enemy. Any questions?"

"I'll need a competent guide, Colonel," Chivington said.

Slough looked at Quint. "Do you know that terrain?"

Quint shook his head. "We scouted along the canyon, Colonel. I've never been up in those mountains."

Lieutenant Colonel Chávez of the First New Mexico Volunteers spoke: "I know that terrain, Colonel. I'll volunteer for the mission. Will you come too, Jim?"

James L. Collins was a volunteer aide-de-camp to Colonel Slough. Prior to the war he had been an Indian agent. He had fought at Valverde, then left Fort Craig to come north with the militia. He had been with the skirmishers at Apache Canyon and had been captured, then released after Cook's charge. He smiled. "A pleasure, Colonel Chávez, a pleasure indeed. Your force will have to be infantry, Major Chivington. You'll never be able to get a mounted unit over those trails. It's difficult enough for men afoot."

Chivington's command parted from the main column at nine-thirty in the morning. Regular Army Captain William H. Lewis led the first battalion, composed of Companies A and G of the Fifth U.S. Infantry, Company B of the First Colorado and Ford's Independent Company of Colorado Volunteers. Captain Edward W. Wynkoop commanded the second battalion of Companies A, E, and H of the First Colorado. The command total was 430 men.

The trail was rough and rocky. They followed it for about eight miles as the sun climbed toward its zenith. They kept on, pushing their way through the tangled brush, scrub cedars, and piñons. Colonel Chávez turned off the trail to the right, back toward the canyon.

It was almost half after one o'clock in the afternoon when Chávez stopped and turned to Major Chivington. "You can see Johnson's Ranch from that rise ahead, Major."

"Go ahead, Kershaw," Chivington ordered.

Quint, Luke, and Anselmo worked their way through the clinging brush, then went to ground just short of the crest. They edged forward and looked down from the thousand-foot elevation. There it was—Johnson's Ranch. The Santa Fe Trail cut across the open ground passing the ranch buildings. The wagons were lined up. An artillery piece was on one of the higher hills. About one hundred Texans were visible.

Anselmo placed a hand on Quint's forearm and pointed with his other hand to the right. "Pickets," he whispered.

They faded into the underbrush. Three Texans seemed absolutely unaware that over four hundred Federals were hidden not too far below the crest. One of them looked up into the muzzle of a Sharps rifle. He opened his mouth to yell, then saw the cold-looking eyes of the scar-faced man holding the rifle. He closed his mouth. He slanted his eyes to right and left. Two more Federals had risen up out of the brush with cocked rifles in their hands.

Major Chivington with Colonel Chávez and Captains Lewis and Wynkoop joined Quint and Luke on the crest. Quint handed the major his powerful field glasses and silently indicated the tempting view far below them.

"By God! We've got them now!" Captain Lewis exulted. "That must be their whole damned supply train and horse herd!"

Chivington grunted. "But where are the rest of them?"

Quint shrugged. "Only one possibility, Major. They've advanced about full strength through the pass toward Pigeon's Ranch. By now they should have met Colonel Slough's command."

Chivington was doubtful. "Supposing we go down there and they turn? We'd be heavily outnumbered, with no way of escape."

"It's a risk we'll have to take," Captain Lewis said. "If the Rebels are beaten by Slough, they'll have to return this way for their supplies and horses in order to retreat. If they defeat Slough, he'll have to retreat, and the Rebels will need the supplies and horses to pursue him. Either way, we must destroy those supplies and horses."

"Granted," Chivington agreed, "but supposing there are Rebel reinforcements marching this very minute from Santa Fe or perhaps Galisteo? We'd be trapped between two forces then, instead of one. We could stand to lose our force. In that case Colonel Slough would be greatly outnumbered.''

Quint studied Chivington. It wasn't lack of courage that was holding the big man back from attack. He had fought like a mad bull at Apache Canyon, head down, pistols blazing in both hands and an extra pair held under his arms. It was probably the fear of failure, which had wrecked more than a few promising army careers.

Chivington noticed Quint studying him. ''Your opinion, Captain Kershaw?''

''Hit them now, sir. We can send scouts out along the road both ways who can give us the alarm in case of enemy approach. In that case we'd have just enough time to do at least some damage, then retreat up here again. This command could hold off any number of the enemy from up here. It's worth the risk.''

Colonel Chávez nodded. ''I agree, Major.''

''Captain Wynkoop?'' Chivington asked.

''Hit 'em where it hurts the most, Major. Right here and now.''

Chivington paced back and forth. He stopped now and again and reinspected the ranch through the field glasses. He smashed a big fist into the palm of his other hand. It was the signal for which the others had been patiently waiting.

The slopes below the crest were steep, stippled with scrub cedar, piñons, and brush, and composed of talus and detritus, loose rocks, and shattered fragments. The men took coils of rope and slings from their rifles.

Captain Lewis looked at Major Chivington. Chivington nodded.

Lewis cupped his hands about his mouth. ''In single file! Double-quick! *Charge!*'' he shouted.

Over they went, four hundred fighting men, lowering themselves by the linked leather sling straps and ropes in the more difficult places, crawling when necessary, sliding a good part of the way down, leaping from rock to rock, and jumping down to land on loose slopes, which carried them down as though they were sliding on ice. A quarter of the way down, the noise of cascading rocks could be heard far and wide, crashing on the steep slopes, rebounding to strike far below, sometimes shattering into fragments that clattered downhill.

Quint slid down a steep slope, bracing himself with the butt of his Sharps. Far below he could see the alerted Texans running to and fro, gesticulating up toward the descending Federals. Some of them mounted horses or mules and galloped toward the road leading into Glorieta Pass. It wouldn't be long before the main body of Confederates would learn they had been outflanked and their rear was in danger. Gunners were clustering around the cannon on a hilltop.

"They've seen us, boys!" an officer shouted. "Down and at 'em! Devil take the hindmost!"

The Regulars and Coloradoans began to yell and warwhoop. Coupled with the crash of rocks and roaring little landslides, it made one horrendous din. The fieldgun on the hill began to add to the unholy racket by banging away futilely. Solid shot skipped along the lower slopes or rebounded from the hard ground, doing no harm whatsoever.

Then the Federals were on more level ground, rapidly forming under the staccato orders of their officers and noncoms, ready to resist any possible assault. Now and then an enemy rifle popped. The six-pounder on the hill was still firing, but the aim was worse than it had been before.

Captain Lewis and Lieutenant Sanborn accompanied Captain Wynkoop and thirty of his company advancing in a steady dogtrot toward the hilltop gun, rifles aslant, bright bayonets and officers' polished swords glittering in the clear cold sunlight. Wynkoop halted his command on the slope one hundred yards from the smoking gun. The gunners were desperately trying to depress the piece so as to aim point-blank at the Federals.

"Volley! *Fire!*" Wynkoop roared.

Thirty Springfields crashed almost as one. Through the thick, wreathing smoke, six of the eight gunners could be seen falling to the ground. The Coloradoans charged up the hill, yelling ferociously. Captain Lewis was first to the gun, closely followed by Lieutenant Sanborn. The two officers spiked the gun by jamming a ramrod into the vent hole, then rammed a solid cannonball as far inside the bore as possible. With the help of some of the cheering infantrymen they rolled it over the steep crest of the hill. It rolled partway, struck a ledge, rebounded, and fell sideways, shattering one of the wheels, then rolled over and over to the bottom, breaking the other wheel on the way.

The charge on the wagon train was not resisted except for a

few scattered and ineffectual shots. The few guards left at the wagon train had either fled, hidden, or been taken prisoner. Details scattered to search for other Texans, rooting a few of them out of ravines or outbuildings. Most of the prisoners were either sick, wounded, or noncombatants—wagon drivers and cooks. Two of them were officers.

Captain Ford questioned one of the officers. "You mean to tell me, sir, that this handful of the sick, the wounded, cooks, and drivers was left to guard this valuable supply train and herd of horses and mules?"

The officer glumly shook his head. "We had two companies on guard here this morning."

"Where did they go?" Ford asked, looking quickly around at the silent hills about the ranch.

"They ain't hereabouts, Captain. When they heard about the fightin' up the canyon, they took off to join in."

"What fighting?" Captain Lewis demanded.

The officer looked curiously at Lewis. "Why? Ain't you heard? Our boys are whuppin' the tar outta your boys up around a place called Pigeon's Ranch." He pointed toward five men in blue uniforms. "See them? Prisoners captured in Glorieta Pass this mawning near Pigeon's Ranch."

The officers gathered around the five Union men, all grinning because of their unexpected deliverance from the Confederates. A slightly wounded Regular told the story: "We had stacked arms this morning at Pigeon's Ranch and were taking it easy. Our pickets came running in yelling about massed Rebels less than half a mile away. Right after that the Rebels began shooting shell at us. We formed a quick battle line. Wasn't much room for maneuvering, I can tell you. It was like fighting in a bear pit. No place to go but straight forward.

"The Rebels attacked the Germans in the ditch. It was hot and heavy, fighting hand-to-hand, until finally the Germans had to fall back. The Rebels checked our advance on the left and charged our center. We had to fall back and formed a second line of defense right in front of Pigeon's Ranch. A lot of the Rebel gunners were picked off by our sharpshooters.

"The artillery wasn't really much help. It was a real bush-whackin' infantry battle. I was out with our skirmishers when the biggest Texan I've ever seen hit me over the head with his rifle barrel." He raised his forage cap to show the welt on his head. "That was the last I knew until I woke up behind the Rebel lines and they sent me back here."

"You've no idea of how the battle finally went?" Chivington asked.

The soldier shrugged. "It was a surprise on us, sir. All we could do was fight a defensive battle. Last thing I heard our men were still holding the line at Pigeon's Ranch and giving as good as they got."

"Then we've no time to waste!" Chivington cried. "Gentlemen! I want everything here destroyed!"

The supply wagons were fully loaded with ammunition, subsistence, forage, baggage, officers' clothing and gear, and medical and surgical supplies. Teams of men worked together overturning the wagons, which were then set afire. Saddles and slabs of bacon were piled on top of ammunition boxes and touched off. A dense pall of smoke began to rise from Johnson's Ranch. Suddenly the ammunition under the bacon and saddles exploded, sending parts and pieces of pork and leather two hundred feet into the air. A private from Wynkoop's company had been standing too close to the conflagration. The blast of the explosion hurled him backward, wounding him severely. He was the only man hurt on the raid.

"It's time for the worst," Captain Lewis said as the last of the wagons were set afire. He looked toward the deep ravine half a mile away, where the Texans had corraled between five hundred and perhaps as many as a thousand horses and mules.

No one spoke. The sun glittered from the polished bayonets as the Regulars and Coloradoans marched to destroy the entire herd. The herd could not be taken back by the raiders. To turn them loose would allow the Texans to round them up again. It was a pity to kill them, but it had to be done.

The wagons were consumed to the ironwork, leaving nothing but smoldering embers and ashes layered thickly on the ground. The troops stood about silently watching the dying fires. There was no sound from the deep ravine. There the ground was covered with dead horses and mules, their blood thick red on the cropped grass.

"Who the hell is that?" Luke shouted.

A horseman had galloped out of the canyon, coming from the

direction of the battlefield. It took only a matter of seconds for him to analyze the situation, wheel his horse, and race back the way he had come, spurred on by a slug from Luke's Sharps.

"They'll know the story soon," Chivington said. "It's getting late, gentlemen. Bugler, blow assembly. We'll have to return the way we came. We can't risk getting trapped here if the Rebels have more troops on the way. We've done our job."

As dusk came over the land, the troops clambered up the thousand-foot precipice. A towering column of smoke from the burning wagons and stores stained the darkening sky behind them.

A lone officer courier met them. "The Rebels have driven us steadily backward, Major Chivington," he reported. "Colonel Slough's orders are for you to rejoin him as quickly as possible. He needs your support. By the way, sir, the trail by which you marched here is now in possession of the enemy. You'll have to find another way."

"Major, I can guide you back by the way we came, but no other," Colonel Chávez said.

Quint, who had been scouting in advance, came back through the dimness. "Here's a Padre Ortiz, Major. He found us in the darkness. He knows this country well."

Padre Ortiz nodded. "I am priest of the small village near Pecos Ruins, Major Chivington. I'll guide you safely to your people."

The darkness was now intense. They marched slowly over steep pathless ridges and through deep defiles hour after hour. Finally they came out on the main road not far from Pecos Pueblo Ruins. The command was utterly weary, dry-thirsty, and apprehensive about the outcome of the savage battle at Glorieta. It was ten o'clock. They marched until they saw many campfires twinkling through the darkness.

"Ours, or theirs?" Captain Lewis asked quietly.

"Do you want me to scout ahead, Major?" Quint asked.

Chivington shook his head. "If they're ours, it's fine. If it's theirs, we can't go back in any case. If it *is* theirs, we'll soon make it *ours*. Gentlemen, have your men fix bayonets."

They moved quietly through the darkness.

A challenge rang out quickly and was as quickly answered.

Major Chivington's command had reached the Federal position at Kozlowski's Ranch.

Kozlowski's ranch house, outbuildings, and the tents erected near the house were packed with the bloody debris of hard combat—the dying and the wounded. One of the outbuildings was stacked with bodies of the dead, some of whom had been brought in from the battlefield and others who had died of their wounds. Slough's brigade had suffered approximately twenty-five percent casualties during the six-hour battle. No estimate had yet been made of Confederate losses, but it was assumed that they would be much greater. A Confederate major had been brought blindfolded after the battle to the Union position at Kozlowski's to arrange a truce. The day after the battle, Confederates and Unionists mingled at Glorieta Pass, bringing in the wounded and burying the dead. The Texans were short of spades. The Union gravediggers obligingly lent them theirs. Colonel Scurry, commanding the Confederate force, asked for an extension of the truce. Colonel Slough agreed. He was convinced the Texans were too well entrenched in the canyon for him to attack. He had also decided to fall back on Bernal Springs, thirty-five miles east of Kozlowski's.

Most of the officers were aghast at Slough's decision. They knew that Chivington's raid had been a disaster for the Texans. The Federals might have been driven back from Glorieta Pass, but the Confederates had won a Pyrrhic victory. Their losses, particularly in officers, had been a terrible price to pay for their success. Their supplies and transport had gone up in smoke. All of their cavalry and draft animals had been killed. They had expended a great deal of ammunition in the battle, and their reserves had been blown up. Their medical supplies were gone. Their sick and wounded needed care. There was only one place to get supplies, horses and mules, and medical attention. They must retreat at once to Santa Fe.

★ TWENTY-FOUR ★

Dr. Hamilton shook his head as he straightened up after examining Alexander Calhoun's shoulder wound. The puffed flesh about the bullet hole was a purplish color. A malodorous pus seeped from the wound. Alec's eyes were closed. His breathing was short and erratic. His face was flushed.

"Well, Doctor?" Quint asked.

Hamilton pointed to the door of the room. Quint followed him past the beds, cots, and floor pallets all occupied by wounded men. Some of them were dying. The odor of carbolic was thick in the close atmosphere. The doctor walked outside into the cold evening air. He turned and handed Quint a cigar. They lit up.

Hamilton blew a smoke ring. He shook his head again. "That young man should have stayed at Fort Craig. The wound hasn't had proper medical attention at all these past few weeks. How in hell that damned fool medical officer down at Craig allowed him to return to duty is beyond me. And damned if young Calhoun didn't get assigned to Captain Howland's company when he found out it was ordered north to Fort Union, riding all that way and ending up by fighting like a madman at the battle here. Can you tell me *why*, Kershaw?"

Quint shrugged. "Patriotism? Love of battle? Youthful exuberance? Damned outright stupidity? Take your choice, Hamilton."

"I think that last is most fitting. The stupidity of the young."

"So, what's the diagnosis? You didn't ask me out here for a smoke."

"I have my orders to follow the brigade to Bernal Springs.

But even if I stayed here, there's nothing more I can do for him." He looked sideways at Quint. "Do you understand me?"

It was quiet except for the low moaning of some of the wounded and the occasional whinnying of one of the horses tethered to the hitching post.

"To be explicit," Hamilton continued, "there is not much hope for young Calhoun. The infection has gained too much ground. It wasn't a serious wound to start with, but lack of medical attention and improper hygiene coupled with his exhausted condition has made it serious, perhaps mortal. I doubt that he'll last more than a few days before gangrene sets in."

"There's no chance of operating?"

The surgeon shook his head. "We haven't the equipment. In addition, the position of the wound would make any such attempt extremely hazardous and perhaps fatal."

"Would it be at all possible with the proper equipment and better conditions?"

Hamilton shrugged. "It's possible, but not probable. What do you have in mind?"

"Do you know Dr. Thomas Byrne of Santa Fe?"

"I have heard of him, although I have never met him. Some years ago I read one of his papers in *The Medical Journal* relative to the treatment of septic gunshot, edged weapons, and arrow wounds. At that time I believe he was surgeon in the Second Dragoons."

"He is still alive and in Santa Fe, although not practicing at present. If there is anyone in this territory capable of treating that wound, it would be he."

Hamilton studied Quint. "Just what are you suggesting? Santa Fe is still in the hands of the Rebels. It's almost thirty miles from here on rough roads. He might not survive such a trip. I can't permit it, Kershaw."

"Would you let him die?" Quint asked bluntly.

The surgeon shook his head. "Not if I can help it. I've told you what his chances are. Are you willing to risk it?"

"There's no other choice."

"Then take him with my blessing."

They brought Alec out on a stretcher and loaded him into one of Kozlowski's old carriages. Dr. Hamilton gave Quint some sedatives and clean bandages. He watched the preparations for the journey, wondering just what Quint Kershaw's incentive was for undertaking it. Slowly, as he watched Quint's face in the lantern light, then looked from him to Alec and back again, a curious thought came to him. There was a resemblance between the two men. The longer he studied them, the more he became aware of it. It was almost as though the two men had been cut from the same bolt of cloth.

"You'll need orders, Kershaw," Hamilton said.

Anselmo led out three horses for himself, Quint, and Luke. He and Luke placed pommel and cantle packs in position and tied them down. Quint had indicated he would drive the carriage.

"Did you hear me?" Hamilton asked Quint.

Quint nodded. "Can you cover for me?"

"I will!" a voice called out from the shadows. Major Chivington walked into the yellow lantern light.

"But what about your company?" asked the surgeon.

Quint half grinned. He pointed to Anselmo, Luke, and then to himself. "You're looking at it," he replied.

Chivington thrust out his hand. "By the Lord, Kershaw, if you want a future assignment, we of the First Colorado would welcome you."

Quint nodded. "Thanks, Major. It's always a pleasure to be in the company of such fighting men as the First Colorado and yourself." He climbed onto the seat of the carriage and threaded the reins through his fingers. He looked sideways at the two officers. "We'll meet again, gentlemen. *Vaya!*" He slapped the reins on the rumps of the two mules and drove off into the darkness.

"A gentleman and a fighting man," Chivington said.

Hamilton nodded. "Is there anything between him and young Calhoun? Are they just close friends? Perhaps distant kin?"

Andrew Kozlowski stood behind them. "There's a rumor been floating around for some time about those two."

Chivington turned. "Such as?"

"You notice the resemblance between them, Major?"

"I did," Hamilton said.

"But he's the son of Major Calhoun of the dragoons, the one who defected to the South and was with Sibley on his advance from La Mesilla," Chivington said. "Calhoun was the owner of the Rio Brioso Ranch up near Fort Union. He was in New Mexico during the Mexican War.''

Kozlowski nodded. "And before that, Major." He paused. "So was his wife. That was before she married him. That was about the time Quint Kershaw came to New Mexico too." There was something in his tone that caused the others to look quickly at him. "She was, and still is, a beautiful woman," he added. "Some say there was a thing between Kershaw and her, but no one ever knew for sure."

"Be careful," Hamilton warned.

The Pole shrugged. "Like I said: It was just a rumor." He turned and went back into his house.

They reached the Confederate field hospital on the road to Santa Fe several hours after daylight. Luke rode ahead with a white flag of truce on a staff. A Confederate captain stopped them on the road. He walked to the carriage and looked up at Quint.

"I'm Captain Quintin Kershaw, sir. I have a wounded Federal officer here, Captain," Quint said. "I am taking him to Santa Fe for better medical attention. He must be taken there as soon as possible. Can you issue me a safe conduct?"

"Of course. Although why your patient must be taken to Santa Fe puzzles me. Have you not adequate medical officers with your brigade?"

"We do, Captain. However, Lieutenant Calhoun's case is beyond their help. I am taking him into the capital to a Dr. Thomas Byrne for further treatment."

"You're in luck, suh. Doctor Byrne just arrived here half an hour ago to treat ouah boys. In fact, he and many of the ladies of Santa Fe, Federal officers' wives led by Mrs. Canby, Colonel Canby's wife, have turned their homes into hospitals for ouah sick and wounded. Every day some of them come out heah with medicines, soups, and food for the field hospital. You see that wagon theah, the one with the tent cloth nailed across the bed? That was Mrs. Canby's idea when she found out we were short of ambulances to get ouah boys into her home in Santa Fe. She had us nail the cloth like that to make like hammocks for the boys. It's a helluva rough trip to the town, and that sure makes it easier on them. God bless her, she's like an angel. You-all know what she said when some of the Yankee ladies said the hospital she was getting ready befoah Glorieta Pass might be used by Rebels? She said: No matter, friend or foe, the wounded must be cared for and their lives saved if it is possible; they are sons of some dear mothah." He glanced away. Tears were welling up in his eyes. He walked off, then turned. "I'll ask Dr. Byrne to come look at the boy. Did you say his name was Lieutenant Calhoun? It is? Any relation to ouah Colonel Calhoun?"

Quint nodded. "His only son, Captain."

"That a fact? Strange wah, isn't it?"

"Where's the colonel now?" Luke asked.

"He was badly wounded at Valverde. Had his left arm taken off at the shoulder. They took him to the hospital at Socorro. He shot himself to death two days latah. Couldn't live a cripple, I'd say. Too bad. A fine officer and soldier."

"He had a sergeant orderly," Quint said hesitantly. "A sergeant Frank Kershaw. Second Texas. Enlisted at La Mesilla. Did you happen to know him?"

The officer pointed beyond the hospital tents. The sun shone on earth-polished spades throwing dirt atop a long mounded mass grave. "He was severely wounded at Glorieta Pass, Captain. Died late last night. He's over theah." He looked quickly at Quint. "Kershaw! Was he kin to you, suh?"

Quint got down from his seat. "One of my sons, Captain." He walked slowly toward the mass grave.

"I didn't know," the Texan said.

Luke shrugged. "You said it was a strange war," he said dryly.

Tom Byrne inspected Alec's wound. "Mother of God," he husked over his shoulder to Quint. "How long has he been like this?"

Quint told him the story. "I thought if anyone could help him, Tom, it would be you," he added.

Tom shook his head. "Thanks. Thanks, Quint." He turned his head away. "So young. So ambitious. So damned foolish."

"He's not alone in this war," Quint said.

Dr. Byrne accompanied them back to Santa Fe, riding in the backseat with the unconscious Alec. "You heard about Shelby Calhoun, Quint?"

"I did," Quint replied.

The doctor hesitated. "And Frank?"

Quint nodded.

Tom Byrne wisely kept his silence.

The road was lined by plodding Confederates heading for the capital afoot. Some of them wore bandages and limped or had their arms in slings. They didn't look much like the tough bronze-faced young men who had charged McRae's battery at Valverde. That had been a signal victory for them. Apache Canyon and Glorieta Pass had none of the glory of Valverde. It had been a savage hand-to-hand brawl in the bear pit of Glorieta Pass, neither side giving an inch, until the sheer ferocity and desperation of the Texans had finally driven the Regulars and Coloradoans back to Pigeon's Ranch. It had been all they could do, probably the last great outpouring of fighting energy of the campaign. It was difficult for Quint to correlate these tired, sick, gaunt-faced men with the exultant victors of Valverde.

They carried Alec into Tom's *casa* on the plaza. The room always used by Jean when she was in the city had been turned into a hospital room. It was empty now. The last occupant had been an eighteen-year-old San Antonio boy who had died of pneumonia the night before.

"Señora Calhoun is over at the Señora Canby's *casa* nursing Tejanos," José, one of Tom's housemen, reported.

Quint nodded. "I'll get her, Tom," he said.

He walked across the plaza. The townspeople smiled and spoke to him. The Texans watched him silently. Even if any of them had wanted to accost him, they would have thought better of baiting this tall, lean man with the scarred face and cold gray eyes. He carried a holstered Navy Colt and a heavy bowie knife in a scabbard. He looked like he could and would use them with drastic results.

Jean was bending over a cot, bathing the face of a fever-ridden Texan. She seemed to feel Quint's presence before she turned her head to look into his eyes. Christ, but she was lovely! "I don't know why, or how," she said quietly, "but I felt you would come."

He took one of her hands and held it. "I've brought Alec here, Jean. He's at Tom's."

She paled. "Is he all right? He's been wounded, hasn't he?"

Quint nodded. He placed her cape about her shoulders. They walked together across the sunlit plaza, a handsome pair.

She looked up into his face. "Are you all right?"

He nodded. "Shelby is dead," he said quietly.

She turned her head away a little.

"Dave was wounded at Valverde. He lost his left hand and the sight in his left eye."

Her breath caught in her throat. "No more," she said.

"Frank was wounded at Glorieta, fighting with the Texans. He died last night. They buried him near the field hospital just this morning," he continued relentlessly.

They stopped at Tom's door. "And what about you, Quint?" she asked. "Have you had enough of this war?"

He opened the door for her. "Not until it's over, Jean."

Guadalupe was beside Alec's bed, holding a bowl of warm water for Tom while he changed the bandage. He threw the old one into the fireplace. The smell was sickening. Guadalupe was pale, on the verge of being violently sick, but she would not leave. Her great dark eyes were fixed on the man she loved with all her heart and soul.

Tom washed his hands and dried them. "I'll need someone here twenty-four hours a day for the next four or five days. Jean, I know I can depend on you for one."

"I'm here now," Guadalupe said. She looked at Quint. "It's so good to see you, father."

Quint held out his arms to her. She came to him and rested her head on his chest while he held her close. He looked into Jean's eyes. She looked toward the bed. Somehow the wheel had swung full circle. It was just like it had been almost half a year past. That was when he had warned Jean, "*You must keep him away from her, Jean, at least until I return. Perhaps, at that time, he'll be assigned elsewhere. That will give us time. Perhaps he'll lose interest in her and she in him.*"

Alec opened his eyes. "Guadalupe," he murmured.

She ran quickly to him.

★ TWENTY-FIVE ★

It was close to dawn. Someone knocked on the door of Quint's room. He was instinctively up on his feet with cocked Colt in his hand before he was fully awake. Jean was still asleep. He walked to the door. *"Quién es?"* he called softly.

"Luke, Big Red," Luke replied. "Just got back from Albuquerque. Good news."

Quint dressed quickly and left the room. He gripped Luke about the shoulders. "Are you all right?" he asked. "Where's Anselmo?"

Luke grinned. "I couldn't feel better. Headquarters asked to keep Anselmo. The only reason they let me return was to report to Captain Howland about what was going on down south and tell you to get your ass down there to report for duty."

"When?"

"As soon as possible. The Rebels are on the run, Big Red."

"Who is it, Quint?" Jean called from the bed.

"Luke. He's back."

"I'll be there as soon as I get dressed."

Luke and Anselmo had tailed the last of the Texans when they had abandoned Santa Fe on April 10. Sibley had decided to evacuate the capital after receiving the news that Colonel Canby had led his command north from Fort Craig and was in the vicinity of Albuquerque, threatening the small Confederate garrison there. Sibley had been frantic at the news. The brigade could not afford to lose the precious supplies stored in Albuquerque. Further, the Confederates were in the nutcracker between two well-equipped and better-supplied Federal forces and would be outnumbered if the Federals joined the two forces. Sibley left behind several hundred sick and wounded with a surgeon and several medical attendants to care for them. As a final gesture of goodwill he left a thousand dollars for the care of the sick and wounded. The sum was in Confederate bills. . . . A number of Confederate deserters were also left behind, remaining out of sight until the troops had left. All Confederate sympathizers who were in the capital left hurriedly with the troops. They weren't anxious to face Federal sympathizers now that their protection was gone.

Tom Byrne awoke at Quint's call. "What is it, Quint?"

"Luke is back. The Rebels are on the run down south."

Tom sat up. "I'll be right with you."

"I can bring Luke here, Tom."

Tom shook his head. "I'll need to change Alec's dressing. We can all meet in his room."

Guadalupe was dozing in a chair close beside Alec's bed. Quint did not wake her at once. He started a fire while Luke ate quickly in the kitchen. Tom came into the room, followed by Jean bearing a basin of warm water and fresh bandages.

Luke came in munching on a thick sandwich and carrying a carafe of brandy in his other hand. "Colonel Canby heard about the skirmish we had at Apache Canyon, but he didn't know about Glorieta Pass," he began. "I heard he was damned angry about Colonel Slough leaving Fort Union and marching into the pass and right into a battle. His orders had been to avoid any conflict and make sure Fort Union was not left unprotected. Canby didn't want any action by the troops up north until he could join them with his force. Canby didn't know about Glorieta Pass when he marched north up the river route to Albuquerque, figuring to go east through Carnuel Pass and up the eastern side of the mountains. He left Fort Craig April first with about twelve hundred men and four pieces of artillery. Kit Carson with most of his First New Mexico and some of the Second and Fourth was left in charge of Fort Craig. Just below Socorro Canby got the news of Glorieta Pass. He figured on taking Albuquerque then but found out it was too strongly held to assault. He fooled around there making the Rebs think he *was* going to attack, figuring he'd scare ol' Sibley into comin' down there to protect his precious supplies." He grinned. "It sure worked, but Canby didn't know it at the time.

"Our boys built campfires the second night they were there, then pulled foot for Carnuel Pass in the dark, leaving behind only the buglers, fifers, and drummers. The musicians played Tattoo that night, then got to hell outta there in a hurry before the Rebs got wise. They got out of there just in time, because that same night the Fifth Texas came roaring into Albuquerque hunting for Federal scalps. One more day and they would have caught Canby. If Canby had fought there and lost, it would have meant the loss of his entire wagon train, commissary and ordnance, and the Rebels sure as hellfire needed 'em."

Quint nodded. "Canby's got the initiative now."

"Canby finally halted at San Antonio, twenty miles east of Albuquerque. I was nosin' around Albuquerque when I run into Paddy doin' the same thing. He told me Canby was waiting for a Colonel Paul, who succeeded Slough, to march the troops down from Bernal Springs to join him so they could move in on the Rebels."

Quint nodded. "He sent Captain Howland with his company to occupy Santa Fe. They're here now."

"Are any of the Rebels still in Albuquerque, Luke?" Tom asked as he looked up from cleansing Alec's wound.

Luke shook his head. "They're headin' south, slow but sure. Canby should be right behind them about now, pushin' them along."

"Do you think they'll try to take Fort Craig?" Tom asked.

"I doubt it. Kit's got heavier guns on his walls than the Rebs are haulin' with them. Besides, Sibley would be a damned fool to try with Canby tailin' him, ready to pounce when he gets a chance. I hope to God me and Quint can get down there quickly to join him. Those are our orders anyway."

Jean shot a startled glance at Quint. He shrugged slightly.

"God, I'd love to go with you to see the end of this thing!" Alec exploded.

"Not a chance," Tom said.

"How soon will you be leaving?" Alec asked.

Quint could not look at Jean. "As soon as I can. Tomorrow."

Jean did not take her eyes off Quint.

Guadalupe helped Alec sit up higher, bolstered by his pillows. She stood close beside him. He held her hand in his. "Then Guadalupe and I must tell you something, Quint," Alec said.

A cold feeling swept through Quint. Before God, he had kept putting the matter of their relationship out of his mind as much as possible while waiting for Alec to improve. He was still very weak and far from a complete recovery.

Guadalupe smiled. "Are you still in the same room with us, father?" she asked softly.

Quint nodded slowly.

Jean bit her lower lip. "Is this the time and place for your announcement, Alec?" she asked.

"What announcement? How do you know what I was going to say, mother?"

She turned her head quickly away from looking at him. "It's very obvious, son," she snapped.

Alec was puzzled. "If I know Quint he'll be out of here before dawn tomorrow. You know how he is when the drums beat the long roll and the bugles blow the charge."

Jean looked at Quint with stricken eyes. "Yes, yes," she said quietly. "How well I know."

"I'd better get some sleep," Luke said. He stood up and headed for the door.

"Don't you want to hear this, Luke?" Alec called.

Luke heard him; he did not reply. A moment later they heard the front door open and close.

Tom washed his hands in the bowl of water. He looked past Alec and Guadalupe at Jean and Quint. "Do you want me to leave?"

Alec looked quickly at Tom. "But why? What's wrong here?"

Guadalupe looked slowly at her father. For some time she had been slowly recognizing the resemblance of Alec to Quint, particularly the eyes, those same Kershaw eyes her brother David and sister Rafaela had. She knew Quint and Jean were sleeping together. She had heard some servant gossip about their relationship years past, and the renewal of that relationship in the present.

One of the piñon logs in the fireplace snapped, sending out a shower of sparks and charred bits of wood. The sound was inordinately loud in the quietness.

Then Guadalupe *knew*. She suddenly felt stricken. She glanced at Tom. He tried to look away but she held out a tiny hand to place it alongside his cheek, turning his head gently so that she could look into his eyes. *"Verdad?"* she queried faintly.

Tom nodded. A tear crept out of one of his eyes. *"Verdad,"* he replied quietly.

She walked quickly out of the room.

"Guadalupe!" Alec called. "Come back!"

Jean shook her head. "It's no use, Alec. She won't be back. She *can't* come back."

He looked steadfastly at his mother. He suspected something, yet was not quite sure. A coldness came over him. *It was not possible*.

It was Quint who broke the stillness. "Alec, you are my natural son."

Alec stared uncomprehendingly at his mother. "If that is true, Quint, how long have you known it?"

"Since 1846, sixteen years," Quint replied.

"Why have you never told me, mother?" Alec asked.

She shook her head. "I don't know."

"Did Shelby know?"

Jean nodded.

"How long?"

"Almost since the time of your birth, Alec."

"And all these years you've kept the truth from me?" he said bitterly. "I can forgive *that*, mother. I *cannot* forgive you for not telling me sooner when you saw my interest in Guadalupe and hers in me. I never want to speak with you again, or see you, if that's possible."

Jean turned on a heel and rushed from the room.

Alec looked at Quint. "I'm not blaming you. She should have told me years ago."

Quint shook his head. "She was thinking of you, son. To be born as you were, with a prestigious birth, into position and wealth, was a far greater advantage in life than to be acknowledged as the son of a moneyless adventurer, as I was then. Believe me, Alec, it was all for the best."

Alec closed his eyes. "Not to me. But then, you and mother never had the chance to discuss the matter until long after it was too late. For that I can forgive both of you. As to Guadalupe, I feel the same way toward you as I do about mother in that respect." He opened his eyes. "You'd better leave. You've your duty to perform. To soldiers such as us, that is paramount. Good-bye, Captain. God go with you."

The door closed behind Quint.

Tom looked down at Alec. "Fate plays tricks on us poor mortals, Alec. This is a bad one, but you'll outlive it. When you mellow in the coming years you may realize what wonderful people your mother and father truly are. I hope in time you recognize that fact." He closed the door behind himself. The slight jar tumbled the charred piñon logs in a smoldering heap at the bottom of the fireplace. A strangled sob broke from Alec.

★ TWENTY-SIX ★

APRIL 19, 1862: RETREAT

Quint, Luke, and Anselmo forded the Rio Grande at dawn with Paddy Graydon's company. The cold wind was still howling and driving fine sand in obscuring clouds and rolling tumbleweeds at great speed across the terrain. The Confederate camp was just ahead. All the wagons stood teamless, their tilts flapping furiously in the blast. There was no sign of anyone about the camp. Paddy dismounted his men and deployed them in a spread-out fan that closed cautiously in on the camp in a crescent-shaped formation. Quint, Luke, and Anselmo walked with Sharps ready in the company of Paddy. One of the leading scouts turned, cupped his hands about his mouth, and shouted out the news. The Tejanos had pulled foot. The camp was deserted.

Quint counted thirty-eight wagons. The site was a mess, littered with cast-off equipment, saddles, worn-out shoes, boots, and clothing. The blackened remains of many campfires dotted the ground. Half a dozen horses and mules lay dead, their throats slashed through. Poor worn-out devils, Quint thought. The Rebels either couldn't spare the cartridges for the job or had feared to alert the Federals across the river.

Quint pushed aside the rear flap of a wagon and jumped quickly back, raising and cocking his Sharps as a man rose up on his elbow and stared listlessly at him. "You're safe, Yank. I ain't got a gun, and if'n I did I wouldn't have the strength to use it." He fell back with a severe coughing fit.

"Your friends all pulled out, Reb?" Quint asked.

The Texan nodded. "Last night. Their orders were to wear what they could and burn the rest. Each man must carry only his gun, ammunition, and seven days' rations. They packed what commissary rations they had on mule back. Nearly every one drove a packmule or led a broken-down horse. The infantry went first, then the Valverde battery, followed by some caissons, ambulances, wagons, and three carriages, one of them for drunken ol' Sibley hisself. The cavalry brought up the rear."

Quint was puzzled. "The Valverde battery?"

The sick man couldn't help but grin. "The one we-uns captured from you-uns at Valverde. You know—McRae's battery."

"You mean they hauled those guns with them? They'll never get them through the mountains. Damned stupid to take them."

The Texan shrugged. "They set a great store on that battery. When they decided to retreat, some of the officers wanted to abandon *all* the artillery, but ol' Colonel Scurry, he raised a storm. He pledged the six guns captured at Valverde would be saved, no matter the obstacles. He'll do it too, Yank!" He managed a weak grin. "Sure made you Lincolnites look sick when we took it from you when we won the victory at Valverde."

Quint couldn't help himself. "Well, Texas, seems like it'll be all the glory you Rebs will ever get out of this campaign."

Luke and Paddy came up. "There are more of them in other wagons, Big Red," Paddy reported. "Sick and disabled. One of them is dying, poor bastard."

The Texan went into another coughing fit. "You got a cup?" Luke asked him. The Texan nodded. Luke half filled the cup with water from his canteen, then added a solid jolt of brandy to it. "Hope you're a drinkin' man, Reb," he said.

The Texan held out a shaking hand for the cup. "Try me," he suggested.

"We'll get you out of here, Texas," Paddy promised.

"One of the sick boys told me the column was headed southwest to pass behind the Magdalenas and then across the San Mateos to hit the Rio Grande somewheres near Canada Alamosa," Luke said. "They got a Captain Bethel Coopwood who claimed he knows the San Mateos fairly well, at least enough to get them across to the Rio Alamosa."

"I hope to God he does," Quint said.

The area to the southwest was difficult, hazardous, and mountainous, a trackless waste nearly devoid of water. Quint knew it well. His *rancho* was beyond the San Mateo mountains to the west and south. The Texans would find no roads. Their animals were jaded or broken-down. There would be little forage for them and hardly enough water.

"They may never come out of them mountains alive," Paddy said thoughtfully. He looked at Quint. "What do you figure on doing now, Big Red?"

"My orders were to scout the Rebs. They're obviously not here. So we'll trail after them to see where they're heading. Colonel Canby gave me permission to go to the Querencia when and if I was sure the Rebels were retreating out of this part of the territory."

"Makes it mighty convenient, then. You think the Rebs might go to the Querencia?"

Quint shrugged. "It would be out of their way if they plan to cross the San Mateos. But it's the best and most reliable source of good water for about thirty square miles. Then too, there are good horses and mules there for transport and sheep and cattle for rations. We've always kept a good supply of staples in store. They're short on rations. They may need some of my stores to last them through the mountains."

"Well, I guess you three can take care of yourselves. God knows I wouldn't tangle with you, singly or all together."

Quint gripped Paddy's hand. "When you return to the command, tell Colonel Canby we've gone on."

They rode southwesterly from the camp. The trail should be easy to follow. The retreating column would have to follow the primitive road to Nogales Spring. They'd leave a track a blind man could follow.

When Sibley had evacuated Santa Fe and retreated to Albuquerque to consolidate his brigade, Canby had been encamped at

Tijeras, fourteen miles east of Albuquerque, waiting to be joined by Colonel Paul and his command from Bernal Springs. Canby had gotten the news of Apache Canyon, but not Glorieta Pass, on April 1 while still at Fort Craig. He had marched north along the river route with twelve hundred men and four pieces of artillery. They heard the news of Glorieta Pass at Socorro. Canby realized Albuquerque was too strongly held, then marched eastward through Carnuel Pass to effect a junction with other Federal troops at Bernal Springs. His feint at Santa Fe should draw the Confederate forces down from Santa Fe. He was correct in his assumption. In addition, his movement had cost the Confederates their last chance to regain the initiative. If they had fought and defeated Canby's smaller force, it would have meant the capture of his wagon train loaded with commissary and ordnance desperately needed by the Texans. Now they had no alternative but to retreat.

On April 12 almost all of the Sibley Brigade crossed the Rio Grande just below Albuquerque. Green's Fifth Regiment was unable to cross so marched down the east bank to Peralta, where there was a better ford. The Confederates on the west bank bivouacked at Los Lunas nearly opposite Peralta. Green established his headquarters at Governor Connelly's Los Pinos ranch, planning to cross the river the next morning. Canby followed and camped a mile upriver from Peralta. Green had been surprised. He had only five hundred men but held a strong position. The fighting was ineffectual. The Confederates on the west bank were unable to cross to his aid. Green's Fifth Regiment was saved by a seasonal howling sandstorm and the fact that the Federals had not been fed for a day and were almost exhausted. The Texans crossed the river under cover of the storm. At daylight the Confederate retreat continued. They left behind some of their sick and wounded with little food and no medicine or attendants.

Luke turned and looked back along their route. "I still can't figger out why Canby didn't attack Green at Peralta. We'da grabbed a good part of their army there, Big Red."

Quint shook his head. "It would have meant a full-scale assault against a well-entrenched position. Victory would have been glorious but impractical. We would have lost too many men. The territory has been stripped of provisions. Our army is already marching on short rations. We would have had to use too many men to guard the prisoners and would have been forced to feed them as well—on rations we might not have. The only alternative was to let them slip away and follow them to make sure they didn't turn back this way and weren't pillaging. I think their abandonment of their strong position at Peralta means they've had a bellyful of fighting us.''

The day after Green had retreated across the river the Federals marched south on the east bank, both forces in full view of each other. The Confederates halted and camped where the Rio Puerco empties into the Rio Grande. The Federals camped at La Joya. Both camps were in full view of each other. The spectacle of the many campfires on each bank had been a grand and awesome sight to Quint, and he knew he was witnessing history in the making. That night the worst sandstorm of the season roared in. The Federals could not have picked a worse place to bivouac. Before dawn Paddy Graydon and Quint had been ordered to cross the river and scout the Confederates.

Fort Craig was seventy miles below the retreating Confederates and on the same side of the river. Sibley had probably reasoned the garrison there could dispute his passage. Canby would be close to the fort and could easily cross over to aid the garrison. The road down the west bank was poor and thick with heavy sand. Forage and grass was scarce. The animals were weary and much too weak to pull the wagons, ambulances, caissons, and guns as far as Fort Craig. He had no alternative but to head west, then south, to try and reach the Rio Grande miles below Fort Craig.

The Texans marched to reach the foothills. There they stopped to rest among the cedars. From Nogales Spring the trail ran between the dry hills for about fifteen miles. The road was a nightmare of roughness.

Luke was riding point. He held up an arm to halt Quint and Anselmo. He pointed upward. A lone *zopilote* swung in lazy, effortless circles high overhead. Luke dismounted and went forward afoot. A few minutes later he turned to wave on his companions.

A broken-wheeled wagon was tilted to one side off the road. The ground was trampled by footprints and hooves. Blackened circles showed where campfires had burned out. Three bodies lay half-buried. A stiffened arm seemed to point accusingly at the three scouts. Anselmo refused to go near them. Quint and Luke dragged them from the shallow holes. They dug deeper and reburied the bodies, then piled what rocks they could find over them. Luke found a can of gunpowder in the wagon. He poured it over the graves and touched it off. The quick little cloud of smoke drifted off on the cold wind. They mounted and rode from the camp. The *zopilote* was swinging lower.

"The wolves will likely be at them tonight," Luke said.

They rode on the wide trail toward Magdalene Mountain.

Thirty miles from the camp they reached a spring that had nearly been drunk dry. Anselmo dug down into it. He sieved the cloudy brackish water through a towel into a battered bucket left by the Texans. He filled the big canteens while Luke watered the horses. Quint wandered about the camp, poking through the litter. He looked out along the broad trail left by the Texans as they headed south toward the San Mateos. He walked out along it, then stopped. Wheel ruts and hoof tracks turned off from the main trail toward the southwest. He followed them for half a mile to make certain they didn't turn back again toward the main trail. They did not. He could see the single trail for quite a distance. It pointed almost directly west. There was only one place in that direction where water might be obtained, and where there was a place of habitation—*La Querencia* . . .

Anselmo came after Quint. "Querencia?" he asked.

Quint nodded. "Likely. Where else would they be heading?"

Anselmo dogtrotted a ways, then knelt, studying the tracks. He went a little farther to a place where the trail parted to pass a boulder half-buried in the sandy soil. He examined the tracks again, then returned.

"Well?" Quint asked.

"Three wagons, *patrón*. Eight, mebbe ten, horsemen."

"Loaded wagons?"

Anselmo nodded.

"If they were after supplies, the wagons would be empty," Quint mused.

"Mebbe filled with men?" Anselmo suggested.

Quint looked at him. "By God! You might be right at that!"

Anselmo shrugged. "They go to Querencia for supplies, they

might get their asses shot off instead!" He grinned widely. "We go after them?"

Quint shook his head. "Our orders were to make sure the Tejanos were retreating out of this part of New Mexico. They're still here, Anselmo."

They stayed that night at the springs. They could see the faint flickering of campfires in the distance to the south. They saw none to the west, where the detachment had gone. If it was a raiding party, they wouldn't want to reveal their presence.

They moved out before dawn light the next morning. They rode leisurely with many rest stops to smoke and palaver. The Texans were moving slowly. When they started out each day the column was up fairly tight, not much over a mile in length, but by evening it sometimes stretched as much as ten miles. The cavalry usually turned their mounts loose at night to forage. In the morning they sometimes had to walk miles to round them up.

It was Anselmo who came up with a suggestion. "Mebbe we could run them horses off at night."

Luke blew a smoke ring. "So?"

"Then them Tejano bastards would be all afoot."

Luke studied Anselmo. "Just why would you want that?"

"It'd slow them down a helluva lot. Mebbe stop them altogether."

Luke shook his head. "I've heard everything now. Anselmo, *mi amigo*, we just ain't about to do anything to slow them down. The sooner they get their hairy asses outta this territory, the better it's goin' to be for New Mexico."

"Amen," Quint added fervently. "I just hope the bastards enjoy dragging their goddamned 'Valverde battery' through the San Mateos."

They grinned evilly at each other.

Seventeen miles onward the Texans had camped for the night near a spring. The ground was covered with feathers, and the wind had blown many of them into the thorny branches of the surrounding brush like some strange blooms. The source was a lot of feather beds that had been ripped open and discarded. Several rusting iron cook ovens had been dumped in the spring. The usual litter of worn-out clothing, some boots with their soles worn through, and old harness lay scattered about.

They started out late the next morning after their usual breakfast of almost transparent rotting bacon and bread baked in a rusting frying pan they had found at the first campsite of the Rebels. They soaked the bread in the bacon grease. They were getting close to the end of their rations. They had seen no game. The Texans did a laborious fifteen miles that day. They stopped at Ojo del Pueblo, a remote spring. They blew up a caisson, burned three of their dwindling supply of wagons, and destroyed much of their medical supplies. Artillery shell and round shot lay scattered on the ground. The column struck out for dry Rio Salada before dawn the next day, thirty miles on a rough road.

"They won't find much water there," Anselmo said thoughtfully. "What they do find will be brackish."

"Better than nothing," Luke said pleasantly.

"Don't be so goddamned cheerful," Quint growled. "We'll have to drink it too, remember?"

"If there's any left," Anselmo said dryly.

They looked at each other out of the corners of their eyes.

Late in the afternoon they came upon a horse standing splay-legged with its head down off in the brush. Something dark was slinking through the brush. It vanished when Quint and his companions halted their horses on the road. Wolves liked to eat living flesh, Quint recalled with distaste.

He dismounted and walked toward the horse. The gray raised his head and looked pitifully and almost hopefully at him. Quint nodded. "Never fear, old fellow," he said softly. The Navy Colt cracked flatly. The horse hit the ground, dead before the echo died away.

Quint looked back as he mounted his horse. The wolf was already tearing boldly at the still-quivering flesh.

Late in the afternoon Quint made his way up a low saddle-backed ridge and uncased his field glasses. The tail of the column was less than half a mile away, a dozen plodding troopers leading their jaded horses, a sorry excuse for a rear guard. He put the glasses on the strung-out column. It was over five miles long, moving slowly near the foothills of the rugged volcanic San Mateos. The mountains stood diagonally across their route to the south, trending from about north-northwest to south-southeast, over forty-five miles in length, slashed with deep gorges and serrated with jagged ridges. Four peaks of the San Mateos were over ten thousand feet high.

That night they built a small campfire in a hollow on the reverse crest of a ridge and ate the last of their rations. The night was cold. They could see the Confederate campfires sharp and bright against the purple blackness of the towering mountains. Their real trials would begin soon when they crossed the San Mateos. *"They may never come out of them mountains alive,"* Paddy Graydon had soberly prophesied.

A distant thundering explosion shattered the predawn quiet, followed by more than a dozen thumping detonations that thundered along the mountainsides and then died away. The bright red flashes lit up the dark grayness of the false dawn. With the coming of daylight, a thick smoke column rose blackly from the Rio Salado campsite of the Confederates. Beyond the smoke could be seen thin dust rising slowly to be driven by the cold wind. The column was on the move again. The soaring smoke looked like a huge hank of coarse black hair stretched against the light-blue linen color of the morning sky.

Quint counted the still-smoking embers and the scorched ironwork remains of six caissons, nineteen wagons, ten ambulances, and three carriages. Smoking craters showed where six 100-pound barrels of gunpowder had been blown up. Four hastily dug graves were to one side. Anselmo walked into the brush. His rifle roared. In a little while he came back carrying a human arm. He dropped it on one of the graves where a stump showed through the gravelly fill. He looked at Quint. "Wolf," he said quietly. "He won't be diggin' up any more graves."

Quint shrugged. "There will be more as soon as we leave," he said dryly.

The Texans had abandoned or destroyed anything that might impede their progress through the San Mateos. What had started out as a rather orderly retreat from the Rio Grande had now become a veritable rout.

"Now what?" Luke asked. "We're out of rations."

Anselmo came to them carrying a sack. He held it up. "Wormy hardbread and rotten bacon. Enough for a couple of days."

"My God!" Luke exclaimed. "You've saved our lives! Now we can follow these damned Tejanos all the way to the Rio Alamosa." He slanted his green eyes sideways at Quint as he spoke.

"We've come this far, Luke," Quint said quietly. "I'd like to see it through to the finish."

Luke pointed up at the San Mateos. "Through *that*?" he asked. He tilted his head to one side. "We know they ain't ever comin' back, Big Red. We've done our job."

Quint walked over to his horse. He took his reata and tied it to the saddlehorn, then attached the other end to some of the still-smoldering remains of a wagon. He dragged it across the ground and over the four graves, then returned and repeated the process with the ironwork and smoldering wood of a caisson.

"You think he means to go on?" Anselmo asked Luke.

Luke nodded.

"You said they wouldn't come back."

"They won't."

Anselmo was puzzled. "Then why we go follow them?"

Luke looked at Quint. "You see what he's doin', don't you? Them Tejanos he's coverin' up won't ever bother us again, but the wolves will."

"So?"

Luke pointed to the thin dust trail rising above the distant Confederate column. "He just wants to be damned sure them Rebels make it to Canada Alamosa, not because he's afraid they'll be back but because he doesn't want to see them die in the mountains. If there's any way we can help them, he's goin' to make sure we are in a position to do it."

Anselmo shook his head. "Loco. It wasn't long ago he was killin' them off at Valverde and Apache Canyon."

Luke shrugged. "They were enemies then. They ain't now."

Anselmo grinned. "You white men can swap ends faster than a wildcat falling out of a tree."

Luke inspected his black, broken fingernails. "That's what makes us so *special*, my boy."

They made their camp that night away from the dismal campsite of the Texans. Even so, they could hear the wolves and coyotes howling mournfully as they closed cautiously in on the lonely graves.

The Texans reached the Alamosa River at nine o'clock in the morning of April 24. The few wagons they had managed to keep with them and the guns of the Valverde battery were left at the foot of a steep hill beyond the camp. The Texans were just too exhausted to finish the job at that time. That was completed in the evening.

Quint and Luke watched the camp while Anselmo scouted downriver to see if there were any other Confederates in that area. The column was worn out and nearly famished. They had virtually fought their way through the San Mateos. The undergrowth and brush had been so dense that for several miles they had been forced to cut their way through with axes and bowie knives. The Valverde battery and the few wagons they had kept were dragged laboriously uphill by the use of long ropes, only to be lowered into the next canyon, to repeat the process on the other side of it. There were a number of places where it seemed impossible for men to have made their way. The distance from where they had left the Rio Grande until they reached it again was over one hundred miles. It had taken ten days to accomplish the feat with only five days' worth of poor rations.

Anselmo returned late that night. He had found the other Confederate force six miles downstream and had trailed a Confederate colonel and his escort to the Sibley camp. Quint and Luke had heard the hoarse cheering from the camp when the colonel had evidently brought the news of the other force waiting for them with plenty of rations.

Day had hardly broken when the column moved downstream to the other camp. The heavenly aroma of frying bacon, baking bread, and boiling coffee reached the three gaunt, bewhiskered men on the heights above the camp. They suffered intense hunger pangs while waiting patiently for the Texans to move on. Later that day the column marched slowly down the valley toward the distant Rio Grande, proudly hauling their treasured Valverde battery.

Luke scratched inside his filthy shirt. "How many of them you figure are left, Big Red?"

Quint lay on his lean belly, resting his chin on his crossed forearms. "Maybe twelve hundred or so, Wandering Wolf."

They were quiet for a time.

Anselmo looked sideways at Quint. "How many they have when they got to New Mexico?"

"About three thousand. They were said to have about twenty-five hundred at Valverde. A difference of about thirteen hundred from before Valverde and now.''

No one spoke. Quint closed his eyes. Where were the missing thirteen hundred? Buried at Valverde, Apache Canyon, and Glorieta Pass were those killed in battle. Hundreds more had died of disease or of wounds and were buried in many places from Socorro north to Santa Fe and back south again, then from the Rio Grande to the Rio Alamosa, many of them in lonely unmarked graves. Hundreds were still left behind in temporary hospitals and were now prisoners of war. More of them would die on the long journey back to San Antonio.

''They're gone at last,'' Luke said.

The Confederate campaign to capture New Mexico and Colorado, and perhaps in time California, was over.

Quint cased his field glasses. He stood up. ''Time to go home,'' he said quietly.

They led their worn-out horses up the valley of the Rio Alamosa. They did not look back.

★ TWENTY-SEVEN ★

CRISTINA

A broken-down wagon stood beside the road five miles from the Querencia. A wornout Confederate-gray shell jacket lay in the bed. A brass belt buckle with an embossed Lone Star and the lettering TEXAS was under it. Hoof and wheel tracks still showed pointing toward the ranch.

They sat their horses in the cool April afternoon sunlight. ''You recall the three wagons that turned off from the column near the Magdalenas?'' Luke asked.

Quint nodded. "I had a feeling they were coming this way. There was no other place for them to go."

They rode close to the ranch, then waited for darkness. There would be a moon later that evening. When darkness came they moved in closer, dismounted, and went forward on foot, Sharps rifles at the ready. There had been reports of Rebel guerrillas, deserters, and stragglers in and about the Rio Grande Valley, preying on the natives.

There was no sign of life about the Querencia. Two sagging wagons stood near the corral. The horsebreaking corral had twenty horses in it.

Luke looked at Quint.

"There should be a guard on the *torreón*," Quint said.

"*Theirs*, or *ours*?"

"That's what we'll have to find out."

Faint chinks of light showed through the *casa* shutter cracks. The living quarters of the help were dark. Quint pointed to the quarters and then looked at Anselmo. Anselmo nodded, then vanished into the darkness.

Quint and Luke reached the rear wall of the *hacienda*. They peered around a corner to where they could see the squat rounded shape of the *torreón*. No sentry's head and shoulders showed above the parapet. They stayed close to the wall and reached the front of the *casa*. The door opened, emitting a flood of light. The silhouette of a man showed on the rectangle of light on the ground, and then the door was closed. The bar bolt fell into place behind the door. Booted feet grated on the hard earth, and a shadowy figure walked past the front end of the *casa* toward the *torreón*. Quint catfooted around the *torreón* while Luke went up and over the low roof of the tunnel connecting the tower to the house.

A key grated in the door lock of the *torreón*. The man turned quickly and looked about himself as though he had heard something. Quint tossed a handful of gravel and pebbles out behind the man. He turned again. A muscular arm went about his throat, pulling him backward. His carbine was jerked from his right hand.

"Who are you?" Quint asked. He eased the throathold so the captive could speak.

★ 239 ★

The man gasped and choked. "Sergeant Ben Tate, Company B, Second Texas."

"You were here before with Colonel Calhoun."

Tate nodded.

"Why are you here now? Have you deserted?"

"For God's sake, ease off on that choke hold," Tate gasped.

"You make one move or cry out and you'll have a knife in your back," Luke warned.

"Open the *torreón* door, Luke," Quint ordered.

Luke lighted a candle lantern once they were inside. The gaunt-faced sergeant eyed his two captors. "You're Quint Kershaw," he said to Quint. "I saw you at Valverde when we captured your battery."

Luke shook his head. "They've lost the campaign and they're still talkin' about capturing that damned battery."

"Why are you here?" Quint asked.

"I was with the brigade up until we reached a spring in the foothills near the Magdalenas. We had some sick men and others badly wounded who weren't recovering at all. I was in charge of them. I knew we'd have to abandon the wagons in time. We'd never get them through the mountains, at least while loaded with the sick and wounded. I asked fór and got permission from Major Pyron to detach three wagons and an escort of seven men and try to reach here."

"Why here?" Luke asked.

The sergeant shrugged. "Where else could we go? It was either come here for shelter, water, and food or let the sick and wounded die in those damned mountains."

Luke nodded. "Your damned brigade left a trail of sick and wounded from La Mesilla all the way up to Glorieta Pass and back again. We've seen 'em, Sergeant. Buried a few too."

"I hope, for your sake, Sergeant, you haven't harmed any of my people," Quint said quietly.

Tate was startled. "God forbid! Captain, you've a band of angels in that house! The women folk have taken care of the boys as though they were their own."

"How many are in there?" Luke asked.

"Twelve."

Quint was puzzled. "Is that all? Surely you had more in the wagons and as escort?"

Tate looked away. "Twenty, all told, counting me. We buried three on the way. Two died the day we got here. Another last night and one early this morning."

"Jesus," Quint breathed softly.

"How many able-bodied left in there?" Luke asked quickly.

Tate shook his head. "None. The boys in the escort were sickly themselves. That was why they let me take them along. Now every one of them is flat on his back."

Quint hesitated. "What with?" he asked at last.

"Pneumonia, measles, fever, and two cases of smallpox."

A chill went right through Quint. "What type of smallpox?"

"One of the doctors told me, but I forgot."

"*Variola* or *varioloid*?"

Tate shook his head. "It was something like that, but worse than them."

Cold sweat broke out on Quint. Neither Rafaela or Cristina had contracted smallpox. Rafaela had been inoculated. *Cristina had not.* "*Variola confluentes*?" Quint asked at last with an effort.

The sergeant bobbed his head up and down. "That's it! That's it! They say it's the worst kind that can be gotten."

Variola confluentes—a severe form of smallpox in which the pustules spread and run together, sometimes forming a solid scab on the face. In many cases it could be fatal.

Someone tapped on the door. "*Quién es?*" Luke called out.

"Anselmo."

Anselmo came into the room. "The people are all right, *patrón*," he reported. "But they have barricaded themselves in their rooms. They are afraid of the Tejanos and the sickness they have brought. They will not go near the house."

Quint brushed past Anselmo and strode to the front door. He hammered on it with the butt of his Sharps. "Rafaela! Cristina!" he shouted.

It was Rafaela who came to the door. She stared uncomprehendingly at Quint, then with a strangled cry she flung herself into his arms. He held her close. She sagged weakly, and he picked her up in his arms and carried her into the house. The stench of disease was in the close air. He placed her in a chair in the sitting room, then paced through the house, looking into the bedrooms. Pallets had been placed on the floor in some of the rooms. Pale-faced men looked up at the tall, grim Federal officer who looked in on them. Two of them had healing smallpox scabs on their faces.

He found Cristina in their bedroom off the library. She sat dozing in a chair beside their bed. A young Texan was in the bed. His face was one huge scab. He did not move as Quint approached. His eyes were wide open, staring at the ceiling, but they could not see.

"Is she all right?" Luke asked from the door.

"Who knows? She's just asleep now." Quint placed his hand on her forehead. *Mother of God!* It felt hot and dry.

They placed her on a cot in one of the unused rooms at the rear of the house. She opened her eyes. *"Mi alma, mi corazon,"* she murmured. "You've come at last."

They wrapped the dead Texan in the bedclothes and buried him at dawn in the *camposanto* beside the other newly mounded graves. The sick were removed from the rooms in which they had lain, and the rooms were thoroughly disinfected. Every window and door in the house was opened to let the fresh cold southwest wind blow through. Infected bedding was burned downwind from the *hacienda*.

Two days passed. As yet no signs of the dreaded disease showed on Cristina's smooth brown skin. "She'll make it all right, Big Red," Luke promised. The next morning as Rafaela was feeding her, Cristina complained of a severe chill. She had a pounding headache, was nauseated, and her back and limbs pained her. Later she was wracked by spells of vomiting. Either Quint or Rafaela was always with her from then on. Luke and Anselmo rode for Fort Craig, taking an extra horse apiece, to get medical advice and medication.

Rafaela was bathing Cristina when she discovered the first telltale red spots on her face and arms. The next day they showed up on her trunk and legs. The disease was now firmly established in her system. The spots became raised and in a few days changed to blisters, which soon filled with pus.

Rafaela came in with Cristina's evening meal. Quint took the tray from her. "Get out," he ordered Rafaela.

"But it's my turn to stay with her," Rafaela protested.

Quint stood up, towering over his daughter in the darkening room. "Get out, damn you!" he repeated.

"I will not!" she snapped. After all, she was much like Quint in many ways. "You're worn-out, father. Let me stay."

He gripped her by her arm. She winced in pain as he forced her to the door and through it into the hallway. "Get out and stay out!" he shouted. He slammed the door behind her.

"She only wanted to help, Quint," Cristina said.

He shook his head. "It's my duty."

She was silent for a moment. "Is that *all*? A *duty*? Is there nothing else?"

He could not lie to her. She had always wanted love from him, not merely the great affection he had always felt for her. It would be easy enough to lie his way out. He could not do it.

"It's all right," she murmured. "I've known for years how you've felt for me, and for that alone I thank the Blessed Virgin. It was a great deal more than not having you at all."

He turned his head away from her. He was gut-sick and ashamed.

She sighed. "Do you remember the first time you made love with me? On the Rio Brioso. I was only a girl. But a *virgin*. That was what she wanted, the blessed Doña Guadalupe. We lost her, but in so doing heaven gained a new angel."

For God's sake, he thought. *Stop! Stop!*

She did not speak again that night.

He sat beside her through the long dark hours of the night and early morning. It was deathly quiet except for the sound of her breathing. He dozed now and then but always awoke to listen.

It was almost dawn when she spoke again. "Soon you will be free to go to the blonde lady in the north."

The next time he awoke she had stopped breathing.

Cristina was buried in the *camposanto* beside the Texans she had fought so hard to save, knowing full well she was liable to become infected herself with the dreaded disfiguring pox.

Dave returned from Fort Craig with Luke and Anselmo. He had been given a medical discharge. Luke brought Quint's orders. He was to return to Santa Fe to serve temporarily on the staff of Colonel Canby. A force of over two thousand California Volunteers, infantry, cavalry, and artillery was on the march across Arizona, coming to the relief of the Federal forces in New Mexico. They would arrive far too late to be of any consequence in the recently completed New Mexico campaign. The Confederates were slowly being withdrawn from their former Territory of Arizona, and already the advance units had left Fort Bliss to return to San Antonio.

The night before Quint was to leave for Santa Fe he walked in the moonlight with Dave. "I'll take Rafaela with me, Davie," Quint said. "She will be a great help to Guadalupe. I'll leave the Querencia in your hands. Anselmo can stay as *segundo*. There are still many problems to be solved here. I doubt if the Mimbres situation will be settled for some years, so you'll have to hold on here with your front teeth. I'll arrange to get more help for you."

Dave was quiet for a long time. "And what of you, Quint?" he asked quietly. "Will you come back when the war is over?"

Quint looked out across the plains, dreaming peacefully in the moonlight. He looked up at the *camposanto* with its rows of white-painted crosses and especially the one at the end of one of the lines, where Cristina slept. Something was gone, a piece of himself that he knew would never be fitted back into the complex pattern of his being. It was good that his orders would take him away from this place he had once loved, but he would have gone anyway. At present the tragedy of the place was too much to bear. Time, perhaps, would heal the wounds.

"Quint?" Dave asked.

"I don't know, Davie. I just don't know."

Quint, Rafaela, and Luke left Querencia before dawn the next day.

Dave and Anselmo watched them ride off in the dimness.

"Will he come back, Anselmo?" Dave asked.

Anselmo thought for a moment. After a time he spoke slowly, "Some men can't rest. He is one of them."

"Meaning that he will *not* come back?"

Anselmo shrugged. "Who knows? Even the *patrón* doesn't know that. If he doesn't know, how can anyone else?"

The three riders were gone in the dimness. Only the faint sound of the horses' hoofs could be heard, and in a little while that too was gone.

Somewhere on the heights above the *camposanto* a wolf howled, just once.

★ EPILOGUE ★

The Civil War would continue for three more bloody years, but there would not be another Confederate attempt to conquer New Mexico. Glorieta Pass had been the Gettysburg of the Southwest. It had been a tactical victory for the Confederates but due to Major Chivington's raid a disastrous material loss. It was the turning point of the campaign. Sibley's Brigade was in a shattered condition at the end of the campaign. Of the approximately twenty-five hundred men who had composed the invasion force, hardly more than eighteen hundred effectives returned to Texas. When reorganized and brought back up to strength, the brigade fought well, principally in Louisiana. General Sibley was not to lead it again. The Valverde battery, so named by its captors, served well in Louisiana and was said to have been sunk in a river rather than be surrendered at the end of the war.

After the New Mexico campaign, Quint Kershaw and Luke Connors served in Indian campaigns during the rest of the war and for some time after it had ended. Alexander Calhoun recovered from his wound and was granted his request for duty in the East. Rafaela became a teacher in the orphanage at Santa Fe. Guadalupe entered a convent preparatory to taking the veil. Dave Kershaw remained in charge of the Querencia. Catherine Williston's fate remained a mystery. Some say she was never seen again. Others claimed to have seen her still dressed in the quasi-military habit she had worn at the time of her disappearance, riding a beautiful dun mare with a white star blaze. She was always seen in the distance. If pursued she'd ride off with the speed of the winds on the San Augustine Plains. The mare's hoofs seemed hardly to touch the ground, and the sound of her hoofbeats could not be heard. If a pursuing rider began to overtake the pair, they would vanish into thin air. It was the beginning of a legend that persisted up until the turn of the century.

While stationed at Fort Bliss, Texas, in the spring of 1941, my wife, Alice, and I, with others, spent weekends searching for historical sites. Fort Fillmore had vanished completely. The ruins of Fort Craig with the heaps of earth revealing the sites of bombproofed buildings and defensive bastions stood gaunt on a mesa overlooking the Rio Grande. In those days minie balls and other bullets mutilated by impact, brass buttons stamped with the eagle and U.S., and bits and pieces of harness could be picked up at the fort and surrounding areas, as well as at the Valverde battle site upstream and across the river. The relics are still in my collection.

The lonely, seldom visited battlefield of Valverde had a memorial stone placed there in 1936 by the Texas Division United Daughters of the Confederacy dedicated to the Texas Mounted Volunteers, Sibley's Brigade, C.S.A., and those who died there. Another such stone was placed in Glorieta Pass in 1939 dedicated to the memory of the Texans who fought there. In the center of the square at Santa Fe is the Soldier's Monument, erected after the Civil War, which reads on the south side, "To the heroes of the Federal Army, who fell at the battle of Valverde, fought with the rebels, Febuary [sic] 21, 1862." On the west side the word *Rebels* occurs again, a designation of the enemies of the Republic that probably does not occur on such an inscription elsewhere in the nation.

Vaya,
Gordon D. Shirreffs
Granada Hills, California
1983

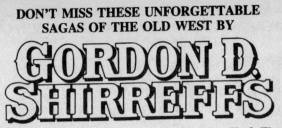